Frank Porter lives in Cambridge, MA, with his wife and small dog. He used to practice law. Now he runs, rows, reads, and writes.

Dedication

To: Ducks and our ducklings.

Frank Porter

Semper Fee

Austin Macauley Publishers™
LONDON • CAMBRIDGE • NEW YORK • SHARJAH

Copyright © Frank Porter (2018)

The right of Frank Porter to be identified as author of this work has been asserted by him in accordance with section 77 and 78 of the Copyright, Designs, and Patents Act 1988.

All rights reserved. No part of this publication may be reproduced, stored in a retrieval system, or transmitted in any form or by any means, electronic, mechanical, photocopying, recording, or otherwise, without the prior permission of the publishers.

Any person who commits any unauthorized act in relation to this publication may be liable to criminal prosecution and civil claims for damages.

A CIP catalogue record for this title is available from the British Library.

This is a work of fiction. All of the characters, names, incidents, organizations, and dialogue in this novel are products of the author's imagination. Any resemblance to actual persons, living or dead, or actual incidents or organizations is purely coincidental.

ISBN 9781788784771 (Paperback)
ISBN 9781788784788 (Hardback)
ISBN 9781788784795 (E-Book)

www.austinmacauley.com

First Published (2018)
Austin Macauley Publishers Ltd™
25 Canada Square
Canary Wharf
London
E14 5LQ

Acknowledgments

Thank you: Ann, Alex, Andrew, Annie, Carla, Don, Jan, Jenny, Joey, Kennie, Lainey, Millie, Rosemary, Tima, and Walter. The infelicities are all mine.

1

I BLAME Hitler for my little brother. After September 1, 1939, everyone knew we were in for it, but what motivated Father? Maybe he thought another child might yet trigger Mother's still-dormant maternal instincts. For whatever reason, Father set to work and out popped perky Edward, four years after me and less than two months before the Japs interrupted morning prayer in Hawaii.

My name is Andrew Millard, Andrew de Peyster Millard, to be precise. The accent falls on the second syllable of my surname. For those who get this wrong, I suggest using 'Milord' as an *aide-memoire*.

What follows is something I started writing in the fall of 1963 when the insufferable Eliot Estabrook Lawrence and I began work at Curtis and Perkins, a fading Boston law firm my behind-the-times New York father told me was one of the two best in the city. I'm not sure how to classify this. A memoir? Probably not. That suggests a certain level of diligence and discipline. More like a series of sequential impressions. A tone poem, perhaps. Why am I doing this? I wish to be remembered. Remembered as I really was. Not as Eliot Lawrence would have it.

Before I go further—a brief aside. I am an only child. However, there was a time when I didn't enjoy that enviable status. During my early years, I was all my parents had or desired. Their first sanctified coupling produced me, a healthy male heir. I was sturdy: destined to survive, succeed, and inherit their severely depleted resources. Sadly, I was often warehoused with a changing cast of hired hands as my parents set off without a 'by your leave' to parts unknown. I retaliated by relieving myself in a 17th century Dutch chest (I come from a distinguished New York family) which was ultimately sold to reduce family debts.

Happily, my caregivers were fun-loving. They imbued me with an almost uncontrollable urge to kick pigeons. They were less successful in getting me on the path to salvation. Despite being marched by Mary and Deidre into and through every R.C. church within toddling distance of our somewhat tattered Upper East Side flat, I never developed a penchant for piety, experienced a call to the cloth, or yearned for a martyr's immolation. I'm told I howled whenever, as a disciplinary measure, I was hauled through the lion house in Central Park.

Sometime in 1942, Father answered the trumpet's call. He and several bored friends, needing a break from wives and Wall Street, took the oath and, after 90 days, were commissioned second lieutenants in the U.S. Army Air Corps. Further stateside training preceded his departure for London and a staff billet at Allied headquarters. From nine to five, Father analyzed aerial photos of German fortifications and during his evenings filled the voids left by absent English officers. Not that Mother stayed home playing Penelope. She was the 4 F's favorite.

Meanwhile, I was stuck with Edward. By the summer of 1944, Mother had saddled me, a carefree seven-year-old, with my millstone brother. Every morning, Mother, enjoying the mobility afforded by her privileged 'B' gas sticker, drove us to the Atlantic Beach Club. She would deposit Edward and me at the pool and, despite the presence of several lifeguards, order me to keep an eye on him. Her final bit of parenting: "Don't tinkle in the pool." Then she'd ascend to the 'poop deck', an open-air watering hole overlooking the ocean that was off-limits to children. She'd give me two sandwiches and, if anyone was within sight, a kiss. The sandwiches, made days earlier and then stored in the icebox, were always soggy and inedible.

My memories of Mother are confirmed by the photo albums I inherited. There she is, in her sundresses, sandals, and floppy hats. Radiant smiles. If she hadn't been my mom, I'd have gone 'hubba-hubba' like her youthful admirers. All I can say to Herr Freud is, "Duh!"

Radar was new in those days, but I was never on her screen. Edward was an occasional blip.

Mother would enter a room and, moments later, the other women would find themselves marooned with each other. However, not everyone saw Mother as I did. That summer, I was hauling Edward along the boardwalk to our bathhouse when I spotted Sally Coleman. Sally was a grade ahead of me, and her pedestal was only slightly lower than Mother's. I worshipped her ardently, but silently. I thought, *Maybe I can unload Edward and splash in the surf with Sally. Wrong.* Sally approached. I was tingling. She whispered, "Your mother is breaking up my parents' marriage." Then she walked away. Some things stay with you forever. Sally never spoke to me again. I knew she'd said something awful. Whatever it was, it had to be untrue. I wanted to defend Mother, but I didn't understand what Sally had meant.

One August afternoon (the 16th, as though I could forget), everyone at the beach heard an unhealthy coughing in the sky. Looking up, we saw a P-47 low over the water. It was never going to make it home to Mitchell Field. Its engine was smoking, and flames squirmed back along its fuselage towards the cockpit. The pilot brought it down just beyond the surf line. The heavy fighter took one sodden bounce and came to rest in cascading sheets of spray. The lifeguards had already launched their boat.

It was a perfect wheels-up ditching, something I'd only seen in newsreels. The pilot had the canopy back, was out of his cockpit, and onto a wing before his aircraft nosed over and sank. He was in the water for barely a moment. Everyone raced to the shore. We got there as the pilot vaulted out of the lifeboat and splashed towards us. He seemed like a deity, the sort of being I was destined to become. Our Icarus turned out to be friendly, relieved, and mortal. He gave me his survival kit but wouldn't let me have his Mae West or his cool ID bracelet. Nor would he tell us about his kills or allow any of us to hold his pistol. Mother was nowhere to be seen.

Then I heard a commotion at the pool. Why hadn't Edward followed me? He was supposed to. People were yelling and milling around. I knew at once that what couldn't happen had happened. I returned to my post, and there was Ed, a miniature version of the shapes we'd seen sprawled on faraway invasion beaches. Someone was pumping up and down on his back, screaming for help that never arrived. None of this mattered to Edward, who refused to move or breathe. Somehow, he must have gotten out of his life preserver. It would have been my fault if he hadn't been wearing it since Mother had tasked me with his safety. Edward had been told to stick close to me, never run on the pool deck, never remove his life preserver, and never go anywhere near the deep end. He must have figured out how to undo the snaps.

That's not how Mother saw it. I could seldom predict her mood after she floated down from the poop deck. Sometimes she was angry, perhaps realizing the war wouldn't last forever, but she was always furious if her stay was cut short. Often she was sloppy, telling me I was her 'little man' and making slurred promises about gifts I finally realized I'd never get. Never believe anything when the sour smell of booze overwhelms the perfume. There was only one constant. I had to stay on my toes if we were to make it home intact. This time, Mother screamed, "Damn you," and walloped me in the puss. As usual, she put a lot into it. I carried her handprint on my cheek for over an hour. Maybe she sensed disapproval among the onlookers, because she did it only once.

It wasn't fair. Even the lifeguards at the pool hotfooted it to the beach. None of my friends had to be nursemaids. Why me? It's a sink-or-swim world, and Edward had elected to sink. It wasn't my fault. I was only a child, and I hadn't done anything. The sin of omission is no sin at all, at least in the eyes of the law. I didn't know it then, but now I realize if anyone was to blame, it was the chief mechanic of the P-47.

How did Mother get this way? She was nothing like her own mom. Would my affectionate grandmothers have treated me as Mother did if they'd seen more of me? Wasn't I all that Mother had left? Wasn't I the person who'd helped draw the stocking seams on the back of her legs? Wasn't I her prop when she wanted to impress men with her warmth? Actually, no. That had been Edward's role.

After scene-stealing Edward was crated and shipped off to Woodlawn, I recaptured the spotlight. People fussed over me for years. I ignored the unkind suggestions that I might have been at fault. For years, I told nobody about my nightmares. They were frequent and varied. Sometimes Edward and Mother would reverse roles. She'd drown and he, grown to the size of the pilot, would beat me to a pulp. Occasionally, it was Edward himself striding ashore. At other times, it was me ditching far offshore with no life jacket or inflatable raft. And always there were sharks and currents sweeping me eastward. Sometimes my chute dragged me under. Sometimes I never got to ditch or bail out. One of my wings would snap off, and I'd go into an uncontrollable spin before auguring into the drink.

In my early teens, a teacher convinced my parents that I should *talk* to someone. It was silly, but visiting the bearded load in Boston was an escape from the stalag-like atmosphere of the faraway boarding school to which I'd been exiled. It was also a chance to stalk girls, take in a movie, and smoke. I allowed the old duffer to persuade me I was blameless and Mother's reaction had been wrong. How anyone could make a living flogging those bromides is beyond me. His job was to make me feel good about myself. He succeeded. Only later did I get it. The Viennese look he affected, meant to signify wisdom and compassion, facilitated hanky-panky with distraught patients and justified hourly rates north of those charged by his callow, clean-shaven competitors. However, he got it wrong when he more or less promised me my bad dreams would go away.

Dr. Prescott did teach me a few useful, if unintended, lessons. Like most boys, I learned to engage in constant surveillance and threat assessment. There were always bigger or older guys who might suddenly take it into their heads to smack the living snot out of me. For better or for worse, I seldom evoke indifference.

It should have been obvious earlier, but Edward's sinking made me add Mother to my watch list. Defuse her or avoid her. If you don't protect your ass, nobody else will. I wonder if that's why I look for the armor gallery whenever I visit a museum.

So many people attribute their failures to childhood episodes. Wimps and copouts. Edward's making like the Titanic would have scarred a lesser man, someone like Eliot. Was I wounded by this? Scratched maybe, but it's long since healed. At an early age, I sensed in Edward an ugly, competitive streak beneath his seemingly guileless charm. It would have ended up poisoning our relationship.

To return to Eliot. His ascendancy began soon after we met in the Framingham, Massachusetts train station before our second-form year (eighth grade, if you have to ask) at the prestigious, if no longer elite, New England boarding school to which Lawrence males had gone for three generations. That spring, he unfairly beat me out for shortstop on our intramural team. He may have regretted doing so since I nailed him a few days later, sliding into second. My handiwork required eight stitches.

Eliot's been blessed by the gods. He's got no enemies, and people don't take his habitual congeniality for weakness. For no apparent reason, everyone is attracted to him as they once were to Edward. I realized even then that being well-regarded by Eliot would be helpful. Like my grandmothers, Eliot appears to put others first. However, it would be wrong to suppose I brought nothing to the table. Being an only child, Eliot needed a bro, and both of us needed someone with whom to talk asthma and baseball, if not pussy. Not that I could ever let down my guard since it was logical to assume that Eliot, once I outshone him, wouldn't hesitate to try and bring me down.

Eliot has been as lucky in love as he's been in everything else. Clare, his divine wife, praises his looks, character, and intellect. Even less plausibly, she enthuses about Eliot's wit and, though I still can't believe it, his metronomic dancing. Clare does this publicly and—as Eliot once confided—privately. She may even have convinced him he's well-hung. However, were I Eliot, I would not be Millard.

I desire Clare. Eliot can't help but sense this, but it doesn't seem to faze him. Little does. Clare should be with me. Virtuous as well as voluptuous, she hasn't, thus far, responded to my subtle overtures. I'm someone to be tolerated but never encouraged. If I weren't her hubby's oldest pal, I'd be banished. Even more annoying, she hasn't betrayed by a wink or a raised eyebrow that her effusions about Eliot are anything but sincere. Her performances are so convincing and so consistent, I've begun to ask myself: might they be genuine?

I sometimes wonder what Eliot makes of me. It isn't easy to get beneath his cheery, can-do mask. Or maybe it isn't a mask. Perhaps that's all there is. Eliot is unbearably agreeable, although I do recall him saying I have the knack of making the one remark you least want to hear to the person you least want to hear it.

Now I must pause for a moment to confess I am enormously pleased with what I have written thus far. When finished, it will settle some scores and air some unclean Lawrence laundry.

What should be the title of my Millard-Lawrence saga? Law firms are not for the sensitive or the saintly. They're about collections, not Kumbaya. This being so, while I considered 'Eliot Lawrence: A Life??', I have selected 'Semper Fee'. I'm saving the title 'Rarely Fi' for my next effort.

So let's get after it. Payback time. Lock and load. Hit the beach!

2

I'VE HEARD Millard's writing something about himself and our law firm. I'm bound to be included, and, knowing him, he'll praise himself and disparage me. He can't help himself. Just like he couldn't help spiking me when we were kids.

So here I go. I shall be guided by Harvard's motto 'Veritas'. For those who haven't gone to Harvard, Veritas means 'truth'.

As usual, I've been procrastinating. I'm just back from my October 1985 trip to Florence, and it's time to fish or cut bait.

In fact, I've done more than just dawdle. Miss Mandible, our head secretary, has helped me find a used Remington and loaned me her own typing manual. To throw her off the scent, I told her I'm writing up my trip.

I've selected the perfect work space. A third-floor guest room which I've fitted out with a straight-backed chair and a table large enough to hold everything I'll need. A setting that should foster productivity. Will the river view distract me? No. Now I'll rub the desk lamp and summon up the past.

Nothing's happening. Days have passed, and all I've done is jot down a few ideas. Haven't hit a single key. I bet Millard doesn't have this problem.

Start filling a page. Don't fret the style. You're experienced enough to know initial drafts are never perfect. Remember that bond indenture which required seventeen printed proofs.

Forget structure. Let it dribble out chronologically.

Why am I doing this? To escape my self-pitying funk. What am I trying to write? Something more fleshed-out than the terse, cryptic entries in my lawyer's diary. But nothing approaching a full-fledged autobiography. Or is it a memoir? What's the difference between the two? Whatever it is, it's to remain private. It would be silly, if not vain, to suppose it might be of interest to others. Also, feelings might be hurt.

All right, the margins are set, the paper's aligned, and the ribbon is fresh. November's almost here. Sit down and try again. Here I go.

In case it's not apparent, I'm a conventional sort. Even my fantasy life is somewhat pedestrian. As a boy, I had a crush on Doris Day. Those European actresses were scary. In sports, I have lived and died for the usually hapless Red Sox and, to balance that frustration, am an avid supporter of my college's teams. When I read, I tend towards biographies of illustrious New Englanders. Being a business lawyer, I subscribe to *The Business Lawyer*. Being middle-aged (48), I subscribe to *The Harvard Health Letter*, and am keeping an eye on a couple slow-growing polyps. My life has become a series of repetitive cycles built around reunions and doctors' appointments.

Back to the past. On Tuesday, September 3, 1963, Rico Belmonte, the most outgoing of the uniformed operators of 23 State Street's classic open-cage elevators, took me to nine, Curtis and Perkins's top floor, the place where the big shots hung out. Rico, for many years a reliable source of unreliable inside information—who delighted in tormenting struggling associates with fables of his stock market triumphs—let me off in the reception area. There before me was the threadbare green carpet, the battered furniture, and the tranquil Miss Landry, about whom Millard is most unkind. I could see myself swimming into focus. She didn't remember me from my interviews, but smiled gently, nevertheless. She took my name and flapped vaguely at a cracked leather sofa that turned out to be as uncomfortable as it looked. I didn't see her notify anyone of my arrival. It being 8:30 a.m. on the day after Labor Day, there may have been nobody around to notify.

My surroundings were Spartan. I found this comforting. It suggested the firm's focus was on substance, not appearance. There were no newspapers or magazines to be seen anywhere. Only a few copies of the *ABA Journal*. I carried my law school briefcase. More like a valise, it contained my law dictionary and what I thought would be my most useful treatises. Not my still-unframed diplomas.

Nobody at Curtis and Perkins advertised they'd gone to the institutions attended by the males in their families for generations. In those days, Curtis and Perkins clients made certain assumptions about the personal and academic backgrounds of their attorneys. My briefcase, purchased at the Coop when I entered Harvard Law School, served me faithfully for several more years until its bottom fell out while I was carrying a set of closing documents through the lobby of the Chase Manhattan Bank. I hated to part with it, but it was beyond repair. Anyway, by then, up-and-comers who took themselves seriously and expected others to do likewise carried attaché cases.

The *ABA Journals* didn't interest me. I couldn't bring myself to read anything. First impressions are indelible, and I very much wanted to get off to a good start. There were only three new associates that fall, and history suggested that probably one, two at the most, would make partner. One was my schoolmate, Andrew Millard, for whom everything comes easily. He's charming in an evasive way. Early in life he'd developed a knack of getting others, especially females, to do things for him. We became friends in boarding school, and since his New York parents never visited, I made a point of bringing him home on our few free weekends. For years, I considered him my best friend. Now I wonder.

So there I was, age 26, in a new, navy blue Rogers Peet suit and well-shined black wingtips, enjoying a late summer breeze from several open windows. Street sounds and low tide smells from the harbor were welcome stimulants in the drowsy atmosphere of the reception area. Window units, not to mention central air conditioning, were still several years in the future.

I had cast my lot with a highly-regarded, 'white-shoe' Boston law firm organized in 1895. When I joined Curtis and Perkins, there were 25 partners and a slightly smaller number of associates, a ratio consultants would later tell us was bound to result in mediocre financial performance. As Millard put it, "Plantations fail when the owners outnumber the slaves."

None of the associates had the remotest idea what the firm as a whole or individual partners earned. This was smart policy. It fostered the misapprehension that each of the partners was important and should be taken seriously. Along these lines, I recall an older one complaining to me that he should have been paid at least $50,000 because he'd collected that amount in fees. I was unimpressed by this analysis. Being a business lawyer, he presumably had some idea of the difference between gross and net.

The partners seemed prosperous, however, so the more self-assured associates assumed they themselves would become so. Even the office directory reinforced this impression by listing the partners' summer houses, most of which were ocean-side 'cottages' on the North Shore. Their names evoked visions of fresh air, sunshine, rattling halyards, and happy cries of 'ready about', 'fore', and 'let'. Millard threatened to call his longed-for but non-existent summer retreat, "La Même F***ing Place."

From our humble vantage points, we regarded the partners as nothing less than demi-gods. Only gradually did the scales fall from my eyes. Some partners, I learned, were more equal than others. Then came the realization that unproductive partners could be deaccessioned.

I saw many derailed between ordination and retirement. Wine and women were familiar culprits. So far, we haven't lost anyone to song, or, as far as I know, to narcotics. There were other temptations and pitfalls. A sense of futility or a hefty inheritance can each, in its own way, sap one's energy. Sometimes management breaks a person's spirit. The death or retirement of a star can lead to the purging of those of his followers who haven't managed to grab a significant chunk of his practice or find a new patron.

Richard Stevens, the other new associate, arrived at nine sharp. Millard sauntered in at around 9:30 a.m. "Always the eager beaver, Mr. Lawrence," said Millard and, staring unwelcomingly at Stevens, inquired, "And *who* might that be?"

Without awaiting a reply from either of us, Millard said, "Eliot, you realize, of course, that life as we know it is over, and the future we'd been reared to expect is now a mirage. Woe, oh woe."

I didn't get that. We were lucky to be here. My promptness had apparently gone unobserved, but I had no cause for complaint. I was about to start my career at a prestigious Boston law firm. I had to support Clare and myself on $7,000 a year, but I knew if I could get to $25,000 I'd be able to do this, educate my children, and consider myself a success. My goal was compensation at least equal to my age times one thousand. I am optimistic by nature.

Mr. Barber, the office manager, arrived well after 10:00 a.m. Would I be that beat-up at 53? He looked like many of the partners. Blotchy complexion. Cheeks with the indented cross-hatching of a lifetime smoker. Wrinkled seersucker suit. Brooks Brothers button-down. Madras tie with a discolored knot. Unshined brown shoes, and possessing, as Millard said, "a beak nearly as large and colorful as a toucan's." Looking neither left nor right, he fled to his office and firmly closed the door. He had, we learned, managed to lose a sinecure in the personnel department of Devonshire Trust Company.

That took some doing. We were still in an era when a Harvard diploma, even diplomas of under-performing legacies for whom Cs were achievements, usually guaranteed tenure and at least a vice presidency at quiet places like Devonshire. After his dismissal, a Harvard classmate found Mr. Barber a home at Curtis and Perkins. His role was to serve as friend and drinking companion to those who'd hired him, somewhat like the ponies that soothe the temperamental thoroughbreds on their way to the starting gate.

We must have waited at least 20 minutes. Miss Landry brought Mr. Barber a cup of coffee. We could smell cigarette smoke, but no motion could be observed behind his frosted glass door. At last he emerged, a man on a mission. Still without acknowledging our presence, he strode through the reception area carrying *The Boston Herald* and made straight for the men's room.

Minutes passed. I heard a chain being yanked followed immediately by the roar of cascading water. The Curtis and Perkins bathrooms with their sound-amplifying marble walls and fixtures would have delighted a Roman emperor. The other appointments were equally imposing: the overhead thunder box, the chain with a wooden pull, the copper piping, and the surprisingly comfortable, sculpted, close-grained toilet seat that Millard calls the 'seat of easement'.

Mr. Barber reappeared, looking serene. At around 11:00 a.m., he reemerged from his office. Rumpled, frayed, florid, and in need of a haircut, he surveyed the new recruits and in a condescending tone inquired, "Which of you arrived first?"

I half expected him to refer to us as 'you wretches'. I raised my hand, something I had learned in the Marines was often inadvisable.

"And you are Mr.?"

"I'm Eliot Lawrence, sir."

"Come with me, Mr. Eliot Lawrence."

I entered Mr. Barber's office. Long and narrow, and barely accommodating a desk, it reminded me of a broom closet. That, I discovered, was what it had started out as.

"Take a seat, Mr. Eliot Lawrence."

I did so.

"It seems you and I graduated from the same college and are, to this day, members in good standing of its finest final club. Small world."

I nodded respectfully.

"Do you have any questions, Mr. Eliot Lawrence?"

"Yes, sir. I was wondering when associates are allowed to specialize and how we choose our specialties."

"All will be revealed in due course, Mr. Eliot Lawrence, and bear in mind that, more often than not, your specialty is chosen for you. Always remember: many are called, but few are chosen."

"I will remember that, sir."

"Now, about your accommodations. Since there is but one remaining single office and since you and I are members of 'The Key', I hereby award it to you."

It was a year or two before I got it about Mr. Barber. He had nothing to do, but nevertheless performed an essential service to his contemporaries. No matter how badly they were doing, none of them would sink to his level.

He was and would remain at the bottom of the barrel. Nor was he going anywhere. He couldn't afford to. In a world of flux and anxiety, he was a comforting constant. Life is scary for underachieving partners. A few departures can transform a relatively anonymous member of the fourth quartile into the next candidate for the scaffold.

Mr. Barber was aware of his role. It afforded him few pleasures other than hazing those recruits he saw as beneath him while ingratiating himself with those he considered his betters. I guess Mr. Barber thought I might survive. It was wrong of me, but I got a kick out of telling Millard he had to double up with Stevens.

A day later, Millard, in his unctuous way, said we should draw straws for my office. I agreed, but only if Stevens was included. We did so, and I won.

3

WHAT I remember most about September 3, 1963 is Eliot's sneaking in before daybreak to scarf up the best office. So like him. Furthermore, I resent the rumors I'm sure he spreads about having taken pity on the sad sack from a broken home. Self-satisfied twaddle. I was anything but sad, and whose home isn't broken one way or another? And then the first-day drama. Look to your left. Look to your right. One of you won't make it. It was obvious from the start who was to be the one: Stevens. His academic credentials were unimposing. His briefcase was Samsonite. He might as well have been wearing a short-sleeved shirt with pit stains and a pocket protector. No sweat. It was in the bag. Stevens was doomed. How long would it take him to realize this? Curtis and Perkins was still operating on the assumption that it could live by well-bred alone.

I recall him turning those moist spaniel eyes towards me and saying, "Mr. Mill-ard, may I call you Andy?"

"No. It's Andrew. Furthermore, Mr. Stevens, you've mangled my surname. Recall, if you will, your instruction in poetry. I am an iamb, and mallard (the duck) is a trochee. Finally, be sure to show more than a smidgen of respect to Mr. Lawrence (he answers to Eliot) whose ancestors had their way with the Wampanoags and their squaws."

Eliot had it made, despite carrying what amounted to a sample case. It would have done credit to Willy Loman, but somehow contributed to his intolerable, clean-cut image. As Eliot often puts it in his complacent fashion, "I feel no need to define myself by consumer products."

The older partners were going to love him. He'd be the dutiful, conscientious son and heir none of them managed to sire. As for me, I had the smarts, the moves, impeccable ancestors, and enviable connections. If only my family hadn't lost so much in the Depression.

Back to Eliot. A somewhat clumsy lineman, he was, nevertheless, elected football captain at the insistence of coaches and faculty who were aglow over his 'sportsmanship and pluck'. Yes, 'pluck', something I'd thought had disappeared with those 19th century boys' adventure books. Eliot was husky and would have been fat had he not been so disciplined. His hair, which he still keeps short, is a nondescript brown—unlike my sun-dappled locks. His eyes are a washed-out blue, not a riveting cerulean like mine. Eliot can never conceal his feelings. His open face can be read by an infant. He has a smile that, strangely enough, is enhanced not diminished by his somewhat irregularly spaced teeth. But then who can dislike a jack-o-lantern? Engaging Eliot. Engaging Edward.

Eliot's success has been so undeserved. He fell into it. His family's name on one of Harvard's innumerable libraries. His first name on a Harvard House for Chrissake. Not to mention several streets in the area and a graceful redbrick bridge over the Charles.

Even worse, both of us have Mayflower ancestors, but mine, I recently discovered, was a servant of Eliot's. Intolerable, but I'm keeping that to myself. Here's how I see it: Eliot, the Puritan; and Millard, the Impuritan.

After school, Eliot sauntered into Harvard, and I slunk off to Brown. My rigid, moralistic headmaster hadn't favored me with the sort of hyperbolic paeans he cranked out for the pious, self-satisfied numbskulls in the bottom half of our class. Eliot said his freshman football coach warned the team it should expect a helluva scrap from Brown because so many of its players were Harvard rejects. My four years at a 'safety school' flew by. I majored in English, took the same courses as Cousin Bruce, and recycled the papers he so thoughtfully handed down to me. Why English? Easy. Dollops of verse, properly applied, can work wonders with soulful lasses.

It's fortunate Bruce was so bright because sometimes there were glitches. When that occurred, I ached to confront my professors. "Look, here's an A for Bruce Channing and now, two years later,

I get a B despite having accepted every one of your niggling criticisms. What gives?" Despite these occasional hiccups, I walked out of Providence with a magna.

Eliot's of decent height, topping out at a hair under six feet. Anyone but Eliot would claim to be a six-footer. Eliot couldn't. But I knew he was hoping because he measured himself regularly until he was almost 30. Eliot got most of his growth early (mine came later, so for years I had to look up to him). This discouraged bullying, and when combined with his middling grades, insupportable popularity, inexhaustible school spirit, and above-average athleticism, made him a deity in boarding school. One smitten French teacher liked referring to him as '*le chevalier sans peur et sans reproche*'.

Eliot once told me he was fortunate to have unremarkable and, therefore, unthreatening looks. The last two centuries have witnessed the erosion of the angularities and anomalies observed in the paintings of his patrician ancestors. That's what can happen when a family stops inbreeding. He is unforthcoming about his appearance, but says he wishes once in his life a girl would look at him rather than his companions. He admits he's never been 'checked out'.

There is another area in which I surpass Eliot. I shall be delicate, but it is obvious to anyone who has observed the two of us in a locker room. As naughty Martial put it, "*Audieris in quo, Flacce, balneo plausum, Maronis illic esse mentulam scito.*" (When you hear applause in a bath, Flaccus, you may be sure that Maro's cock is there.) I, too, am worthy of acclaim and have named my ardent organ, which discharges regularly and puissantly, 'Old Faithless'. I call the rest of my package 'Balzac'.

Back to 23 State Street. Eliot was no doubt thinking selfless thoughts, perhaps reflecting on Martin Luther King's 'I Have a Dream' speech of the previous week. Stevens was glorying in his shiny accessory, while I was delighting in the scandal that had engulfed John Profumo, England's dashing Minister of War. Hilarious to be caught in a dalliance with a scrumptious hooker who fancied KGB agents. In Albion, it's the Tories who entertain us with those delicious sex scandals involving costumes, animals, spankings, and hyphenated names. Here, the Republicans are prigs while Democrats in high places go at it like mink—in my view, one of the few positive things to be said about them. The Profumo mess thrilled me. Could there be hope in other hidebound institutions?

There I sat, like a lobster in its crowded, aerated tank. Soon I'd be seized and, with my taped claws flapping wildly, dumped into the cauldron. As Eliot so perceptively observed, the Curtis and Perkins offices were Spartan. He failed to say they were Bronze Age Spartan. To Eliot this denoted virtue, whereas I was queasy about the financial implications of our décor. It's not encouraging to learn you must turn in the pencil stub before you're issued a replacement. Our receptionist, the comatose Miss Landry, reminded me of a manatee. I could see her in a tropical water world drifting upward, raising her whiskered muzzle above the surface and gently inhaling a mouthful of carrots and lettuce. Then sliding downward in a trail of bubbles. What, I asked myself, do Curtis and Perkins's less somnolent clients, if any, make of Miss Landry?

While Eliot was having his Saul on the road to Damascus moment and Stevens's tail was tucked firmly between his legs, I, the third of the three stooges, longed to slash my wrists. I tried consoling myself with the thought that 1963 wasn't the year to make big bucks, not with the marginal tax rate at 91%.

Law school had kept me from the workplace for three barely tolerable years, but now my sentence, possibly a life sentence, was beginning. What boy has ever grown up hoping to be a lawyer? I'd met a few in law school and wanted nothing to do with them. For me, as I suspect for most studs, it's sex and sports. My advice has always been, 'Listen to your bawdy'.

Believe me, I had thought this through. Dire financial pressure drove me to law school. For years, I had studied my elderly relatives hoping their deaths might defer or, better yet, obviate my entry into the labor market or, once there, hasten my retirement. Their lack of productivity combined with confiscatory death taxes have quashed my hopes. Both sets of grandparents died, and it was evident they'd been as profligate as I hope to become. The trusts from which they received their sustenance allowed them to spend principal, and they had done so with a sense of purpose not observed in my family for generations. Their spineless trustees did nothing to rein them in. Other than some unmatched cuff links and impeccable manners, I've received little from my family besides the personal effects of a great uncle. Sadly, I have yet to figure out how to monetize his collection of split bamboo fly rods and Dunhill pipes.

My parents have been equally unhelpful. What can I add about Mother? Consistent to the end. Her last words to me were "Screw you", and they seemed to be coming from a cave on the far bank of the Styx. It sounded as though Mother was not enjoying herself.

Much to her surprise, Mother had failed to land a trophy husband after her abrupt, tumultuous post-war leave-taking from my father, although she caught and consumed a pair of undersized ones. As a consequence, there was little left for me when she pegged out.

Ignoring for the moment those instances where she overindulged and yelled at me for murdering her baby, I think semifondly of Mother despite her Dewar's-induced mood swings. She often claimed we were best pals. So be it. I even got over it when she bestowed my title 'Lamb Chop' on her third and final husband and reduced me to some lesser cut. What can you do? You take your initial cues from the first living thing you see in your hospital room, burrow, or nest.

My old man was a plodder. Bumbling, good-natured, and ineffective, he maxed out as an Assistant Vice President in a small but tony Manhattan trust company. For the last several years, he's been loving his dementia in a lock-up that's consuming the last Millard resources. What's not to like? Every television program's a hoot, and it's a kick to sit around bare-assed singing *Ten Thousand Men of Harvard*.

If only Edith had been as advertised. I was young and had assumed that, except for the nouveau-poor Millards, being in the studbook meant big bucks now, not generations earlier. How silly. Why had my parents invested so much in teaching me golf, tennis, sailing, squash, skiing, bridge, backgammon, and forks while leaving me untutored and vulnerable in the high stakes game of gold digging?

Edith, the apparently highly-sexed, high-net-worth Kentucky lass may have been Bennington College's only virgin. How was I to know that her family was being kept afloat by a towering stack of daddy's high-interest demand notes? Edith's treasury was empty of bullion, but her vault was as well defended as Fort Knox. I met her at a party in Newport. That, too, was promising. During our first dance, as we were in the 'getting to know you' phase, she told me she was interested in a Harvard senior, who, she implied, was mad for her.

I casually asked for the name of my rival. It was Sir Eliot. Suddenly, I was on her like a limpet. Had competitive juices been more than a figure of speech, I would have needed to towel off. That still-unravished chubby deb, that foster-child of bourbon and blue grass had a yummy, slightly squishy Rubenesque allure. There was little doubt Edith was in season, but most importantly she was, temporarily at least, Eliot's and, therefore, fair game.

I had the band play *My Old Kentucky Home*. We chatted. We waltzed. We trotted like foxes. We smoked. We drank. We flirted. I sparkled. Edith invited me to the Derby. Her daddy's very-own (soon to be repossessed) plane would pick me up wherever I wished. I would stay at her house in Louisville. It was all on her. After a few pro forma protests and a wholly insincere offer to pay my own way, I yielded.

Time for a drive along Bellevue Avenue. We parked. The moment seemed propitious. The moon was in the seventh house. Jupiter was aligned with Mars. I laid alongside, made deft use of my grappling irons, and loosed my boarding party. I was the conflation of Drake, Nelson, Cochrane, Aubrey, Hornblower, and other sea dogs, real and imagined.

I squeezed, shaped, and kneaded her like someone about to throw a pot. I burrowed like a fervid gopher, but Edith, well-versed in siege warfare, was well-defended. Her breastworks fell, but my ram was denied. He never got to batter, foiled by, of all things, a girdle. Stalemate.

We retreated to our respective corners. When the bell rang, I bounded forward. Soon Edith was bobbing and weaving like her fellow Kentuckian, Cassius Marcellus Clay. I was overmatched.

Edith possessed that bred-in-the-bone southern knack of bringing you to a gasping, panting boil and suddenly declaring a ceasefire. My assault was beaten off. Alas, I was not. That all-too-familiar ache seized my nether regions.

During the next break, Edith rearranged her protective layers while repainting and re-scenting herself. She regarded me appraisingly. How did I stack up?

"If mah daddy were here, Mistah Mahlaad, I can tell you just what he'd be saying."

"What would he be saying, you divine thing?" I gasped.

"He would look you square in the eye and say, 'What are yoah intentions, suh? Honable or dishonable? You hahdly know mah dautah.'"

Being determined to go where Eliot had failed to tread, I tossed her my troth and continued to march. The drawbridge fell, the portcullis rose and the citadel threw open its gates. "Oh! Oh! Oh! Yeaaaah!" My siege engine discharged its awful load. Edith was mine. Eliot, for once a loser but always the good sport, agreed to be my best man.

Father showed up in boater and white bucks. With his secretary, whom he passed off as his 'colleague'. Mother couldn't make it. She was cruising in the Aegean with Seton of the pencil mustache and belted trench coat. But Mother had not forsaken her surviving cub. She sent me a telegram.

> *Dearest Lamb Chop:*
>
> *I'm sick at not being with you today, but count me in for number two et seq. It goes without saying that you've got a standing invitation to all of mine. I'm sorry to be missing what's bound to be a real toot. Edith's papa's sure to pull out the stops 'foah' his 'dahling'.*
>
> *Now a splash of advice from your wise, old mum. Don't wait too long before you stray. Infidelity deferred can, I've heard, be difficult to initiate.*
>
> *Your loving mother.*

> *P.S. Generous Seton snagged one of the two suites with balconies, and then he nabbed us seats at Captain Sven's table for the entire trip. I've got high hopes for Seton.*

Within a year of our wedding, Edith's mother died of liver failure, and her father, shut down by his bank, went into Chapter Seven. Depression and the bourbon she used to combat it erased Edith's already diminishing sex drive. In no time at all, the Edith I had wed vanished into the body of a boozer with a cask for a torso and sticks for arms and legs. Next, she began evolving backwards from butterfly to caterpillar. Given the brevity of our marriage and the absence of issue, our parting was quick and relatively inexpensive. My great uncle, he of the fly rods, would have understood. Merely a case of catch and release.

Deprived of my place in the Kentucky squirearchy, I took the law boards, scored brilliantly (besting Eliot, I might add) and followed the lead of other directionless contemporaries. There, after my gap year, Eliot and I reunited at Harvard Law School. While I'd been courting and discarding my starter wife, Eliot served six months in the Marines, and taught English on a Pima Indian reservation where he met and won the heart of a fellow do-gooder, the incomparable Clare.

4

ANY WRITING of this sort should contain a word or two about one's childhood. Isn't that the way it's done? The child is father of the man and all that. Boys born in the late 1930s, like Millard and me, were raised on tales of Achilles, Hector, Galahad, Robin Hood, and Hawkeye illustrated by Howard Pyle and N.C. Wyeth. Myth and fiction provided our heroes while the real world supplied us with villains. Who could fail to be moved by Roland, nephew of Charlemagne, defeating the Saracens and dying with his face towards the enemy? Stuffy as it may now seem, comic books were not allowed in the Lawrence house. Banned in Boston, so to speak.

When our fathers went overseas in World War II, we assumed command at home. Before email there was V-Mail. I have many of those tiny gray letters confirming I was the man of the house, the acting commander-in-chief. Some of my friends held similarly exalted positions.

We took our responsibilities seriously. We were vigilant and well-informed. Maps of the European and the Pacific theatres covered our bedroom walls. Colored pins showed the last known location of fathers, uncles, cousins, and older brothers. Models of P-38s, P-47s, P-51s, B-17s, B-24s, and other U.S. aircraft hung from our ceilings. We could recognize the silhouette of every Allied and Axis plane.

We did what we had to do. We armed ourselves with knives, slingshots, and Daisy Red Ryder Western Carbine air rifles. There was even the odd shotgun or .22 our distracted fathers had forgotten to hide before shipping out. Several of us had gas masks. I found a pearl-handled .25 caliber Colt, shells, and a magazine in an unlocked toolbox. I loaded the magazine and slotted it into place.

I felt like General Patton, with whom an uncle was serving. Patton always wore a pearl-handled Colt. Sometimes two.

Had the Nazis parachuted onto the Boston Common, they would have been set upon by a legion of steely-eyed seven-year-olds prepared to defend their mothers, their younger siblings, and their family pets. We were not a geriatric home guard. We were a somewhat undersized Praetorian Guard.

Then came the first disappointments. For years, I saw myself batting cleanup and playing center field for the Sox, starting my ascent to glory—which would include several MVPs and a number of world championships—just as the great Ted Williams was taking his last cuts. By the time I'd turned 13 in 1950, I realized that even the minor leagues were beyond me.

Nevertheless, I was still certain I'd excel in some fashion. It was up to me to carry on the Lawrence name and begin replenishing its coffers.

I find some solace in recalling a time and a place where to be above average at everything was to be king. I am talking about the Marines, where the slight of build, though quick and endowed with endurance, lacked the strength to cover long distances carrying a machine gun or the base plate of a mortar, while the muscular giants pooped out on hills and pull-up bars. As Mister-Above-Average, I was numero uno for a brief shining moment, even beating Duke's best quarter miler in a 440 run in combat boots after an hour of exercise and harassment.

I was also pleased to discover that I possessed a modicum of leadership ability. Right after boot camp, I was shipped out to the storied First Marine Division in Camp Pendleton, California and given command of a four-man fire team, the Corps' smallest tactical unit. It was me and three shifty-eyed teenagers.

One starless night, my fire team and five thousand other Marines embarked on landing craft and were ferried out to the transports anchored offshore. We reached the side of our designated ship, secured a landing net, and, on our squad leader's command, began climbing, making sure, as we'd been trained, to keep our hands on the vertical risers.

None of us expected we'd have to climb *up* one of those things. Our progress on this heaving contraption was snail-like. Then one of my Marines froze. He wouldn't move. He wouldn't speak. What next? Give him a direct order? Ream him out? What would Chesty Puller do?

I sidestepped over to him and asked a fairly obvious question. "How's it going?"

No response. Just shaking. He'd entwined himself in the landing net.

"Can I give you a hand?"

"I can't make it."

"Sure you can."

In addition to his rifle and his other gear, my paralyzed Marine had a heavy roll of communications wire slung over his shoulder. "Can you make it if I take the wire?" I asked.

"I'll try."

We managed the exchange without braining anyone below us, and, with me pushing on his rear end, we got to the top, over the gunwale, and flopped onto the rolling deck.

Next morning's descent was a piece of cake. My trooper carried his wire and stormed the beach like a Marine.

All this is to say that by the time I met and married my beloved Clare I was convinced, after doing an interim unaudited review of my life to date, I would in all probability be able to protect and provide for her and our children. I was, nevertheless, forced to acknowledge I might never be enshrined in Cooperstown or earn an Oscar, an Olympic medal, a Pulitzer, a Nobel, or a Field Marshal's baton.

5

WORMWOOD AND gall. I recall sitting in that beat-up reception area with dust motes floating in the sunny, slow-moving air. It was as though I, Comte de Millard, was in a tumbrel on its way to the Place de la Concorde. Edith was to provide me with a sedentary life of sensuality and sloth, but she had failed most grievously. Therefore, I had to make my time at Curtis and Perkins as easeful, brief, and lucrative as possible. I needed to put myself in charm's way, in a position where I would meet a cross section of women, each of whom was financially secure and needed an Andrew de Peyster Millard to complete herself. How best to realize these goals?

Could litigation be my path to riches? If you fail but have any credentials, you can often wangle a judgeship. Do the fat litigators get appointed to food courts, I wonder? I could have been a star in litigation. I possess physical grace, a commanding presence, an arresting voice, a quick wit, and an unerring sense for the *mot juste*. And how exhilarating to make matters turn out as I decree, not necessarily as they should.

Even now, I thrill to the observation of Genghis Khan: *happiness is crushing your enemies and hearing the lamentations of their women.* But not at the cost of my evenings, weekends, and vacations. The louts in real estate repel me. Bankruptcy? Ruffians all. Labor law? The province of the loud and uncouth. Divorce? Interesting. Gossip, naughty secrets, and a procession of wealthy, needy, distraught women. Fish in a barrel. On balance, though, too messy.

Business law? I'd need to brush up on my golf. While erratic off the tee, my short game's fantastic. Trusts and estates: my fallback position, my Brown. Yes, business law. I'm glib. Engaging. Versatile.

If I was to get anywhere, I needed a mentor—and who better than Ezra Clark, the firm's waning but once effulgent star, a man whose wishes were still commands on the three floors occupied by the firm he'd once dominated? How to showcase my ability and my commitment? Wholly apart from Eliot, I had to move quickly because, based on my observations, it wasn't clear Ez would make it to Christmas. I studied his habits. He was a creature of habit. Regularity was his watchword. I learned the times of his arrivals, his departures, and his trips to the hospitalities. I hung about on the ninth floor, our Olympus. I made it my business to cross old man Clark's unsteady path at least once a day Monday through Friday and twice on Saturday mornings when I was my most aggressively cheerful.

At every encounter I'd bark out a crisp yet deferential, "Good morning, Mr. Clark," throwing in a snappy 'sir' in order to differentiate myself from the other sycophants. To hammer home my message and acknowledge my humble station, I'd add, "Andrew Millard, sir." It took me at least a dozen such ambushes before I received any form of acknowledgment and another few weeks before my jaunty salutation produced anything approaching recognition.

I sprang my trap at 10:00 a.m. on Thursday, November 14, 1963. I know because I recorded it in my lawyer's diary. Ez Clark never got to his office later than 10:05 (frighteningly early for someone his age). At that hour, he was usually Rico's only passenger and, therefore, vulnerable. I was lurking in the ground floor lobby, 'studying' the building directory when he negotiated the revolving door and tottered toward Rico's outstretched hand. I scuttled into the elevator before Rico returned with his burden.

Rico propped our senior partner against the back wall. He wrapped four unsupple, claw-like fingers around the safety rail, assumed his position, and checked his passengers. Then he squared away his visored cap, faced front, levered shut the outer door, closed the grating, took the joy stick in one gray gloved hand, and, with an authoritative semi-circular motion, rocketed his battle star into the billable empyrean.

I had little time to act. Rico was expressing Ez to nine before offloading me in steerage.

"Good morning, Mr. Clark, sir. Andrew Millard."

He half turned in my direction. It took him two floors to bring me into focus.

"Good morning, Mr. Millard. I'm not certain we've been introduced. Ezra Clark."

"Yes, sir. I know who you are."

"You're new here, aren't you?"

"Yes, sir, I am."

"What do they have you doing, Mr. Millard?"

"A little of everything, sir. A great deal of memo writing. Many, many trips to the Social Law Library." Sigh.

A promising but unintelligible sound from Ez. "Do you have any idea yet as to what you might be good at?"

"Yes, sir. I sure do, sir."

We had reached nine. Rico had the elevator perfectly aligned with the floor. Ez shuffled forward and debarked. I considered but rejected the idea of offering him my arm. That suck-butt Rico might get away with it, but not me. I followed him from the elevator. The nearly bald Miss Landry inclined her ample upper body in a gesture of submission and respect.

"Transactional work, sir."

"Really?"

Who knew, but that was the term being bandied about by the more savvy-looking business associates. "Yes, sir. Absolutely."

"In that case, come see me tomorrow."

"Yes, sir. I'll be there."

I sensed my audience was over. Not wishing to press my luck, I bowed and shuffled backwards toward the elevator. Was that a sneer on Rico's face?

At 10:15 a.m. the next morning, I was in Ez's office looking into his watery eyes. Did I want to end up like him?

With a face resembling a scrotum after a cold shower, Ez appeared to have been recently exhumed from the Valley of the Kings. His doleful canine expression suggested he might have been distantly related to Anubis. Had his brains been removed through his nostrils and his viscera laid to rest in canopic jars, or was this

36

the unavoidable consequence of over 50 years in a law firm? What happened to Ramses Clark at night? Was he injected with fresh embalming fluid, wrapped in fine linen and laid to rest in a sarcophagus with good lumbar support?

There was something else, a not inconsequential something else if we were to work together in close proximity. He reeked. When you got within range, your head was snapped back by a sharp, penetrating odor. Just what happens when a stone hits your windshield. How to describe it? Putrefaction comes closest. Was it contagious? Where was Mrs. Clark when hubby doddered off to work?

What could have been the source of this stench? Cigarettes? Decaying, unbrushed teeth? That must have been it. However, it was impossible to identify the offending teeth as all of them appeared to have been fused together by a grayish green substance that over time had hardened into a floss-proof carapace.

And what was expected of me if Ez collapsed in my presence? Were associates supposed to administer mouth-to-mouth?

"Mr. Millard, would you like to…" Puff. "Work on a…" Pause. Smoke leaked from his mouth and nose. "Deal?"

Crossing my fingers as I leaned forward and looked my most engaged, I replied, "Yes, sir, Mr. Clark. Absolutely."

Ez studied his cigarette as he considered my response.

I am unused to maintaining an alert and respectful demeanor when revolted.

A dry hack followed by another, more liquid sound. A cross between a wheeze and a death rattle. I slid backwards in my chair.

"We are going to represent the underwriters…"

I liked that 'we'. Clearly he meant the two of us.

"Of First Mortgage Bonds—" he picked up a Hydrox cookie from the plate beside his blotter and nibbled, "of a Massachusetts electric utility." He paused and gawped. "An investor-owned electric utility." Ez withdrew a handkerchief from his sleeve and flapped at the crumbs.

I could tell the old prick was wondering if I'd grasped the significance of the utility's being investor-owned. I hadn't, and what's more, I didn't give a rat's ass. I'd find out later. Time for a servile nod.

Ez cleared his throat. Violently. Disgustingly. Before his handkerchief could intercept it, something wet and globular flew from his mouth at a velocity approaching Mach 1. It touched down damply in the indemnification provisions of the underwriting agreement at which he'd been staring.

Struggling to control myself, I looked away.

"Pay attention, young man," croaked Ez.

"Yes, sir. Absolutely, sir."

"Have you ever—" he blew at an ash on the broad lapel of a double-breasted suit that was probably out of fashion in the Coolidge administration, "worked on a…"

What, for Chrissake, what? I'd hardly worked on anything. Sweet Jesus, I'd just gotten here.

"Public offering?"

"No, sir, Mr. Clark."

My sharp ears picked up the soft sibilance of escaping gas. I bit my lip.

"That will be all, Mr. Millard."

For now, I assumed.

As I left, I observed my mentor rearranging his privates.

Next morning I spied Eliot sprinting for the stairs. "Where's the fire, big guy?" I drawled.

"Mr. Clark wants to see me," said Eliot.

6

MY FIRST few weeks at Curtis and Perkins (henceforth I'm calling it 'C&P') were spent on unrelated assignments for a variety of partners in different fields. So were Millard's. It was hit or miss. New associates are like chum flung off a fishing boat. Would we attract any big fish? In that well-mannered era it was unthinkable to go knocking on the doors of partners you wanted to work for. You might drop hints, but basically you hoped to be noticed and waited to be asked. Like a girl?

The result of my labors was invariably a memorandum which usually failed to provide a conclusive answer to whatever question had been posed, but was, I hoped, sufficiently well thought-out to avoid having me written off as partnership material. For many memo writers, the primary objective is avoidance of blame and passing off uncertainty as balanced judgment. I did my best to provide answers.

After about a month, I received what I considered a real-life mission, one that would take me out of the office and away from the library.

It began with a call from Mr. Clark's secretary. Mr. Clark would like to see me if I was available. Indeed I was. Mr. Clark was something of a legend among securities lawyers. He had single-handedly created the firm's business practice and, in the 1930s, became a recognized expert in the New Deal's securities legislation, which enabled him to develop a nifty Wall Street practice 200 miles north of Manhattan.

I was intrigued with Mr. Clark because both my grandfathers died before I was born. I'd had no contact with elderly males. In those days of life tenure, C&P had a varied assortment of ancients. I was fascinated. To me they were a different race. They were living, breathing examples of what I might become. Looking back, I see my youthful self as a visitor to Jurassic Park.

Not to be callous, but a lot of our grizzled veterans were cautionary tales, caught in the slack tide between uselessness and helplessness. However, most of them were or had become gentle creatures with kindly dispositions. Our ninth floor was like a petting zoo where you fed farm animals pelletized grain and let them tickle your palm with their rough tongues and leathery noses.

My most touching recollection involved a dotty old thing who wandered the corridors smiling at one and all while simultaneously playing pocket poodle and humming old show tunes. One day he entered a conference room where a meeting was in progress and expelled everyone because, said he, he'd reserved it weeks earlier for an important gathering of his own. Nobody had the heart to object. They collected their belongings and left while the gentleman in question sat at the head of the table and gazed serenely out over the harbor as he awaited the arrival of his dead clients.

My curiosity about the elders was unbounded. Sometimes you'd catch one grazing, but generally they were as hard to spot as shy nocturnal mammals. A puddle under a urinal told an alert tracker that a senior had just passed through. Millard and I laughed about these accidents. I remember thinking, will I be here long enough to sprinkle the tiles myself?

Shuffling between their offices, the bathrooms, and the elevators, these men, Mr. Clark excepted, arrived late and left early, often in taxis their secretaries had called in advance. The last chauffeurs had disappeared a few years before my arrival. They were wraith-like beings bundled up like children in overcoat, hat, scarf, mittens, and rubbers or galoshes even when this wasn't called for by the weather. They clung to their large offices until the EMTs arrived with a gurney.

Mr. Clark welcomed the opportunity to work with the young, and you could tell his life, his whole life, was the law. "What a weirdo," Millard said. I was told Mr. Clark had a long, if somewhat detached, first marriage, which, being childless, left him with more time to concentrate on his financings. His wife had died in 1962.

Some months after noticing her absence, he married the widow of a Harvard Law School classmate. Evidently, the newlyweds understood the drill. She was content to pass her remaining years as she had the preceding ones—playing bridge with her friends, themselves widows of Boston lawyers. Not my idea of a wife.

Off to Mr. Clark. I armed myself with two ballpoint pens, in case one of them ran dry, and the standard-issue yellow pad. I put on my jacket, shot the cuffs, checked my appearance in the nearest reflecting surface and sprinted from my cubicle on seven to the ninth floor where Mr. Clark occupied a cavernous corner 'room' with a working fireplace. En route, I ran into Millard who couldn't resist making a fresh remark about my seeming agitation.

Yes, I was anxious. I wanted to practice business law, and I assumed C&P would only allow one of its rookies to do so.

Mr. Clark's office felt like a seldom-visited museum with its occupant a well-preserved specimen in an otherwise empty gallery. Somewhat glassy-eyed, he'd have been at home among the disintegrating stuffed animals in Harvard's Museum of Natural History. He and his surroundings were neat and spare. His spacious office contained a few items of heavy dark furniture. Eight freestanding wooden bookcases with sliding glass doors were arrayed along the walls. These contained a complete set of the *Harvard Law Review* and various treatises, including a thorough and surprisingly readable work on trust indentures which, on Mr. Clark's death, passed to David Farnum, and, upon his retirement, to me.

Mr. Clark's desk was a lonely atoll. It was flanked by a straight-backed side chair. Two wooden arm chairs faced the desk. All the chairs were covered in the same dark horsehide held in place by brass tacks, none of which appeared to be missing. This was before the days of fripperies such as sofas and coffee tables. What, if anything, Mr. Clark had on his walls, I've long since forgotten. There were no family photographs anywhere. The floor was covered with the same thin green carpeting used throughout the firm, except that Mr. Clark's was, like his desk, scarred with cigarette burns.

His door was open. Mr. Clark appeared to be napping or studying a document. I couldn't tell which. Hoping not to startle him, I tapped gently on the door frame and received a nod and what I took to be a fleeting but welcoming smile from a diminutive man who combined the alert expression of a squirrel with the stillness of the Great Sphinx. Mr. Clark had a tidy, well-tended face. All extraneous hair had been erased.

He wore wire-rimmed spectacles resembling those now returning to fashion. Despite the attention paid to Mr. Clark's appearance, up close he exuded a sharp, unpleasant odor (tobacco?) which I couldn't place.

Mr. Clark was calm and cordial. Months later I learned that this quiet man, who during the time I knew him, seldom raised his voice, had once been feared for his temper and impatience. However, even in his 70s, Mr. Clark was accustomed to being obeyed. When engrossed in drafting or negotiating, Mr. Clark would throw his burning cigarette on the floor. He'd shout "Pay attention" at anyone who distracted him by putting it into an ashtray. His subordinates learned to remain seated and keep focused on business while monitoring the thin plume of smoke rising from the carpet like a Lilliputian's campfire.

Despite the Surgeon General's warning, Mr. Clark puffed away until the end. As I soon learned, the only interruptions Mr. Clark tolerated were his secretary's prompt 11:00 a.m. and 4:00 p.m. appearances with his cup (not mug) of tea and two Hydrox cookies.

I advanced and took the proffered seat. It's been 22 years, but this is how I remember it.

Mr. Clark said nothing for several seconds. It was a companionable silence. He had attained a state of mystical inwardness, and appeared to have shed ambition, desire, envy, greed, lust, pride and, I am sure, several other vices. Sloth had never been an issue. Was I in the presence of the State Street Lama? I felt warmly towards Mr. Clark, but I hoped I wasn't seeing myself 50 years hence.

Then he cleared his throat. "We haven't been introduced yet, Mr. Lawrence." Pause. "My name is Ezra Clark, and I've been told you did good work for Harold Downing's grandson."

I thought I had, but you can never be sure. "Thank you, sir."

"Young Downing doesn't strike me as very promising."

I realized I had to slow down and allow Mr. Clark to complete his thoughts. He was looking at me intently. How should I respond to his observation about my client, an observation with which I was not inclined to disagree?

"Tom's not stupid, sir, and, I believe, with a little coaching he could succeed at something."

Mr. Clark nodded. "I've met your classmate, Andrew Millard…"

Mr. Clark floated off somewhere then drifted back.

"It was most peculiar. For several weeks, I kept bumping into him. I'd never seen him before, and then I couldn't seem to avoid him."

Was I too late? Had Millard gotten the nod?

"I'm not sure Mr. Millard's cut out for business law…"

"Andrew Millard is very able," I replied. Mr. Clark thought about that for a moment.

"Able, you say?"

Silence. Although I didn't know the expression at that time, I could see no point in 'bidding against myself' so I said no more about Millard.

"Would you be interested in my line of work?"

"Very much so, sir."

"Do you think you'd be any good at it?"

"I'd do my very best not to disappoint you, sir." Was that the faintest nod?

Several minutes passed. Mr. Clark's cigarette charred the edge of his desk. Unperturbed, he flicked it onto the rug, finished his first cookie, and passed the plate to me. Another test? No way was I taking the senior partner's last Hydrox. I smiled, shook my head, and told him I'd had a big breakfast. Had I committed a faux pas? Had I been rude? Was this like declining sushi in Japan? Mr. Clark didn't seem offended. Relieved, if anything.

Waiting until he'd finished his second cookie, I said, "I'd be honored to work on your deals."

Mr. Clark weighed my answer. Had I overdone it with 'honored'? Thankfully, I detected nothing that could be interpreted as disapproval. Had I made the team? I was touched by his tentative smile.

"I'm glad to hear that, Mr. Lawrence. Mr. Millard told me that you were headed into litigation."

I said nothing, but Millard and I were going to have a little talk.

Without waiting for a response, Mr. Clark pressed a button on his phone and, as though popped from a toaster, a spindly lady appeared in his doorway. She knocked, entered, hesitated, and advanced, holding a spiral pad in a trembling, gloved hand.

"Get me Farnum," yelled Mr. Clark.

His secretary winced and withdrew. Moments later, Mr. Clark's phone rang. "Clark here." He slammed the handset back into its cradle. Evidently Mr. Farnum was not at his post.

Mr. Clark told me we would be representing the underwriters in a sale of first mortgage bonds of an investor-owned electric utility. Mr. Clark did not seem upset when I asked what he meant by 'investor-owned'. Other lawyers would be called in as needed.

Although I didn't realize it at the time, the days of two partners and an associate working on routine financings were numbered. The clients would be screaming, "Old man Clark's worthless and so is his stooge, Lawrence. One capable guy can handle it." They would object to subsidizing my apprenticeship. And who were all those other people? Did they add value?

Mr. Clark outlined the deal. His secretary gave me the underwriting documents from the utility's previous issue. Mr. Clark told me to read them and give him my thoughts at 10:00 a.m. the next morning.

It was a stressful 23 hours. Aside from my obvious insight that the documents needed to be updated, I didn't have much else to say about them. Fortunately, Mr. Clark's expectations were low. He walked me through the papers. I had few questions. Mr. Clark spoke slowly. There were relaxed pauses between his utterances, pauses during which he puffed and communed with the muse of public offerings.

It was like being in the presence of an oracle. When Mr. Clark finally spoke, what he said was invariably worth hearing. It was mean of me, but I couldn't help but think Mr. Clark made a lot of scents. Ha. Ha. Through it all, I was touched by his willingness to initiate yet another novice into these ancient mysteries.

The next day I tracked down Millard.

"Something's bugging me... Andrew."

"And what would that be?" said my unruffled friend.

"You told Mr. Clark I wanted to be a litigator. That was total B.S."

Millard didn't miss a beat.

"Down, big fella. Quite the contrary, actually. I told Uncle Ez you'd be a natural in his tiresome field, but I didn't say 'tiresome' as you may have guessed. Next?"

Millard's room is the only one in the firm with a mirror. He was attending to some errant locks.

"Ez got it ass-backwards. One of the many reasons I steered clear. Anything else?"

That shut me up, but Millard wasn't done.

"You owe me big time, Tiger, but if you like, I'll remind him of what I said."

"Sorry for the mix-up, and—thanks." Millard smiled benignly. Should I have doubted him?

Mr. Clark evidently approved of my meager contributions, but several months passed before I was pulled into his orbit. During my probationary period I was, like Millard and Stevens, at everyone's beck and call. It was fabulous training. Back then, as the one rookie in the corporate department I was expected to master the new developments in my field. All the fledgling businesses were dumped in my lap with the dumper hastening off to more lucrative enterprises. I was to figure out what needed doing, do it, and bill it. It was taken for granted I would collect 100% of time charges, and disbursements, no more, and certainly no less.

Then came DataCentric, Inc., a company palmed off on me by an associate who considered it beneath him. How was I to know Al Hendricks, its president, treasurer, and sole stockholder was a sleaze?

After ignoring my invoices and entreaties, Hendricks called with a proposition. "Eliot, my man, we're experiencing a temporary cash flow problem, so tear up your annoying bills and accept my once-in-a-lifetime offer. The DataCentric shares I've sent you will be worth a bundle when we go public, next year, at the latest."

I returned the shares and watched helplessly as Hendricks took his business elsewhere, leaving me holding the bag for over $3,000 in lost C&P revenue. That was a lot back then, more than 43% of my starting salary.

Had I committed a capital crime? Millard was gleeful. He ribbed me for weeks about my high horse and his low one. Usually in public. Few of my other colleagues were sympathetic even though keeping those shares would have cheated the firm and been grounds for immediate dismissal. Some of them, thankfully, not all, just looked at me and shook their heads. What effect would this have on my career, I remember wondering? Why hadn't I talked with Clare or Mr. Clark beforehand?

When I told Mr. Clark about my blunder, I thought he might read me the riot act. He didn't.

"You've learned an important lesson, young man," said Mr. Clark, "and you've learned it early and at small cost. Size up your clients immediately and never stop reviewing your initial assessment. Maybe you got it wrong. People change. So do organizations. Usually for the worse." Mr. Clark looked inward and seemed to dissolve like his cigarette smoke. Then, genie-like, he reappeared.

"Establish billing rules early. If you make a mistake, and mistakes are inevitable, face the damn music. Admit it, apologize, and offer to reduce your fee before you lose the client."

This was the only time I'd ever hear Mr. Clark swear. He looked tired, and it was clear he hadn't been inspected before he left home.

"One moment," Mr. Clark said. He got up and disappeared for ten minutes. I had nothing to read, but I could see the harbor and the Custom House Tower from his office. Mr. Clark returned.

"Would you like a cigarette, Mr. Lawrence?"

"No thank you, sir."

"I believe I will."

Mr. Clark's Parliaments reposed in a cork lined silver box which Miss Bosworth, his secretary, locked up at night and refilled with fresh cigarettes every morning. She was also responsible for keeping his carafe full of cool (not cold) water.

"Where were we?" Mr. Clark asked.

"We were discussing clients, sir."

"So we were. Yes. Yes. Remember this." He aimed his cigarette at me.

"As you no doubt learned in law school, every rascal is entitled to vigorous representation, but that doesn't carry over into our (I liked that) line of work. Have nothing to do with shady businesses. Even if they pay promptly and in full. We are what we eat."

Mr. Clark leaned back in his chair. He smoked and thought. Was he finished? I couldn't very well ask. Nor could I leave. Had he forgotten about me, and what about the cigarette that appeared to be glued to his lower lip? He pried it free without drawing blood and dropped it on the carpet. I studied it out of the corner of my eye.

"We were talking about clients, weren't we, Mr. Lawrence?"

I nodded.

"As I was saying, avoid the bad apples. They'll infect you. What's more—"

There was no more. Miss Bosworth tiptoed forward with his 11:00 a.m. rations. Time to rise and depart.

"Thank you, Mr. Clark."

He may have given me a tiny wave, but by then the cookies had his full attention.

I can't remember how many transactions it took before I thought I was making the slightest contribution. Mr. Clark constantly emphasized four things. Don't quibble about someone else's infelicitous drafting if it works. Learn what is and what is not negotiable. Do not ever try to re-trade a deal. Never forget Boston's a small town; if you misbehave, people remember and make you pay.

Mr. Clark was fading fast, but each new deal was a pick-me-up. Its restorative qualities would temporarily arrest his decline. I worked on his last deals together with whichever partner was the heir apparent to the account. The number two man and I maneuvered Mr. Clark into and out of taxis and through revolving doors. Escalators were a particular challenge. His balance was gone. I had horrid visions of our senior partner toppling into the mangle and being shredded before my eyes. Mr. Clark was a slight man, as difficult to steer as a skiff in a strong wind. It would have been easier to carry him. Mr. Clark, who cherished his independence, accepted our help with a graciousness I hope to duplicate when I become infirm.

Without warning, Mr. Clark stopped coming to the office. I had no idea I'd never see him again. I remember our last session (I'd finally become 'Eliot'), and wish I'd expressed my gratitude. Only his contemporaries and oldest subordinates were welcome in the hospital. I was told that on one visit, Mr. Clark was sitting up in bed staring at the top sheet. Holding it close to his face, he murmured, "This airline deal is really complicated."

"Don't worry, Ezra (few people used his first name), I've got it under control," said his guest. Mr. Clark nodded, smiled, fell back on his pillow, and dozed off. David Farnum, who hadn't worked with Mr. Clark as long as others, told me he thought it wise to introduce himself when he visited. Mr. Clark looked at him and said, "Farnum? Yes, he was all right."

The entire firm mourned Mr. Clark, and for a while the place seemed rudderless. That was a false impression. As senior partner, Mr. Clark was nominally in command, but administrative matters bored him, and the place had devolved into a loose federation of semi-autonomous principalities. Shortly after he died, those who'd worked for Mr. Clark (I was the last associate to do so) were reminded of him once again. Each of us received a $750 bequest. Why that amount? Five hundred dollars, insufficient? One thousand dollars, excessive? Who knows? For me, it was a windfall. This was before bonuses, when annual pay increases were measured in hundreds of dollars.

I was lucky to have gotten my start with Mr. Clark. Unfortunately, his death left me without a powerful mentor.

7

ELIOT'S INTO old man Clark's worsteds. So what about moi?

Do he and that prissy old fart presume to talk about me? Any clown can do business law. Just mark up the friggin' papers from the last deal. Like reworking Cousin Bruce's English papers. How challenging. I doubt that Eliot's 'drafted' an original sentence since he's been here.

I never got it with the drippy books Eliot read as a kid. All that twaddle about Galahad et al. No comics? And what about skin mags? Who pulls his pud over Maid Marian? Eliot's heroes never got rich and, despite a lot of exertion, never got laid, at least not in print. You can cram your courtly love. Those damn damsels never put out.

My idols were those slicked-back, fast-developing Latin-American students who'd been packed off to our New England gulag. Where have you gone Ernesto, Eduardo, and Edmundo? You with your sleek, pomaded black locks. Your scented aftershave. Your roguish, European, multi-breasted blazers. You were rhythmic brilliance on the dance floor. All of us would stand and gawk as you tangoed our prim dates into the lilac-scented spring evenings and returned them flushed and disheveled.

But, alas, the presence of girls among us was all too infrequent and the pressure generated by your jizzum buildup cried out for regular release. You were much like the productive South-American oil and gas wells that financed your years in our joyless Protestant enclave.

During those long dry interludes, you suave rogues engaged in prodigious bouts of unabashed self-abuse. Sometimes you avoided tidying up by wanking out the window, frequently in time to the admiring applause of your fans gathered below in the quadrangle.

Sometimes you played the prankster and made fervent love to your roommate's pillow leaving him to deal with the residue of your exertions. Some of you may even have been as big as—OK, bigger than—me.

How could anyone expect you to pass your courses when all your energies went into inspired onanism, smoking, and desultory games of soccer at a time when that was the refuge of those who couldn't cut it on the gridiron? But why did it matter when your padre ran the secret police and had millions stashed in Zurich? What has become of you? You never come to reunions. You never contribute to the alumni fund. Are you in exile? Did you die in a coup?

By fifth-form (junior) year my burden had become intolerable. There are only so many ways you can choke your chicken. I was like a sergeant inflicting corporal punishment on his privates. Try as I might, I was unable to score with any of the well-fed, well-bred, well-chaperoned debs we met at those deadly holiday dances. Even shop girls who were doing it like rabbits rejected my overtures with unconcealed contempt.

Providentially, we had an urbane classmate, now deceased, who had savored pleasures that to most of us were recurrent fantasies. Pierre, who spent his post-college years in drink, drugs, and high-stakes backgammon, led me and two other friends—not including Eliot, who I am certain went to his marital couch as a homo intactus—on Operation Libido Freedom. Bring on the forbidden fruit. I wanted sin, and I wanted it at once. Even if it involved paying wages.

Pierre had the phone number of a Miss (I'm guessing) Merwin, and knew the password that would admit us to her bower of bliss. There is now some disagreement among the surviving novitiates as to whether it was 'Ralph with a Crew Cut' or 'Red from Princeton'. No matter. Anyone familiar with the military knows that for security reasons, passwords, like codes, are changed frequently. While Pierre had visited several ladies of Miss Merwin's calling, she was, in a manner of speaking, virgin territory.

D (as in deflowering) Day arrived. Pierre called and arranged our group appointment. We were determined to be punctual. Who knew, there might be a line. We set off for our virginectomies. Even though we'd imbibed a little Dutch courage, our stomachs were in knots. Not to worry, Pierre knew the ropes. We arrived, were buzzed in, and trudged, not bounded, up five flights of filthy stairs. In response to his knock and an uninspiring "Yeah?", Pierre identified himself as a friendly. We heard deadbolts snapping back, keys turning, and chains rattling. The door was opened by a skeletal apparition in a soiled bathrobe. With her lifeless yellow locks, she looked like a dispirited dandelion. She displayed no welcoming behavior. These days we would say she lacked marketing skills and confine her to the library. No client contact for her.

Where, I wondered, were the silk mules, the fishnet stockings, the see-through undergarments, the garters, and the luscious décolletage one saw in the lingerie ads that so inflamed me? This was not the cheery, traditional bordello we'd seen in our cowboy movies.

Like Miss Merwin, the setting was a downer. No incense. No beaded curtains. No slinky music. No tea. No sympathy. Not even a well-thumbed *National Geographic* featuring half-clad aborigines. No come-hither looks. No touching. Miss Merwin possessed the raw animal vitality of someone working overtime at the registry of motor vehicles.

Time to set the batting order and hand in the line-up card. Pierre, we conceded, was entitled to lead off. The rest of us played scissors, paper, and rock. I got stuck in the cleanup slot, checked out the reading materials, and settled down with an outdated edition of the Dartmouth alumni magazine.

Pierre gave us a jaunty nod and disappeared. He reappeared half an hour later, his tie in place. The rest of us were suitably impressed. Quite the performer. Batters two and three averaged about fifteen minutes each. I heard nothing except the sound of running water. No delirious outcries. Why not?

I heard a halfhearted, "Next." I was up. After a pause to steel myself, I knocked, entered, and was greeted by the cadaverous Miss Merwin. She was on her back. There was no turning back. She beckoned with a nicotine-stained index finger. "Be positive," I told myself. "Channel Dr. Peale."

All would erotically unfold in an atmosphere of languorous carnality. Instead, she flipped open her faded robe and there it was. The fabled fissure. She put aside her comic book but not her Juicy Fruit while she outlined the options and the cost of each. Since this was my first outing and I was unfamiliar with the electives, I settled on the introductory course. Miss Merwin named her price, and, without any haggling, we reached an oral understanding.

"So, what's your name?

"OK, Patrick. You don't have to whisper. Your pals can't hear you. Ever done it before?

"Nah? OK, I could tell.

"So, don't just stand there. Take 'em off and let's have a gander.

"Yes, everything. Toss 'em over there. On the chair. Not on the floor. You live in a barn, Patrick?

"OK. Keep your socks on.

"Not bad. Not bad at all, Patrick. You're going to make the girls very happy. But why's it hiding? I won't hurt it.

"OK. This isn't working. We've gotta do something or we'll be here all afternoon.

"Relax, Patrick. Where you from?

"Round here? You don't sound it. Not a bit. Well, how's about those Yanks? Creamed the Bums again, didn't they? My old man's from Brooklyn, the prick.

"OK, you in college?

"Not yet. You're just a junior. Well, that thing of yours isn't a junior. Where you want to go?

"Yeah, I mean college.

"Nah, skip that dump. Even if Patrick Senior went there. They're all pansies. Yale or Dartmouth maybe. Yeah, Dartmouth. They grow 'em big and horny up there.

"What say we get going? Junior looks like he's waking up."

Then she marched me to the sink, turned on the water, and scrubbed me roughly.

Miss Merwin, whose nickname we subsequently learned was 'Slats', was hardly the schoolboy's dream. I had no opportunity to hone my amatory skills. I never got to unzip, untie, unbutton, unwrap, unsnap, undo, untuck, or unfold. As they say in police procedurals, she assumed the position, slid a stained pillow under her bony haunches, told me, quite unnecessarily, that certain areas were off-limits, and directed me to proceed.

"OK, Patrick. All aboard.

"Yeah, on top. This is beginner's class, lover. You got to pay extra for that special stuff."

After some ineffective dowsing with my divining rod, I am relieved to say that Miss Merwin got me properly aligned. Until that moment, I'd felt like Jacques Cousteau trying to maneuver an undersea probe into the Mariana Trench. Despite my guide's lack of gusto and her superfluous ground rules, I'm pleased to report I achieved my objective. I had committed sexual intercourse, at least as it's defined in the Uniform Code of Military Justice, where all that's required is "penetration, however slight".

"What pipes and timbrels? What wild ecstasy!" Not!

So, what was it like, my long-anticipated coming-of-age? Both overdue and premature, and I trust Pierre negotiated a volume discount. I'd hoped this experience would leave me feeling like a depraved voluptuary—a Marquis de Sade. No, more like a handyman who had made quick, no-nonsense use of his plumber's snake. But was I discouraged or pessimistic? Never. It was a start.

Back to the uninspiring present and Uncle Ezra. In gushing about his mentor, Eliot forgets one of his more memorable lines. It competes with 'the check's in the mail' and 'I'll respect you tomorrow'. Since before I arrived, Ramses Clark, like most of the old dodos, has been mumbling, "I'll retire the moment I start to slip."

And where does that leave me? With trusts and estates. My shelter from the stormy blast and my more driven contemporaries. At least, I don't have to sit downwind from decomposing Clark. My choice, if such it is, suits me perfectly and saves me from direct competition with my nemesis. It has not escaped my attention that trusts and estates lawyers seem immortal and stress-free. High blood pressure among this lot is as rare as scurvy. Those at Curtis and Perkins (hereinafter referred to as 'Curtis') are particularly long in the tooth, sustained perhaps by colonic irrigation or advanced cryogenic processes. This foretells great opportunities for those in their late twenties. Perhaps there are things an ambitious lad can do to hasten the elders' departures.

Trusts and estates, owing to a low enlistment rate, welcomes those who've been found wanting in or have no appetite for the more fast-paced practice areas. Ironically, many of them are having the last laugh on those self-styled hard chargers.

The immediate challenge was to persuade my seniors that, despite possessing a Y chromosome, I nevertheless wanted to join these gentle, slow-moving ruminants. I'm not being rude. These guys struggle to kill time. There's not much to do. As an estate planner, you draft the instruments (or, to be more precise, exhume them from the form file) and await the inevitable. Then, if you've played it right, you double-dip as executor and as attorney for the estate.

While so many of my decisions, such as my first and second marriages, have been based on inadequate intelligence, I've been careful in choosing my life's work. Curtis's crown jewels are the hundreds of millions of dollars under the trusteeship of a fortunate few partners. Once you've snaffled or inherited a piece of this [in]action, you're immune from anything short of a total—and I mean total—mental collapse, a felony conviction, indiscretions with the inappropriate, or expulsion from one of a handful of clubs. You can go on a lifetime sabbatical; and as long as the sluggish beneficiaries don't regain consciousness, you'll pass the years in genteel inactivity helping yourself every three months to a percentage of their assets. A hint of Parkinson's? A whisper of dementia? No biggie. Now you can bond with your customers.

Snagging a fat trust practice was the objective towards which I crept late in 1963. After perfecting my solemn mortician's act—this isn't as easy as it might seem; it's sometimes difficult to distinguish the earnest from the witless—and cloaking my ambition, I am pleased to report that after only a few years of crawling, cringing, and coat-holding, I was enthusiastically welcomed into the club. I was trustworthy.

My business is death. My income depends on it. Death is my life. The first coffin I saw was Edward's. Since then I've become a connoisseur of caskets.

The wisdom of my choice was confirmed when one of our senior T & E lawyers, wanting one for himself, caused Curtis to adopt a sabbatical policy. Realizing their presence was purely ornamental, my departmental colleagues began a disorderly rush for more salubrious climes. Several of the more pompous talked of 'improving' themselves while they were away. It amuses me to observe that no lawyer in any other department has ever taken a sabbatical. They realize that if they're gone for over a month some other partner will poach their customers.

8

I SPENT six months in the Marine Corps after college. Almost everyone my age who had relatives in WWII felt he owed Uncle Sam a piece of his life. In fact, I've often thought I should have given more, particularly when the Marines were getting chopped up at Khe Sanh in 1968. I served during a peaceful decade. Not much was happening in 1959. Korea had been over for six years and Viet Nam hadn't heated up.

Once I realized the Marine Corps' syllabus didn't permit the DIs to intentionally kill or maim me, I reveled in boot camp and was unperturbed by our tormentors. Our training combined elements of schoolboy athletics with pre-adolescent summer camp where I took riflery and archery and picked up rudimentary woodland skills. We learned to read maps, use the compass, and move undetected (at least sometimes) from point to point. I remember crawling through goldenrod trying not to sneeze. I discovered an object wasn't Marine Corps clean unless it "sparkled like a diamond in a goat's asshole". What a kick.

My months in the Crotch (as we cheerfully referred to the Corps) remain more vivid than the years, even the recent ones, spent at my desk. C&P time is fuzzy and generally unremarkable. I couldn't begin to tell you, without consulting my diaries, how 1970, say, differed from 1980.

The Marines clarified my vision of what I wanted in a wife. Growing up, I observed many marriages. Some looked tolerable; few seemed enviable. Then I met Major Hastings, a career officer or 'lifer'. Having gone to my alma mater is not necessarily a plus in the armed forces, particularly the Marines. You must prove yourself at every new command. Show them you're not an Ivy League wimp.

That was fine with Frank Hastings, whose size and aggressiveness discouraged challenges. He'd played varsity football with happy abandon and flown Corsairs in the same reckless fashion. Finally, he was grounded for persisting with such typical airdale pranks as flying under bridges, often inverted. The classic World War I aerial maneuvers were, he claimed, a sure cure for hangovers.

Major Hastings and I hit it off from the start. At the end of my tour and in a serious breach of military protocol, he invited me, a lance corporal, to his house for a farewell dinner. Since we were both Harvards, the dinner should have been polite and decorous. Since we were both Marines, it wasn't. After a full hour of cocktails, we advanced (Marines always advance) to the dining room and there, confronting the Major, was a plump roast chicken. He emitted a blood-thirsty cry and lunged at it with his carving fork. Every Marine is trained in hand-to-hand combat, but that doesn't mean an inebriated field-grade officer can necessarily subdue an agile chicken on a slippery platter. After several failed efforts to immobilize his elusive foe, he picked it up in his bare hands, called it an awful name, and hurled it through a screened window.

Did his wife upbraid him? Was she enraged? Mortified? After all, they had company of a sort. No. She laughed in a wonderfully affectionate way, got up and gave him an emphatic smooch. I can't remember what we ended up eating, but the chicken was left outside for the coyotes. Give me a wife like that, a woman who would love me, no matter what. And I found one, even though when I mentioned this incident to Clare, she said Major Hastings was violent and his wife must have been drunk. Maybe so. But I owe him a lot. He provided me with an infallible way of assessing people. He called it his foxhole test. Do you want that person next to you when, literally or figuratively, 'Luke the Gook' or 'Link the Chink' (that's what he called them) comes at you with burp gun blazing? I would have cleaned up the Major's language, but I cannot fault his premise.

The day after the chicken-as-grenade meal, I went from a military reservation to an Indian reservation. I signed up to teach English on a Pima reservation outside Tucson. I know it sounds corny, but there I discovered joy. And I knew it at the time. She was wearing dungarees, a checkered shirt, and a bandanna. An impish Dale Evans cowgirl look combined with wit, intelligence, and a sweet nature. She was not a classic beauty. She was something better. Lustrous, and without intending to, she upstaged the girls who were and perceived themselves to be gorgeous. Plus, she was from Boston.

From the beginning she looked, sounded, felt, and smelled perfect to me. Her generous features took up her entire face. Like Audrey Hepburn's. I even loved the way she yawned. She tolerated me. Thankfully, there were a number of factors in my favor. We were constantly thrown together. All the volunteers ate in the same mess hall, and there was little male competition within a hundred miles. Had we met at a dance or attended classes together, I would have been lost in a welter of better looking, more promising beaux. Clare was wildly popular, but she wasn't vain or mean like the typical goddess. To use an antiquated term, she was not 'stuck up'.

Her suitors tried to stay in touch even when she was in the desert. She had already declined several marriage proposals, but I didn't learn this for years. Her modesty increased her appeal. Quite honestly, I could visualize nothing but misery without her, but, perhaps fortuitously (although I didn't think so at the time), I was my usual tongue-tied, awkward self. I went so far as to buy one of those silly shirts with snaps instead of buttons. She giggled.

I knew I'd get nowhere pleading, pursuing, or pouring out my feelings. Unfortunately, I never had the opportunity to save her from a rattlesnake, and, as always, my possibly-interesting observations came to me days later. So I gave her a lot of space without realizing I was doing so. Don't, I kept telling myself, become completely tiresome. Don't read too much into a generous disposition. Don't overthink everything. Stop replaying every conversation. Leading Marines was easier.

While I am unable to recreate many of our conversations, I cannot forget my sense of lumpish unease. I recall saying, "Isn't it nice we've read so many of the same books and seen so many of the same movies."

I may have hit bottom with, "What's your favorite color?" Clare was kind, and instead of crushing me, drew out of me a long and no doubt tiresome monologue about the teams on which I'd played and the colors of their uniforms.

When I'd finished and fallen silent, she volunteered, "Wouldn't you like to hear about my triumphs?"

"You bet." Listening was easier.

However, even Clare had trouble staying within my somewhat constricted conversational comfort zone. One day she said, "What kind of music do you like, Eliot?" Since I didn't listen to it, sing it, or play it, that was a stumper. Thereafter, Clare went back to feeding me meatballs over the center of the plate. Not the time to let her know my oldest friend claimed to be an 'organ virtuoso'.

Clare admitted later to having been aware of my adoration and amused by my snail-like courtship, if courtship it could be called. She never acted bored. Nor was she ever cold, abrupt, or sarcastic. I was like a stray that wouldn't leave her porch. Since she couldn't bring herself to muzzle me, neuter me, put me down, or send me out for adoption, she finally gave up and kept me. Eliot Lawrence—rescue dog.

That's how it happened. Later she admitted she'd hurried me along.

As though I could forget. One evening towards the end of August when it looked as if our relationship might make it to Boston intact, I asked her, "Have I told you about my friend, Andrew Millard?"

"Yes, Eliot, you have. I'm beginning to think he may be your only friend."

"Well, he's not, but I should warn you, he'll be after you."

"Really?"

"Yes. After money, Millard's only interested in a lady's…"

"Don't you share *that* interest, Eliot?"

"Yes. Of course. But with Millard, all that matters is their…"

"Then I should be safe, shouldn't I?"

"Good God, no. You're perfect."

"How would you know, Eliot?" she said in a tone I'd never heard before.

Well, I was correct on both counts. Clare was perfect and Millard would be unable to control himself.

Thankfully, our relationship didn't just survive. It flourished. Millard preened and strutted, but I won despite his telling her, in what Clare insisted was a joking manner, that she could always 'trade up'. In the end, Millard was a good sport, so I made him my best man. He's never been more animated or attentive. Something else: one of my sweetie's many kindnesses was never suggesting she could have done better. She didn't have to.

Next came law school, about which I'm saying very little. Not that those three years were entirely forgettable. I have vivid memories, few of them good. The atmosphere was, as advertised, toxic.

Then there were the self-absorbed professors. They were more concerned with their outside income and public exposure than their unlovable, grade-crazed pupils.

As Millard put it, "Some of them will make time for their more adoring students to inhale their brilliance."

Millard was endlessly amused by our profs. If memory serves (and it probably doesn't) he described them somewhat as follows: incorrigible publicity hounds inveighing against law students selling out to soulless corporate law firms, while they're chasing the same business and lifting pages if not entire chapters from lesser academics who, in turn, 'internalize' passages from yet more obscure eggheads. Millard claimed to have gotten law review grades and said, "I laughed when they invited me to toil for that tiresome magazine."

C&P, when Millard and I got there, was relaxed and unstructured. Formal orientations were years away. There were only three rookies and not much to orient us about. We were each issued a lawyer's diary, a yellow pad, an office directory, and, if we were lucky, more than one pencil and maybe a ballpoint pen. It was assumed we'd figure out how to record our time. The custom, when I started, was to report in fifteen-minute increments.

We were told nothing about time requirements because there weren't any. You would have to be pretty dense, however, not to catch on quickly. As a group, the C&P lawyers didn't stress themselves, but most felt obliged to observe the dying convention of being seen in the office for a half day on Saturday. I hated this triumph of form over substance. Wearing sports jackets and flannels rather than suits was scant consolation. We didn't accomplish much, and it ruined the weekend.

I almost forgot, each of us got a desktop blotter. We could choose the color: blue, green, or crimson.

I approach the next topic with a high degree of skittishness. It did not escape my attention that, despite a few southern accents, the C&P lawyers all looked, dressed, acted, and sounded much like me. There was little diversity or, as Millard would say, "few invasive non-native species". All I can say about this subject is that the C&P demographics just happened. I'm sure it wasn't calculated. Nothing much was. There are those who insist that some of our partners were bigoted. I believe they are wrong.

Millard loved needling me. "Do you think our southern partners are just *lactose* intolerant?" he asked. Then he would claim C&P had slipped. The best minority lawyers had more exciting options. I do not mean to give it short shrift, but I suspect people from different backgrounds might sneer if I tackled this vexed subject. So I won't.

To get a better idea of my first year at C&P, I might mention its holiday celebrations. They were pre-*Plessy v. Ferguson*, both separate and unequal. The staff was relegated to our library. These proceedings remained orderly until the elderly bookkeepers, who were acting as bartenders, got soused. They freshened their own drinks while pouring for others. Millard discovered one of them out cold in the dumbwaiter. When the oldsters faded, the young bloods from the mailroom seized the bar and dragged the prettier secretaries into the stacks.

My first Christmas party, the one for associates, took place at what was then regarded as Boston's best restaurant, which at different times in the past had been a stable and a brothel. It served the finest *ancien cuisine,* as Millard liked to call it. Heavy, solid, and delicious, it clung to the ribs and the arteries. The festivities began with a seemingly interminable cocktail hour. Those were the days when men were men, and all of us tucked into the high-priced brands we' couldn't afford to buy for ourselves, the hundred-proof brown medicine that was gradually destroying the partners' lives and livers. While so engaged, we wolfed down handfuls of hors d'oeuvres. This was how the other half lived, and all of us, myself included, couldn't get enough of it.

There was a certain animus at this event. Since C&P was among the firms not paying a Christmas bonus, the mission of Millard and his ilk was to consume its entire bottom line in one sitting.

After cocktails we sat down, and the more boisterous began hurling food at the geeks. Millard cried out for serving wenches, but all our waiters were male. At this point in the evening, we were our most entertaining selves, quite unlike the slobbering wrecks some of us soon became. The female associates, who of course had been invited, took pains to absent themselves and preserve their reputations.

Although we weren't oenophiles, we knew oen (Ha Ha) came in different colors, and this was not the night to be monochromatic. We also understood pink wine was for mama's boys and it was sophisticated to have a different wine with each course. In making our selections, price was, for many, the only criterion. Some of us consumed about a pound of shellfish and then turned to our entrée or entrées. Lobster Savannah was and still is the most expensive dish. I saw one of my colleagues slip a well-béarnaised filet mignon into a jacket pocket.

Next, dessert. At least one baked Alaska per person. We didn't overlook cigars, and some of the gluttons ordered an entire box. Finally, brandy. The restaurant assigned one waiter to every three or four of us. It was barely enough. Many of my fellow associates fasted in preparation for this binge. Accidents occurred, but the waiters were discreet in tidying up and finding cabs for the ambulatory. I don't know where they stacked the unconscious.

The partners' Christmas lunch is still held at the same club. The partners leave the office around noon. Some of them struggle back after four and go through the motions of returning calls and attending to urgent business.

The only event to which all lawyers are invited is our field day. For years, it's been held on a June Friday at a North Shore country club. The location was chosen to accommodate the large number of partners who summered thereabouts. The South Shore wasn't considered.

Field day is rigidly structured. It begins early with the golf tournament. Everybody plays. No exceptions. No complaints. Each participant is required to drive off each tee. Then it becomes alternating shots. This is stressful if you're playing with an important, short-tempered, low-handicap partner. There are always spectators at the first tee. Many are accomplished hecklers. In the view of the seniors, non-golfers do not belong at C&P. Maybe this will toughen them up. A gentleman should be able to break 100 on a course of average difficulty. This attitude is needlessly unkind to non-golfers like Stevens.

It may not be worth mentioning, but, after two years at the firm, I discovered Millard consistently understated his ability (very rare for him) so he'd be paired with one of the firm's lowest-handicap, most influential seniors. This gave him a can't-miss shot at one of the silver trophies.

As of 1985, Millard had bagged five or six and charmed everyone with his witty, self-deprecating, off-the-cuff acceptance remarks. During that period I, as a one-time runner-up, brought home a ceramic coffee mug. I'm holding off on my order for the velvet-lined trophy case.

I remember calling Millard on this maneuver. He was dismissive, "Eliot, my son, remember Chapel. Never puff yourself up. The meek shall inherit the earth, preferably at a time of low estate taxes."

Golf is followed by a leisurely liquid lunch, the beginning of the end for some of the weary older partners. The festivities resume in the afternoon. Golf for those who are still alive in the tournament. Others play tennis. Some rest up for what's coming.

Everyone assembles around 4:00 p.m. at the traditional location for softball. Sometimes the proceedings are livened up with a fracture. The patient, if he isn't already drunk, engages in self-anesthetization on the way to the local hospital. The walking wounded are expected to return for dinner, on crutches if necessary. David Farnum, who'd seen combat in WWII, did just that.

After softball, we colossi stride back to the clubhouse recounting our triumphs. Most of us, not having spent this much time in the sun since the previous summer, are parboiled. On the way to the locker room nearly everyone downs another beer to see them through showers and towel snapping. We are now at about the 20-mile mark of this marathon, but the hardest part is still ahead—cocktails, then the banquet, more cocktails, then entertainment, still more cocktails, wrapping up with poker, bridge and/or spirited singing around the piano. Off-key but never off-color, despite Millard's best efforts. Millard knows several stanzas of 'Fuck 'em all' and has, I must admit, a pretty fair voice. Finally, the drive home for those who have not been decanted into a taxi or interred in one of the club's upstairs bedrooms.

Entertainment is provided by the youngest class of associates. They parody the partners. Over time, these performances have become as rigid and stylized as kabuki. While the skits themselves can be savage or benign, certain partners are featured every year. Looking back, I realize the most talented performers fled C&P. They had too much flair and vitality for our profession. As the firm became increasingly coed, the field days ended with activities involving pairs. Millard says he can still coax a blush from the cheeks of one of his 'favorites' when he alludes to the slippery leather upholstery in a certain Lincoln Continental.

For those who don't live on the North Shore, the day's greatest challenge is getting home without doing injury to themselves and/or others. I do not usually overindulge, but I remember a return trip where each vehicle ahead of me appeared to have multiple sets of taillights. The patron saint of lawyers (Millard says he's 'St. Shyster'), must have been looking out for us. Though it's statistically improbable, C&P has not, as I write this, suffered a single KIA after field day. Knock on wood. And, yes, absurd as it may be, I miss some of those skits.

9

YES, I endured being Eliot's best man. He only did it to show me up. It matters not. Time is on my side. There's something else; it's Eliot's attention seeking pro bono work he yaps about all the time. He's not, however, the only Curtis attorney concerned with fair play and committed to righting ancient wrongs.

I am not one to dodge the tough social issues. Issues that are awkward to discuss, such as reparations. Not to sound self-interested, but I have a legitimate claim for reparations. My family traces its roots back to ancient Saxon stock, and I have an airtight case against the French for what they did to my hardworking forebears on October 14, 1066, and thereafter. I have researched this matter thoroughly and plan to draft a complaint against the Republic of France, M. de Gaulle, as successor in interest to William the Conqueror, and everyone named Norman. It will claim damages somewhat in excess of $1,000,000, a fair and modest amount representing damages of a mere $10 plus interest compounded quarterly at LIBOR (London Interbank Offered Rate), assumed for this purpose to be an eminently reasonable 2% per annum.

Here's my theory. According to the Saxon Register, my free-born ancestors Edwin and his wife Edwinna were, during the summer of 1066, living at peace in the earldom of Wessex. My forebears inhabited an unspoiled paradise. No herbicides. No pesticides. No man-made emissions. In my mind's eye, I see the industrious Edwinna productively engaged in a commercial enterprise. Perhaps she owned a shop. The Venerable Bead? She could have been selling a line of woolen knickers known as Boudicca's Secret and other items that were the 11th century predecessors of the clothing now found at Orvis, L.L. Bean, and the like.

This, then, was the green and pleasant land of the WASCs (White Anglo-Saxon Catholics). We've since learned that the bones of people buried in England around 1000 are those of a strong, tall, and healthy race living in an unpolluted countryside on a diet that produced sturdy limbs and healthy teeth. Yes, healthy teeth. So thank you, Mr. Conqueror, for cavities and those snaggly English smiles. Your only contributions to the land of my progenitors were sneers and snails, not to mention great opportunities for endodontists, orthodontists, periodontists, dentists yet to be prefixed, and meals soon to be prix fixed.

This happy idyll ended forever on that awful October Saturday. As we know, Harold's forces were ultimately undone by William's unsportsmanlike use of cavalry and archers. I have reason to believe Edwin was captured and deported to a French foie gras factory. His house was burned, his crops trampled, and his livestock became hors d'oeuvres and entrées.

There can be no question about Norman culpability, and all I'm seeking is the monetary value (conservatively estimated) of my ancestors' lost property. I am not asking for triple damages, punitive damages, damages in respect of pain and suffering or loss of consortium. I might be persuaded to drop my suit if I'm allowed to open a casino on the old family land.

Contrast the Conqueror's vile behavior with that of my Dutch ancestors who paid fair market value for Manhattan.

Enough for now about my grievances. Now let me speak of Ruth, my reliable girl Monday through Friday and always on weekends.

My tale starts with a partner from a decidedly 'brown-shoe' firm—who, for purposes hereof—I have dubbed Attorney Thomas. While effective in court, he was, like so many litigators, haughty, opinionated, and standoffish. His isolation may have derived from his dark college years. The self-regarding Thomas had attended a rah-rah institution in the boondocks where the highest art form was the well-wrought beer can pyramid, and the most prestigious campus organizations were the frats where the brothers passed four years upchucking together.

I feel obliged to report I'm unable to verify the following story. So what. I revel in slander, slurs, and innuendo. I adore gossip. I collect it, embroider it, and disseminate it.

On the memorable evening of which I speak, one of the night secretaries had been instructed to leave a document on Attorney Thomas's desk. Finding his door closed, she knocked once, and, hearing nothing, entered. There on her knees with her back to the door was Ruth, the gentleman's comely, resourceful personal assistant who—among her other accomplishments—was an honors graduate of Katherine Gibbs.

Facing the door and sitting forward in his swivel chair, which he'd moved from behind his desk, was Attorney Thomas. He was holding a licensing agreement which he hurriedly lowered over Ruth's head. Dazed and speechless by what she'd beheld, the intruder withdrew quickly. She couldn't say whether Attorney Thomas did likewise. This tale quickly made its rounds, taking precedence, even among the most committed attorneys, over the reading of advance sheets.

This episode proved beyond a reasonable doubt that Attorney Thomas deserved to be at his lesser firm. Any Curtis attorney, well, any Curtis attorney other than Stevens, would have had the manners to stand and give Ruth the chair.

My source told me Ruth had been fired. Well, natch. Where would we be if partners got into hot water for that sort of thing? She could be mine if I moved quickly. I did so. What an interview. The 20-year-old Ruth was breathtaking. Literally. She breathed life into that word. So round, so firm, so fully-packed. Her sparkling green eyes said, "I am a devil." Her luxuriant, red, pixie-cut hair responded, "I am a naïf." Her body whispered to me, "You'll never do better." One and two are correct. As to three, time will tell. I tried her out on a mildly off-color joke. She neither giggled nor looked away. Bold of her, and back to me.

"I have high hopes for us, Miss Donohue, but you understand, I assume, that you'll be on probation for several months."

Without blinking she looked at me and said, "I understand my position, Mr. Millard."

How cheeky. How magnificent.

It took me only a few weeks to get Ruth on board. I arranged for the reassignment of my secretary, Millicent Bowelback, a dour middle aged woman with an inflexible disposition and a wandering (unfortunately, I'm not speaking figuratively) eye. She was the first employee I ever sloughed off. What's more, she richly deserved it. A pal told me what she'd said when he called about a squash game, "Mr. Millard's in his office with some redhead, and the door's closed."

Was I turned-off or put-off by Ruth's alleged antics with Thomas? No and no. America's the land of second chances, so I generously assumed the burden of Ruth Donohue's redemption.

We clicked from the get-go. She's smart and efficient, but best of all, she's fun. Serene on the surface, molten underneath. Ruth even laughs when I refer to her monthly outages as the Curse of the Bambino.

What happy times we're having. I'll never tire of her. Such naughty wit. We burn the midnight oil and the candle at both ends. She withholds nothing. My colleagues are stiff with envy.

Wait. Having reread the preceding effusions which, I confess, were written immediately after a particularly invigorating romp, I am compelled to add these, more balanced observations.

It's not all cakes and ale. Ruth can be a brat. I've given up on her mastering the tea ceremony (she's no more proficient on the three-stringed shamisen). Just yesterday she broke my only decent saucer. Hand-painted Minton. One of the unmatched odds-and-ends I discovered in Nana's pantry after her final stroke.

I must have scowled when she brought me Lipton (yes, really) in a Boston College mug, because she cocked a hip, lowered her limber lashes, and whispered, "Do I displease you, Mr. Millard?"

"What's become of my Earl Grey, Dearie? And my biscuits?"

Pouty silence.

So passive-aggressive. "It's always something, Miss Donohue, isn't it? Why is my tea never warm enough, or sweet enough, or creamy enough? And now the Jesuits. On a mission, are we? Enough. Speak to Miss Bosworth. She handled these matters for Ez Clark. Handled them perfectly and respectfully, I might add."

"But I handle more than your tea bags, Mr. Millard," smart-assed the difficult Miss Donohue.

Thereafter, I made my own and, now and then, rinsed the effing cup. I should keep reminding myself: anger, annoyance, and arrogance never get you laid. Ruth's impudence is, I'm afraid, the inevitable consequence of breaching the master-servant barrier.

10

IT'S FUNNY how time smooths memory's rough edges. Except for the last few years, I've never been truly miserable, but we all gloss over the bad times. Clare and I knew we were happy and hoped the children were too. There'd be mornings when we'd wake up and discover that each of us had joyful dreams about the other. Once Clare asked me, "How old was I? What was I wearing?"

I said, "I can't remember any of that, but it was you."

Clare replied, "How funny. You were physically indistinct, but vividly present."

Clare and I weren't fooling ourselves, so I can see our early years together as they really were. There was no extra money, but I was certain I could provide for Clare and however many children we might have. I was fit, and if by some chance I didn't cut it behind a desk, I wasn't afraid of blue-collar work. I remember mentioning this to Millard. He gagged. I wasn't frightened by the idea of physical labor nor the people I'd be working with. I'd held summer construction jobs as a boy and felt at home with my fellow grunts in the Corps, even though many of them kidded me about my expletive-free language and the fact I didn't sound like other Bostonians.

It's impossible to avoid discussing money when you're a wage slave, but thinking back it amazes me how little we knew about or concerned ourselves with C&P's financial condition. The firm seemed invulnerable. Boston's starting salary was $7,000, Wall Street's about $2,000 more. It wasn't much, but I reminded myself that Mel Stottlemyre, the Yankees' sensational rookie, was only making $500 more than me. Business school graduates started higher. That irked us. We are smarter.

How frequently would we get pay increases? How large would they be? What would I be making in five years if I made it that far? Most important, what did partners make?

When Millard, Stevens, and I reported for duty, it was sink or swim. Each associate had to find or develop his own niche. Otherwise you could be grabbed for the least desirable jobs by the least successful partners. Stevens, who caught on more slowly, was treated poorly. He was the dumping ground for the firm's subrogation cases. It was dead-end work. Ask anyone. However, some of us flourished in this climate of benign neglect.

My first-year review was instructive. In November of 1964, several weeks after I expected it, I received the dreaded visit. Standing in my doorway, clipboard in hand, was the dapper, vested Archie Northwick, a time-on-his-hands trust and estates partner who'd had the associates foisted off on him. Mr. Northwick got this assignment because of his empty Rolodex and the erroneous, in his case, assumption that trusts and estates lawyers have superior people skills. In the military this assignment would be considered light duty consisting as it did of hosting semi-annual, mixed-grill lunches at the Parker House for himself and his charges, and delivering a series of two-minute performance reviews at which each associate would be told the amount, if any, of his next year's compensation.

Since Cravath (no need to say more) hadn't raised its starting salary that year, I knew with certainty the amount of my increase. Back then, Cravath, Swaine & Moore determined associates' pay for New York and the rest of the country. There was a ritual. When Cravath deemed it meet and right so to do, it would announce a higher salary for its incoming class. This decision would be greeted with groans and vows to hold fast by partners everywhere. The resistance was short-lived. Wall Street firms which considered themselves players and hoped this view was shared by their clients would grimace and sullenly fall into line. Then the provinces would capitulate, taking care to maintain as large a gap as they could plausibly justify between themselves and the New York spendthrifts.

I'm not sure whether Mr. Northwick had any friends, but he harbored no warm feelings towards anyone who was still optimistic about his future.

I was on the phone, but Mr. Northwick kept knocking, and when he had my attention, made insistent hanging-up signals.

"I'm sorry to interrupt you, young man, but I'd be grateful for a moment of your time."

"Of course, Mr. Northwick."

"Let me see," he said, studying the clipboard of destiny.

"Would you like to sit down, sir?"

"I won't be long," said Mr. Northwick running an accusatory finger down the column of names. "It's Lawrence, isn't it?"

"Yes, sir, it is." Was that really necessary? There weren't that many of us and everyone's name was on his door. Gold letters outlined in black. Very snappy.

"It's that time of year, Mr. Lawrence."

Even Millard would have refrained from saying, "Duh!"

"Next year, should you be with us for the entire year, you will earn $7,800 which, I might add, is more than twice what I made my second year here."

"Thank you, Mr. Northwick."

Wow! I'd skipped the standard first year raise. Eight hundred dollar raises were reserved for second-year associates. I had broken away from the pack and was feeling surprisingly well-disposed towards Mr. Northwick. But why wasn't he smiling, and where were the compliments and assurances?

"Any questions, Mr.… Lawrence?"

"No sir, but I was wondering if you have any suggestions for improvement."

"I do not. Good day, Mr.… Lawrence."

Odd, I thought, but surely the raise spoke for itself.

As soon as Mr. Northwick left I called the nursery school where Clare was working. Could this mean I was being treated as a third-year associate and might expect to make partner after six years, something that had never occurred at C&P? Clare shared my excitement. She said she wasn't surprised, but wondered out loud about the absence of commentary. Not to worry. I was off to the races. Millard and Stevens had received the standard increase. So as not to lord it over them, I said I'd gotten $600 as well. Just a thoughtful white lie. I'm glad I did so. A day or two before we were to receive our bigger paychecks, Mr. Northwick returned. He said he wasn't sure but he might possibly have read my increase from the wrong column so he just wanted to 'reiterate' (his unforgettable word) that my raise was $600. I waited to tell Clare until I got home.

With a laugh, Clare said I should be paid twice as much as Millard, gave me a big hug, and said this would be a funny story for our first child who was soon to join us in our tiny apartment on Walnut Street. Eliot was thoughtful enough to appear on January 10, 1965, right on schedule but too late for a 1964 deduction. I decided (at Clare's urging) that it might seem a bit elitist to name him Eliot Estabrook Lawrence, V, even though that's what he is and I so admire Olivier's Henry the Fifth. Instead, I compromised on III, not Junior, since there were, at the time, two living E.E.L.s ahead of him.

It would never do to show them this, but someday I must tell the children more about their young mother, their smart, funny, beautiful mother, the woman they no doubt saw as a mom, not as a dish. If she'd cared less about us, she would have outshone us. Clare would have flourished at almost any graduate school. She learned things quickly and easily. She understood situations and personal dynamics. She knew how to lead while seeming not to. She never made enemies. We might have more money if I'd stayed home and Clare had taken on the outside world. Sometimes, she regretted not doing so. Thankfully, she made us her first priority.

I loved taking her to the movies, usually the first show. I hated to miss a weekend. It was blissful just sitting together in the dark for two hours. When we went with other people I made sure we sat next to each other.

I feel badly about what Clare gave up for us. No sooner had she gotten her head above water with Eliot than dear, willful Cecilia, a.k.a. Ceci, appeared on October 3, 1966. Millard looked as though he could use a little cheering up after Edith (life with Maud wasn't looking much better) so I made him her godfather even though he chose not to have me as his best man the second time around.

I used to think—when I get established and the children can fend for themselves—Clare could finally spread her wings. We never let her. Oh, yes, we said it was her turn. She should return to school. She should write. Or paint. She might consider voice lessons. But she realized we still needed her. Collectively, we made this clear in small but unmistakable ways. We wanted her to remain a part of us, an everyday, if not every hour, part of us. She seemed happy playing the role she'd perfected. Sometimes there were clouds of wistfulness, but they were soon dispersed by her sunny nature. Nothing approaching resentment. It would have taken a saint to have refused what Clare offered so willingly. So we didn't. In fact, I sensed we were often in competition for her.

Back to my inescapable worry. All in all, I'd gotten off to a good start. There was, however, a 1965 episode which concerned me. It involved a cocky senior associate.

In my opinion, shared by many, Michael Sturdy was a jerk. Unfortunately, he was a rarity that bordered on the exotic, an associate with some paying clients of his own.

"Mr. Lawrence," he said in his self-important fashion. "I have an assignment for you... May I?" he said, stepping into my office and pointing to my guest chair.

"Of course, fire away."

"That was an apt response, as you will soon discover."

I waited, trying to think of him as I did Mr. Clark. By then I'd discovered Sturdy was one of those associates who find it necessary to abuse and defame their younger colleagues. In firms the size of C&P, men like Sturdy are rightfully fearful about being passed over if there are better prospects in the same practice area just ahead of or right behind them. I vowed I'd never treat juniors the way Sturdy did.

"You are, no doubt, aware of what has come to be known as the Tonkin Gulf affair."

I nodded.

"My farsighted cousin, who owns a number of warehouses at

Logan Airport, intends to cash in. He has directed me to organize a Massachusetts business corporation which he proposes to name 'Air Funeral Service, Inc.' I'm delegating that task to you. You can handle it, can't you?"

"Yes."

"Excellent."

"What exactly is this company going to do?"

"I thought you might have guessed. It's slated to fly the stiffs back from 'Nam.'"

"And make a ton of money doing it?"

"We are not talking about a non-profit."

I considered telling Sturdy to go fuck himself, but that would have been injudicious. Then I thought about claiming I was over-booked. That would have been wiser, but instead I said, "Michael, I'm afraid this one's not for me. I may have served with some of those men. I hope you understand."

Sturdy got up, gave me a bleak look, and said, "You bet I understand. I hope you do too."

11

MOST THINGS are black and white with Eliot. If he likes you, he'll lay it on with a trowel. If he doesn't, you're toast. In Eliot's eyes, Clare's a saint. A saint who renounced worldly acclaim to devote herself to him and their sprouts. I'll give him this much, Clare is smart and cultivated. She'll be off to graduate school and, I suspect, a new spouse as soon as her children are launched. She'll end up running something with as light a touch as she uses on her unconscious husband. Then there's the beauty thing. Clare's a dish. Why's yummy Mummy squandering herself on Eliot? No doubt Eliot wonders the same thing.

Another thing about Eliot: he's a penny pincher. He considers himself prudent. In fact, he's cheap. Clare sighs and tells me she's lucky to have a hubby who's so concerned with their collective welfare. She tries to justify his parsimony by describing the profligates and plungers who've squandered the Lawrence assets. What hokum. Eliot's a skinflint. Here's proof: Eliot and I shared a secretary during my pre-Ruth months at Curtis. We agreed to split the cost of a joint Christmas present. Eliot volunteered to get it during a lunch break. I acquiesced. When Eliot returned he told me he'd bought a pocketbook. Assuming he'd gone to pricey Newbury Street, I was stricken. Associates couldn't afford such presents for their mistresses, let alone their secretaries. With a grin, he announced I owed him 'two fifty'.

"You're shitting me," I screamed. Then the turkey proudly displayed the brown plastic purse he'd bought from a peddler in the Combat Zone for $5.00.

What have I gotten myself into? I am less sanguine about my firm's prospects than rose-tinted Eliot. Where's our business to come from? Most Curtis partners don't venture outside their social stockades. It's scary out there. Who knows what brutes lurk in the forests west of The Country Club. Goths? Tartars? Sometimes they make timid overtures to known quantities, who've been vetted by having been admitted to one or more approved clubs. Schoolboy chums are prospective clients, but you're an idiot to expect remunerative business from a Vice President still known as, say, 'Bunny'.

Few of our safe choices ever climb high enough to dole out even routine legal work. None claw their way to the top where the plums are dispensed. The high-hanging fruit is out of reach. We chase the wrong people. Also, 'chasing' is too vigorous a concept; we dither, we amble. It's like the courtship of sloths. We don't care for this sort of thing, so we're easily deflected. When we encounter an obstacle, we put aside this distasteful form of money grubbing. We weren't raised to hawk produce like street vendors. We applaud ourselves when we land $500-a-year clients such as Wenham Saddlery or Manchester Yacht Brokerage.

Which brings me to yet another annoyance—the inability to hustle like the hustlers we are. I'm talking about my racket's absurd ban on advertising. Combine that with our comatose elders' penchant to doze by their phones (most of them consider business cards to be degrading) and it's a chancy future for those of us who stand to inherit nothing.

As one might suppose, Eliot sees it differently. There he sits, gazing professorially over his horn rims and chiding me yet again with one of his favorite canards, "Andrew, we are members of a profession."

"And what the fuck does that mean? It certainly suits our geezers who despise the ambitious."

But Eliot bores on relentlessly, "Let me remind you, Andrew, we were sworn into an ancient, and I believe, honorable guild. Do bankers swear to anything? Do businessmen? We are charged with maintaining the rule of law." He purses his lips and continues, "We are autonomous practitioners possessing valuable and specialized expertise and part of a responsible community with countless shared values."

He said that with a straight face. "We have but one shared value, pal, our distributable net income."

"Not so, Andrew. Consider our pro bono work and our worthwhile civic undertakings."

"Gimme me a break. We do that crap for show, and we fob it off on those with low rates and empty time sheets."

"That's not how I see it, Andrew."

"Arrrgh."

12

SOMETIME IN the late '60s, I realized more was happening at C&P than the practice of law. Despite what Millard might say, I am not completely oblivious. I've heard of those music festivals where people took off their clothes in public. I've read about the lost souls of Haight-Ashbury. However, I tend to be one of those last-to-know types. I've never been interested in office politics or gossip, and it's easy to resist temptations that do not tempt.

If I was to support Clare, Eliot, and Ceci, it was essential to make partner and to do so, I supposed, meant no more DataCentric foul-ups or foul-ups of any kind. I was confident that if I kept doing what I was doing, partnership would be mine at the regular time. In the meantime, I had no problems carrying the bags for a group of men I liked and respected—even those who, Millard said, had passed their "sell-by" dates. The idea I might do better at another firm or in a different profession never crossed my mind. Once or twice I had offers from New York shops, but without fail, I set the amount needed to move me above what was being offered. I had fetched up at C&P, and I was determined to succeed there on its terms which I assumed were fair, reasonable, and coincident with mine.

When each workday ended, I recorded my time (I did this instinctively, knowing I could never accurately recreate yesterday, let alone last week or last month as many of my colleagues seemed able to do) and went home to Clare unaware that a goodly number of associates were, as I walked up Beacon Hill, carousing with the more gregarious members of our staff. As for me, I was already feeling guilty about missing so many of my children's bedtimes. Clare would get on me about dragging in at 8:00 p.m. hungry, tired, and grouchy. So home I went. As soon as possible.

Then something out of the ordinary occurred. It involved a paralegal. Paralegals were a new breed in the '60s. The first ones were bright, enterprising secretaries who had developed specialized skills and, at less cost to the client and no loss of competence, could perform routine tasks which would otherwise have fallen to associates.

Gloria, the corporate paralegal of whom I am writing, was pretty, friendly, chatty and, how should I put it, well-built. Furthermore, she seemed to be aware of her charms. Unless your radar was malfunctioning, you couldn't help but notice her. She had an interior office just across the hall from mine, and we sometimes found ourselves at the photocopying machine together. I sort of looked forward to these chance meetings.

Gloria was a witty girl, and one day she caught me by surprise when she said with a serious (Or was it mock serious?) expression, "Mr. Lawrence, are you aware of the dark, out-of-the-way places you can photograph with these machines?"

I believe I blushed. Then she began coming into my office to chat about the Red Sox or invite my reaction to something happening at the firm. These visits seemed completely harmless.

At the time of which I am writing, I had a rubber plant in my office. It had become droopy and discolored. One day Gloria, who had a more vigorous specimen, said, "Let me take care of yours too, Mr. Lawrence." It would have been rude to decline such a friendly offer. So I didn't. Thenceforth, she undertook the task of watering it and stripping off its dead leaves. She even bought plant food. Naturally, I reimbursed her.

She would show up at least twice a week with scissors and watering can, wearing a cute green apron, which she said "matches my thumb".

My plant responded enthusiastically to her ministrations. No more limp leaves. One morning as I was struggling through yet another bond indenture with the aid of what was now Mr. Farnum's treatise, Gloria appeared carrying a handful of paper towels. Some of them were moist. "May I?" she said, looking at my plant's dusty leaves. When she finished gently wiping and drying them, they were radiant. Something about the way she performed this task distracted me from my indenture. I should add, in my own defense, it is not difficult to distract indenture readers.

Then one day she ventured into an area theretofore out of bounds. She was removing a yellow leaf when she looked me in the eye, rose from her revealing crouch, and said demurely, "May I raise something of a confidential, personal nature, Eliot?"

Eliot? Oh, boy. Millard had been asking me whether I noticed the 'enticing pruner's crack' when Gloria was attending to my plant. How could I say no? I said something neutral like "Of course". I assumed there was a problem involving her family, her landlord, or something like that. It wasn't.

She said, "Mr. Millard's an old friend of yours, isn't he?"

"Andrew Millard and I have known each other since we were 13."

Gloria approached my desk. "I've always looked up to you, Eliot," she said looking up at me.

"How can I help, Gloria?"

"I don't know how to put this delicately, but your friend's been making unwelcome overtures."

"Unwelcome overtures?"

The modest Gloria was apparently going to leave it at that. My response to her accusation was a feeble "Oh" or "I'm sorry to hear that". I didn't ask for particulars, but I promised to look into it at once. She smiled gratefully and left.

What now? How had I gotten into this mess? What on earth had Millard been up to? I had always thought of him as the smoothest of the smooth, and I'd never heard a word of complaint, directly or indirectly, from any of his conquests or from those few—according to him—who'd turned him down.

We've always had our share of cretins in the office, but, whatever I may have thought (and still think) of the way he sometimes behaves, Millard is not one of them. When he's unwelcome, I assume he withdraws with a wink and a twinkle. As he would have said, had the phrase been in use at the time, "No harm, no foul." These days the conduct of which Millard stood accused would result in immediate financial consequences, the severity of which depends almost entirely on the size of the miscreant's book of business. The smaller the one, the bigger the other.

There was no point postponing the unpleasant task for which I'd impetuously volunteered. I couldn't concentrate with this awkward situation unresolved. I turned over the document I'd been reading and sought out Millard. He was alone in his office. I cleared my throat. "Gloria tells me you've been saying things to her."

"Gloria who?"

I just stared at him while he smoothed his hair.

"OK, what kinds of things?"

"You know what kinds of things. Things she doesn't want to hear. Things she doesn't want to do." Silence. "Well?"

Millard's response was unexpected, being neither the proud admission nor the casual denial I'd expected. It was a quizzical expression. After a moment he began to snort, snorts turned to laughter, laughter became howls. Tears flowed. When he brought himself under control, he explained. "Glorious," he said, "was a 'sexual artiste'. She was ardent and athletic, possessing boundless energy, endurance, expertise, and enthusiasm." A few hours with her, and the Pompeian murals, the Indian cave paintings and whatever I'd read, experienced, or dreamed would all seem rather ho-hum. "She gives la belle Ruth a run for her money," said Millard.

"She is *so* creative; after one particularly delightful romp she used magic markers to draw an intricate Greek key pattern on Old Faithless. I give her my highest recommendation. Five mattresses. Sign her up. Get her on your staff. Spend a little time with Glorianna, and Clare will be yours forever."

I resented the last bit. Despite what Millard may think, I'm no slouch in that department. Even now in 1985, at age 48.

Millard said his account would be endorsed by all but the most out-of-it C&P associates. I stood there slack-jawed, the utter fool. Then he counter-attacked telling me I was way off-base championing Gloria. "Pull your head out of your ass," he said. *What could I reply?* I raised my hands in surrender and left his office. *Was it possible I'd been taken in by her? If so, why?*

I corroborated Millard's story with one of our cretins. He echoed Millard's recommendation, ungallantly remarking that Gloria's breasts were five times the size of his wife's. I'm not exaggerating. Those were his exact words, "Five times."

The next day I got a call from Millard.

"I've got something for you, Galahad. Hot off one of these new machines."

Naturally enough, I was suspicious. I went to his office, and Millard handed me a picture of something. But what? I studied it carefully. My God, it couldn't be, but I could tell from Millard's delighted expression it was. Yes, a picture of… I can't write the word. Around the edge in red block letters were the words 'WISH YOU WERE HERE!' And yes, the exclamation point was… Enough.

"Glorious asked me to give it to you," said Millard.

I felt like such an idiot. How could I ask her about the picture? Was it really of her? Did she, in fact, ask Millard to give it to me? I still get short of breath thinking about that episode. Was I being used? Made fun of?

Gloria, when I saw her next, acted as though nothing had happened and nothing had changed. So did I. Twice a week she tended my plant, and we avoided dangerous topics.

I remember our last conversation. Out of the blue, she invited me to have lunch with her. I panicked. "I don't do lunch unless it's family, friends, or clients."

She looked hurt or angry, I couldn't tell which. That night I left my rubber plant by the service elevator. Next morning it was gone, and Gloria stopped visiting me.

In addition to being upset by the Gloria fiasco, I now had a bigger worry. Had I allowed pride to jeopardize my family's well-being? Wasn't I being self-centered in saying what amounted to 'Nuts' to Michael Sturdy? And then failing to conceal the disgust I felt about his project. The satisfaction I experienced while telling him to piss off was vainglorious and possibly fatal. Was it also an indication I'd be ineffective as an attorney?

13

I YEARNED to find out how Glorious was doing with Eliot. Bringing him down in flames would make her a double ace, and six of her nine Curtis conquests were married. I kept asking myself, is my buddy actually getting a little? Or did it really end the way he said? Glorious could never keep her mouth—or anything else—closed, but she clammed up about Eliot. I believe she had a soft spot for him just as I had a hard spot for her.

Some weeks later, I asked Ruth about her. It's one of the few times I've seen Ruth furious.

"That disgusting little tramp. Our worst troublemaker. And I really resent your pet names for her. Thank God, she's left us." Then she added, and this is one of the reasons she's so neat, "For greener mattresses."

Glorianna was a diversion, and Ruth is a delight, but I need wealth and liquidity. Besides, Glorissima made me nervous. She was unpredictable. She might lift her skirt in the corridor. She was someone for whom the concept of 'private parts' was utterly alien. She knew too much and talked too much. Now she's causing an uproar somewhere else.

As I see it, there are four get-rich strategies: make it, marry it, inherit it, or steal it. Scratch three, downgrade one to doubtful, hold four in reserve, and concentrate on two. Away all boats!

How, then, could someone as 'with it' as I have fallen for Maud? Hadn't I learned anything from my time with the once-fair Edith? Evidently not. There were, however, a number of extenuating circumstances.

At the top of the list was her feckless daddy who was killing time plowing furrows in the wine-dark sea in a succession of the latest and largest Hinckleys, crewed by ascoted leeches who couldn't afford their own boats. Maud's parents had a house in Hobe Sound. Like several of our partners. Need more be said? Without confirming it, I concluded Maud must be the beneficiary of one or more plump trusts. Wrong. In my own defense, didn't I have every reason to suppose that when Maud referred to her analyst, she was talking about her securities analyst, not her psychoanalyst? Few women from Maud's background get shrunk. She was a stolid Wellesley grad, not some high-strung Cliffie.

Then, too, Maud bore a superficial resemblance to Clare, and worse, she struck at an auspicious moment. When we were introduced, I was experiencing a rare and blessedly brief sexual drought. Nor can I forget her sneaky tactics. She inflamed me with her 1950s behavior. Here we were in the middle of a carnal tsunami; maiden heads were rolling, but I couldn't make it to second base.

Though I inferred it wouldn't be materially different from what I'd disinterred on earlier digs, I ached to lay bare what hid beneath Maud's jutting cable-knit sweater and pleated skirt. Was it just Maud, or Maud as augmented by cotton and sponge rubber? This was simultaneously an insult and an incentive. As intended. Account must also be taken of wounded pride, frustration, and the concern it might get around town that I, A. de P.M., had been denied. Insinuating myself between Maud's legs became my quest for the Northwest Passage.

Our courtship lacked gentleness and gallantry. Our conversations were perfunctory and to the point. We talked about doing 'it', but never fitted act to words. After yet another night of being unable to slip anything between her unyielding thighs, I blundered horribly. I implored her to be mine forever. I had to have her. I was like a bibliophile looking at a crisp, clean, tight first edition in its original calf. She accepted on the spot (on the sofa actually) before I could reconsider, retract, or retain counsel.

I sometimes wonder whether a person in my condition has the legal capacity to contract. There must be some ancient common law defense based on an inflamed libido. What about entrapment or statutory relief modeled perhaps on the automobile lemon laws?

Without running a Dun and Bradstreet on her, I'd decided Maud was more than capable of supporting me.

Once again, I let my Byronic impulses override my inner Adam Smith. I disregarded the most basic advice fathers give to sons, "Never play poker with anyone called 'Doc', never patronize a diner named 'Mom's', and never sleep with a woman whose problems are worse than yours."

I thought I'd discovered someone very special, as indeed I had. She had the physical perfection described if not possessed by those whose personals appear in exclusive periodicals, such as *Harvard Magazine*. With her slim figure and great rack, she looked almost top heavy. But don't worry, Ralph Nader, unlike the Chevy Corvair she was impossible to roll over.

Lastly, I was awed by her youthful mastery of a facial expression usually seen only on women of a certain age who have spent a lifetime in the performing arts. It could be described as a 'maybe you can come hither look'. It says, "I am mysterious, unfathomable, and inscrutable, at least by you."

Only after it was too late did I tumble to the fact that this expression was also saying, "While men *and women* may have had me in some crude literal sense, all of them were but passing fancies; none of them has come close to possessing the essential me. I've had many lovers. I've had countless admirers. Of course you are enchanted. How could you not be?"

Why, then, have I trudged to the altar with two women who, despite outward appearances, didn't like men? Fortunately, I never learned whether either of them cared for children. Once again, I was governed by the wrong organ. I followed my own advice and listened to my bawdy. Since he'd been a Jonah at my first wedding, Eliot was not my best man when, in the spring of 1964, Maud and I tied the knot, a slipknot, thank God. By then, Father was confined to quarters, and Mother was at a spa in the Berkshires with cucumber slices on her eyelids. She left me this message: 'After a lifetime of caring for others, it's now Mom time.'

To flesh out this depressing montage, I must report that no sooner had we settled into our less-than-palatial Beacon Hill flat than we stopped having sex—with each other. Both Maud and her dress size are ballooning as she envelops herself in more and more of herself. She is unashamed and continues wearing stretch pants, even in public, as her mass and displacement increase exponentially. When it isn't contained, her abundant, liberated body is housed in tents. Not pup tents, but billowing, gaily colored shrouds decorated with the signs of the zodiac and Mesoamerican fertility symbols.

Late breaking news: she's stopped shaving.

This marriage has outlasted my first one, but I don't give it much longer. Maud's turned odder still. She's examining herself—you can probably guess where. The latest fad. No admittance to me her husband, but here she is with mirror, penlight, and speculum spelunking in a cavern now measureless to man. She's studying every arête, couloir, and terrain feature of her interior. I wouldn't be quite as upset if she'd leave it at that, her grotto and her primitive tools. But no.

She's commandeered our second bedroom, transformed it into her private observatory, and opened the doors to her same-sex buddies. I am unwelcome in this gynecocracy. Many's the night I return from my labors at Curtis only to find a TV dinner melting in the sink. The door to The Room is closed and bolted from the inside. I hear angry, strident voices. Once or twice I listened. Some of their cackling was about me. Often these aliens annex the entire apartment. My appearance is greeted with scowls or averted eyes. When I gently object to this treatment, Maud tells me many of her friends have been hurt by men and says I should be more understanding.

I am beginning to receive sardonic comments from friends and colleagues. Andrew de Peyster Millard, an object of mirth. Intolerable. In the office, I remain cheerful, cooperative, and always willing to lend a hand. Inwardly, I'm a caldera of rage and mortification. Finally, at around 2:00 a.m. on a grim February morning in 1967, I sat bolt upright in my lonely bed. It was so over.

I strode into The Room where Maud had been sleeping since she'd seized it like the Sudetenland. As I suspected, she was not alone. Disdaining to acknowledge the creature sprawled next to her,

I announced, "It's over, my love, and, being the gent I am, it is your choice whether to remain or depart. Your call. I am indifferent."

"You can leave my room now, Andrew. I shall tell you our decision in the morning."

Maud decamped. She remained with me only long enough for her and Helga to winterize Daddy's fishing cabin on Lake Sebago. Then they were gone. Maud is out of my life, but not out of my wallet. If only those two could get hitched I might persuade a probate judge to modify our separation agreement.

All in all, I feel quite ill-used by the women's movement. First they crash our law schools. Then they infiltrate our firms. Now these gorgons are shrieking for partnerships while, at the same time, howling about balanced lives. Gimme a break. Nobody who makes a difference wants a balanced life. I may commit these thoughts to paper. The working title for my diatribe is 'The Testicle Dialogues'.

Nor is Ruth the sympathetic pal I have every right to expect when I grouse about Maud. All she said as she winked and high-heeled out of my office was, "I warned you about blimps in Birkenstocks, Mister Millard."

Some of this is my fault. It was foolish to have once again married someone of limited means when I had at my fingertips detailed information about a representative sampling of Boston's richest women. After Maud, I shall restrict myself to ladies whose orientation I determine in advance and whose net worth I establish from a careful, if after-hours, review of the financial information contained in the Curtis trust files. How could I have overlooked this gold mine?

Being a man of principle, I shall concentrate on well-connected ladies to whom principal, gobs of principal, has already been distributed. I've even thought briefly about taking up with someone whose warranty has expired. Not that I would diddle anyone in a hospice. Doing so might make it difficult to persuade the partners I'm the right sort. Another thought crossed my mind. If I snag a lady with at least five million free and clear (my 'fuck you' figure), I can tell Curtis to piss up a rope.

Meanwhile, Eliot keeps rolling along. He lives in a warm happy cocoon. One that I, in my rare maudlin moods, sometimes begrudge him. Eliot and Clare are delighted to share their happiness. In fact, like so many love birds, they feel obliged to do so. I am their favorite victim, being among their friends, the one most in need of a wholesome, nourishing home-cooked meal consumed in a stable, loving environment.

Blessedly, these evenings are over early. The pattern is identical. Clare and Eliot make goo-goo eyes at each other while ignoring me and my need for liquid refreshment. Starting soon after his birth, Quintus would be displayed in his crèche on the dining room table. He'd gurgle, display his tongue, make spit bubbles, and emit vile smells. Eliot alleges those toothless grimaces are smiles, smiles that indicate vast reservoirs of character, intelligence, and wit. Hah, I suspect this is how the dauphin tells us he's letting go in his pants. Poor Eliot, wait till he sees my bairns.

And so began those BYOB dinners.

I can't forget them. Usually it's Clare's most daunting casserole: a mound of desiccated pork chops, spread-eagled on a bed of charred rice, accented with fragments of tomatoes, onions, and peppers. The dish, a monochromatic gray, reminds me of Mathew Brady's photographs of the Confederate dead. If I escape 'Pork Chop Ecstasy', I'll be confronted by Clare's other standby 'Tuna-Mushroom Bliss'. Clare cranks out dozens of these terrors at a time. Sometimes they spoil, sometimes they sprout colorful growths. Thus far, I've avoided the emergency room.

Eliot's in heaven. He finds Clare's Joy of Cooking creations ambrosial. Even the 'gourmet' vegetable dish to which Clare subjects all her guests all the time—wilted (this was before 'wilted' meant something other than overcooked) string beans garnished with demoralized nuts. For myself, I favor the recipes in The Joy of Sex. And that's what consumes me as I watch Clare move gracefully about her kitchen. She's the only edible dish there, and has somehow avoided the distracted, disheveled look favored by so many new moms. Yes, I'd wolf down cubic yards of her casseroles to remain within her force field. How soon will she realize which one of us is the Best Man?

Then little Ceci arrived, and suddenly Clare's cooking seemed almost palatable. I even volunteered to shovel goo into the engaging child. One evening I raised the stakes. I smuggled a Dixie Cup into that sugar-free kitchen.

"I've got something for you," I said to my goddaughter.

"What is it, Uncle Andrew?"

"Something you never get at home."

"What? What is it?"

"Ice Cream."

"What kind?"

"Vanilla."

"Vamilla?"

"Yes, vamilla."

"For me?"

"For you."

"Ceci, you know we don't eat ice cream in our house," said Clare as she marched in on us.

"Just this once?" I pleaded.

"Yes." Clare can glare. "Just this once."

Ceci and I grinned at each other.

Thereafter, my arrivals at Chez Lawrence were greeted by passionate cries: "Vamilla! Vamilla!"

At one of these feasts I whispered to Clare that hubby was spending what looked like a lot of non-billable time with a certain dark-eyed Gloria Angora.

14

I NEARLY forgot. Michael Sturdy disappeared in March of 1967. Hooray. He never stopped in to say goodbye. I heard he went with a real estate developer and told his few friends here they were idiots to stay at this 'dead-end' firm. Good riddance. I never learned whether he jumped or was pushed. It would have been better for me if he'd left under a cloud, since I'm sure he bad-mouthed me because of our tiff over Air Funeral Service.

I can hear him now, "I'm not sure Lawrence is right for this place. He appears to have a history of not getting along. Not what we're looking for, I'd say."

I never learned whether that company got off the ground, so to speak.

Enough about my insecurities. One of my favorite activities during those happy times was hitting baseballs. If we were on a road trip Clare would indulge me. She'd allow me to take a few swings at any pitching machines I spotted. I'd often plan our itineraries with this in mind. Clare would read in the car while I took my hacks. Once I fouled a ball into my face. Brilliant. The bridge of my glasses was driven into the bridge of my nose. It was messy and left a scar, now hiding among my wrinkles. Clare suggested I might consider a driving range whenever I felt this urge. Golf balls were less likely to assault me.

I have a ritual when batting. It's October 15, 1946. St. Louis. Seventh game. Top of the ninth. A half inning earlier Slaughter pulled off his 'mad dash' from first. Pesky screwed up. The Cards lead us 4-3. He'd never have scored if Dom had been playing.

York and Doerr lead off with singles and, instead of Pinky Higgins, up steps 'Long Ball' Lawrence. I toss aside two of the three bats I'd been swinging. Man, I looked good in the on deck circle. I go to the rosin bag, crush it, hurl it to the ground, and step in there. If I dug in any deeper you'd just see my cap. Harry 'the Cat' Brecheen, their so-called ace, has nothing, and he knows it.

The Cat's first offering is high and tight. I expected that. No biggie. I'm still crowding the plate. Then he gets cute on me. He steps off the rubber. OK. If that's the deal. I hold up my left hand, step back a couple of paces, knock the dirt off my spikes, and then I'm back in the box. Rice, who's catching in place of Garagiola, is getting lippy. I squirt tobacco juice on his shoes.

Brecheen shakes off a couple signs, nods, and tries to smoke one past me. Sorry, Cat. Big mistakearoonie. I turn on the ball and get all of it. Yessirree. A lot of quiet sportsmen in Sportsman's Park as Long Ball crosses the plate and is engulfed.

Now it's 6-4 Sox, and that's the way it stays. Earle Johnson shuts them down in the ninth with yours truly notching the final out with a leaping, twisting, over-the-shoulder, in-the-web-of-the-glove grab just before crashing into the wall in dead center.

15

IT'S CRUNCH time for the last of the Millards. Time for the hurry-up offense. I once had a blasé attitude about making partner. No longer. Neither Edith nor Maud has provided me the wherewithal to hang it up before I turn thirty-five. In December 1970 the partners will be considering Eliot and me for admission to the firm on January 1, 1971. I have omitted Stevens. He'll be gone by then. He'd be stupid to hang around for his inevitable humiliation.

Looking at the tote board with the election 18 months away, I'd say my odds of success are favorable but only slightly, 60/40 at the outside. Three negative votes would sink me, as would the failure to receive thumbs up from at least 85% of the partners. I'm sure I haven't made any implacable enemies (How could I?), but I don't have the feeling of being swept forward on a tidal wave of enthusiasm. I need more. I need vociferous, influential fans.

Now there's the horrid possibility of being deferred. This is a cunning, newly-instituted device by which the firm grinds another year or two out of useful worker bees who lack the self-assurance to reject this degrading status. Stevens? Sure. But not me. A passed-over de Peyster? Not bloody likely. It would be intolerable to watch Eliot's triumphant entry into Jerusalem with me in the mob scattering palm fronds.

I have a year and a half to sway the electorate. Ample time. It's merely a question of presentation. There might be a couple areas in need of some slight buffing, but I'm indispensable. It only remains for others to acknowledge this truism. Then there's my image. There may be a few who question my commitment to the law in general and to Curtis in particular. Sourpusses, all of them. I'm 'outstanding' in every category. As Eliot once (and only once) said, recalling his days in the Marine Corps, "Out-fucking-standing." Eliot's uncharacteristic obscenity turned on the proverbial light bulb, a bulb that is burning with the intensity of a magnesium flare.

My idea is inspired. It's bold. Given my environment, it's a sure winner. My image will be transformed. I will become the new Messiah. Eliot will be on palm frond duty. The suspicious geezers will be putty in my hands. I, the noble stoic, will evoke the words of Horace, "*Dulce et decorum est pro patria mori.*"* Might I be overdoing it? No. I am not a believer in the unadorned lily.

Next on my wish list is a different sort of spouse. High time I get that right. I'm 32. My seed has been scattered across the Commonwealth. Thankfully, it hasn't germinated. But how am I to overcome what might be suggested by two spectacularly unsuccessful marriages plus innumerable discreet (I hope) dalliances? Not the traditional credentials for a ponderous, cold roast trusts and estates partner. I need a presentable third wife and I need her pronto. By June of 1970 at the latest, so that when the partners vote, I'll be mistaken for Eliot.

Though we seem to be well into the Age of Aquarius ('nefarious' is more my line) and I am all for peace guiding the planets and love steering the stars, the third Mrs. Millard needs to be respectable, retiring, and rich. Well-endowed financially and anatomically. An insatiable (all right, barely satiable) sex drive would be appreciated, likewise a dirty mind as long as both are kept under wraps. Mustn't arouse the envy of those repressed Curtis worthies shackled to their plain-faced, blunt-spoken, badly-dressed frumps.

Would it be possible, I wonder, to find a wife who would not only burnish my image but increase my value to Curtis? Why not? It would be one of the dividends of attaching myself to a wealthy trust client. Message to the partnership: 'Treat me with kid gloves or Miss Got Rocks and her millions sashay down the street to another firm taking her dear Andy with her.' And yes, if she were rich enough I'd let her call me Andy. I have roughly a year.

---

* Those for whom I am writing won't need a translation.

But, what about Clare? When can I begin my creeping tender offer? Yes, I've disparaged Clare and laughed at her blind, uncritical adoration of Eliot. That was the sourest of grapes. I can't begin to calculate the number of hours I've fantasized about her. I've scattered my Clare reveries among countless billable matters. To not charge for those hours would put me out of the running for partner. Giving myself the benefit of the doubt, I may average between 1,200 and 1,300 hours a year that the sticklers might consider billable. These are enhanced with about 500 hours of creative time-keeping and several hundred more camouflaged under a number of deliberately uninformative headings: 'Pro Bono', 'Administrative', and 'Professional Reading'. This gets me to the magic 2,000, an extraordinary commitment.

I have tried, with no success, to purge myself of this obsession. I ask myself repeatedly, "Why Clare?" My reasons (she's not Mother, she's Eliot's, she's special in lovely, hard-to-define ways) strike me as insufficient. She's not rich, and Ava Gardner is hotter. But still... This is an unproductive inquiry. I am not introspective. Who wants to see himself clearly? As others do and yet...

Certain images linger. This is the most recent: a steamy April evening with A. de P. M. on a 'vanilla' mission to Chez Lawrence.

We had that day, without coda or overture, made an abrupt but typical New England transition from storm windows to open windows and billowing curtains. The tulips had exploded, and frenzied moths were humping every unprotected light bulb.

Clare answered the door. Gone was her worn, gray chrysalis. In its place were hot pink flip-flops, tailored white pedal pushers, and a delicate white t-shirt adorned with Matisse flowers which I would have loved to arrange and rearrange.

So, there we were, frozen in place in the vestibule; me, my elevated heart rate, and Ceci's ice cream dripping down my wrist.

All I know is this: I must surpass Eliot, and I must have Clare. And, though she doesn't realize it yet, she must have me. Someday, she must ask herself, "How can I endure what could be half a century with that earth-bound lump?" And I, a Gemini, an air sign, will be there to answer, "You can't."

Meanwhile, I shall train. I have yet to have my way with a married woman. However, before lamenting this gaping void in my CV, I remind myself I'm not much over 30, and I've been diverted by law school and my sometimes less-than-fervent efforts to succeed at Curtis. I have the perfect candidate, however. The dissatisfied and unsatisfied wife of a floundering associate. Adultery at last. I've looked forward to it since becoming an adult.

Ah, Stevens. I had him pegged as a loser from the moment I saw him in '63. He isn't officer material, but the powers-that-be have strung him along. He's diligent, but that's never enough. He has churned out quantities of motions, interrogatories, and other commodity-type work and is seen as a fully-depreciated duplicating machine. It's not surprising he's turned bitter. His surliness has sealed his fate, and his eczema keeps him in the library. Nobody tolerates a disfigured grump with no billings.

Curtis, like most first-tier firms, adheres to the 'up-or-out' policy. You make partner in seven years, or, barring an occasional deferral, you're gone by the time your more able peers are anointed. The firm can't have sullen laggards blocking the ascent of stars like me and, I suppose, Eliot.

Poor Stevens. After a series of less-than-candid annual reviews, he's been given the word, and the word stinketh. It ain't happening for him at Curtis. He's on his own. No outplacement. No hand-holding. Unlike the Wall Street firms that find foster homes for their castoffs in the law departments of their clients, Curtis has no disposal sites for its low-level waste. Hello, anxiety.

Then comes the short, unhappy life of a lame duck. A pariah. For a few months, nothing changes. The condemned keeps doing what he's been doing, and the bilious Mr. Barber looks in periodically to inquire how the job hunt's proceeding. The chivvying then increases in frequency and ugliness with pointed questions about when your office, which has taken on the air of a leprosarium, will be vacated. Is this cruel? Not a bit of it. Stevens is damned lucky to have started off at a place like mine; it will be the only decent entry on his résumé. Particularly with that Samsonite briefcase which looks as though it's met its Delilah. Stevens, whose libido has gone the way of his self-respect, should have seen it coming. Everyone else did. Including his pissed-off wife who knows she latched onto a loser.

Having my way with Jane Stevens has taken all the skill of using worms in a stocked pond with no natural food supply. It's been a healthy diversion from the stress induced by my precarious situation at Curtis. Jane's discontent and restlessness are writ large. She drinks too much at parties. Her behavior's brassy and borderline louche. Too much perfume. Too much make up. Her attire is suggestive. No. Blatant. Whenever I look at her, she's staring back at me.

I've touched her, brushed up against her, and 'invaded her space' at every opportunity. I've broached forbidden subjects. We both know what's coming next, but she stands her ground. So brassy.

No surprise. It took only one call. "Hello, Janey, it's Andrew."

"I guessed it might be. Always a pleasure, Andrew. Always."

"Can you get your hubby? We're working on something together."

"You know I can't, Andrew."

"Why's that?"

"You know why."

"I do?"

"Andrew, Andrew, Andrew. You're such a cutie. I told you, quite pointedly I thought, at Curtis's last drink-'em-up, that Richard was away this week. Don't tell me you've forgotten."

"Do you miss Dick, I mean little Richard?"

"Such a one-track mind, Andrew."

"Back to us, dearie. Isn't it a shame we didn't get to talk more at the party?"

"What would we have talked about, Andrew?"

"Maybe we could figure that out over lunch. What do you say?"

"I say 'tomorrow', Andrew."

"I read you loud and clear. How's about the Ground Round on Soldier's Field Road in Allston? Just the place for two friends to have a relaxed get-together. Is noon good?"

"Perfect."

"What's more, it's renowned for its cuisine." That provoked a promising belly laugh.

I love clandestine meetings. Were I a Scot, I'd found a clan of that name. Lunch plus a couple pops was fast and inexpensive. We weren't really having a meal together. We were taking on fuel. We knew the agenda. When I placed the motel key on our table, she smiled. My kind of girl. We left her car in the restaurant parking lot and took mine the few hundred yards to our love nest. The last thing I'd wanted was a slow walk and a possible change of heart.

I'm glad the drive was brief because Jane began taking liberties with my right ear, squeezing the produce, and sparring with my boxers. She unwrapped herself for the few moments it took us to interrupt our groping and stumble from the car to our room. A fortunate reprieve. She'd had me on the brink. In fact, there'd already been some seepage. Note to self: *never wear light-colored trousers on expeditions of this nature.*

Opening the door, I said, "My apologies for the uninspired décor and the view of the dumpster." She gave me a knock-off-the-crap kind of look.

Poor Jane. After meeting people like me and Eliot, it must have been obvious she and Stevens weren't going anywhere as a couple, and Stevens, given what was arrayed against him, wasn't going anywhere at Curtis. Jane was enraged. She'd been cheated, and someone was going to pay. This made her sensationally impersonal in the sack and confirmed my long-held hypothesis that anger is an infallible stimulant of peak physical performance. She loathed her husband. Sex with him was unthinkable.

Our first coupling was silent and savage. Payback for both of us. For her, a combination of lust, guilt, and rage, concluded with a final, gratifying tremor. For me, a glorious workout culminating in an explosive, albeit dishonorable, discharge. I nearly went anaerobic. Outside our motel, as Harry Parker's well-drilled Harvard crews rowed by on the Charles, I matched them stroke for stroke. At last, an 'A' for Andrew's forehead.

Driving back to the Ground Round, she said, "Now I suppose you'll want to discard me."

"Maybe so," I replied, "but I'll need you, or someone like you, in a few days."

She sniffed.

We 'did it' some more. The preliminaries never varied. Same lunch. Same motel. Usually twice. Sometimes thrice if one of us was particularly angry or had gone without for a while. For each of us, the other was a desirable object. I used this as a time to experiment. To learn and grow. It was like studying for the bar exam. My cram course. But she was right, in a couple months it palled.

I've kept things at a low simmer with Clare. Our paths cross frequently. I engineer seemingly unplanned encounters. When we meet, friendly hugs. Fraternal kisses. When embracing, I avoid contact below the belt. Last week, August 16 to be precise, I stopped by to give my goddaughter a silver rattle that belonged to my grandmother's grandmother. Though she was a bit old for it, the three-year-old Ceci nevertheless shook it with delight.

Both mother and daughter thanked me. Then, out of the blue, Clare said, "Isn't today…"

"Yes, the 25th anniversary…"

"I'm so sorry, Andrew." Our eyes met, and neither of us looked away. Had it finally happened?

"Thanks, but it was a long time ago."

"I understand, but have you ever talked about Edward?"

"Why would I want to do that?"

"Not with your mother? Not with Edith or Maud?"

"Would you have?"

"Have you ever considered seeing someone?"

"I'm always seeing someone."

"Come on, Andrew."

"We don't do that."

"I suppose not."

"You remember Maud, don't you?"

"Of course."

"Did her a fat lot of good, didn't it?"

"Well…"

"Case closed. Meeting adjourned."

"I'm sure you'll get it sorted out, Andrew."

"I believe I have. And now I'm going to read to Ceci."

"She loves that."

"I'm glad. No more Go Fish, though. The imp's been creaming me."

My goddaughter and I settled down with an old favorite. I'd hardly begun when Ceci said, "Actually, Uncle Andrew, I'm getting tired of Mr. and Mrs. Mallard."

Fun's over. Back to the sweat shop. Eliot confided to me he'd been criticized by Tobias ('Toby') Saunders for being literal, pedantic, and excessively detail-oriented. Evidently, Toby felt Eliot lacked 'flair'.

Flair is Toby's stock in trade. Toby, one of our few colorful partners, is noisy and facile, a 'loud waters run shallow' sort of person. He has a quick mind and unlimited resources. His family owns most of a mid-sized Southeastern city. Then he married some *real* money. Details and the mundane concerns of little people are beneath Toby, whose pre-tax income I've heard approaches $2,000,000 before he records his first hour. And much of it's tax-free. Problems bore Toby. He dismisses them with delicate backhand flicks of his fingers.

Toby spends little time at Curtis, and except for his breezy arrivals and departures, has made no impression here. He's proved that someone can control several hundred million dollars in trusts and still be on semi-permanent sabbatical. To my knowledge, Toby's only contribution to the firm is the legend which appears on the memos he leaves in his wake: 'Dictated but Not Read'. Curtis provides Toby with mild and intermittent intellectual stimulation and is a convenient oasis at which to recharge his batteries between fishing trips.

Eliot disapproves of Toby. What's more, Eliot can't conceal his feelings, and I'm sure this was what precipitated Toby's criticism.

Then, eureka! If the enemy of my enemy is my friend, why then shouldn't Toby be my Ez? By sponsoring me, he'd be kicking sand in the face of my rival while developing his latent nurturing side.

It's my duty to make certain Toby is fully briefed on Eliot. With only a little prompting, Toby asked for my candid opinion of Mr. Lawrence. He appeared concerned with Eliot's lack of creativity.

"Eliot and I have been friends, close friends, since the second-form. I'm a big fan of Eliot's and, as such, may not be entirely objective."

Toby favored me with a knowing look. "I respect your loyalty, but do your best."

I hesitated.

"We must put the firm first," Toby added.

I managed a pained expression. "You're right, of course."

"And?" said Toby, arching a well-trained eyebrow.

"Eliot's hard-working and reliable. Nobody could go too far wrong using him on routine corporate work."

"Thank you, Andrew."

Curtis provides perfect cover for Toby. It's an irreproachable Boston brand. He can consort with idlers and layabouts, but avoid their early deaths by periodically holing up and drying out at Curtis. Law firm as spa. His healthiness may be a problem, however. Toby's relative temperance and moderation make it likely he'll be hanging around Curtis long past the time I must establish myself as a big biller or settle for the bleak and uncertain existence of a service partner. We have no mandatory retirement age, and Toby, in his late 50s, looks smug, vigorous, and, damn him, immortal.

Toby went into trusts and estates for all the right reasons, the primary ones being the absence of stress and the irrelevance of personal presence. There's little to be done, and what there is can be handled from afar or ignored indefinitely. Moreover, trust 'work' is all inside the box and behind the curve. Mirror the standard indices and snooze. I long to follow in his footsteps, but for now, my nose must split time between the grindstone and Toby's posterior.

I've resigned myself to months of arriving before nine and hanging around until well after six with particular emphasis on being visible at the opening and closing bells. I've practiced the 'hang-a-spare-suit-jacket-over-your-chair' ploy. I intend to observe the abhorred tradition of Saturday mornings in the office. The attorneys, in their Harris tweeds and flannels, look as though they've just popped in from the grouse moor.

Which reminds me. In matters amatory I liken myself to a double-barreled shot gun—equally gifted as an over-under or a side-by-side.

Yes, I've buckled down. I decode Toby's memos and carry out their always incoherent and often conflicting orders, concealing my annoyance at their tone. I nearly uproot my forelock in his presence.

Toby's introduced me to a sampling of his trust beneficiaries, but to them I am merely a fungible, faceless fixture, someone they may assume is a member of their caste but no different from any of the other anonymous apprentices Toby produces to do their bidding. I must distinguish myself. But that will have to wait. For the moment, I am little more than a genial errand boy with no prospect of being written into their instruments until I make partner. Toby has me where he wants me, but then he has everyone with a net worth of less than nine figures where he wants them.

My bowing and scraping, while nauseating to observe, is paying off. I've become Toby's primary gofer, stooge, and coat holder. I've gone so far as to tell Toby his work fascinates me and I'm 'up' for as much of it as he's willing to send my way. I remain insecure, however. Toby could turn his beams elsewhere, and I would shrivel and die. There are several unscrupulous associates who would willingly step into my wingtips and supplant me in a trice. What's worse, one of them is female, and, there's a growing sentiment among our more wooly-minded elders that females might make acceptable partners. Ridiculous. You can't kick ass in open-toe shoes.

In fact, Toby has never ordered me to grovel. He doesn't have to. What with all my fawning, I'm surprised he doesn't call me Bambi. Thank God he's straight, but if he weren't, I'd work around it. When Toby's in residence and technically on duty, he takes day trips to pursue blues and stripers, though this is far less elegant than the salmon-killing he enjoys in Scotland, Iceland, and New Brunswick. Toby demands help on these plebian, low-budget outings. Nobody who knows Toby and isn't at his mercy ever volunteers.

I soon learned why.

My first summons to play with Toby came in late June. He popped in on a Friday. "Let's haul some lunkers out of Buzzards Bay tomorrow. The boat's all set."

Short notice, but Andrew de P. Millard accepted with pleasure the kind 'invitation' of Mr. Tobias Saunders. In fact, I rose for the bait like a starving blue. What an opportunity to crawl into Toby's creel. God, maybe he'll drown and leave me some walking-around money. Look what Eliot received from the moderately well-off Ez.

My hangover and I climbed the granite steps of his Beacon Street house at 6:00 a.m. Toby and I gathered up a handful of rods that hadn't been unrigged, cleaned, or disassembled in years. A salt-encrusted lure with rusted hooks hung from an eyelet on each rod. I took it upon myself to pull off the desiccated remains of last year's sand worms. We piled the gear into Toby's Land Rover and set off for Padanaram.

When we got to the boat yard, Toby's Boston Whaler was being backed into the harbor. This was its first outing of the season. Toby claimed the motor had been serviced and was ready to go. I was dubious. Indeed, our craft's floor was still covered with decaying leaves and several inches of brownish water. I grabbed a sponge and began sponging. A peek into the future? Then I led the boat around to the dock and loaded our tackle.

Commodore Saunders ordered me to "shove off". Thankfully, he was talking about the boat. The engine caught on the first try. We were on our way. Belay that. As Toby turned towards open water, the steering cable snapped, the engine coughed, spewed smoke, and went into cardiac arrest lasting for what turned out to be a month. Being only 50 yards from the dock, we returned under our own power, using as our means of propulsion the single broken oar with which Toby's craft was equipped.

This summer I've made hay when the sun shone and when it was overcast. I am Toby's deck hand and golf wallah. I've done everything but pipe him aboard. We've caught some scup, but mostly I polish the boat like the lad who became the 'Ruler of the Queen's Navee'. On the links, I see myself as Toby's cardiologist, on call to reduce his strokes. My other jobs are to retrieve his errant drives, improve (and ignore) his lies, take a dive on the eighteenth, and act as an enabler for his imaginative scoring. As a reward, Toby has given me his most recent cast-offs. It's been hard enough to lose to Toby using my father's hickory relics. What now?

No more carping. Toby has sponsored me at his in-town eating establishment and a pair of country clubs frequented by the bulk of his clients. As part of this package, he's paid my initiation fees and promised he'll cover my dues until I make partner. Actually, he didn't put it quite that way. Toby said he'd underwrite me until January 1, 1972, one year after my anticipated ascension.

Some might wonder whether I'm ashamed of prostituting myself. Silly question. What business do they think I'm in? And who would have guessed it, stiff-backed Eliot seems jealous of my good fortune, although he's expressed it as disapproval. Another reason I've jumped at Toby's largesse is because I remember the admonition of a senior partner who said everyone should join their clubs while young and relatively unknown. Good advice and I didn't take it personally.

Becoming the clubbed and clubbable Millard has been merely one of my 1969 summer initiatives. It's been a momentous July for me and my country. On the 18th, Edward M. Kennedy had his swim off Chappaquiddick. On the 20th, Armstrong and Aldrin walked on the moon. On Thursday, July 24th, Andrew de Peyster Millard marched resolutely to the nearby recruiting station and enlisted in the United States Marine Corps. 'The Crotch', as Eliot and other insiders, affectionately (?), called it. Yes, you heard me fucking loud and clear. And to put All-American Eliot in his place, I volunteered for Officer Candidates School and told the recruiter (as well as everyone at Curtis) I was determined to become an infantry platoon commander. A grunt. The tip of the spear. Oooh Rah!

How do you like them apples, Eliot? You and your pitiful, peaceful, pussyish six-months at Camp Pendleton. The Curtis veterans, all of whom had been REMFs (rear echelon mother fuckers), are awestruck. Teary-eyed almost. Who is this young Hector disdainfully turning his back on partnership and financial security? Who is this reincarnation of our Founding Fathers risking life, fortune, and sacred honor? Patriotism runs in my family. I had an ancestor who fled on Patriots' Day.

My announcement has scorched, seared, and singed all opposition to my candidacy, like napalm on troops in the open. This *ruse de guerre* has required meticulous preparation. For several months,

I put it about that I was disturbed by the way things had been going in Nam. I'd become distraught when Khe Sanh was on the verge of being overrun. We were facing an American Dien Bien Phu. The Marines were being used as bait to lure the dinks into a kill zone. I even trotted out Samuel Johnson's "Every man thinks meanly of himself for not having been a soldier".

Gunny (this, I learned, is how Marines address a sergeant whose insignia consists of three chevrons with a pair of rockers enclosing crossed rifles) was as surprised as everyone at Curtis. Whatever he thought, he wasted no time. Here was a live one, at least for the moment.

The setting was more depressing than 23 State Street. Four or five polite, polished, hairless robots in low-rent space overlooking the Granary Cemetery. Beat-up metal desks. Folding chairs. Flickering fluorescent lights. Every wall painted a woodsy green and adorned with depictions of jarheads practicing their craft with bayonets, Ka-Bars, and sharpened entrenching tools. Scary? Fucking A! And the accessories: discolored coffee mugs and sawed-off shell casings overflowing with smoldering cigarette butts. Much staccato swabby talk about 'bulkheads', 'decks', and 'overheads'.

The beta dog who answered the door said, "Corporal Sweeney, sir. Let me introduce you to Gunny."

Gunny was enthroned with his back to the view. He was wearing four rows of ribbons, several metal badges, and a name tag. If his shirt hadn't been skin tight, it would have listed to port. His trousers (for Chrissake, don't call them 'pants'): sky-blue with a vivid scarlet stripe running down each leg. The chicks must so get off on them.

One couldn't help but notice the scar that traversed his right cheek. What a showboat. Actually, I'd love a scar like Gunny's if I could get it without pain or risk.

Gunny arose. "Welcome aboard, sir." His hand shot out towards my solar plexus. Was he testing my reflexes?

"Thank you Gunny... Doyle." He returned my right hand intact.

"What can I do for you, sir?"

What the fuck do you think, I thought. "I'm here to sign up, Gunny."

"Have a seat, sir. The smoking lamp is lit."

"Eh?" What would make this grim prick smile? A fatality on Tremont Street?

"I'm sure you know it'll be tough, sir."

"That's why I'm here, Gunny Doyle."

"You're a college grad, aren't you, sir?"

What in the name of Christ, do I look like, thought I. "That's affirmative, Gunny Doyle. Brown. Down the road in Prov." A less than chummy expression told me, yes, Gunny had damn well heard of Brown.

"You'll be shooting for a commission, won't you… sir?" A disdainful glance at my scuffed shoes. Screw him.

"Roger your last."

Yes, I was being flip. Gunny didn't care for that. I could tell because he made his forehead almost disappear by dropping his low-hanging hairline to within an inch or so of his dense, uninterrupted eyebrow. Afterwards I learned that Gunny's behavior was quite out of order. The Marines call it 'silent contempt'. Had I realized this, I'd have straightened him out on the spot.

Infantry lieutenants were in short supply, and if Gunny could deliver one he might be able to delay his own return to I Corps. While the brain-dead partners swallowed it, Gunny gave me a fishy look, but it didn't slow him down. We blew through the paperwork. He had no problem with Brown. I was a prize. He wanted me hogtied and delivered to Quantico before I came to my senses. I took the oath looking poster-perfect. Steely-eyed. Ramrod-straight. Bring it, da fuck, on.

"Would you mind if we expedited the physical, sir? Corporal Sweeney can drive you over to the Chelsea Naval Hospital chop-chop," said Gunny.

Hell yes, I want to go. The sooner the fucking better, said my body language. Had they known what was heading their way, those gook muthas would have been shitting their skivvies. Sweeney appeared. He told Gunny that transportation awaited and all systems were 'go' at the hospital. We saddled up and moved out at flank speed. Most definitely chop-chop.

Crossing the Mystic River Bridge, my heart began to flutter. First of all, I've never liked heights. They terrify me. Second, something might go wrong. My bum knee should keep me safe on State Street, but what if the rules had changed? What if the medical criteria had been relaxed? Things weren't going well 'over there'. Relax, I told myself. In a pinch, you can always trot out your asthma.

Corporal Sweeney hustled me into the examining room. My doctor was a smart aleck Princetonian. He stopped what he was doing when Sweeney told him I was a volunteer. As he thrust his rubber-clad forefinger into the heart of darkness, he said with a grin, "Princeton tigers really enjoy doing this to Brown bears." Then he banged on my bad knee. I howled. He manipulated my leg. I grunted in pain. Very much the limp upper lip. "Forward march," he snapped. I struggled across the room, with my knee clicking convincingly. He winked when he pronounced me unfit for active duty, the wise-ass. However, he was good enough to provide me with the paperwork needed to substantiate my noble but failed attempt to offer myself to my country and my 'Volk'.

Corporal Sweeney drove me back to Tremont Street. Gunny was unhappy, but I was a civilian so he damn well had to call me 'Sir', not 'Maggot'. I could see nothing to be gained by lingering, but I did grab a poster for my office. A reminder to my draft-dodging peers. I gave Gunny a manly handshake, looked him in the eye, reiterated my disappointment, and bugged out.

Forgetting my disability, I fairly skipped the few blocks back to Curtis. I composed myself before entering 23 State Street. My buddy, Rico, asked me how it had gone. I shook my head, looked stalwart, and pointed to my knee. Rico patted me on the shoulder. One stud to another.

I went directly to Toby's office. He wasn't any Ez, but he'd have to do. It was 4:30 p.m. on a July afternoon and, against all odds, Tobias Saunders was at his post. I dropped the medical papers on his desk, favored him with an expressive head shake, and, with shoulders drooping, left his office. Toby stopped me. He bucked me up. "Good show, Andrew, jolly good, absolutely first rate." I almost said I regretted having only one afternoon to give to my country. Instead, I nodded curtly and returned to my hooch.

Have I done enough? Can I, at last, rest from my labors? Not by a long shot. The odds have shifted in my favor, probably conclusively, but polls can be unreliable. I must keep sailing to the sound of the guns.

Too bad for the jarheads. I'd have been such a star. I see the cameras rolling. MGM. Big budget. Technicolor. The legendary 'Howlin' Mad' Millard is down. There I lie, crumpled at the summit of some numbered hill, swathed in discolored field dressings, my shattered Thompson at my side. I've taken the objective, saved my platoon, neutralized several bunkers, and cut down swarms of anonymous, shrieking, buck-toothed fiends in round-lensed glasses.

Now I have little time. My plasma bottle hangs from an upended M-1. John Wayne and Aldo Ray look down on me with concern and non-homoerotic love. The Duke hands me his Lucky, "Have a drag, Hoss." Meanwhile, back at Pearl, a virginal Ava Gardner is lighting a candle for me in the All Faiths Chapel.

On cue, I moan, "Mother."

Then I cry, "Cut." Why, in the name of all that is holy, would I want her?

16

IN OCTOBER 1969, Clare and I moved into my family house at 118 Beacon Street. It may have been rash because there was no assurance I'd make partner, and if I didn't, we couldn't afford it. Clare was unenthusiastic. In my opinion, however, it was the proper place for us to live. My parents, a.k.a. Papa and Grammy, had vacated their 'once-fashionable' (as Clare said) four-story, bow-front granite house and moved into the spruced-up summer place in Prouts Neck. Clare had been dreading this. She was unimpressed that the house had been in my family since my great grandfather's time when the land was reclaimed from the tidal flats of the Charles. Even being on the water side of Beacon Street wasn't enough.

"Why must I leave our nest on Beacon Hill and be entombed in a mausoleum?" asked Clare. "Who wants to be stuck in a moldering pile hemmed in by college dorms?" This was one of our few discordant times.

I got my way, but it cost me dearly: gallons of paint, new rugs, refinished floors and furniture, up-to-date wiring, central air conditioning (I had initially proposed a few fans and a window unit for the master bedroom), a deck, and a fancy kitchen even though it meant sacrificing a Lawrence treasure: the coffin-sized soapstone sink. Within months, Clare made this house as happy as our apartment had been.

17

BACK TO the mating ritual. I've discovered a purebred filly and need to hurry if I'm to cover her by next summer. There are, however, a number of tiresome preliminaries. Alice Edmunds will not, I suspect, willingly slip away to a Las Vegas wedding chapel. Every social nicety must be observed. At least my trust department research will prevent a repetition of earlier miscalculations. I still need an introduction, but that will be easy to arrange since the Edmunds' money is in Toby's capable hands from whence I see it proceeding in due course into mine.

Like a coach studying game films, I've analyzed Alice's tendencies. She'd gone to a southern finishing school where the only creatures of color were the horses. But Alice surprises people. She's an intellectual. The first woman in her family to earn a college degree. She and her two geldings matriculated to a now-defunct junior college and then finished with a home economics degree from a moribund four-year institution. After so many years of scholarship, enough was enough. There aren't many graduate schools with stables, so it was back to Dover for Alice and her mounts. Besides, Alice scoffs at advanced degrees. They are, in her own words, 'redundant and unnecessary'. Since completing her studies, she's been clip clopping about on the Edmundses' well-tended acres. After considering the options available to liberated women, Alice opted for matrimony. Anticipating a stampede of proposals, she and her parents set the bar high.

While it isn't necessary to slay a dragon or sing ballads beneath her turret, every suitor is expected to buy into certain Edmunds myths. Alice is special, Alice is an important member of a still-important family. Alice is an ASAP (Anglo-Saxon American Princess) and we must remember: Alice is *not* stupid. She's a superb equestrienne and could, I'm certain, whip my ass in squash.

Mr. and Mrs. Edmunds expect to have significant input in their daughter's selection of a husband. They won't accept some stripling or someone on the make, no matter how good his odds. They require a known quantity—somebody who's proved himself, preferably in the marketplace. It would be desirable, but his money needn't be old, only abundant. He must, however, pass an optics test. It's important their daughter's intended looks at ease with a cashmere sweater tied loosely around his shoulders. Sockless in his loafers. No gut, but a slight paunch is acceptable as long as it's carried above the belt.

Alice's husband needs be well-mannered, meaning he needs unlimited tolerance for tedium. Alice is not, all admit, a sparkler. Despite her limitations, Alice is accustomed to being pursued and admired. Though the unaccountably self-assured Alice has never desired or been desired, she somehow believes she's desirable, and has been carefully shielded from those who might not have drunk the Kool-Aid.

For unfathomable reasons, Alice also expects to be listened to attentively. She requires the floor and requires it frequently. You can tell when she feels neglected.

Suddenly, Alice will interrupt and seize a sentence, one that can be twisted into a subject on which she feels qualified to declaim. Her range is wide. She can choose among private schools, Mayflower families, sailing, racquet sports, certain breeds of dogs, and horses, horses, horses. It's like being in the streets of Pamplona. The earth is trembling. You hear a faint drumming of hooves. Then louder. Too late. Alice is on you—snorting, goring, and trampling. Resistance is futile. You are facing at least fifteen minutes of payback for your callous inattention.

The way to Alice's heart is through her jodhpurs. I feel obliged to display my horse-like qualities. I must bond with those beasts. Truth be told, I dislike horses, and ponies, for that matter. I can never tell what they're thinking. They sense this and reciprocate my sentiments. If I'm to hang out with large, hard to read quadrupeds, make them soft-eyed cash cows.

You can bust your ass riding, and where's the reward that offsets the risk? It quite eludes me. Furthermore, they produce too much crap and are totally high maintenance. Like wooden boats. What about fiberglass horses?

Fucking horses. They scare the piss out of me. Look at what happened to my idle, clumsy, uncoordinated classmate Brad. He dips into his trust fund and buys an athletic jumper. Jumpers, I'm told, need to be jumped or they get disagreeable. Bucephalus—yes, Bucephalus—was no exception.

So here comes my fleshy friend, thundering towards a stone wall. He must have seen himself riding down Persians or maybe leading the charge of the Scots Greys at Waterloo. Brad and his riding crop cleared the obstacle. Bucephalus took a pass.

Instead of sabering fleeing infantry, Brad crashed, impaling himself on his crop. It entered his body next to his collarbone and proceeded due south until only a couple inches were protruding beside his neck.

Brad never passed out. Somehow, he arose and lurched a few hundred yards to the neighboring golf course, where he persuaded a terrified caddy to summon an ambulance. Brad's novel form of self-mutilation made the career of a till-then-anonymous young surgeon who saved both Brad and his riding crop. Brad has shown me his portfolio of stills, slides, and x-rays. I think of them whenever I consider mounting Alice or one of her unpredictable pets.

Alice's financial condition is robust. Clare's is anemic, but in her case I'd waive that requirement. Ten million now with more on the way enables even the most discriminating to overlook minor imperfections. Enough grousing, Millard. Mucking out stables and playing equerry beats walking point under triple-canopy jungle in Nam.

Despite her predilections, Alice isn't horse-faced. Her body's shapely and well-toned. Her bloodlines, going back generations through sire and dam, are impeccable. That's more than sufficient in the land of paddock and pasture.

In my hour of need, Toby came through for me again. Right after Labor Day he throws a bash for his favorite customers, welcoming them back to the Commonwealth from their damp and drafty summer cottages. A celebration of the rentrée. Time to put away the Nantucket Reds and get one more party out of the venerable madras jacket before Harvard plays da Cross. Most of Toby's customers know each other, so this is a way to reconnect with friends who, having scattered from Seal Harbor to Siasconset, have been deprived of each other's conviviality since the Memorial Day diaspora.

I guilelessly suggested to Toby he use some of the younger Curtis lawyers to liven up his parties. Every cruise ship has an assortment of polite, well-groomed Apollos to amuse the crepey-skinned ladies and attend to those with Crone's Disease. Toby might wish to offer the same services in case any pre-menopausal customers should appear. You didn't want the next generation getting the idea there might be other, equally accommodating, trustees out there. In fact, I helped Toby with the invitation list. He thought my idea of providing a stag line was spot-on. With what I took to be a smirk, he asked if I might be able to attend. By chance, I was available.

Alice Edmunds came. This was no surprise since I'd personally mailed her invitation and found out from Toby's secretary she'd accepted. I made a stunning first impression. I was attentive. I plummeted to her level of discourse and steered the conversation to her strengths. She talked, and, God save me, I listened. I recall her recounting every spell-binding detail of her childhood carsickness episodes.

I'd even done a little research about the Triple Crown and was able to speak semi-knowledgeably about the races and the tracks. Alice was impressed. She had, of course, visited each of them. I can't say it was love (or even desire) at first sight. I had anticipated this, but I am willing to unclothe almost any woman once. You never know.

Alice Edmunds must become the third Mrs. Millard not later than next Labor Day. It's important for the Curtis partners to sniff, touch, and observe the suitably married Millard for a few months before he stands for partnership. I will present them with a socially-connected princeling who, but for his bum knee, might be returning to Boston in dress blues, sword, and decorations for valor. I've always wanted to be 'mentioned in despatches', but maybe that's just for Brits.

I swung into action. Alice got the full treatment. It included a Hermès scarf, the cost of which I took as a tax deduction. I've gotten a lot of mileage out of scarves, and I'm talented at matching them to the recipient's complexion.

I am not proud to admit we did it for the first time in her barn. Alice is always most energized after a ride. I chose a mild October afternoon, left work early, and met her with a bottle of bubbly and two champagne flutes. Romantic that I am, I told her we were celebrating the one-month anniversary of our meeting. I wouldn't say the phlegmatic Alice was deeply moved. She was appreciative, but she expected to be appreciated. She parked her horse and undressed it. Then she spent half an hour fiddling around with the damn thing. Finally, we sat outside together in the late afternoon sunshine. I had staged this well. "Season of mists and mellow fruitfulness," you know. We polished off the champagne. I could have used a chaser, but I pressed on. We began nuzzling.

So much for that. We went inside. Stale air. Straw and dust. I began coughing. Out with my albuterol inhaler. This was a multi-puff episode. My airways were closing. Alice took no notice. She pointed to a pile of saddle blankets. I was struck by their aroma. Nasty, but when in Dover… I took my time spreading them out. My breathing began to recover. I could stall around no longer. Tally ho! She required help with her cinch, her boots, and her unbreachable breeches. Horses don't engage in foreplay, and neither did we. Thinking of Clare helped.

Our first frolic was literally a roll in the hay. As such, it had elements of the Belmont Stakes, the longest of the Triple Crown races, known to devotees as the Test of the Champion. A mile and a half. You need speed and stamina. Patience helps too.

Alice won the toss and bade me lie down. She has a good seat. Her traditional forward position, proper weight distribution, and efficient use of the aids resulted in a harmonious unity of horse and rider.

A fast track. Fractious at the gate, I settle in a good position along the rail and move quickly into contention. Approaching the final quarter, Alice has me under a light hold. We've nailed it. I'm ready to surge. Alice is roaring, "Yes! Yes! Yes! More! More! Now! Now! Now!"

Seconds later, she's yelling, "Whoa! Whoa! Whoa!" Sweet Jesus. I give way grudgingly. Suddenly she goes to the whip. "I'm ready. I'm ready. I'm ready. I'm there! Yes. I'm there."

With one furlong to go, she cries wolf again. "Soon. Soon. Not now. Pleeeeese, NOT NOW!" I falter. We're crawling down the stretch. I'm losing ground. The crowd is booing. They're shredding their pari-mutuel tickets.

Back to her stout left hand urging. She's raising welts. "More! More! Oh, more! Yes! Yes!" I've got the lead. "It's now. It's reeeeely NOW!" I'm full-extended. I let fly. She stands in her stirrups. "Oh, YES!"

"That was wonderful," gasped Alice. "Still is," I whinny gallantly, summoning up a couple last disingenuous thrusts.

Yes, I finished high in her gallop ratings, but I couldn't wait for a bath, a rubdown, and a pail of oats.

Since we've done what we've done, we must be in love and, therefore, must get engaged if we're to continue doing it as I ardently insisted we must. So there I was in the winner's circle. I'd worked damn hard for my blanket of white carnations.

Before telling the world of our engagement I bought Ruth a pretty salmon-colored scarf at Filene's Basement. Next, I'll get Alice a bridal bridle. Then I urged my intended to begin monogramming everything with what would be her new initials. The more she marks, the harder for her to bolt. The Edmundses are pleased to underwrite an appropriately gaudy engagement party. I'm relieved. Alice's parents haven't been the obstacles I'd expected. I'd worried they might balk at their chaste daughter (a misdiagnosis; I was not her first, unless something had parted on one of her rides) becoming the prize of a two-time loser in the matrimonial stakes. Thankfully, father Edmunds was overwhelmed by my act of selfless patriotism. Having been in uniform in WWII—he never went overseas—he prides himself on his ability to recognize a fellow warrior. So, who better than me for his precious Alice? Also,

I bet he secretly worries his Alice might end up with a hubby who really is a groom.

Everything is falling into place. In an effort to fit in, I've taken to wearing saddle shoes while Alice's parents have gone so far as to rummage through their safe deposit boxes for a fitting rock. Alice deserves only the best, and that's what her doting parents have provided. It's a whopper—an emerald-cut diamond in a platinum, art deco setting. Thank God I don't have to spring for that. I slipped it onto her finger, promising that when I came into my own—by which I meant her money—I would buy her an even gaudier one. My little speech would have done credit to Cyrano. What's more, it resulted in the one instance of lively sex I ever had with the woman who was to become my third but not, I assumed, my last, or even penultimate wife.

Then Eliot comes along and inserts his judgmental nose into my affairs. I'd kept him in the dark about Alice and me. I didn't want him spooking her. But now he hunts me down.

There he is in my doorway wearing his sappy 'I just got laid' smile. Instead of congratulating me on hitting the trifecta, he plays Dutch uncle.

"I've known Alice Edmunds for years," he said. "In fact, I escorted her to a lot of parties, and I don't think the two of you are well-suited."

Did he really expect an answer to that crap?

"She's pretty, she's well-born, and she's certainly well-off, but she's never struck me as particularly warm."

Warm. Schmorm.

"What's more, her range of interests is rather narrow, even by my standards. With the best intentions in the world, I still find it painful to converse with her. Forget books. Unless they're about horses."

I could tell he was about to get preachy on me.

"Most important, you might hurt her. I like Alice and her family and wouldn't want that to happen."

Then he really tore it.

"Besides, I'd have thought you, of all people, would have learned the wisdom of the expression 'marry in haste, repent in leisure.'"

What a hand job. I kind of lost it.

"Could it be that my old friend Eliot Estabrook Lawrence the Fourth of the once-wealthy Lawrences is a wee bit jealous his pal's set for life?"

You could anticipate his response.

"Believe it or not, Andrew, I'm thinking of your well-being, not my own."

My ass.

I pressed the secret buzzer and seconds later my phone rang. I ignored it. Next came a respectful knock and there was the all-business Ruth. She let Eliot finish his sentence.

"Mr. Cabot's holding on line three, Mr. Millard."

"Which one, Miss Donohue?"

"Mr. Lysander Cabot, Mr. Millard."

"I better grab this one, Eliot."

Ruth returned to her station, and the two of us engaged in some inspired telephone improv long enough for Eliot to take the hint and depart. Ruth can do a wicked high WASP accent.

Events are proceeding apace. The engagement's been proclaimed in traditional fashion, and the wedding's set for May 16, 1970, the Saturday before the Memorial Day weekend. The entire extravaganza is to take place on Squire Edmunds's spread because the drive from Trinity Church to Dover is too taxing for many of the spavined guests. There will be two giant pavilions, one sacred, one profane. One for tying the knot and one for tying one on.

Ruth is unwilling to bless my dynastic union with Clan Edmunds. On the contrary, she's being downright pissy. The day after meeting Alice, Ruth insinuated her sultry self into my chambers.

"You really prefer *her* to little ol' me?" my unabashed Doll Tearsheet pouted as she stepped out of her heels, placed five twinkly, stocking-sheathed toes on the arm of my chair, and gave me an unobstructed close-up of my favorite vista—the garter belt, the auburn groove, and the grandest of grand canyons. Top that, Ansel Adams!

"You still want to marry her?" said Ruth.

"Darling love vessel, the only way I can afford *you* is to marry Alice."

That got a grin and a tickle from my honey. I wedged the usual chair under the door handle, and ordered the drummer to sound 'beat to quarters'.

An aside: as we gained confidence in our workplace high jinks, we shed more and more of our clothes. Finally, Ruth lost patience. "Andrew, would you please remove those less-than-arousing over-the-calf, cable-knit socks? There are times when male hosiery doesn't do it for me." I couldn't confess that Slats let me wear my socks.

What could I do but comply?

Now it's late autumn, and Alice is spending more time with her horses. There is one niggling concern. How to ensure I inherit Toby's trusteeships? Toby, I'm afraid, has no intention of doing the right thing by anointing his successors. Who does? Life is good, and Toby has every reason to believe he's got at least fifteen years to make up his mind. That's the traditional pattern among trustees. Talk transition but cling and clutch. No trusts, no leverage. No leverage, and management casts you from the Tarpeian Rock. For whatever reason, undoubtedly his own amusement, Toby has been good to me. But suppose I'm just a passing fancy? Looking behind me, I see at least two associates who'd have no qualms about rustling my cattle.

One of them, as I've mentioned, is female, a cunning, attractive little tart. She's industrious. I'll give her that. This distinguishes her from the rest of us idlers. She has suggested Curtis break with tradition and promise 'wills within a week'. Bad precedent. Worse, she's brilliant about concealing her ruthless ambition behind a lacy veil of deceptively agreeable manners and is deft at cadging lunch invitations from certain partners. Soon she'll be putting the moves on Toby—my Toby.

This devious Miss Macbeth of the high heels, well-cut clothes, and steel-trap mind must be 'scotched'. I thought her layers of inexpertly-applied dark eye shadow would do it, but so far it hasn't. Even though she looks rather like a raccoon. Meanwhile, both of us are revoltingly nice to each other. She tells me how much she is rooting for me to make partner, while I provide her with advice I hope will be her undoing.

Time to crank up the rumor mill. Surely, we have enough misogynists who'll welcome the chance to think ill of this polished young woman who wants to crash their party. She can't be dismissed like so many other female associates who require instruction in deportment, dress, and depilatories, and who in a crisis behave as expected by quacking harshly and then rushing about in their stockings being hateful to one another. Yes, I outfoxed the vixen. I planted some stories and watered them tenderly. Miss Know-It-All got a crappy review and departed.

Then the gods smiled on me again. I have always enjoyed walking over the Hill to work. It gives me a sense of prosperity and provides a certain amount of exercise. Usually, I take Beacon Street, passing Toby's house, one of the clubs he's enabled me to join, the State House, the Athenaeum, and then down to my State Street salt mines. I've always been conscious of Toby's house, its solidity, its location, its view of the Common.

This particular December morning Toby's vertiginous granite steps were covered with a nearly invisible sheet of ice. There'd been a rainstorm the night before, followed by a sudden, unexpected drop in temperature. Now a cold rain was falling. The brick sidewalks were equally treacherous. I noticed a bucket of rock salt on Toby's front stoop. I paused for a moment and moved it out of sight. Didn't want my mentor tripping over it.

It takes several hours for news, even momentous news, to make its way around Curtis. Someone gets the word. It may or may not be relayed to an important partner who may or may not dictate a memorandum to be typed, revised, reproduced, dropped off at each secretarial station, and finally delivered to the lawyers.

I didn't hear of Toby's accident until almost lunchtime. Nasty: a severe concussion, a broken hip, and a compound fracture of his right leg. Toby'd been taken to Mass General, where he couldn't receive visitors or take phone calls. I am the first to send him flowers and a note. I've thrown myself into the task of holding the fort and letting Toby's most important customers know there will be no interruption of service.

The partners, few of whom are looking for extra work, are

relieved and impressed by my initiative. I can be counted on. Toby's customers are thrilled by my responsiveness, particularly my speed in returning phone calls, one of the areas in which Toby is particularly lax. It's not hard to seem attentive when your plate's nearly empty.

So, Toby won't exhaust himself, I've arranged to be the only person from the office who visits him in the hospital. Certainly not that foxy little schemer. A healthy guy can get some kind of randy lying around in a hospital bed. I spend nearly an hour a day with Toby. We work on everything together. Toby's accident has taken a lot out of him. Might he now be willing to transfer some of his trusteeships or at least ask me to share his 'burdens', if I dare use that word?

I've been tactful lest my solicitude be correctly interpreted. I also had a practical suggestion. I told Toby I was aware of the sensible firm policy requiring trustees to be partners. Eminently reasonable. But what about this? Toby needs help, so why not appoint me as a co-trustee now and I, in turn, will execute and deliver resignations to become effective, when accepted, in the event I don't make partner by January 1, 1973. Yes, I've cut myself a little slack timewise. No matter how things turn out, I expect to be indispensable in three years. This plan sounded fine to Toby, and he sold it to his docile colleagues. Nobody crosses Toby. Bold Millard. Canny Millard. I wish I'd prevented Toby's accident, but lots of folks came a cropper in Boston that day. All the streets and sidewalks were dangerous. Toby wasn't the only person to take a pratfall.

It's been a productive winter and spring. By May, I'd been written into trusts worth close to half a billion dollars. Alice and I have been inundated with gifts. Nearly every one's covered by representations of horses. The tribe into which I'm marrying rivals the Mongols in horsemanship and literacy.

A week before I was to re-perjure myself at the altar, the Edmundses hosted an intimate dinner party. After dessert, Squire Edmunds summoned me to his study for what I assumed would be the traditional man-to-man chat. And why not? The perfect opportunity to get to know his daughter's exceptional catch? As usual, I was slightly buzzed. How else could I get it up for the obligatory postprandial coupling?

The high octane Rémy Martin slid down easily. The Monte Cristo drew perfectly, and the combination transported me far from Dover. It was all good.

"Mother and I are so glad our Alice finally found a real man," purred the Squire.

Instead of responding, "Miraculous, isn't it?" I did my best Eliot imitation. Stalwart. Modest. Protective.

"One of these days I'm getting you onto a polo pony, my boy," said the expansive Squire.

I nodded in agreement. "Might be damn good fun," said I. *No fucking way*, thought I.

The atmosphere reeked of bonhomie. Even the Stubbs horse looking down from the wall seemed to be smiling. What on earth made me say, "Henry," (I'd never called him that before) "I'd do anything for our dear Alice."

"I know you would, Andrew," responded Henry. "And, now that you mention it, there's a little something we can take care of before we rejoin the ladies. Won't take a second."

The next thing I knew the snake produced an anonymous manila envelope from which he withdrew a document with the innocuous title, "Agreement."

How could I have been so trusting and open?

"Just the usual. Here…" He thrust a serious-looking Parker pen at me. The kind used for unconditional surrenders.

I flipped through the pages. There weren't many. No need for many. It was hideously clear-cut. Alice's money, together with the income therefrom and the accretions thereto, remained Alice's, and if we split up, I got jack shit. A prenup.

Should I pour my cognac on his bald dome? Should I stick the Parker pen up his fat ass? No, better yet, the business end of my Monte Cristo. I was enraged by his innocent expression. The sneaky prick.

"Come along, Andrew. Let's get back to the party. I'll be your witness." My perfidious fiancée had already signed, and her signature had been witnessed by someone I knew to be an obnoxious, no holds barred 'family lawyer', as those dickwads like to style themselves.

Be cool, Millard. Just a bump in the road. Soon enough you'll have her begging you to shred the damn thing.

I gave Henry no satisfaction. With as much jauntiness as I could muster, I took the offending pen, scribbled something I hoped would be sufficiently illegible to disclaim, and handed over my declaration of dependence.

We rejoined the ladies, and I really hit the sauce. Old Faithless took the night off.

The wedding itself went off like clockwork. It was far more elaborate than either of my first two. Squire Edmunds had ponied up. Since my entire life had been and would soon again become a merry bachelor party, I saw no need to have one in this instance. Instead, my groomsmen and I drank a toast in the stall where it all started. One of them talked of my 'stable' relationship. The horses looked on, but kept their counsel.

And then: a revelation. Those poor trusting beasts. For centuries, they'd been central to us. We loved them. They loved us. We rode them into battle. In a pinch we ate them. Now they're irrelevant. At best, ornamental. Rendered so by us. Are they disheartened by their reduced status and diminished numbers? Am I to be riffed?

Having Eliot as my best man at a wedding attended by over 400 of the right sort added the perfect note of solemnity and legitimacy. There we were—two rising stars of the Boston legal firmament. Pillars, both of us. Both of us married to Cliffies. I at least had the sense to select a Briarcliffie, not the more astringent Cambridge variety. With giants like us coming along, Curtis was poised for lift-off. Oh, partnership election, where is thy sting? So I raised a glass to moi. Unlike Richard III, I had a kingdom and all the effing nags I could shake a crop at. For the record, I drew the line at leaving the service on horseback.

There was one discordant note. As I feared, Mother came. How could she resist carpet bombing such a target-rich environment? What an opportunity to rustle a head or two of Brahmin bloodstock.

Alas, Mother miscalculated. She rolled up in a limo and was sheathed in enough sable to inflame a Moscow call girl. Perfect for The Breakers in high season. A year-round no-no in Dover, MA. Later in the festivities, she insisted we dance together. *How adorable,* she thought. *How horrifying,* I thought, *to be confronted by acres of exposed maternal chest.* Sophocles had it wrong.

18

THE UNFORTUNATE Stevens left C&P shortly after Millard's wedding to Alice Edmunds. He and his immodest wife, Jane, got tight at the reception and behaved badly. How sad. It would have been a chance to show a little solidarity among the three musketeers who'd enlisted together. I tried to encourage Stevens, but he was having none of it. He'd gotten bitter, and I sensed he may have been experiencing marital problems. Poor guy. It never rains but it pours.

While we hadn't spent any time together outside the office, I'd always been fond of Stevens. He was loud. His short-sleeved shirts raised eyebrows throughout the firm. And yes, his sideburns were a bit much, even by '60s standards. But Stevens had a good heart. He worked hard and cared for his wife, whose flirtatious behavior at firm events boded ill for their marriage. From a professional standpoint, Stevens was a competent litigator, but the knock on him was he couldn't handle big appellate cases. Not that we see many big appellate cases. Stevens came to the wrong place. He didn't get a fair shake. Shouldn't someone have looked harder at him in the first place? In fact, Stevens found a job at a plaintiff's medical malpractice firm. He did it without any help from C&P.

As for Millard, he certainly showed his best side. His attempted enlistment was one of the bravest, most selfless acts I've ever seen. I was proud of him. It's funny really. Ever since Khe Sanh, I had the same feelings. However, unlike Millard, I did nothing. Guilt over my inaction increased with the news that Major Hastings had been blown to pieces by a booby trap. Millard, I thought, put us all to shame.

I must also mention Millard's marriage to Alice. She's a fine girl from a top-notch family. A good egg. Despite some misgivings on my part, I could see the Lawrences and the Millards becoming close. Clare's response: "Let's talk about that some other time."

I've been pals with Millard since we were 13, and I'd never seen him happier. Edith was alluring. We Yankees are susceptible to those southern girls. Their syrupy accents are seductively exotic. But Edith scared me. I sensed I was supposed to say I loved her, then we'd go to bed, then we'd be engaged. All this on our second or third date, and if that didn't happen she'd move on to someone else. Poor Millard. As for Maud, who could have guessed what she'd turn into? Not me. Nothing in her upbringing would have suggested it. What was it Maud once said to me? "Always keep an eye on your friend when he's playing with his hair."

But who can fault Millard for his mistakes? Nobody's perfect. Look at his mother. Then Millard reinvented himself. He started over with a clean slate—a model for all of us.

I hadn't wanted to worry Clare about my prospects, but 1970 wasn't easy. Except for some mildly disparaging comments by Toby Saunders which I couldn't discount, I'd gotten uniformly positive annual reviews, and after my fourth year was assured I was "on track". However, I remembered Stevens telling me he too had received favorable evaluations. He said he'd been flabbergasted when the rug was pulled out from under him. As for me, ever since the screw-up with my first compensation increase, I'd been nervous about my standing. I never dared ask the partner reviewing me what others were making, but each year whoever he was told me I was earning the most ever by an associate at my level. I decided to live with that and keep my fingers crossed. No matter what happened, I had Clare.

Nevertheless, it was risky to assume I was out of the woods. What if everyone remembered DataCentric? The company's been doing well, and its new lawyers enjoy bragging about how it 'outgrew' us. Then there was Air Funeral Service. And how about Papa's mental deterioration? Should I have been more open about him? Might someone suggest that early-onset dementia runs in the Lawrence family? Nobody at the firm knew about this but Millard. He wouldn't tell anyone, would he?

It was tough sledding. There'd been an awkward and potentially damaging incident. Last year, a couple of the older corporate lawyers nominated me for partnership. Unfortunately, they'd miscounted the number of years I'd been with the firm. This caused confusion at a partners' meeting. I am told a few of those present were resentful about what they perceived as a heavy-handed power play—an effort to break with tradition with no discussion or advance notice.

"What makes Lawrence so special as to warrant early admission?" someone asked. Every viable partnership candidate was presumptively a star. When the situation was clarified, my premature candidacy sank beneath the waves. I could have used a damage assessment. My loudest supporters were not necessarily the people I wanted pleading my case. Most of them didn't measure up to Millard's champion. If only Mr. Clark had been alive. Also, I was worried people might think I had engineered this maneuver myself or was presenting an ultimatum. I am not a squeaky wheel by nature, at least not on my own behalf.

I date my sleeplessness to that premature nomination. God knows what the partners were thinking, but it was unwise to tamper with tradition at C&P. Tough nights. I'd wake up after a few hours, go to the john, slide back in next to Clare, and try to compose myself. More often than not I'd give up and go to a guest room with a good reading light. Then I'd be pooped and off my game the next day.

During that period, I found financial statements to be reliable sleeping potions. I didn't have the nerve to visit my doctor and ask for something to get rid of the tic in my left eyelid. Probably just as well, he might have sent me to a shrink. I didn't want that in my file. Litigators must have their own favorite knock-out drops. And someday I'll ask Millard what he uses. Forget it. He'd never admit to doubts even though his gnawed fingernails betrayed him.

Until then I'd always been confident that if there were only room for one partner from the class of 1963, it would most likely be me. That was no longer true. Millard seemed to have vaulted ahead. He reminded the partners of his patriotism by speaking Marine. When he complimented them on their attire (yes, he did that), he referred to their neck ties as 'field scarves'. Even so, I couldn't have been more pleased for him. He had it sewed up. Millard must have thought so too because his fingernails reappeared. Maybe I should have asked him to put in a good word for me. But Millard can be hard to figure. He's up. He's down. He can be a bear, a bipolar bear. Ha. Ha.

I think it's fair to say I had the right to feel moderately bullish about my chances. I'd never be as good as Mr. Clark, but I believed that with continued effort I could hold my own with most of the corporate partners. Clare was great. She laughed at my misgivings, particularly my concern that Millard had passed me in the last furlong, as Alice might say. I told myself to stop worrying. But I couldn't help wondering what I'd do if I got turned down.

Well guess who came through for me? None other than A. de P. M. There I was, hiding in my office sweating bullets. Enter Millard.

"It's a done deal, buddy," he said.

Huh?

"I've spoken to Mr. Toby, and now he's on board. In fact, he's spreading the gospel. I fed him a line about your new clients, your long hours, your dedication… all that crap."

"You pulling my leg?"

"No way. Tobias and his millions, his vote delivering millions, are now, thanks to me, squarely in your camp. You may have to chase bluefish with him, though."

What would people have thought if they'd seen me hugging Millard? Instead, I thanked him and shook his hand. Millard had aced the foxhole test.

I admit I was still concerned until one of the partners I barely knew said, "Toby Saunders has been talking you up, Eliot."

December 15, 1970 was the big day. Millard and I both made it. I was told there were no negative votes or abstentions in either case. What a thrill. Millard and I had been tipped-off the partners were assembling at 5:30 p.m. Neither of us was about to leave the office before learning the outcome. I must have called Clare three times that afternoon. I don't know what else was on the agenda, but the meeting was gratifyingly brief. Millard and I were summoned and then welcomed into our first partners' meeting with a standing ovation. What a relief, Clare was fabulous. She told me I needn't have worried. The announcement was, as I knew it would be, snazzy. Engraved on the highest quality stock, it read:

CURTIS AND PERKINS
ARE PLEASED TO ANNOUNCE THAT

ELIOT E. LAWRENCE
AND
ANDREW de P. MILLARD

HAVE THIS DAY BECOME MEMBERS OF THE FIRM
[NAMES OF THE OTHER PARTNERS]
JANUARY 1, 1971   23 STATE STREET
BOSTON, MASSACHUSETTS

19

OF COURSE, Eliot likes the damn announcement. His name comes first. It's ahead of mine on the stationery and every other listing of Curtis partners. What's worse, considerate Eliot is taking pains to assure me that the order in which our names appear isn't merit-based, only alphabetical. Then he really gets under my skin by claiming the listing makes sense because he got to the office ahead of me on September 3, 1963. He thinks this is funny. I can tell because he says, "Ha. Ha." I almost wish loser Stevens had made it so I wouldn't be tail-end Charley. Get over it, Millard. There'll be new partners coming along in twelve months. Hell's teeth. How can I forget it? Unless something happens to him, I'm doomed to be behind Eliot forever.

So why did I convert Toby to Eliot's cause? First of all, Eliot had it made, and I've never been one to kick against the pricks. Next, I could at last afford to be magnanimous, but most important, how could I tolerate Curtis without him and Clare? I must have her and, if I'm stuck here for long, Eliot will be a useful, if unknowing, ally.

20

I MADE it, and, as I promised Clare, I stopped smoking. For good, it looks like. Praise be. My tic vanished and sleep returned. Set for life, I assumed. I was looking forward to having the new Andrew Millard as my partner. It had taken us slightly over seven years, which, of course, is as long as college and law school combined. What happened next? I didn't feel transformed, but I'd have been shattered if I hadn't made it.

Then and there I promised myself I wouldn't forget the ordeal of the last couple years. What must it be like for associates who never receive the assurances and support I'd gotten? Poor Stevens had become a lush by the time he left. As for his wife…

My life had changed for the better. Clare and I would be able to scrimp less, if only a little less. Fewer hand-me-downs for the children. Maybe the two of us could get away together. Somewhere besides our parents' summer places. Would there be enough for tuitions? How about braces? I had started at $7,000. In 1970, I made almost $21,000, and I hoped my first year as partner would bring me at least $30,000. I remember when I thought $25,000 would put me on easy street.

Time to look ahead. Should I settle in for the long haul? No, that's too passive. Mr. Clark was proud of spending his entire career at C&P. Had the time come to vault into something more remunerative, more worthwhile, or more exciting? If I didn't, would I, at the end of the day, feel as though I'd done enough, accomplished enough, and dared enough? If I stayed, would I end up being wheeled out of my office and taken down to the building's loading dock in the service elevator?

Who was I kidding? It's fun to pretend you have countless

options, but, as I guess is obvious, I'm not the most adventurous person. I liked C&P. If something spectacular came my way, sure I'd consider it. If the firm changed I'd try to figure out what that meant to me and to the atmosphere of the place. But who can predict the future? I was content and, if I kept at it, I expected to prosper. None of the partners looked as though he was broke.

When I thought about my future at C&P, there was a lot to be excited about. For one thing, the firm moved into a new building at 40 State Street about six months after Millard and I made partner. It was 38 stories tall and had over 20,000 square feet per floor. The exterior was glass and pink granite. Spare and severe. All right angles. Lifeless. We took three entire floors and had options for more.

Boston was on the move, and it was thrilling to be moving with it. However, I missed the idiosyncratic intimacy of 23 State: the old-fashioned elevators, the fireplaces, the windows you could open, the cavernous bathrooms, the doormen and Mario, the 80-year-old shoe shine boy, who'd knock on your door once a week. I missed Rico, who took me upstairs on my first day of work and regaled the associates with sea stories of his stock market coups. Rico shrank before our eyes. Age and self-service elevators combined to do in my effusive friend.

Our new quarters were cheesy. Too much glass. Too much chrome. We weren't a sales outlet for Danish modern. On the other hand, the new, jumped-up law firms were trying to look as though their founding hustlers had stood tall against the Redcoats. Dark wood. Leather armchairs. Yellowing maps, sometimes in foreign languages. Recently-acquired paintings we were to assume were portraits of the name partners. Heavy curtains. And prints of sailing ships everywhere.

I no longer roomed next to Millard. We were now grouped by practice areas. Millard seemed peeved when I ended up with a better office on 21 (I could see a slice of the Harbor) than he'd gotten on 19. I liked reminding him the lesser practice areas get the lower floors.

These offices could have been considered transitional because they carried forward vestiges of the *ancien regime*. The 'executive suite', comprising the southeastern corner of the 21st floor, was our Versailles. The older partners were quartered here and looked after by slow-moving secretaries of their approximate age. Located just off the reception area, it had its own entrance and men's room. This gated community was off limits to all but its residents. I couldn't decide whether it was the gold coast or an elephants' graveyard. Our more vigorous elders wanted no part of what they saw as a hospice, and after a few deaths, the executive suite began to fill up with riff-raff. It even got to the point where people waiting in the reception area would use its bathroom.

And then there was our senior partner's office. One of his windows could be opened, the only one in the building. He demanded this. As for our furniture; I liked the comfortable old pieces. Millard said they looked as though they'd come from Goodwill and favored trading them for tax deductions. Thank heaven we didn't. It would have been so wasteful. I was particularly fond of an antique table which had about 10 legs. We still have it. It's impossible to sit at it without banging your knees. I must not forget our many sets of the *Mass. Reports*, which Millard dismissed as "chipped, cracked, dented, faded, foxed, ripped, rubbed, soiled, and torn". Sometimes he overdoes it. Finally, the portraits of our two founders. We kept them even though Millard says Mr. Perkins looks as though he's having the 'big one'.

The ritual of signing the Curtis and Perkins Partnership Agreement meant a lot to me. I did so on January 4, 1971, the first working day of my partnerhood. It was a momentous act. I was officially part of the team, and hoped I'd strengthen it.

The Partnership Agreement provided for a management committee which was "responsible for the general management of the firm". New partners were eligible. Very enlightened, and I say this not just because I was elected to the committee in 1972, the first year I was eligible. I could tell Millard was disappointed at not being considered. He got angry when I told him his time would surely come. The management committee elects a managing partner to serve a four-year term.

A quick digression about the partners' monthly lunches. I'd been expecting something more collegial. Here's the way it worked and still does. The eldest grab the seats at the end of the table nearest the windows. As appropriate, the youngsters end up below the salt. C&P is not like the Marine Corps, where the officers eat last. Quite the contrary. The food starts at the head of the table.

Our elders are uninterested in denying themselves, so the platter is sometimes meatless by the time it reaches the likes of me. They probably think: *those pushy whippersnappers have scores of lamb chop-eating years ahead of them.* Some of the oldsters undoubtedly feel inadequately compensated by the upstarts who are now slicing up the pie—so they ignore the injunction about revenge being a dish best eaten cold. There might be nothing left by then.

That said, this was one of the happiest times of my life. I'd gotten what I'd struggled for and, though I was troubled by the absence of a pension plan, I hadn't yet experienced the 'is this really all there is' letdown.

21

I SHOULD be ecstatic, but I'm not. It was in the bag from day one. Yes, I've drawn even with Eliot, but I feel the way I did on September 3, 1963: ready to open a vein. Over seven damned years and here I remain. Lovely. I'm still working for a living. Strike that. It really isn't work, although our little cabal of trustees yammers it is. We turn up the volume starting in late November as compensation decisions approach.

I'm partially consoled by knowing how I'd feel if, inexplicably, I hadn't made partner. Deeply ashamed. To the outside world, make that a narrow slice of the Boston establishment, becoming a partner at Curtis is still considered a big deal. If only they knew. I can't believe what Eliot said to me. "Aren't you proud to be here, Andrew? I am."

Even more provoking, the sanctimonious twit claims to have quit smoking, "Just as I told Clare I would," he tells me. Well, up his. Maybe I can get him onto grass.

All is not lost, however. Ascending to our cells one morning, I said to Eliot, "Please thank the divine Clare for her witty 'Congratulations on Making It' card. It's a scream."

Eliot's mumbled response was painfully unconvincing to me and, I am certain, to the others in the elevator. So. Clare hadn't told hubby of her billet doux. What had she written, he was wondering but couldn't bring himself to ask (in fact, the card said virtually nothing and was signed 'Affectionately, Clare and Eliot', but that was between Clare and me). This scene will be all over the firm by noon, and by the close of business it will reek of scandal. Elevators are such splendid petri dishes of gossip.

Relatively speaking, I have it made. I don't need to and don't intend to do fuck all. My trustee gig is an annuity funded by the oldest money in the Commonwealth. The dollars keep rolling in. Take a sabbatical. Take several. Nobody will notice. I don't even have to be a stock picker. We've always had a couple of analysts (security analysts) for that, and trustees are never faulted if they don't wander too far from the other sheep. Unlike Eliot, I don't need to drum up business. I don't need to lecture, to publish, or be active in bar associations or worthwhile organizations. Never being wound up, I never need to unwind.

I will lift a glass, many a glass, to dear Toby who looks as though he won't be around much longer. Accidents can do that. His beneficiaries are questioning Toby's commitment and competence, and I am compelled to tell them their concerns are not without merit, as we lawyers like to put it. Toby's 'work' has begun flowing to me, and I'm not sure he really cares. I do not intend to grow my business. That would require me to hustle, and hustling isn't something de Peysters do, at least not since Augustus de Peyster made his bundle in Nieuw Amsterdam real estate during the 17th century.

My customers love me. Picking their pockets is a no-brainer. Every quarter, we trustees stuff our paws into the cookie jar and extract one fourth of the annual fee which grows as the trust increases in value. We earn our money the old-fashioned way. We help ourselves. Painless. No yipping clients protesting the bill. None of those impossible-to-win arguments about staffing. If you use low-priced help, you're running a boot camp for clueless recruits. If talent's too expensive or too numerous, you're gouging. In either case you're accused (correctly, in most cases) of trying to blot up excess capacity. My customers seldom grumble, but if they do, I twinkle and suggest, "Life's greatest good is the prompt and cheerful payment of legal fees."

Even better, trustees aren't expected to know squat. As one of Eliot's Parris Island DIs told him, "I taught you everything I know, and you don't know shit." Just get some nerd who knows a little tax law to tweak the standard forms, then sit back and let the good times roll.

On another subject, I detest our new digs. It's Holiday Inn without the flair.

It is said Eskimos have countless words for 'snow'. Our decorator, bless her vibrant palette, has an equal number of ways of saying 'brown'. We are brutalized by beige, tormented by tan, terrorized by taupe, done in by dun, and assaulted by acres of ochre. The brown comes at you from all directions. It is cruelly uncompromising. It's on the walls, and it's underfoot. It invades your lungs, and it sticks to your shoes. Welcome to Death Valley.

Our carpeting is of a thickness I would estimate generously at not more than 1/32nd of an inch. Our walls are covered with delicately framed pressed flowers, which we got for a song when a Junior League gift shop on the North Shore went belly up. They give our offices the look of a genteel powder room. Those conference room walls not made of glass are decorated with an understated blue fabric on which one can detect sinuous milky forms. What do they represent? Spermatozoa? The troubled souls of departed partners? If so, what are they telling us? "Raise your rates? Stop making payments to my grasping widow?" There is yet another inspired stroke. The bargain-basement bathrooms make their own dramatic but ambiguous statements. Bus terminal? Halfway house? At least someone, wearing rubber gloves I hope, tossed out the caked toothbrushes of the long-departed. And why green urinal cakes? Yes, it's Boston, but this is Curtis and Perkins, for heaven's sake.

We have spared every expense. I can only hang my head, but I have promised myself that if I have the misfortune to be here at the time of our next move I will make the place worthy of me.

As might be expected, Eliot is upset by one of our few innovations.

"It sends the wrong message," says he.

The 'cot room' is a tiny, windowless sanctuary in the executive suite. The 'cot' is, in fact, a comfy bed. A place for the duffers to snooze and gratify their unspeakable cravings in private. The executive suite's locked at 6:00 p.m., and only a few of us have keys. I am one of the few. Ruth loves the cot room's liberating privacy. For added security, she always brings a door stop. A significant upgrade over the tilted chair.

Face it, I'd be lost without her. Miss Donohue keeps the Millard legal engine lubricated, tuned, and firing on all cylinders. But our relationship has its tiny strains.

Yesterday morning I turned the page on my desk calendar and staring up at me was an unfamiliar name. One of my elevator conquests?

I have this game. Situate me on a lift with a promising honey and, more often than not, I'll have her name, phone number, and at least a coffee date before the first of us to do so, debarks.

OK, think like a journalist, numb nuts. WHO is Sue Driscoll? WHAT had we cooked up? WHEN and WHERE were we doing the cooking? WHY was the only question I could answer with reasonable certainty. I drew a blank. No way around it. I buzzed my generally personable personal assistant.

"Ruthie dear, what can you tell me about Sue Driscoll? A new client, I presume."

Ruth glanced at my calendar, stuck out her tongue, and, in a less-than-respectful tone said, "Counselor Millard, that was my reminder to initiate legal proceedings against Richard Driscoll. Shall I commence the process?"

"I would be grateful, Miss Donohue." Ruthie flounced out so endearingly.

Yes, she can be damn annoying. And unpredictable. And ornery. Like a camel. Sensitive and submissive one moment but rebellious and intractable the next. When a camel becomes angry with her (the best riding camels are female) rider, he can sometimes mollify her by surrendering an article of his clothing that she will tear to pieces before allowing him to remount.

Quite perversely, Ruth has balked at handling my checkbook and shopping. Even after I reminded her Miss Bosworth had gratefully performed those tasks for Ez Clark. Ruth snorted angrily, and for a moment I feared she might kick or bite.

"That sad, sweet thing," said Ruth. "She waited 50 years for the dried-up creep. She even lost weight for him. The old fart never noticed. He never thanked her. And he left her nothing. Not even a crummy keepsake." A pointed look.

I should have let it go, but I didn't. "Old fart? Mind your manners, Miss Donohue."

"Wasn't it you, Mr. Millard, who taught me truth's an absolute defense to a charge of slander?"

What will it take to tame her? Must I sacrifice a pair of my slim-cut, monogrammed, Egyptian cotton boxers to her vindictive hooves?

22

I WAS firmly rooted in the present during my first year as a partner. My time had come, but was I ready? David Farnum discovered he had colon cancer (he ultimately beat it) and abruptly retired. He gave me Mr. Clark's indenture treatise, and some day, I'll need to find it a good home.

Suddenly, I was first violin on the Northeast Power Company (an investor-owned public utility) account and several others which I didn't think would be mine for at least another decade. A Northeast bond issue was headed my way. Beware of what you wish for or believe you're supposed to wish for. I was also concerned the firm might decide I needed more seasoning or worse, wasn't up to it. That would be humiliating. For better or worse, we had no leadership, so nature just took its course. Clare was her usual reassuring self. "Look around," she said. "Who would they think of putting in your place?"

Clare was correct. I was to remain numero uno. Here's what I told myself. There's no reason I shouldn't be able to carry it off, even though it might help if I had a few gray hairs. I've studied the law and the industry. I understand corporate finance. I know the company inside out, and I've got a handle on the players. But will I be taken seriously?

After brooding about it for several weeks, I brought up The Card. The card Clare'd sent to Millard and hadn't told me about. I'm afraid I was less than subtle.

After listening to my pathetic whining (Millard will misinterpret the card, he'll make too much of it, he'll tell others, etc. etc.), Clare skipped across the room and hugged me. "Darling, you can't, you really can't think I am—or ever have been, or ever could be—attracted to Andrew. He repels me on so many levels. You simply must trust me. You're mine, and I'm yours forever. Whether you like it or not. So there. And never forget, you were the one who made him Ceci's godfather. Your idea entirely. I objected. You said it would add meaning to his life.

"And, since I'm in the confessional, I sent a card to Richard Stevens telling him how sad *we* were that he and Jane were leaving. You approve, don't you…? Thank you.

"Did Andrew tell you the card was from the two of us…? I thought not. Now, let me ask you something… did he or Alice send you anything…? Just what I thought."

It was time for me to stop worrying that bone. "Thank you, Sweetie."

All went well on the bond deal until I received the first draft of Northeast's prospectus, the document which, if it hit the fan, would either save our collective tails or land us in the 'brown stuff' as Millard calls it. Maybe bankruptcy. Possibly prison. It needed a lot of work if I was going to get any sleep before the statute of limitations expired. In fact, Northeast and my client thought it was great as it was. Upbeat. Positive. A fine 'selling document'.

The first conversation with my client Neil Johnson, a managing director of Ernst and Woodward, the underwriter, was a portent of things to come. I gently suggested to Neil the prospectus was unduly bullish. In fact, it was dangerously one-sided. It as much as promised clear sailing ahead. I said we needed to disclose and highlight the risks. What's more, we shouldn't bury the caveats in the notes to the financial statements. They needed reasonable prominence together with a balanced assessment of what might happen if the risks became reality.

"For Christ's sake, Lawrence," Neil erupted. "Why the hell don't we hang it up now? Call it quits. Tell Northeast we can't peddle its lousy paper. You know what would happen? Fucking Drexel would do it in a heartbeat.

"Let me outline the facts of life. I'm not interested in delays, cost overruns, or the difficulty of clearing the evacuation plans. Nor do I want you using phrases like the 'rate of employee burn-up' when we're discussing radiation exposure. Spare me. If that crap goes into the prospectus, the bonds get downgraded to junk and the company pays an interest rate the shylocks couldn't get. That's bullshit. Let's get this frigging plant built and into rate base, pronto."

Then Neil Johnson laid his cards on the table. "No fucking way am I getting replaced by another bank because I can't control my pigheaded lawyer."

Oh boy. My first and last deal as honcho. Lose this account and find another day job. The word would get around. No hard-charging New York investment banker wants to be represented by some stick-in-the-mud Bostonian anyway, let alone one who doesn't know what side his bread is buttered on. We'd represented Northeast's investment bankers since the 1930s, when Mr. Clark snagged the account. His two successors had hung on to it. Now comes loser Lawrence.

As I saw it, my only options were: cheerfully roll over or devise some way to spread the blame for truth-telling. I couldn't have all the annoyance directed solely at me. So I phoned Tony Markham, my counterpart at Baker & Richards, Northeast's outside counsel, a well-respected, old-line Boston firm. I'd done a few deals with Markham and sensed he might be sound, someone who possessed a backbone. I'm sounding self-righteous, but I was scared.

I suggested there were problems with the prospectus as drafted. It seemed unwise to characterize it as fraudulent or fundamentally misleading. Go easy. Markham's client was the author of the offending first draft. Weren't there a couple areas that could use a little tightening up? What about those overruns and delays, the opposition by important politicians, the resistance of the regulatory bodies, and the growing sense Northeast had bitten off more than it could chew?

Markham was not opposed to discussing these matters, and listened politely as I outlined my proposed fixes. Being an attorney, he was, of course, compelled to 'improve' what I'd suggested. I'd counted on this and had purposely overstated some of my positions knowing I could gracefully give ground but still have a document which would enable me to continue sleeping with Clare and not just see her at irregular conjugal visits.

In relatively short order, we had the outline of our joint screenplay, and I had Markham believing it was all his doing. "Great idea. Well put. A nice touch. Brilliant paragraph." This and more I exclaimed, as my ideas bounced back at me.

Next, we were onto the stage directions. We decided I'd raise the issue of cost overruns, and before I could be shouted down by both clients, my new ally would gently interject, "Let's hang on a moment. Lawrence may have something." Then it would be Markham's turn to lead off, and I'd chime in with support leavened with constructive, collegial modifications. And so we would 'spontaneously' proceed to our prearranged conclusion.

That's the way it happened. Misstatements and omissions diplomatically rewoven into reasonable approximations of truth. We succeeded in manipulating our clients, and I was ultimately vindicated with hosannas from my partners when the lawsuits following Northeast's bankruptcy were summarily dismissed.

As expected, Millard, who was irked by my legerdemain, took credit for helping me devise those bullet-proof prospectuses. He evidently forgot suggesting we incorporate C&P. As he so loyally put it to our partners, "That way we can leave the liability where it belongs—with those who bungled the Northeast deals." I'm grateful to my partners for not hanging me out to dry.

There were additional challenges. Partnership and the changing times conspired to alter the way I conducted my practice. For years, my traveling companions had all been men. I was comfortable with this. However, the world wasn't standing still. Several of our best associates were women, and they resented being excluded, particularly from New York trips. They refused to believe they weren't missing important opportunities. Finally, the day of reckoning arrived.

Carol Holmes had worked on several deals with me from beginning to end. Her skills were first-rate, and she hit it off beautifully with our clients and those on the other side of the table. Carol is one of those rare lawyers who always makes things go more smoothly. People remember her deals with pleasure. Many lawyers turn every transaction into a fight to the death. Not Carol. How could I not take her to New York since she'd done so well and was eager to go? By the way, I probably wouldn't have mentioned this trip, which I admit was a little dull, if Millard hadn't told people I'd "gotten my end wet on a road trip to the Big Apple".

The idea of traveling with Carol made me anxious. I'd spent very little time alone with her in the two years we'd worked together. What would we talk about? We'd be cheek by jowl on planes and in cabs. We might have to eat together. After work. At night. I hate to seem stilted or stuffy, but I certainly didn't want Carol getting any wrong ideas.

Carol was from some out-of-the-way place in the Midwest. She hadn't gone to an eastern college and didn't look athletic. I sensed she knew little about the Red Sox despite having lived in the area for six years. However, she was a quick study and may have realized that success in corporate finance called for at least a rudimentary knowledge of certain important eastern institutions.

Clare was funny about my coming trip, wondering out loud whether she was in danger of losing me, suggesting she might come to New York and spy on me like one of my partner's wives who had slunk down to Bermuda to shadow her husband at C&P's first retreat. Her fieldcraft was poor. She was observed, and hubby became a laughing stock. Clare knew she was making fun of me and being wicked. She could always make me blush in a way she said indicated a fib or an impure thought. How unfair. She claimed to be the only woman with whom I was completely at ease. Absurd.

As always, Clare was helpful. "Carol," she said, "is as concerned about the trip as you. After all, she wants to succeed, and you're the partner. There's no reason to suppose your pleasant, respectful relationship won't continue past the close of business, is there, Eliot?"

A trip filling me with misgivings was regarded by Millard as an opportunity. He insisted Carol was 'ripe' for an affair, but Millard thinks every woman is 'up' for an affair. "Let me enlighten you," said Millard. "Carol has surpassed her drab hubby. She's sailed past him in compensation and stature. She's yours for the plucking."

"Want to impress the stolid Carol?" he continued. "Go the boarding area, chat up a wreck in a wheelchair, attach yourself to her, and scuttle onto the plane ahead of all the sheep."

Carol and I finished early and got to the Hilton (Millard always laughs at my choice of hotels) before 5:00 p.m. We had agreed to have dinner together. How could we not? In a generous moment I consented to eat at a Chinese restaurant. It wasn't that bad. I used a fork. Carol helped with the menu. We had enough to talk about (even if none of it involved sports). When I checked out the next morning I noticed, while reviewing the bill, that I'd called Clare four times to keep her posted on my doings. Clare was amused. Millard found it pathetic.

23

SUCH CRAPOLA. Business lawyers catch all the breaks. They slip away whenever. Even when it's not legit, those inventive snakes dream up conferences or closings, scoop up young things needing guidance, fly first class to five-star hostelries, doctor their time sheets ('attention to due diligence' is one of their favorite entries), and lay everything off on some nodding customer.

I have few such opportunities. What's wrong, someone might ask, about cultivating withered widows in Hobe Sound in February and the Vineyard over the Fourth? Plenty. Having horizontaled themselves up Net Worth Mountain, these canny shrews are seldom taken in by my solicitude. To them, I'm no more than the anxious aliens who service them and their bougainvilleas or rhododendrons, as the case may be. I'm ignored, and the female help is warned to keep its distance.

Therefore, I was more than a little ticked off when the exuberant Francesca accompanied Eliot to the Annual Meeting and Educational Conference of the Association of American Finance Attorneys. Eliot himself told me little about this, his most distressing out-of-towner. He may have worried about people thinking he'd strayed. Whatever. The unexpurgated version of this saga deserves broad dissemination.

AAFA is a solemn organization whose membership is comprised of lawyers from firms—the hunters and in-house lawyers at financial institutions—the quarry. These gatherings are barely controlled feeding frenzies with Eliot-types making nice and their in-house counterparts keeping their legs crossed while fending off those of our hungry brethren whose behavior exceeds acceptable bounds of crassness.

I'll never comprehend what possessed my levelheaded friend to yield to Francesca's importuning. Francesca, however, is difficult to resist. Eliot should have taken sensible Carol. She'd have meshed perfectly with the thoroughly-domesticated AAFA members. Instead, Eliot allowed himself to be seduced—professionally, at least—by the hot-blooded Francesca. God, how I wish I'd been there.

This was a huge gamble by Eliot. He was trying to jump start a Curtis practice area languishing in the post-Clark doldrums. He must have thought he could do with a little flash and sparkle. This interminable two-day meeting was his year's most important event. A command performance. Eliot always attended, and he showed up for every panel, cocktail party, and meal. He deserved a medal. His citation would begin: "For conspicuous patience in the face of overwhelming tedium..." Now he knows what it's like living with Alice.

He pressured young Curtis lawyers to join the organization, and forced the retirees to stay on until they reached intensive care. It was essential to create the impression Curtis had mass and a deep bench if it wanted more institutional business. The result: practice area packing. Everyone does it. While most firms draw the line at fabricating attorneys and listing the deceased, it's SOP for every anemic grouping to swell its ranks with the names of colleagues from wholly-unrelated fields of law. At least we don't list our messengers.

Eliot stayed at the mediocre, moderately-priced New York hotels at which these programs were conducted. How else could you mingle and how outrageous to stick the firm with a larger bill. Some of those most active in dissipating Mr. Clark's practice would sign up for the program but take rooms at the Pierre or the St. Regis, where they'd molest the mini bar and savor the skin flicks. They might attend a few of the presentations, but wouldn't be caught dead fraternizing with the customers after working hours.

Francesca was not your generic Curtis attorney. In fact it was obvious to all but Eliot that Francesca was not long for the law or Boston. Francesca had great expectations for herself and they didn't include shuffling along in flats at the beck and call of customers. For Francesca, toning it down meant taking off her anklet and doing up all but the top three buttons of her straining, deliciously sheer blouse. I had tried with a predictable lack of success to lure Francesca into trusts and estates. Fat chance. Nor was she interested in me. Ouch. Why did Francesca want to work with Eliot? Eliot dealt in 'green goods'.

Meanwhile, Francesca was having a ball—many, in fact—at Curtis. She consumed young male associates. The two of us would have been a natural combination, but I fell between the cracks. I lacked wealth and status and was too old (over 30), she incorrectly assumed, for non-stop copulation.

Francesca and I developed an entertaining, if for me frustrating, relationship. I learned a lot about my colleagues' prowess and those whose 'packages' diverged significantly from the norm. We would lunch together regularly at Trattoria Angiolino in the North End, tantalizingly close to her apartment.

It was a hot afternoon in that earthy, not-yet-yuppified neighborhood. Francesca was not overdressed. Moreover, she was discharging a heart-stopping scent composed equally of natural and artificial fragrances. We were facing each other across a speck of a table and had just polished off a carafe of the dangerous house red.

"So, Andrew," cooed Francesca, amping up her ocular candlepower. "Am I correct in assuming you find me attractive?"

"You are not incorrect," said I, returning fire with my high-voltage baby blues.

"But don't you fancy that Julie Andrews look-alike, the depressingly virginal Clare Lawrence? Don't you bet that in the boudoir she's more Plimoth Plantation than Victoria's Secret? Word gets around, you know."

How could that basilisk have guessed? "She might do in a pinch," I laughingly replied.

"In a pinch, indeed. Don't trifle with me, Mr. Millard. I'll not be trifled with. Come now, which of us is more alluring?"

"Both of you have your points."

"At this precise moment, which of us would you prefer to undress?"

Francesca's nyloned thighs murmured to me as she crossed and recrossed her legs. Tie me to the mast. "Since you put it that way…"

Francesca looked triumphant. "I thought so. Now, which of us is brighter? While considering that question, recall my perfect board scores and my gift of repartee; Clare is somewhat flat in those and other departments."

What could I do but bow in humble submission?

"And finally, Mr. Millard, which of us do you suppose will amass the larger pile of worldly goods?"

"No contest, but Clare…"

"No more about the divine (your word), but, I suspect, prudish Clare. Has that school marm ever showed you anything like *this*?" said Francesca, leaning towards me.

I downed my last swallow of plonk and sat transfixed.

Francesca kept leaning. She passed 45 degrees and there they were, her swaying, liberated free-range glories. I understood the feelings of "stout Cortez when with eagle eyes he stared at the Pacific". Francesca continued her descent until her herness was resting on the back of my right hand. If only my pinioned fingers had been housed in ball and socket joints.

"We're not done yet, Mr. Millard. I wish to know how I stack up against the comely but commonplace Ruth."

"May I deliver my judgment at your place tonight?"

"No you may not, my priapic Paris," chirped Francesca, nodding to my trousers and chortling, "Res ipsa loquitur."

That tore it. It was self-help or a cold shower. "Excuse me, Francesca." Blessedly, there was an empty stall in 'Signori'. It would have been awkward attending to myself at the exposed wall fixture.

On my return, Francesca looked me over, nodded, and said brightly, "All better, now?" And added, "I've thought of Clare's perfect Caribbean destination," I scowled. "The Bay of Prigs," giggled Francesca.

That's Francesca, the force of nature Eliot took with him to AAFA's 1972 fall gathering. It would have been comradely of me to warn Eliot. I didn't. Before they left, I asked why he'd selected Francesca for this all-important mission. Eliot admitted she was somewhat rich for the blood of most AAFA members, but he believed in giving women a chance and was convinced her high intelligence and ability to get along with people (his words) would carry the day. Eliot told me Francesca had agreed to blend in.

From what I've gathered, that event has become the stuff of legend. I have pieced together this account from conversations with the two other Curtis attendees. As always, it was a Thursday/Friday affair.

The program was held in a nondescript function room, with the attendees nodding off at tables facing the panelists. Those who remained conscious drank the iced water, sucked the hard candy, and/or doodled on the handouts. The outside lawyers sat near their customers and remained glued to them, sometimes for the entire two-day session—like minders. Since there was plenty of room, it was accepted practice to leave an empty seat between you and your captive. This custom seemed silly to Francesca. So she ignored it. None of the males objected.

By Thursday's cocktail hour, several in-house attorneys had inhaled lethal lungfuls of Francesca's perfumed spores. They were convalescing at the bar. Pacemakers were working overtime. Defibrillators were still in their infancy. The lesser females were gathered in a disapproving knot at the side of the room.

Francesca's entrance was unprecedented.

She had changed from her stylish, obviously expensive business suit into something less confining. It was black, loose, and low cut with a hemline that ended at mid-thigh. A pendant was poised above a crevasse capable of swallowing an entire dog sled and team. Francesca had traded in her workaday shoes for a pair of black slingbacks that added at least another inch to her already majestic self. Her nails were a startling carmine. Her anklet had made its triumphant return. The blast effect was multiplied by her toe rings.

Yes, toe rings. Specfuckingtacular. Priceless exposure for our little Boston firm. I must ask Francesca what they meant. Their placement. Their design. Is there a secret language of toe rings? Is there a 'toesetta stone' to unlock their secrets?

It was feeding time at the waterhole. Nobody dropped his drink, but Eliot swore he heard sharp intakes of breath as Francesca ambled into the sheep fold. Never before had breasts been implied, let alone displayed at an AAFA event.

Our bird of paradise was in her element. I think of Mother in her prime. Francesca accepted a martini from one overwrought conquest and a cigarette from another. By now, Eliot was convinced he'd been ruined. He retreated to his room, called Clare, and told her he would for all time be known as the guy who brought a hooker to AAFA's annual meeting. What would become of them and their children? Clare, Eliot told me, was calm and reassuring, telling her distraught hubby he was respected tonight and would be tomorrow, that his clients were as fond of him as he was of them, and all would be well.

Stout fellow that he was, Eliot returned to the fray in time to see two of AAFA's most influential in-house lawyers escorting Francesca to dinner. Francesca did not consort with the negligible. Eliot seated himself at the same table in hopes he might be a moderating influence. He told me he was so upset his marketing instincts deserted him. "Halfway through the meal I noticed I was sitting between two lawyers from a competing firm."

Eliot was squirming. "Our table was the loudest there, and we put away many more than our allotted two bottles. Trying to put the best face on the situation, I sprang for supplemental rations and, at Francesca's insistence, included a magnum of champagne."

Eliot considered himself lucky it stopped with a magnum. Francesca had said, "It'd be jolly to work through the Old Testament from Jeroboam to Nebuchadnezzar."

Everyone at the table was mesmerized. Service was impeccable, with the waiters jostling each other for the chance to hover over Francesca and hyperventilate. Eliot said, "Ours was the last table to finish and, as chairs were being pushed back, Francesca landed her haymaker."

Knowing New York, Francesca recommended a club in the Village, and ordered her tablemates to accompany her there. Forthwith. Her motion that dinner be adjourned to said club was unanimously approved with much table-pounding. Eliot felt obliged to vote 'yes'. Francesca assured everyone they'd have a blast. According to Eliot, she said, "There's music, there's dancing, there's stripping, and there's an open mike for the uninhibited."

Eliot took Francesca aside and begged her not to bankrupt or disgrace the firm. He also begged off, pleading fatigue and the need to be 'bright-eyed and bushy-tailed' when he delivered his 8:30 a.m. report at Friday morning's business session.

If he slept a wink, I bet Eliot dreamed of peddling pencils on State Street.

If it weren't for Francesca the tale would have ended there, but that girl is not one to put her light under a bushel or her bush under a lightweight. She was nearly breathless when she slipped into my office at the opening of business on Monday. I passed on to Eliot a redacted version of Francesca's odyssey.

As Eliot slunk upstairs to the sleep Francesca had murdered, the eight exuberant males from her table found themselves a pair of taxis and headed downtown. Since none of her companions opted for the front seat, Francesca parked herself on the emaciated lap of a senior attorney at a New England life insurance company. Who says Yankee lawyers are uptight and inhibited? Francesca reported feeling "stiffening, stirring, and thrusting. I was kept from sliding off and perhaps injuring myself by two large hands placed firmly on my hips, gnarled, aged hands which, perhaps not coincidentally, positioned me so as to best receive an insistent message."

This is what Francesca said happened next. "Morale was sky high when we got to the Bashful Minx, and it went off the charts when I said the party was on Curtis. I seated myself next to the gentleman on whom I'd wiggled for 50 blocks."

Francesca paused for dramatic effect. Not that she needed to. "It was only a moment before I detected knobby fingers advancing resolutely inland from my knee. I made it easier for the old dearie by opening up the fairway and giving him a little more maneuvering room for his less than supple members. He'd require help if he was going to hole out in par." She had to be kidding. Didn't she?

I closed my office door. Francesca rolled on, "Thinking only of the benefits accruing to Curtis, I embarked on an exploration of my own. It was gratefully received by my dinner partner who tried unsuccessfully to maintain an impassive expression as I, the dexterous (I was in fact using my right hand) Francesca, without even bothering to demonstrate my facility with zippers, brought him to and over the top while making small talk with the codger on my other side." Why was she torturing me?

Francesca was coy and unforthcoming when I asked her to identify her new friend.

She had her thralls back a little after 2:00 a.m. Feeling restless, she went down to the hotel bar for a nightcap. In her words, "There, thank God, I found an energetic young fellow—no, he wasn't an AAFA member—who finished off what my elderly solicitor had set in motion." She told me she'd considered knocking on Eliot's door. Francesca knows how to twist the blade.

Someday I must ask Francesca whether women interrupted in medias res experience the same well-nigh unendurable ache we do in those circumstances. And what might they call it, I wonder?

Eliot filled me in on Friday's happenings. He was exhausted and agitated when his alarm went off, but our boy doesn't stay upset, and he doesn't hold grudges. I cherish mine.

Friday was a new day, a day to chase business and repair any damage caused by Francesca. Eliot got downstairs in time for some customer-stroking at the continental breakfast. He delivered his report which he alleged was well-received. The business meeting was typically short. The treasurer declared the Association solvent. The slate of nominees was elected without demur, and it was on to Friday's first panel, a discussion of the 'bankruptcy exception' in legal opinions. Pass the No Doz.

The panelists were three learned partners from good-pedigree Wall Street firms, the kind of guys who do high-visibility bar association work and are seen by the unperceptive as credits to our racket. Guardians of our jurisprudence engaged in the most indirect marketing which, of course, is the most effective variety. Theirs was a scholarly, disinterested quest for truth. They might well have been named Poverty, Chastity, and Obedience. Francesca's not an early bird, so Eliot figured he'd be safe until lunch.

Eliot told me he was about to nod off when the speaker paused and stared fixedly over his half-lenses. Great God Almighty. Francesca was striding purposefully up the aisle. Was she really going to sit between him and his client? In the front row? That's affirmative. She had changed back into her suit and her less arresting shoes. Most of her buttons were buttoned. The anklet was gone, but not the perfume. Eliot could only speculate about the toe rings. At least they weren't visible.

There was a stir among the panelists. The monks renounced their vows. While they may have forgotten their prayers and incantations, it was clear they remembered Francesca. The speaker resumed, and the other two made a show of concentrating on their brethren's profundities. But their eyes betrayed them. A plague on legal opinions. It was beaver-shooting season for the distracted truth-seekers.

The speaker was losing his thread. He coughed. He consulted his notes. He poured himself a glass of water. He invited questions. He employed the traditional oratorical device of rotating his head to include his entire audience. Eliot wasn't fooled. No siree. He noticed the speaker's calm and reflective gaze pausing for increasingly longer intervals on the shady glen his co-panelists found so inviting.

Eliot could only pray Francesca was wearing underwear. Why he wasn't begging for a peek is beyond me. Naturally, I had the same question. I was not shy about asking. You may be able to guess her answer. It was a playful toss of her luscious black tresses. Was she now? Did she ever? She knew I wanted to beg for a look-see, but I resisted. "You've seen all you're going to see, Randy Andy," said Francesca.

Eliot's customer list swelled during the six months after Francesca's two-day run in Manhattan and plateaued at this new higher level after she'd left Curtis for New York. She fled Boston, but has remained in my Rolodex. Lucky Eliot. Francesca could have ruined him, but did the opposite. Whoever heard of a fairy godmother with toe rings?

Back to Drearyville.

The gloom I feel about partnership, not so much the making it, but having had to make it and then endure it until, perhaps, senescence, became worse when Alice brightly announced she was scheduled to foal in June. What a one-two punch—a life sentence to the salt mines on January 1, 1971 and six months later another disaster. And me in my prime at 34. Is it time for a second walk to the recruiter's office? This time for real.

Clearly, Alice had violated our pact. She'd shuffled off her intrauterine coil. It would have been ungallant of me to suggest remedial action and I didn't. In fact, I didn't consider it. The world deserves more Millards. And the Edmundses have plenty of dough, even if little is trickling down to me. However, my stalwart behavior did not prevent Alice from later claiming it was only her tears, protestations, and liquid assets that stopped me from dragging her off to an un-air-conditioned Tijuana abortion parlor. In fact, I was curious about what might come of my union with a daunting equestrienne. A centaur?

Here's what happened. Arthur, as foretold, was dropped on June 15, 1971. He should have no trouble surpassing Eliot's unexceptional Quintus. Stan joined us on September 15, 1972. I never have problems remembering their birthdays since they fall on the dates of estimated tax payments. By the time of Stan's appearance, I was thoroughly spooked. Was Alice going to keep doing this to me? Were we to be lampooned as Dover's only practitioners of the rhythm system? Alice saw it the same way. Her faint maternal instincts having been satisfied, she took the required steps to end her breeding. There's no way I'm doing likewise. Someday I may have to support myself on stud fees.

My lads are, I am ashamed to admit, about as interesting as the larvae from which they oozed. My six-year-old goddaughter, on the other hand, is a different bundle of electrons. Vibrant, responsive, bright, and willful, she reminds me of—me.

I offer my godfatherly services whenever Eliot's out of town. Double dipping because I also get face time with Ceci's mom while her biological father's choking down room-temperature Chinese take-out in stress-filled Manhattan conference rooms. Naturally, I'm on my best behavior.

Upon arriving at 118's daunting oak portal, I'll announce my presence with a distinctive 'ring-ring, ring-ring, ring-ring'. Seconds later the door will be dragged open by my ebullient gnome yelling, "Vamilla! Vamilla!"

I remember the evening I gave her the blue-and-yellow dress. The one with the embroidered butterflies. After admitting me, she raced upstairs, changed, skipped back down, and executed an endearingly clumsy pirouette.

"I love it, Uncle Andrew. I'm an Easter egg."

"Do you like the pretty, scrunched-up front?"

"Yes, I do, and I believe it's called smocking."

Clare laughed.

"You've spawned a prodigy," I said.

"Eliot and I have, Andrew." I sensed a certain severity in her tone.

Ceci and I read together in that formal front room, the one that's hung with Lawrences and furnished with a jumble of 18th century originals, 20th century reproductions, and a pair of faded samplers. "Don't let Daddy make me sew," said Ceci.

Quintus, humorless and literal like Papa, usually slinks off to his coin collection, leaving me with Ceci and Clare. Perfect. My two favorites.

"What a shame Daddy never finds time to read to his Ceci," I'll remind them.

"Your father's working much too hard, and he hates being away from you, me, and your brother."

"Your mother's right, Ceci, but Uncle Andrew works just as hard as Daddy and *he* always makes it home in time to be with Arthur and Stanley before they go to bed."

"When Uncle Andrew goes in a few minutes, you can leave Daddy a message telling him about tonight and reminding him how much we love him."

I look at Ceci, sigh, and close the book. "Fun's over, dear girl."

"When can you come again, Uncle Andrew?"

"Whenever Mommy lets me."

24

ON A sad (but predictable) note, it looked as though Millard and Alice were coming unglued. I suppose I could have run a conflicts check. Joke. Actually, Millard was behind schedule. Neither of his first two marriages lasted nearly this long. But neither Edith nor Maud was, or was likely to become, rich. Clare and I became used to certain telltale behavior. She'd get phone calls from Millard's wives and his surrogates. They sought advice and information. "What is Millard really like?" "Does he mess around?" "What happened in his earlier relationships?" "Does he give scarves to all his ladies?"

Some of the women talked to Clare about drink and depression. "How do I cut down on the Smirnoff?" "Should I double up on my Elavil?" My cagey friend sold many of them on the notion he wasn't to blame. He was upset. He was confused. He needed to 'see others' while he 'found himself'. One hoodwinked woman said we should support 'poor' Andrew. He wasn't 'himself'.

It's pointless to get angry with Millard. One of my colleagues characterized him as unalloyed appetite. He told me of sitting next to Millard at a banquet where, almost singlehandedly, he polished off a platter of crabs' legs, lobster, shrimp, and oysters. Still unsated, he scrabbled among the tails, claws, shells, napkins, toothpicks, parsley, cutlery, and melting ice for any edible leavings. Millard's face, he recalled, was a picture of grief and longing whenever a waiter carried away any uneaten scraps.

I'm glossing over the rest of the wretched '70s. The Arab oil embargo. The unholy union of economic stagnation and galloping inflation, a.k.a. 'stagflation'. The '73–'74 bear market and a prime rate that climbed to over 21%. For me, the nadir of the disco decade occurred when the Yankees emerged from their Horace Clarke years, crawled back on top in '77 and repeated in '78. There must have been a dozen of us squeezed into Millard's office listening to that horrible playoff game. Why had we gone there? Because we assumed we'd win and get to heckle Millard.

When mouthy Nettles caught Yaz's game-ending foul pop, all of us scuttled away without a word. There was total silence broken only by Millard chanting, "Bucky Dent! Bucky Dent! Bucky Dent!" He still does that on special occasions.

Then there was that damn case. It's bound to do grave harm to our profession.

25

GOD, I love the '70s. The screwing rages on unchecked with the flower children of yore inspiring those too young for Woodstock. The bad-ass Yankees with Billie, Bucky, Reggie, and Sparky kicked some major ass while, earlier in the decade, Yankees pitchers Mike Kekich and Fritz Peterson swapped wives. How about a Family Values Day in the Bronx?

Then along came *Bates v. Arizona*, the Supreme Court decision that finally deconsecrated our 'profession' by letting us advertise. In a split decision, our right to puff and mislead was discovered to be protected by the First Amendment. Thank you, learned Justices, for discerning the Founding Fathers' original intent.

We considered the implications of this case at a partners' lunch. No surprise, there was a chorus of barking, honking, and harrumphing from the geriatrics who had not already nodded off. Sounded like feeding time at the seal pool. Guess who joined this chorus? Yes, you win a dead mackerel. It was Eliot.

I was feeling my oats. By then I'd wriggled into enough trusteeships to be immune even if Alice went belly-up, financially speaking, or invoked her prenup. Secure in my impregnable citadel, I arose and rapped for silence. Demitasse cups clattered into saucers as my partners carefully put down their macaroons.

"Oyez, oyez, oyez," I boomed in my best parade ground voice. "How many of you have heard of 'marketing'? To be clear, this is not about provisioning our larders, a subject about which none of us is, I trust, qualified to speak.

"I am talking about getting our message to high net worth consumers of legal services. Baptizing all New England in the name of Curtis and Perkins." Now I had their attention.

"As a result of this inspired decision, we can shed our fusty inhibitions and tell it as we like. Without our customary dawdling, we must appropriate funds, hire a huckster, and focus on the areas we wish to promote." Not that there are many worth promoting.

"I see myself spearheading this initiative and I visualize…"

"Excuse me, Andrew," said Eliot, pushing back his chair. "Isn't it time we got back to our clients?"

I was unperturbed by the murmurs of assent. My time approacheth.

Meanwhile, it's imperative I make my sentence here more remunerative. We're lagging the competition and, if that comes out, we're screwed. What, aside from brighter lawyers, more eminent customers, and greater effort, makes other places so much more profitable? There must be short cuts. Only dullards go by the book.

26

ONE OF the few positives of the '70s was the firm's adoption of a defined benefit pension plan. A wonderful decision that reduced the incentive to grab as much as you could whenever you could because that's all there'd ever be. Win Winthrop, one of our most respected and highly-compensated (the two don't always go hand-in-hand) senior partners, was wise enough and gracious enough (and perhaps rich enough) to insist the pensions be equal. As he put it, "Everyone's served honorably, and there's no good reason to carry the workplace differentials into retirement."

I was proud and relieved and told Mr. Winthrop so. The pension was set at $50,000 and included cost of living adjustments. Splendid.

However, for those of my older partners who saw C&P as their refuge and ultimately their rest home, the cost of the pension plan—mandatory retirement—was prohibitive. I'll never forget stooped Archie Northwick's expression when he realized he'd be seeing his Mary more often than the occasional Sunday. None of them had a Clare.

If this were an old movie, you'd see the pages flying off a calendar. I spent those years proving myself as a corporate partner, one deal after another. Often, I'd be away a week or so every month. I missed too many of Ceci's plays and recitals. This wasn't a problem with young Eliot who, like me, is less outgoing.

Finally, the deal would close and next came the all-important question of whether I'd get paid, and, if so, when and how much. Then it began all over again or at least I hoped it did. A couple weeks before each deal closed, I'd get anxious if there weren't others in the pipeline. When there weren't, I'm afraid I came down hard on the children. Groundings would increase in frequency and duration. Meals were tense. My lecturing grew more tiresome. Thank heavens for Clare. She understood my life in the office, and offered encouragement plus helpful suggestions for damping down antagonisms and being more empathic, whatever that means. She reminded the children of my difficult schedule.

Enough. I couldn't allow myself to remain in a funk. People were counting on me, and I had everything that really mattered. Now back to the family and a new decade.

OK, Ceci turned 14 in 1980, and the honeymoon was over. One night she said, "Daddy, you're living in a bubble." She then accused Clare and me of being 'self-absorbed goody-goodies' and me of being 'strict and inflexible'. Ceci followed that with, "And why hasn't Mom done anything for herself?" If that weren't enough, she informed us we were fortunate to have produced such an insightful child.

I was perplexed by her flinty, uncompromising realism, not to mention her black turtlenecks, black jeans, and biting contempt for makeup. She'd been such a warm child. What happened? It wasn't many years ago that young Eliot was my pride and Ceci was my joy.

Clare assured me it was a phase and suggested I relax. In any case, Ceci declared, quite ponderously I'm afraid, that bubbles always burst. To demonstrate her depth and understanding, she added, "And so they should." She expected me to change the subject or brush her off as I did whenever she started lecturing me. But I must have been tired. Or maybe I'd had more than my usual ration of two watered-down bourbons.

In the gentlest possible way, I said, "I really like bubbles, Ceci. Always have. Bubbles are great. No disappointments. No sorrow. Give me a nice sturdy bubble any day of the week. The longer it lasts the better."

A pause to let it sink in.

"Unfortunately, they don't build them the way they used to. More's the pity. Why wouldn't I want to get everyone I love (I must have been quite overwrought to have used that word) into a bubble? Doesn't a good provider always have a pair of bubbles in his garage?"

I believe I went back for another Old Crow. I wasn't done yet, and something made her pipe down. Maybe it was a signal from Clare.

"Happiness. You're never issued a lifetime supply. It can't be manufactured and, like electricity, it can't be stored."

I could tell Ceci hoped Clare would silence me. She didn't.

"When it's gone, it's gone. The longer I'm happy, the more anxious I become. That's the reason for the curfew and the dress code you resent. Your mother doesn't feel that way, but I do."

As I recall, Clare smiled, accepted a second Dubonnet and, holding hands, we led our children into the dining room for a delicious pot roast dinner. If I were Millard, I'd talk about what fun Clare and I had afterwards. But I'm not.

The next morning, I was finishing breakfast by myself after an invigorating jog along the river. Dearest Clare was taking a shower, the children were noisily preparing for school, and Sandra, the ancient cocker spaniel we'd adopted from Clare's ailing parents, was snoring on her pillow. It was perfect. Then suddenly it was fragile and impermanent. Sandra couldn't last much longer. And what about us? I was devastated.

Episodes like the foregoing reinforce my decision to keep this entirely private. I have no wish to upset my children or anyone else. No point in mentioning the Coop episode.

27

PRAISE GOD for Ceci.

The other day she called on my direct line and said, "Andrew," (some time back, 'Uncle' had fallen away like a vestigial tail) "I'm sure you're busy, but may I read you what the headmistress just wrote on my report card?"

"Sure, but how did you come by it?"

"Daddy's desk."

"I'm all ears."

"Just remember, Miss Monger's a creep. She scowls whenever she sees me."

"I recall you telling me that."

Ceci began to read. "Cecilia is a great frustration. She is talented, but obdurate. Cecilia should be receiving straight As. However, she received three Bs, two Cs, and a D in Health and Hygiene, where she persists in being unkind to her teacher, the unfortunate Miss Schmidt. In addition, Cecilia can be a disruptive force throughout the school."

"I hear you, Ceci. You might think about cutting the overweight Miss Schmidt a little slack, but, other than that, when does the bad part begin?"

"Thank you, Andrew."

"Here's my advice, Ceci. Bank your flame a little. And, not to be tiresome, do something about those grades. We don't want your brother screaming 'safety school' as you slink off into the weeds as I did."

These morale-building sessions usually followed Ceci's grading periods. After her last one, I laid down the law. "Stop beating up on yourself. You're light years ahead of your peers—and peeresses.

Look at your brother, you've even got him running scared." Note to self: I've never called him Quintus to anyone in his family.

"Really?"

"Yes, really. I'd hate to have you as a younger sibling baying at my heels. Remember when he spotted you with a fistful of his coins? Rather than running away, you rushed towards him, faked one way, scooted the other and left him standing there screaming. I witnessed it."

"God, I'm awful."

"Not a bit of it, and, while I'm at it, is it OK to keep calling you Ceci?"

"Yes, Andrew. You don't treat me like a baby."

How I love bucking her up and how easy it is. She protests too much.

Clare helps too. Unlike so many beautiful moms, she has no need to upstage her daughter. I remember how upset Clare became when someone suggested they could be taken for sisters. After hearing that, I was worried momma might get a buzz cut and go all 'Cambridge' on me.

Now it's back to the well-groomed land of hares, hounds, and horses. The land with milk and honey blessed.

Sometime during this period, I became aware of the brisk trade in spouses taking place around me. I liken this phenomenon to the classic Wall Street bond swap where the object is to alter maturity, quality, and/or yield. After testing the market, I was both delighted and surprised to discover Alice was marketable. She was carted off with evident relish by whatever luckless laird drew her car keys from the fondue pot. I can still see their sunburned faces, eager grins, and nipped-in hacking jackets. Away they'd spur for a few chukkas. *Lucky me*, I thought, until I realized what was on offer was little different from what I was trying to divest.

Fortunately, I have other consolations.

However, you can't take anything for granted. Not even man's best friend. I've been most cruelly betrayed. By Malcolm. Malcolm and I've been best buddies ever since Edith left him with me after our 1960 split-up. Malcolm's my Scotty. We've been tight for over 13 years. He's a confirmed bachelor. I made this decision for him when he was nothing more than a noisy ball of black fluff. As a consequence, his life's been considerably more tranquil than mine.

Malcolm has always been there for me. He's stripped life down to its essentials: eating, making waste, playing ball, snoozing, and vociferously defending me against other dogs. He is, in all respects, the well-bred gentleman: no leg-humping, no crotch-diving, no public erections, and no eating of or rolling in nastiness.

My pal has seen, heard, and smelled more than most dogs, but until this sad episode, he'd never spilled the beans. His constant presence irritated Maud and Alice, but his centrality is non-negotiable. Unlike Eliot and my wives, Malcolm is never hostile or accusatory. Maybe Malcolm is one of the reasons Maud moved out. If so, bravo Malcolm.

Alice objected too, but I told her, "If I tolerate your equine proclivities, you must allow me my pal." As a concession to Alice, I moved Malcolm's plaid cushion from our bedroom to the master bath. He noticed, favored me with a hurt stare but didn't sulk. Alice reluctantly agreed that the door between the bedroom and the john would always be open. Malcolm is not to experience isolation.

Sadly, Malcolm's beginning to show his age. His hearing and eyesight are failing, and he's developing a limp. He isn't making smells, but Alice will be on me when he does. Despite it all, Malcolm insists on being where the action is and that, combined with his infirmities, was the problem.

I've never liked being alone, so I often have company when Alice is away. Ruth's my default position. When the weather's good, as it was that night, I instruct Ruth to bring her bathing suit. This is a standing joke because, after playing Burt Lancaster and Deborah Kerr on that Hawaiian beach, we invariably skinny-dip. Then it's into the terry cloth robes Alice snitched from The Four Seasons on our wedding night.

Ruth and Malcolm have become tight. Sometimes she brings him treats, or toys, or something in tartan for his wardrobe. It wasn't always thus. In the beginning, Ruth froze when she heard Malcolm yawn or burp. She never fully relaxed until she realized Malcolm wasn't watching. He doesn't care. We aren't throwing a ball, so we're irrelevant.

Saturday morning, I noticed that Hector, my Trojan, wasn't in the bedside ashtray where I thought I'd dropped him the previous night. After breakfast, I left Ruth at the railroad station. When Alice returned, the place was shipshape. The rest of the weekend was unmemorable. I hung with Malcolm while Alice jumped fences, or chased foxes, or something.

But Malcolm was off his feed. Literally. Mopey and out of sorts. Uninterested in the ball. Refused his supper. Where was the unconditional love? That night Malcolm vomited, thoughtfully on the bathroom floor. By the time I noticed, he'd licked it up. Malcolm's a stud, but he whimpered when I patted his belly before turning in.

After an unproductive, early-morning walk, Malcolm joined Alice and me in the kitchen. Something was amiss. Not that I blame him, but Malcolm was avoiding his bowl. He squatted, staring into space. Both of us were alarmed since he'd assumed the pooping position.

When Malcolm has to go, he walks to the door making sure I notice him. He doesn't bark or whine. In his younger days, he'd bounce. But there he was. In the center of the kitchen. Straining. If I'd had any sense, I would have slipped a newspaper under him. I wouldn't have made him move, not in that condition. I'd never seen a more focused creature. But focused on what? Nothing was happening. More contractions and then the sound of escaping gas as something shot out from beneath Malcolm's rigid tail. It was Hector. There's no accounting for terriers' tastes.

Alice looked from it to me and said, "Did Malcolm enjoy it as much as you did?" As for Malcolm, he looked proud and relieved. He and I had a heart-to-heart talk about his performance. Dear Malcolm. Although I didn't appreciate it at the time, he helped me lose Alice. Malcolm soldiered on for another two years after this unfortunate episode. In fact, he lasted a year longer than Eliot's sad-sack spaniel. Malcolm understood mortality. His last act was to lick my hand as the needle was going in.

28

IT'S ESSENTIAL to devote equal time and resources to your children and not play favorites, but sometimes that's tough. Ceci can be such a handful compared with her brother, who is good at everything and does what's expected. Here's what I mean.

I love family tennis. Clare and young Eliot against Ceci and me. Usually Ceci and I win. That Friday night was difficult. After finding out what everyone had been doing, I asked the children whether they were up for our regular Saturday match. Young Eliot responded with his customary good cheer, "You bet, Dad."

I turned to Ceci and caught her scrunching up her face and giving her brother the finger behind a butter plate she was using as a shield. Clare was smiling. I couldn't believe it, but she was. What behavior from a 15-year-old.

Ceci's mood was not improved by her brother's provocative, "Come on, Ceci, you know you'll love it, you always do."

To which my daughter responded, "It's much more fun playing with Andrew." That hurt. Yes, it did.

Well, we had our match. Ceci and I lost in straight sets. I think she threw it. We only won the games I served, and not all of them. I was so upset I double-faulted a lot. Who wouldn't, when his own partner/daughter called him on a foot fault?

After we got home, Clare said to me, "Did you observe the play of our brilliantly perverse daughter?"

"What do you mean? Of course I observed it. We got creamed."

"No, Dearest. Ceci lost each of her points in a way that differed from how she'd lost the preceding one."

I didn't get it.

"Ceci'd whiff, then she'd smash it out, hit it into the net, drop her racket, or launch a rocket into the game on the neighboring court. Then she'd vary the sequence."

29

SPEAKING OF departures, *muchas gracias*, Señor Toby. Malcolm's was more painful, but you, my friend, launched me into T&E, underwrote me at several clubs, and festooned me with customers. Then you died. Your funeral was the occasion for my public debut as honcho of our marketing committee. Trinity Church. A fabulous stage with good acoustics.

Toby, you had three speakers: me, one of your witless childhood pals, and another old duffer with whom you liked to wet a line. By the time I finished, they'd been eclipsed and forgotten. I did you proud.

My initial response on being asked to speak by your matter-of-fact widow was: How do I get out of this? Most short-sighted. You were over, but your customers lingered on and on. There was no honorarium, but I'd be performing before a packed house.

I opened with the heavy stuff: Toby's exemplary 53-year marriage (before penicillin the philandering dog would have died of the pox), his industry (indolence), his nurturing (self-centered) ways, and his concern with social reform (reduction of capital gains rates).

I had them snuffling. Then I changed speeds and lightened up. I made much of Toby's bespoke threads and colorful bow ties, intimating somewhat incorrectly that he'd bequeathed me his collection, including the one I was wearing at that moment—in fact the ingrate left me nothing. Bold, boisterous, and wildly effective. Just what was needed after speakers one and two. The audience, Clare included, was in the palm of my hand. And there was Eliot. He looked irked and was wearing, if you can believe it, the double-knit suit he'd bragged about finding in Filene's Basement. Why hadn't Clare burned it?

Stevens came too. Sat near the front. Slightly, only slightly better dressed and accompanied by a woman more his speed. Damned if that impudent loser wasn't smirking at me. Then I spotted two barely-conscious near-decedents who were rapidly eroding into mid-eight figure estates. A few weeks later, I signed up both of them. Thank you for the bully pulpit, Toby.

Ah, the cyclical nature of life. Toby withers. The 16-year-old Cecilia blossoms. Just yesterday that peppy but self-critical girl said to me, "I'm too outdoorsy and the freckles don't help. Boys look at me and see a lumpy, braces-wearing, zit-faced jock in scratchy wool."

Then her eyes said, oh, contradict me, Andrew. So I did. Full empowerment. "No, no, Ceci, you're enchanting and growing more so."

She called me at home two days later. "Absolutely," I said. "I'd love to fill in for Daddy, but where is he?"

"Still at the printer?

"On a Saturday morning?"

"Another Northeast Utilities all-nighter? Lucky guy."

"Eleven o'clock?"

"I'll be there.

"And which of you and your mother gets to partner with Pancho Millard, the lithe, limber Latin lefty?"

"You poor girl.

"That's the price you pay for having me take Daddy's place.

"Of course, I'll stretch. See you at 11."

As pre-ordained, it came down to the 10th game of the third set. Five-four with Pancho serving for the whole enchilada.

A rocket. Slack-jawed Quintus hadn't even moved. Fifteen-love.

A cookie ball to Clare who blooped it into the net. What gives with that? Thirty-love.

Quintus—or should I say E-minus—was ready this time. And pissed-off. My partner was readier still, flying across the court and redirecting Q's smartly-stroked return into his nuts. Ceci giggled. Like her mother but different. A brief injury time-out. Forty-love.

I intentionally double-faulted. It must have been obvious. Ceci gave me an exasperated look. So did Clare. Forty-fifteen.

My booming first serve was out by a mile. Quintus crept forward. The fool. I uncorked a screamer that spun the racquet out of his hand. Game. Set. Match.

Ceci went into the victory dance I'd taught her so long ago.

The pale but lovely Clare consoled her son, congratulated her daughter, and gave me a distracted wave. What had happened to that spark between us?

30

IT BEGAN with a phone call less than a week after what Clare assumed had been her routine May 1983 physical. Just as I dreaded. Could she come in for a few 'purely precautionary' tests? Purely precautionary my foot. The results were crazy. There must have been a mistake. A major screw-up had occurred, and I was going to get to the bottom of it. Instead, I received the usual runaround. I blew up at Clare's doctor when he said he'd discovered a 'mass'.

I didn't like the guy. He was competent but remote. His patients weren't people. They were interesting or not so interesting intellectual puzzles. He was unused to being challenged. I wanted, as they say in the Corps, to tear him a new asshole. It took him a week to come clean. In the most elliptical fashion he told me Clare was dying. "Nobody beats that kind of cancer," he said. The lazy jerk. Clare never disagreed with his pessimistic diagnosis. I wanted Clare to fight, but she seemed more interested in soothing me.

Something had to be done. The doctor demurred. I asked him about surgery, about new medicines, about innovative treatments. No, no, and no. He said he'd confirmed his conclusions with several colleagues. They'd been unanimous. Well, they hadn't spoken to me, and they were damn well going to. They did. Evidently, Clare's doctor was being straight with me.

This was unendurable. Who else could I talk to? Was Mass General overrated? Did big donors receive this shoddy care? Every visit is followed by a solicitation, the implication being: you cough-up or get attended to by the junior varsity. Were the doctors brushing me off? Did they give a damn? They'd keep collecting their fat fees no matter what happened to my darling girl.

Was I being negligent? Cheap? Should I look into concierge medicine, whatever that is?

How many opinions should I have gotten? I was being a pain in the ass. So what? There had to be other options. Clare was not going to die. She couldn't die. I would not permit it. Time would stop. The film would be reversed, and Clare would be herself again.

Weren't there clinics in Switzerland? What about Mexico? Wasn't Baja California filled with places offering hope to patients with advanced-stage cancer? Didn't they provide a last chance for those who'd been condemned to death by egotistical MDs? Hadn't I heard of a facility in Rosarita, just south of San Diego? The only doctor who seemed at all engaged said we shouldn't consider foreign alternatives. They would break our hearts.

I was not persuaded, but events moved quickly, and soon it was too late for Mexico. It was too late for another Boston hospital. For several days after I'd moved Clare into Mass General, I pretended to myself that, despite the swaying IV bags (they looked like sleeping bats), all would be well. She would heal of her own accord. Clare indulged me in this fantasy, but I could tell she was flickering. I'd gotten her a spacious room with a view of the river and tried to turn it into our bedroom with photos, books, hair brushes, knick-knacks, her favorite music, and her nicest nightgowns. I knew how much she wanted to be pretty for us. I thought seeing her tennis racket would help so I brought it in as well. I was of two minds about flowers.

Across Storrow Drive, the chewed-up playing fields and paths were alive with joggers, rollerbladers, walkers, cavorting dogs, and interlocking softball games. Sunbathers sprawled beside the river, which, at that point, was wide enough to accommodate the often-contentious mix of powerboats, shells, and sailboats. How could anything bad happen in a room with such a view?

I would visit Clare before going to work, let her rest, come back for lunch, and then return for dinner, bringing something to replace her drab hospital fare. She never told me not to bother, but always said she'd eat it later. Then I'd close the door, get carefully under the covers, and stay there until she went to sleep. The nurses kept away. Sometimes I'd go home. Sometimes I'd fall asleep by her bed. Ceci,

Eliot, and I made sure Clare was never alone. In the beginning, there were many visitors.

After what some might characterize as denial on my part, Clare said we had to talk. Not talk, but *talk*. Exactly what I couldn't face. By now Clare was eating hardly anything, and it didn't matter to her where it came from. She had too many tubes in her to allow us to snuggle so we held hands and I tried to be optimistic and helpful. I watched carefully to make sure all her apparatus was properly reattached after she was disconnected and moved around.

One evening, after helping Clare take a couple swallows of her dinner through a straw, I felt the faintest pressure on my hand and saw her staring at me. Drugged and exhausted, she reminded me of her lousy prognosis. It was of rapid decline into a coma of indeterminable duration. Being alive but cut off from us terrified her. I dreaded what she was about to say.

"It's almost time for me to go. Not today. But soon. I'm ready. So are Eliot and Ceci." She stopped and made me look at her. "And, whether you know it or not, so are you."

Clare was tired. Several minutes passed before she said, "Besides, you must be getting sick of my casseroles."

That was Clare's next-to-last joke.

"Please help me, Dearest."

I could only nod dumbly.

"Also, you must remarry."

I shook my head.

Clare dozed off, and I came unglued. I wanted to wake her up and tell her she had to stay alive, no matter what.

Getting what was needed wasn't as difficult as I'd expected. A member of my college class who I remembered as a science geek was one of the rising stars at the hospital. I was surprised when he told me he'd heard about Clare's condition. His condolences seemed sincere. We talked of old times we hadn't shared. Then he looked at me expectantly. I told him Clare was unable to sleep, and the morphine, while dulling the pain, was making her nauseated. He understood.

I collected the pills from him the next day. He wanted to deliver them personally. Holding the bottle, he warned me that taking more than one or two a night could be harmful, and a significantly larger dose (I've forgotten how many) would be fatal. He wished me all the best and, seeing my reaction, gave me a hug.

I told Clare she didn't have to worry. Everything was set, but please not yet. She smiled and nodded. She tried to apologize for being such a trouble. We talked about the children. By this time, playing cards had become too much, so I began reading her Jane Austen, something she'd recommended I do on my own for years. What a safe, orderly world. Not unlike the one I had failed to create for my family. We didn't make it to the halfway point of *Pride and Prejudice* so I'll never know how things turned out for Elizabeth Bennet. It's a lovely book, but I couldn't pick it up again. I left it in the hospital.

It's never the right time. Would it have been any easier in winter with silent, empty fields and the river fringed with ice? In my usual fashion, I let Clare make the decision. I couldn't. Although barely able to speak, she said, "Counting back from a Saturday service, brings you to Monday or Tuesday at the latest."

"Tuesday, please Tuesday." Clare nodded.

I asked her how she thought I should tell the children. She said she'd already discussed it with both of them and they'd agreed. Oh.

That evening Clare handed me a four-page list, and I started to put it in my briefcase.

"No, no. Please read it out loud, Dearest. Otherwise, you'll forget."

I did as I was told. The first section was about me, my health, my doctors, and my medicines. Next came relatives and friends. Clare reminded me of birthdays, anniversaries, and certain personal matters. I had the financial side covered, so she didn't go into that. There was a page about 118 Beacon Street that Clare told me she had grown to love despite her initial doubts. She had learned the house's secrets and reminded me of the location of its arteries and organs. Also included was a list of those involved with its care and feeding. Then she enumerated the items that should not go into the microwave. My marching orders ended with this final, unnecessary directive, "Don't forget me, Sweetie."

After I'd finished my assignment, we talked about the children, particularly Ceci. Then Clare said, "And now I want to mention your friend Millard."

She raised a hand and said, "Please don't say anything, Darling. I'm a little tired and this won't take long."

I nodded.

"Keep an eye on him." Clare smiled, and I tried to. "Your friend even hinted you were fiddling around with that paralegal you told me about. I laughed at him, but knew how upset you'd be if I'd told you what he'd said. And don't forget, he owes you, not the other way around. Maybe that's why he's so resentful underneath his good cheer."

Clare rested. Then she fell asleep.

I suppose Clare knew she'd have to orchestrate her leave-taking as she had so much else. Young Eliot and I were virtually paralyzed, although I'd taken it upon myself to make sure her will and trust were in proper order. I'd even reserved the church and tended to several other god-awful details. Ceci and her mother were driving the bus. The children and I worked on Clare's service. Millard would be an usher, but not a speaker.

Then the dreaded Tuesday was upon us. We had invited a few special friends without telling them it was their last visit. The day passed too quickly. Clare's nurses were subdued. The ones she'd given presents thanked her again. Eliot, Ceci, and I took turns reading to Clare and to each other. None of us ate. All of us cried. As I am doing as I write this. I could tell Clare was thanking us as she took her evening medication. It was growing dark on the river as the last sculler glided upstream into the twilight. We sat with Clare through the night. When the sun rose over the harbor we were only three.

31

CLARE DIED on August 14, 1983. None of that 'passed' shit.

I've had no trouble remembering the date since it was just two days before the anniversary of Edward's last swim 39 years earlier. Eliot and I were both 46. It was pancreatic cancer. T and E lawyers know death. In less than two months she went from the desirable Clare, to a husk, to the Lawrence family plot at Mount Auburn. Eliot took it poorly, but he never had my inner strength. So dependent. So clingy. Clare spent most of her life propping him up. Eliot and I both needed Clare, but he tried not to show it.

When the chips were down, Eliot flat out lost it. Calling third-world clinics. Demanding more tests, as well as countless additional opinions. I felt like telling him to cool it. One look at Clare was enough. He was never going to hear a surgeon tell him, "We got it all."

I could never get inside Eliot's head, but Clare's death was what he most dreaded, proud as he was of his ability to control events and safeguard his flock. He also worried about finding someone to help him protect her as he declined. Such a micromanager. Then the unthinkable happened. He failed.

All Eliot ever said about Clare's death was she had "Once again, forgotten her purse and, if she doesn't come back for it, I look forward to bringing it to her".

I played an insignificant role in Clare's service. This slight infuriated me. Why was I passed over? Funerals can be downers if you're not at the mike. Moreover, I'd have reduced the melodrama. There wasn't a dry eye in the house. There was maudlin poetry (some of it composed by the speakers). And a capella singing. And a quartet accompanied by a dulcimer. And the inevitable guitars. And endless rambling remembrances. So emotional. So '60s. You might as well have been at a third-world disaster site. Would it be possible, I wondered, to find a pitch-perfect Republican folk singer?

Mona Tucker, a recently-divorced member of our circle, with torrents of makeup cascading down her uplifted face, enveloped Eliot and proceeded to drench and discolor his shirtfront. But Eliot will not be wanting for female companionship. Uncle Andrew's on the case.

As I sweltered in the nave, I diverted myself with ideas for my own service. It will be unforgettable, if profane. Should I give Eliot a bit part, I asked myself? With any luck, he won't be around for it, I answered.

Eliot's send-off will be my masterpiece, even better than Toby's. For undiluted delight, nothing beats a solemn reading of the Twenty-Third Psalm at the service of a fallen rival. My frothy, irreverent remarks are always well-received. They generate warm laughter, gentle eye dabbing, and many, apparently sincere, compliments. I'm a whiz at self-effacing self-promotion. I might even put it out there that Eliot's oft-mentioned Mayflower ancestor was my guy's servant.

Why is it impossible to regulate the temperature of churches? I can always make it through an Episcopal quickie in relative comfort, but this was something else. Even without prayers, hymns, readings, or communion it consumed damn near two hours. So, there I sat dripping and wondering why some functionary hadn't cracked a window. Then I reminded myself: don't knock it. Funerals are marketing opportunities. A sense of impermanence and large concentrations of assets needing meticulous attention. I love them. Funerals generate urned income, and babes at burials make me tombescent.

Unwelcome thoughts enveloped me. Like filthy, nodding pigeons. I shooed them away. Better no hereafter than returning as, say, a Morris Dancer.

Could I have misinterpreted that look Clare gave me on the 25th anniversary of Edward's final belly flop? Little happened between us in the ensuing 14 years. Could her eyes have been saying, "I understand you too well?" Not, "Be mine." No. I needed only a little more time.

Thank God for the foxy minister whose stole framed a Himalayan chest which cried out to be scaled and adorned with fluttering Buddhist prayer flags. Hanging from her neck was a cross on a braided chain, a chain so long that the icon dangled in space like a mountaineer who'd lost his footing, fallen, and found himself swaying at the end of his climbing rope.

I caught her eye as she processed past me, and I caught the rest of her outside the church.

"Andrew Millard... I'm a childhood friend of the Lawrence's."

"Yes, I know. I'm Faith Roberts. Friends call me 'Pokey'. Clare and I became very close towards the end."

"So, Pokey, tell me, when did you go to divinity school?"

"After I got let go by Saks. And I'd been there for nine years."

Sachs? Wow, that's cool. But I've always heard it called Goldman. Had I missed something? I tried consoling her. "Don't be cast down, Pokey. It's impressive to have hung on there for nine years. So cut-throat. Very few last that long."

"Particularly in gloves."

"Gloves? A new hedging instrument? An exotic derivative? Are they publicly traded? I've always admired Goldman. It's the most innovative shop on the Street."

"Are they publicly traded? Are you making fun of me, Mr. Millard?"

"OK. And before divinity school?"

"I rode Patsy in Central Park and attended Miss Hewitt's Classes."

"Where the girls greeted their headmistress with a curtsy?"

"That's right."

"And then post-graduate work at Saks Fifth Avenue?"

She tossed her blond tresses and hissed, "Yes, and I hope that satisfies you."

I was anything but satisfied. Ms. Roberts, despite her attractions, leaked a viscous piety that extinguished desire and inspired flight. So I fled. One equestrienne is enough.

Why was I unable to divert myself? How could I with idiots spewing banalities like "She's in a better place". My ass, a better place would have been here with me, not feeding the worms. We'd have been perfect together. Look what she did for Eliot. I remember him saying that without Clare, he might have become an alcoholic philanderer. I responded, "An admirable objective, but you don't have it in you."

Eliot and I had lost the person we most wanted. However, Eliot still had what I never would. Memories. But memories are fragile and changeable. Particularly those of the insecure. Could Eliot use a little reminding of the flamboyant skier who was Clare's first, and perhaps only, real love?

How, I kept asking myself, could I be grieving for something I'd never had? But then, how can you really grieve for anything else?

32

MERCIFULLY, I have the children. Though only 19 and 17, they were stalwart companions. I tried to help them with their grief and not burden them with mine. Luckily, I also had C&P. There was a great deal going on, and I welcomed distractions. Soon I became the sort of person lawyers crave as a partner, if not as a friend. I was all work. Having no particular desire to live any longer, I was running on habit.

My hours soared as my spirits sank. I was averaging over two thousand billables a year and spent several hundred more helping with the modernization of the firm. Since I didn't bother recording all my time, I was seen as a model of efficiency. Millard told me to back off. I was making him look lazy. He said, "Keep up your obnoxious behavior, and I'll be expected to produce an estate plan in something less than the six-plus months I've conditioned my customers to expect."

At times like this, I'm reminded of Clare's warning about Millard, but whenever I'm tempted to give him the back of my hand, I recall that night in our fourth-form year. Millard was my roommate. I hadn't wanted him, but our headmaster insisted and told me to 'shape him up'. He was small, sneaky, and thoroughly abrasive. In addition, he was detested by a group of sixth-form losers on whom he'd hung cruel but devilishly apt alliterative nicknames. I still remember them, as does everyone else. 'Booger Brown' springs to mind. Speaking of nicknames, we were known as 'Wheat' and 'Chaff'. Since Millard was mine, I felt duty-bound to stand up for him.

Those sixth-form weasels must have gotten at least tacit approval from the headmaster for what they did.

As the rules prescribed, Millard and I hit the sack when the lights snapped off at 10. The next thing I remember was somebody shaking me and yelling, "You're coming with us, Millard." I was confused and unresponsive. That really pissed him off.

One of the others screamed, "Move your ass, Millard." Then my bed was dumped with me in it. Time to rise and shine.

The sixth formers, all of whom were wearing pathetic black masks, realized their mistake. Before they grabbed Millard, I began hollering, "Help! Help!" Neither gutsy nor original, but that's what came to mind. I could have used some assistance, but Millard was disinclined. He'd drawn the covers over his head.

Thankfully, the sixth formers, dogs that they were, were wavering. Doors along our corridors were opening. I yelled some more, "Come on, fourth formers, give us a hand."

That seemed to do it. When I was certain they were high-tailing it, I threw a bottle of that gooey white hair tonic at them, missed, and broke a window. I should have fessed up, but I didn't.

The hall master and his flashlight turned the corner to a chorus of slamming doors. Millard hadn't budged and it was obvious why he hadn't. He'd ruined his pajamas and our room stank. Neither of us covered himself with glory that night, so both of us kept our mouths shut and our windows open. I figured we were kind of stuck with each other.

I hope my children understand and are relieved by my inability to discuss my private life with their mother. The same goes for my relationship with them. While I may have sometimes been remote and demanding, I care about each of them more than I can say. What's more, I care about them equally, and I so wish Ceci would stop referring to her brother as Quintus (Where did that come from?) or the dauphin and needling me about primogeniture.

Let me just say that Clare and I were happy in all the many ways married people can be happy. She delighted me. We adored each other's company and couldn't stand being apart for more than a few days, at least that's how I felt. Nobody can ever take her place. Anything more on that subject would, I'm afraid, inevitably lead to a discussion of her illness and death, events too painful to revisit.

I behaved erratically in the days after Clare's death. I wouldn't let the children touch her things. I couldn't even throw out her medicines. What would she wear, what would she take when she walked back into our lives? If her stuff's around, she must be too.

The children were a comfort. It would have been intolerable without them, but I'm afraid what I really had was work. For a while, I lost them. I'm so sorry.

Not that I noticed, but within weeks of Clare's death, all our houseplants died. After they silently rebuked me for several weeks, Ceci gave them the heave-ho. Clare was the only gardener in our family. I vowed to do my best for Spooky, our cat (Ceci's cat, actually, but she'd outsourced his maintenance to Clare). I could tell he was dubious. First Sandra disappeared, then Clare. One of us must have left a door open, because Spooky hit the bricks. He must have figured he was better off freelancing.

I was down, but it helped greatly when Eliot made it into my first choice and, I presume, his. Lawrences have gone there since the early 18th century. He was only across the Charles, but might as well have been west of the Mississippi. Ceci had another year at school. Despite her brilliant test scores, she seemed determined to get mediocre grades.

I was too tough on them. Maybe tougher on Ceci, who accused me of being even worse than I'd been when Clare was alive and I had no time for anyone but her or, as Ceci claimed, the 'heir apparent'. They didn't get it. After their mother's death, they had to be perfect. Cheerful. Obedient. And immortal.

At least Ceci pulled her grades up.

I expected her to follow young Eliot to Harvard but still live at 118 Beacon Street. She defied me, went to New Haven, and flourished in that unattractive city.

I should count my blessings. What would it be like having a child like Stanley Millard who was just suspended from school for kicking a teacher?

How time drags when you're in the dumps. I was happy to go to the printer in the evenings and hold the fort at C&P on weekends and holidays. I didn't have much of a social life, and I wasn't much of a social asset. I wish I'd kept up with more of my Harvard pals.

I recall a well-intentioned fellow lecturing me about what he called the 'stages' of grief. Assuring me it was an orderly process with a distinct beginning, middle, and end. What a fool. He never lost a Clare.

As it happens, a lot's been going on at C&P since the mid-seventies, when our net income was slightly under $50,000 per partner. I'm glad I hadn't known the firm's economics when I signed on in 1963 or when I made partner in 1971. Our financial condition was thrown into bleak relief when we computerized our time and disbursement records.

The turmoil over a new, theoretically objective, compensation system led directly to the first of what has now become a biennial retreat. Law firms everywhere were withdrawing from the fray for a few days of self-scrutiny, somewhat, Millard said, like Maud.

Our retreats have become increasingly scripted. Spontaneity has never been encouraged, and now it is forcefully suppressed. Retreats are risky. One firm disbanded immediately after its initial retreat. In their search for shared values, the partners discovered only mutual aversion.

We've had our tense moments too. On our first retreat, a pair of our ablest but most destructive colleagues drew up a list of partners they would, given their druthers, summarily discharge. It included about a third of us. Thankfully, not me. Not the best way of getting the oarsmen to pull together. Since then, C&P has been haunted by the specter of a hit list. The managing partner says there isn't one. I don't believe him.

Certain issues dominate our retreats. Among the favorites are: billable hours, billings and collections, firm governance, financial analysis, and long-range planning. At one retreat, we enumerated our core values. They looked like everyone else's and contained only a passing reference to ethical standards. I am disappointed there has never been any emphasis on 'doing the right thing'. Tremendous pressure is exerted to produce billable hours, but nobody has ever said over-recording will not be tolerated. At the other end of the spectrum, our core values don't say a word about making money. A peculiar omission. It's as though our primary obsession doesn't exist.

33

OUR RETREATS have become dismally low-budget. We used to fly off to a semi-tropical paradise, far from home, responsibilities, and prying eyes, except for the poor sap whose suspicious wife trailed him to Bermuda and stalked him like a ghillie. We'd relax on the plane with a few pops, chat up the stews, and meet them at a club on Friday night. Our first retreat was a kick. As we were leaving for the airport, one of the hotel's housekeeping staff loudly accosted Tommy S. and presented him with a pair of rhinestone-encrusted 'fuck-me' sandals found under his bed. Nor can I forget the original hit list. If anything, it was too forgiving.

That was then. Now it's a dispiriting two-hour bus ride to discounted, off-season New England resorts. Magical evenings in Bermuda have been replaced by leafless, lifeless November nights on Cape Cod. The shutters are closed, and the streets are empty. How can you avoid getting lucky in Hamilton? And who scores on the Cape after Columbus Day?

We change sites. We change facilitators. We never change the message. After the brain washings, we split into mind-numbing break-out sessions. Spare me.

Here's a rhetorical question. What's the point of retreats? Answer: retreats are used by management to perpetuate itself, coerce submission, reprogram the recalcitrant, and marginalize the wayward. And rightly so. The purpose of our retreats can be summed up in a single word—'more'—and only a fool would ask 'More what?' It's usually presented more stylishly, thinly disguised within the most recent iteration of our strategic plan. Why are we so coy? The theme of our next retreat should be 'Bill all that you can bill'.

Sometimes we actually do something. At our 1984 retreat, we finally croaked our unfunded pension plan. Most of us were thrilled. The elders and foot-draggers like Eliot grumbled about 'betrayal'. It was a smart move financially, and who cares if it destroyed our last vestiges of togetherness. Dumping the pension plan placed a healthy emphasis on the here and now. Since you will receive nothing from the firm after you leave, you should focus on getting what you can today and stop brooding about the hereafter. Let the future take care of itself. Insufficient unto the day are the profits thereof.

Personally, I never allow the retreats to get me down. I have learned to keep off the ridge line, make supportive noises about our visionary leadership, applaud the new direction in which we're drifting, and loudly announce how 'excited' I am to be part of the resurgence of my revitalized firm. Hallefuckinglujah! What, me, worry? The zealotry will abate within six months. The book burnings, stonings, and witch hunts will peter out until the next retreat.

From my perspective, the most corrosive features of the '80s have been the inhibitions spawned by AIDS, the worry we'll all be bought by the Japanese, and the emergence of the new morality. Overnight it seems, hallowed patterns of speech and behavior have become actionable. We are being deprived of our baronial prerogatives. The Round Heads rule. Old Faithless is unaffected, but the louts are less lucky. These are the dweebs who could never get any on their own, who hoped their status as partners would open doors theretofore closed to them. They persist until reported to our ombudsperson and punished.

One of these clowns playfully asked an unplayful associate whether *all* her hair was such a lovely shade of brown. Perfectly innocuous, right? Not on your tintype. It cost him $10K. If he'd had more collections he'd have skated.

Let me make something clear. I fully support management's efforts to stamp out vice at 40 State Street. As evidence of my bona fides, I commissioned a limited-edition button reading: 'Don't Hump the Help'. Did any of this cramp my style? Don't be silly. I just avoid the humorless and concentrate on what the military refers to as 'situational awareness'. We still have plenty of chicks who dug and continue to dig the status quo ante. None of them wishes to peg out without having been 'hit on' by the cool guys.

Enough of that.

Now Clare's dead, and Ruth, a delectable 40, seems to have intuited that Alice is off the tenure track. Ruth is energized. Shortly after Clare's death, she said, "It's horrible when a marriage like the Lawrences' is cut short."

Leave it be, I thought.

"I happen to know of a red-headed hottie who'd be delighted to give you just such a long-term deal."

That got Ruth a smile but little more.

However, she is hard to deny. The next day my dazzling helper burst into my sanctuary.

"Guess what, Andrew?"

"Surprise me, fairest of them all."

"Now we've got something else in common."

Oh, dear. "Tell all."

"I just got my sheepskin."

What was she talking about? Had I just been stuck with the cost of a fancy coat? An Antartex?

"A college degree, you dope. Finance. First in my family. Like Mr. Lawrence, Harvard. The Extension School."

She assumed a beguilingly triumphant pose. "Let me show you." Exit Ruth.

She raced back moments later with her framed diploma. "Aren't you proud of me?"

I held up my proud mask and nodded, "Always, My Lovely." She was so cute, so optimistic.

Enough. Focus. Curtis needs a shot in the arm, in both arms. Our sphere of influence extends north to Newburyport, west to Worcester and south to Sandwich. To the east, the Atlantic, but admiralty's out of our depth. We need infusions of high-billers, even if they come with some warts. Why else would they join us?

34

CLARE DIED over two years ago, but she's never left my thoughts. I remember someone calling out, "Hi, Sweetheart," as I was crossing Beacon Street. It was Clare's voice, inflection, and customary greeting. It came from somewhere above and behind me. I stopped and looked around, hoping. It was a woman in the third-floor window of a graceful brownstone. It wasn't Clare. Several cars were honking at me.

Funny about resemblances. Ceci's looking more and more like her mother. If only she had her disposition.

I've begun going out. An extra man is useful, I'm told. And I suppose I qualify even though I have trouble breathing when I think of Clare. I am usually seated next to some woman I've known and avoided for years. Many of them make me shudder, especially those who say they 'can't stand the idea of stepchildren' or announce they 'aren't into babies'. How tender. Just as bad are those who can talk of nothing else. I'm always looking at my watch and thinking how lucky I was. What's more, I'm steering clear of scary Mona Tucker, who wants to take me to the symphony.

Clare never looked old to me. These women do. Notwithstanding they're the same age Clare would be. I don't know what to say to them, and I was struck dumb when one of them said, "How does it feel to live without your wife?"

My tablemates and I observe the rituals. They ask me about Eliot and Ceci, and I'm pleased to repeat the same positive news. Thankfully, my children were young enough not to have been ruined by the '60s and '70s although they sowed a few of the proverbial wild oats. I remember Eliot's getting tipsy at a Head of the Charles Regatta before he was old enough to drink legally. And Ceci received a speeding ticket. Several, actually. Other than that, I'd say they've done fine and have never behaved like Millard's two hellions. No. I'm not being truthful, even here. Ceci's been worrying me for years. I wish I saw more of her.

Sooner or later, one of the women sitting next to me will inquire about C&P. The only information of interest to a non-lawyer relates to matters the canons of ethics prevent me from disclosing. I'm not really sure I have an accurate picture of C&P. It seems less and less like the firm where I'd been so happy for 20 years. In this regard, it's only fair to say that many of my partners would cry 'Thank God' for the changes. Certainly, Millard feels that way, and he's thriving despite his annoyance at never having been elected to the management committee.

Not all of what we've lost is intangible. After a long squabble, the partners voted to scrap our pension plan. Millard led the charge. This is the first major issue where I've been on the losing side.

Certainly my tablemates don't want to hear about the C&P pension plan. It would be rude to force that on them, so I try to learn something about their lives. Some of these women mistake my inquiries for expressions of interest. One of them put her hand on my leg. Like most guys of my vintage, I never developed the knack of politely fending off members of the opposite sex. When I was young, boys took the lead and became accustomed to being rebuffed.

I don't want to spend time with these women, or see them with their clothes off. So, I've increased my hours at the office, play more squash (mostly doubles), and may sign up for the Orvis Fly Fishing School. Thankfully, I've kept a handle on the booze.

I tell the children little about my social life. They must realize nobody could replace their mother. Are they upset by my behavior? Do they think I'm having sex with these women? Do they assume I'm incapable of sex? Are they relieved I'm going out, and might become less of a bother?

They seem to think I can't look out for myself. Ceci produced my grandfather's genealogical notes and suggested I might get a kick out of organizing and updating them. Then she gave me one of those ancestral fan charts. I realize she thinks I'm dull, but come on.

In the meantime, I'm still waking up two or three times a night. No gentle breathing. No reassuring mound. No familiar face on the adjacent pillow. Would I be less miserable if I didn't huddle on my side? No. That empty space belongs to Clare.

Perhaps my greatest pleasure at that time was captaining the C&P softball team. I played catcher. I figured I'd do the least damage there (base stealing wasn't allowed) although I longed to reclaim my childhood place at short. We were better than respectable, and acquitted ourselves with honor in the Bankers, Brokers, and Lawyers League. This was unusual because the financial institutions, in addition to being larger, attracted better, if not smarter athletes, leaving the law firms, except us, to wallow around in second division. Millard told Alice he was our first baseman, but he's never been to any of our games.

I always wore my spikes. I love their snug feeling. They improve my play, and, having once been drilled by Millard, I take pains never to hurt anyone. If only I could play softball every day from the time I leave the office until I return the next morning. And on weekends.

35

I'LL GIVE him this. I've never heard Eliot mention a play one of his teammates calls the finest he's ever seen at any level of sports. He told me my eager friend caught a foul pop after chasing it up a rickety aluminum grandstand. He can still hear Eliot's clattering spikes. Everyone thought he'd break a leg if not his neck, but he never took his eye off the ball. That's my boy. He was pleased when I dubbed him 'Lord of the Flies'. Had I been present, I'd have disallowed his catch by ruling the stands out of bounds.

36

THERE IS, I am afraid, no other way of putting it. The children became pests. Led by Ceci, they decided I needed a change, and not merely 'a change of venue' as their 'uptight' father might put it. Something life-altering.

Ceci said I'd stopped taking care of myself.

Utter nonsense, but only a warm up for what was to come.

She informed me her English class had just finished *A Room with a View* and she thought, why not Florence? Young Eliot pronounced it an inspired choice. Together they decided that, with any luck, Florence would do as much for me as it did for Forster's heroine, Lucy Honeychurch. They gently suggested there were places of interest outside New England. To get me into the right frame of mind, Ceci dug up her great-grandmother's 1904 Baedeker, *Italy from the Alps to Naples*. She assumed I would love deciphering our forebear's marginalia.

The children persuaded me to sign up for an Alumni Association tour. Surely I would be among kindred spirits with whom I could fret about Yale's strong-armed sophomore quarterback. Then they suggested there might be some unattached ladies who would appreciate me, their 'dear but uncultivated' father. They said Clare had wanted me to find a kind-hearted woman who loved her own children and might, therefore, love someone else's. It would have been better if they hadn't let the genie out of the bottle. Sometimes it's best to leave bad enough alone.

No self-respecting corporate lawyer takes off 11 days in October. The fourth quarter has just begun, and we're getting in deals which must close by year-end. Lucky Millard, he can disappear whenever he wants for as long as he wants and never be missed.

However, sometimes my children cannot be denied, and I did feel a few stirrings of excitement. I'd never taken a tour, never wanted to, but being a Harvard tour I was sure to be surrounded by smart, interesting people—maybe even some cheerful women. In this regard, I remember being intrigued by my half-day in Florence during the summer after my junior year. I was dutifully impressed by Michelangelo's David, but can't remember what else I saw there except I know it wasn't the Mona Lisa. She's in Paris.

Despite my children's enthusiasm, I remained apprehensive until I was assured FedEx would be able to find the Hotel Ghiberti, even though it's located on a tiny piazza that doesn't make it onto every city map. In fact, the location was almost perfect—midway between the Duomo, *i.e.* the Cathedral, and the Piazza della Signoria, the home of David* and those other spectacular statues (I must always remind myself not to spell this word 'statutes'). My spirits rose further when I learned I could get the football scores without incurring the cost of an overseas telephone call. If only my stomach didn't betray me.

Ceci ordered me to go easy on the pasta.

The overnight flight from Boston to Paris went smoothly, so did the connecting flight, and, miracle of miracles, my bag and I made it to Florence together. I asked our guide whether any Renaissance painter ever did an 'Adoration of the Luggage'. Ha. Ha. Our tour began, in what I was told was the customary fashion. At 6:00 p.m. we gathered in one of the Ghiberti's less attractive public spaces for what was billed as 'a festive welcome reception'. It wasn't festive, but it was free. We met our tour leader and introduced ourselves to the group. My initial assessment was correct. Not one of the men had been in my class, and none of the unattached ladies was my type.

One of them spoke only of art. She monopolized the guides and talked down to the rest of us. I'm sure she considered me a low brow. She seemed put out when I declined to come by her room for a drink.

---

* After writing this, I learned that I'd been looking at a reproduction. For those who are interested, the real McCoy (the real McDavid) is in the Academia.

Another woman, who was several years my junior, didn't take care of herself, and I made a huge mistake with number three when I made what I thought was a witty remark about the Sabine women. Her response was, "I don't do rape jokes."

For purposes of this journal, I see no point in listing everything I saw. My notes can be found in a folder labeled 'Florence, 1985'. My greatest pleasure was returning on my own to the Saturn Room of the Pitti Palace. I spent at least 45 minutes walking back and forth between two quite different Raphael Madonnas. The guards may have thought I was planning a desecration. I was unnerved by the intensity of my feelings, particularly when I thought of Clare and our babies.

After a week in Florence, I began to miss Boston and my customary routines. I hadn't met anyone I wanted to keep up with, but I really enjoyed Forster's novel, which Cecilia had slipped into my bag. If only its title didn't make me think of Clare's room at Mass General.

In the end, I 'did' Florence, visiting palaces, churches, and museums, not to mention loggias, piazzas, and salas, but I did not find what I was looking for. And probably never will.

One of my 'at leisure' evenings consisted of a solitary (I'd received no dinner invitations) meal in the Piazza della Signoria, sipping, as Forster put it, "bitter coffee out of a tiny cup as shadows filled the violent bronze and marble world of the Loggi dei Lanzi". Hard to be upbeat on what I'd discovered was the site of Savonarola's auto-da-fé, and bringing my grandmother's Baedeker only reminded me she was dead.

Going home won't be easy. I sense people muttering, "Time for him to get over it and move on. It's been how long, now?" I'm trying not to wallow, and I don't want to appear self-indulgent, but, in some weird way, I dread getting over it. Regardless of what Clare might think, wouldn't that be a betrayal, an admission she's replaceable? In short, I felt worse than before I left.

Certain days will, I'm afraid, remain exceptionally painful. Her birthday, our anniversary, the holidays, and most especially the 14th of August. Constant reminders.

My only laugh came from those raunchy underpants. The ones depicting the crotch of Michelangelo's David that are, I am told, sold throughout Italy. I still have the pair Millard gave me before this trip. Trying to buck me up, he urged me to "model these for one of your more lively companions".

Millard could probably have used some cheering up himself. Before leaving, I learned his boys got picked up for joyriding on the Mass Pike. Arthur was only 14, and their car (Millard's BMW) was full of beer. He didn't help himself when he brushed off the state trooper with, "My attorney father, Andrew de Peyster Millard, a senior partner at Curtis and Perkins, specializes in police brutality cases." Millard will be fine though. He blames his children's misadventures on their mother's genes.

37

WHATEVER MAY or may not have transpired in Firenze, Eliot's trip hasn't had the desired effect. He has not been reborn. His children having failed to pep him up or hook him up, it's up to me. Eliot's treading water. He's still the sorry hangdog who makes almost daily trips to Clare's grave.

He should have known. Just as the dying resent the healthy, so too the angry and dissolute gods cannot abide happiness or fidelity in mortals. Eliot pissed them off.

There's something else. Yes, it's hearsay, but a little bird told me Eliot was spotted leaving the skin flick near North Station. Has my worthy friend become one of those dudes hunched in the back of the theater with a raincoat over his 'lap'? I must intervene. The office has become his entire life, and if he continues on this path he, not I, will end up running the place. That wouldn't do.

I have just the right woman. In fact, I've had her regularly, and that's becoming a problem. It's not as though I'm dumping defective goods. Jeannette Tisdale passes all but the net worth test. Well, maybe I'm exaggerating.

Jeannette's getting impatient. Her financial clock is ticking. Although Alice and I are foundering, I'm not ready to split and take on Jeannette. In fact, I don't see her as spouse fodder—for me. Bossy, demanding, and, so obviously, on the make.

We are too much alike. Not only does she remind me of Mother, she even made the absurd claim that her mum had more lovers than mine. The last thing I want is "a gal just like the gal who married dear old Dad".

Jeannette's fond of telling me she'll make my life miserable if she doesn't get her way. I have no reason to disbelieve her. She must have a solvent husband. Now. She'd prefer me, but Eliot's at hand and will have to suffice.

I could place Jeannette easily. It would be as simple as arranging a worn-out greyhound's adoption in Cambridge. She makes a great first impression and with my coaching has developed what I call her 'geisha routine'. A quick learner, she can, in an instant, change from savage to submissive and—if you don't know better—loving. A Venus man trap.

When I broached the subject of Eliot, she flashed me her most unguarded expression. Frightening.

"Here's the way to bag Eliot Estabrook Lawrence. He needs someone who needs him. He must have tasks to perform. Like a sheep dog. Any questions?"

"Yes. Does he dress as nicely as you?"

"Of course not."

"What's he drive?"

"A Chevy, always has."

"A 'Vette?"

"No, a wagon."

"Oh… How old?"

"It's nicely broken in."

"Does he belong to a health club?"

"Yes, but he doesn't go there very much. Still, he's pretty fit…"

"Does he dance, do weed, or go on cruises?"

"No, no, and no."

"Does he like to…?"

"Eliot will make a devoted and possibly ardent hubby. Not in my league. But serviceable, I suspect. You'll have to bring him along slowly, though. Don't startle him. He keeps talking about some wanton who tried to drag him off to her room in Firenze, that's Florence."

"Smart ass… What's he worth?"

"Well, he's very worthy, and you could energize his inner Galahad by letting it slip that some dirt bag managing director's coming onto you."

Jeannette found the feigned innocence routine surprisingly easy. She opened her kimono gradually. And in short order Eliot was hers. Having done unspeakably pleasant things with an innocent, Eliot had no choice but to do the right thing. Without delay. Just to make sure there'd be no backsliding, Jeannette gave Eliot to believe she was great with Lawrence.

Jeannette's still not sure about Eliot in the sack. Yes, he seems adequately vigorous for a 49-year-old and yes, he still does it—but only weakly, weekly. Jeannette realizes she'll need some between-meals snacks. I closed the deal by reminding Jeannette that Eliot was a peer of the realm and assured her we'd still have regular get-togethers. I fibbed about my deteriorating relationship with Alice, from whom I've been getting virtually nothing physical or financial for many moons.

Helping Eliot with his needs puts me in mind of my 22-year-old goddaughter. Her mother's gone, she's wowing them in New Haven, and I'm in the boonies with Alice.

We had such fun back then. Ceci was about seven and, as I recall, engagingly bossy. Daddy was off on what became a week-long closing in Toronto. I'd bought her a hat with bunny ears. My goddaughter's mother was perched on the sofa in such a way as to afford me an unsettling glimpse of thigh. Intentional?

Ceci and I were on the floor playing gin rummy. As usual, she was winning. How could she not? My mind was elsewhere.

Ceci needed and still needs to win as badly as I do, and I encouraged her to celebrate her victories by parading around the room, pumping her arms, and tootling on an imaginary brass instrument.

I'd just finished dealing another hand when I noticed Ceci had fallen silent. Her concentration was almost frightening.

"I like your shirt, Uncle Andrew."

"Thank you, Ceci. You have good taste. It's made of fine cotton and comes from Italy."

Ceci nodded and studied her hand.

"Uncle Andrew, I want to tell you something."

"What is it, Ceci?"

"Gin."

She and her mother giggled. So did I. Ever the good sport.

38

PERHAPS I'VE misjudged Millard again. I suppose it's possible. I remember Clare warning me about him just before she died, but isn't Millard entitled to the benefit of the doubt? Could my dearest wife have been expected to get things right in those circumstances? Sure, he's competitive, but it's nothing personal. It goes with the LLB.

Soon after the third anniversary of Clare's death and after I began writing this, Millard introduced me to Jeannette Tisdale, who happens to be a pretty fair tennis player. Jeannette is only 30, but our age difference doesn't seem to bother her. At least she's never mentioned it, and she must know how old I am. As luck would have it, she's out of her 20s.

For several months, Millard's been talking about an anonymous lady he's trying to unload. Some may consider me obtuse, but it occurred to me to wonder if Jeannette Tisdale and the mystery woman might possibly be one and the same. Looking Millard in the eye, I asked him directly.

"Good God, no. Out of the question. Jeannette's a personal client and more like the daughter I've always wanted. Taking advantage of her would be unconscionable."

"Promise?" I asked him.

Millard put away his comb.

"Word of honor," he replied.

Jeannette and I have done some fun things together. I've taken her to the U.S.S. *Constitution,* and she's fascinated with its success against the English frigates. Military history is one of her hobbies. Not that I would think of criticizing her, but Clare never took an interest in that subject. Jeannette says it would be "a kick" to tour the Civil War battlefields with me. Maybe take in an air show. Terrific.

The two of us play tennis against Millard and Alice. Despite Millard's thunderous first serves (the velocity of Millard's serve is increasing as his third marriage deteriorates), we always beat them. Jeannette was, after all, the captain of the Colby tennis team. I'm proud of these victories and pleased to have maintained my concentration. Jeannette's marvelous figure in a tennis dress is a sight to behold. Furthermore, Millard is never at his best when playing with Alice and on the receiving end of her barbed remarks about his game and his physique. I recall her saying, "Andrew, you may be immobile, but you cover a lot of the court, nevertheless."

After one particularly strained afternoon, Millard offered me a drag on a shapeless, hand-rolled cigarette. I knew what it was and declined.

These matches are good fun, and I know Jeannette pulls her punches when serving to Alice. Jeannette's a sweetie and a good sport to boot. You can't say that about many girls who work for Merrill Lynch. The four of us usually have drinks and dinner together after tennis. Then I drive Jeannette back to her Beacon Hill apartment.

For the longest time, nothing happened. Jeannette would give me a fast peck on the cheek after I'd escorted her to her door. Now and then I'd receive another. I could never figure out whether or not I was going to get the second kiss. Nor could I figure out why I had or hadn't. Our quiet routine was fine with me. Sometimes I thought it might be nice if we did a little more, but then I'd get sad and nervous. Things were best left as they were.

After a month or so of leaving Jeannette on her stoop the way I'd dropped off my college dates, Jeannette said we were being silly and invited me in. I accepted. Her apartment's neat as a pin. Just the way Clare kept 118 Beacon. I liked that, but I wasn't really sure about those shelves full of figurines. "Hummels," she called them.

Anyway, I had a glass of wine and then another and another. Thereafter, matters became a little confused. Not wishing to frighten her, I said, "I ought to be getting along." I was startled by her reaction.

"So you want to leave me," she said.

"No. No, of course not, but I really should go," I stammered.

"Don't you think I might have a view on whether you stay or leave? You've got a great knack for making someone feel good about herself, haven't you? You've been here less than an hour. Don't you like being with me? And, by the way, why haven't you ever had me over to your home? Aren't I good enough?"

I didn't know how to respond so I said, "Maybe we've had a little too much vino." I thought calling it 'vino' instead of 'wine' might lighten the mood. Boy, was I wrong.

"Speak for yourself, Mr. Lawrence."

Was she making fun of my background? As Millard might have said, I really screwed the pooch.

"Can we talk about this tomorrow?" I asked.

My question was cut off by the slamming of her bedroom door. I took that to mean I should leave.

Something certainly happened on my next visit. My behavior was inexcusable, and I'm afraid Jeannette may have been appalled, perhaps traumatized. She'd never seen me like that. However, Jeannette appeared willing to forgive me, to write off my conduct to a tougher than usual match (it went five sets) and a third glass of chardonnay. Sometimes it's tough to be a 'chardonnaysayer'. Ha. Ha. Jeannette's an old-fashioned girl. Innocent. Especially for an investment banker.

I'm a wimpy drinker. Just white wine. If you toss in enough ice and club soda, almost any white slides down painlessly. Shortly before Clare's death, Millard produced what he told me was a 'Margaux'. He chortled about 'stealing' it from an ignoramus shopkeeper for 'a lousy 75 bucks'. That seemed awfully expensive, but Millard was correct. It was perfection. Unlike anything I've had before or since. I suddenly realized what all the shouting was about. After that, every red I tried tasted like vinegar so I stopped looking. Could Jeannette be my second bottle of Margaux?

On our next date, it seemed to be assumed I'd come upstairs and we'd do the same thing. We skipped the wine and went directly to her bedroom, undressing en route. I did nothing to put on the brakes, particularly after seeing her black underwear.

Afterwards, she said something I'd never heard before, "You

really know your way around a woman's body." Followed by, "I think I'm falling in love with you, Eliot Lawrence."

Do I feel the same way? I can't tell. Should I stop seeing her? That would be caddish. She might be devastated. I've certainly made no promises. On the other hand, I've issued no disclaimers. Can I retrace my steps and once again become Jeannette's weekly tennis partner? And nothing more? Do I want that? What if Eliot or Cecilia find out about their father and his inappropriately young woman? Weren't the '60s and '70s supposed to have made this easier?

I've heard people are inclined to be more open, truthful, and compliant right after having sex. So, I came at it obliquely by noting Millard was known as the consummate ladies' man. This sally elicited an encouraging response to the effect that I was the only man who could possibly "excite" (I loved that) her. And she didn't qualify it by saying something like—the only man my age.

Why didn't I have the decency to leave it at that? But no, I pressed on. Had she ever gone out with Millard? Jeannette didn't act guilty or evasive. Hurt was more like it.

"My darling Eliot," she said, "I'd have told you as soon as we met if I'd so much as held hands with your friend, who, by the way, has none of your charm or vigor."

What a nice choice of words and how wonderful, after almost 50 years, to be found sexy. I am completely reassured and would be on cloud nine, or maybe ten, if I could only forget my churlish interrogation.

Jeannette hasn't pressured me to do anything, but… It sounds corny, but maybe I'm the first with Jeannette. I understand you can't always tell. That would put matters in an entirely different light. Also, this could look awful to my colleagues and the outside world. Eliot Lawrence carrying on with a young client—someone entrusted to him by one of his partners. Have I broken any laws? This isn't my practice area. Don't I remember something called 'palimony'? Should I be considered a fiduciary? What a scandal.

Jeannette, bless her heart, said nothing of the sort. However, some weeks later she mentioned the possibility of a little Lawrence. That stopped me cold. When can a woman tell? In the meantime, cad that

I am, this new relationship is proving to be giddy and restorative. I am torn between shame and exhilaration. One thing is certain. Much as I might like to, we simply cannot carry on in this fashion indefinitely. I must propose.

She will decline, almost certainly in the nicest possible fashion. Then if she isn't pregnant we'll go our separate ways, and she can find someone more suitable. If she's pregnant, of course we must get married. If that's OK with her. I respect Jeannette's right to choose, but I'll be haunted by the loss if she terminates our baby. I haven't told Ceci or Eliot. What good can come from disillusioning them about their father? Another reason this journal must remain confidential. Or what about this—place it in a time capsule to remain sealed until the expiration of the maximum time period permitted by the Rule against Perpetuities?

I shouldn't mention it. It's almost certainly unfair. But I can't get it entirely out of my mind.

Returning to 118 after our last date, I decided to take an overdue look at my *Wall Street Journal.* When I opened my briefcase (I still have trouble calling it an attaché case), I noticed my brokerage statements were all higgledy-piggledy. I'm an orderly sort, and I don't usually leave them that way. In fact, I don't remember opening this month's statement. But I must have. I'm glad my account's not at Merrill Lynch.

After our next adventure (a swan boat ride), I told Jeannette we had to talk. I almost didn't, because doing so would remind me of Clare and *talking*. I picked a bench in the Public Garden. She looked at me trustingly. My proposal was, I am afraid, unpolished. I sounded like an unprepared first-year law student.

I stammered out something like, "On the one hand, I will be pleased if you'll marry me. In fact, it will be grand. On the other hand, I will fully understand if you choose not to do so. There is, after all, a 19-year age difference between us, and it would make perfect sense for you to choose someone of your own generation, someone who will understand you better than I, someone you won't have to prop up in his dotage." I made a point of not talking about the possibility of a child.

I kept my fingers crossed, but was prepared to accept whatever Jeannette decided. It would have been wrong to pressure her. If she chose to have our child, then I'd insist we marry with the promise I would support it and grant Jeannette a divorce whenever she wished. I paused, not entirely sure what I expected or wanted to hear. To my astonishment, she accepted then and there.

Unconditionally and, I believe, enthusiastically. I presume this means she will have our baby, and we will keep it. Am I doing the right thing? Have I atoned for my base behavior? Am I being a stand-up guy? What will Eliot and Ceci think? I'm sure they'll love Jeannette and our baby, because Jeannette tells me repeatedly she knows she will love them.

How wrong one can be. For years, I'd assumed it was all over for me in the romance department. And to think I owe it to Millard. Now I'm going to get after that managing director who's been 'harassing' (I believe that's the current usage) my intended.

As best I can tell, there are only two reasons to marry. Because you can't live without her, or because honor demands it. Looks like I'll have covered both bases.

39

JEANNETTE'S A hoot. She wondered out loud how many balls she'd have to pick up in her low-cut tennis dresses before Eliot got the idea. Would one, or perhaps both, of her tanned, untethered orbs have to spill out on center court?

The lovebirds married within a month of Eliot's proposal. Naturally there was chatter in our circle about the short time period between the first news of their relationship and the wedding. Tongues wagged. Eyebrows rose. Those given to gossip said my buddy didn't seem at all like the Eliot Lawrence they thought they knew. The Eliots of the world wondered if they'd been taken in. People more like me said, "Hooray for Eliot. Some young stuff might do wonders." I was Eliot's best man and introduced him to Jeannette's parents the day before the wedding. The ever-positive Eliot was heard to describe them as "a refreshing change from our usual crowd".

One of the many services I performed was to assure all and sundry this was a love match, and the happy couple had yet to make up their minds about children. Tactfully, I made it clear it wasn't a shotgun wedding. You see, I knew it wasn't. I'd experienced a moment of dread when Jeannette dropped the baby bomb. There might, after all, have been doubt about its paternity. DNA and all that.

The week before his wedding I considered suggesting a prenup to Eliot. Then I reconsidered. It might imply I knew too much. Anyway, Eliot would decline, favor me with a pitying look, and say something like, "Maybe for you Andrew, but not for me. It's so untrusting and unromantic. Besides, I haven't got that much to protect." I tried, Lord knows I tried.

As it was, all three of us were happy. Eliot was oblivious. Jeannette and I were discreet. The world smiled approvingly at the charming couple, particularly at Eliot, who had soldiered on so bravely following his loss. Less than a month after the ceremony, Jeannette had her quiet 'miscarriage'. Both of them were devastated, but Jeannette managed to snap back quickly.

Jeannette was rather curt in her brief after-action report on their honeymoon. Something about hubby's lumpish inflexibility regarding sides of the bed.

On other fronts: I can't believe the news. My favorite young friend is going out with Quintus's hopeless pal, Sam Morris. Father Lawrence is pushing it hard. How could he? Such a mismatch. Sammy barely made it through one of those formerly all-girl colleges that will accept any swinging dick with a trust fund. Strike that—any swinging dick but Arthur or Stanley.

At work, the 'Roaring' '80s were good to me (my Curtis compensation topped $300,000 by the end of the decade) and a nice warm-up for the spectacular '90s. Eliot is, quite appropriately, moving from dominance to decline.

More and more trusts are coming my way as our elders either give up their ghosts or become too far gone even for my line of work. I am also getting more efficient at relieving the codgers of their best customers. We call it 'transitioning'. And a fine thing it is until it happens to you.

Even better, I'm developing a reputation around town as someone who makes things happen. Diversion of assets is one of my specialties. I think of it as a refinement of the clumsy art of undue influence. The epicenter of this endeavor is, as everyone knows, Florida, with its crafty practitioners and gullible, lonely, unprotected seniors. It's more challenging in New England, but if you're looking for a master, I'm your man.

The key is to foster dependence. Once his instruments have been satisfactorily redrafted, the decedent-in-waiting must be sequestered, figuratively if not literally. Remember, isolate the elderly and hand-pick their caregivers. You don't want relapses or recantations, and you must protect him from folks he's just cut out. Surround him with those who will benefit from his death, and make sure he understands you're the only one who cares. Everyone else is plotting against him. The aged are so susceptible to the idea of conspiracies.

To a large extent, I'm self-taught. There aren't many practical, flexible, and imaginative estate planners. Most of us are an amalgam of sheep and lemmings. Occasionally, someone will devise a new tax scam. All those he's scooped will cluck disapprovingly about the uncertainty of its legitimacy and benefits while shamelessly copying it. As for myself, I've never quibbled about backdating documents, and I pack the most customer-friendly notarial seal in the east.

Working with me is rewarding. I have persuaded many of my customers to be more generous to charities. After lives of self-dealing and betrayal, they tremble when pondering the hereafter, particularly those of the less-forgiving faiths. I have a consoling casket-side manner. I understand their anxiety and encourage it. Then I offer to ease their spirits and get their names engraved on tablets other than their gravestones. The executive directors of several of Boston's most revered eleemosynary institutions are among my allies. These worthies have me, and me alone, to thank for a number of new galleries and significant additions to their endowments and permanent collections.

In return, my obliging executive directors have offered me board seats, making it clear they are freebies. I have provided two of these gentlemen with unattached, well-off ladies to serve on their boards and, in one instance, to replace the spouse he improvidently acquired before he developed an itch not just to conserve but to possess. Being on these boards and being a fixture at their A-list functions exposes me to yet more wealth, which I redirect like an irrigation system. I am, of course, familiar with the tight-fisted holders of Boston's old money. It's the parvenus I pursue. Boston's traditional watering holes have been fished-out.

Here's how I reel in those hungry arrivistes. Rule One: none of those nobodies gets through to me on his first few tries. Ruth and her now plummy Oxbridge accent hold them at bay while stoking their ardor.

"I'll see if Mr. Millard's available. Please excuse me. Once again, your name is... Ah yes, Shea."

"But not one of the Sea Island Sheas?"

"No, he seems to have slipped out on me. You need to see him at once? I'm so sorry; he's booked for the fortnight. Can you give me some dates and times that work for you next month?

OR

"No, no, no. Mr. Millard's always away Derby week. He has so many friends in Louisville.

OR

"I'm afraid not. Mr. Millard's availability during that time period depends entirely on whether the salmon are rising on the Tweed. Yes, the Tweed."

Once a date's been set, Ruth rings off with, "And, of course, Mr. Millard will expect his customary retainer."

It takes about six months to get into my Rolodex. Meanwhile, the waiting list continues to grow.

I help the uncultured. I assist them with 'croissant', 'vichyssoise', and other tongue twisters. They've made their bundle and now, as always, they want to age it and be taken seriously as patrons and connoisseurs. They crave respect and status. Not to mention deference from persons other than their corporate toadies. They and their lovely, reconditioned wives yearn to appear on the so-called society pages in taut skin, matching teeth, and properly-fitted evening clothes.

They wish to be made much of, to have their opinions solicited and then, God save me, taken seriously. Finding themselves beyond their depth when it comes to literature, music, art, wine, attire, conversation, manners, and taste, they are happy to spend big to mask these blemishes. I help them in their comic efforts to catch up. I clothe them in couth. In effect, I'm running an exclusive finishing school with a high tuition and no financial aid. 'Refinement's Within Reach' is our motto. None of them would understand a Latin one. The mission of my academy is to reduce the number of persons to whom its students feel inferior.

When they enroll, most of them remind me of Dennis Kozlowski of Tyco renown. They are eager to bury their snouts in the trough, divert their investors' cash flows, and, like modern Medicis, commission heroic ice statues with vodka gushing from their frozen peckers. I suggest there are classier ways to squander other people's assets. I remind them that being known as a philanthropist and mixing with the right celebrities can, at the time of sentencing, mean the difference between community service and 'Club Fed'.

I assure my pupils they'll be able to circulate among the swells and cognoscenti without drawing a snicker. I cultivate the fallow. For the most presentable, I ease their way into formerly unattainable clubs, clubs forced by cruel financial necessity to drop breeding from their admission requirements. I teach them how to slip cash to a maître d' in a subtle but noticeable fashion. I'm pleased with my sideline of fabricating patricians. Raising these rootless specimens is like hydroponics. Or think of me as a refinery. I take in crude and pump out premium.

Some of the most creative faculty members of de Peyster Prep are the executive directors of prominent 501(c)(3)s. One of them functions as a tutor/valet, educating and outfitting his charges while exposing them to the mysteries of Thucydides, thread count, and tissue paper. Recognizing what I've done for him, his annual thank-you letter contains a thoughtful typo that adds two deductible zeroes to my trifling contribution.

And now a caveat to those who aspire to follow in my path. Beware of cunning clerics, and be particularly chary of sects deploying female priests.

I speak from sad experience. Some months ago, one of my dotty customers, whom I was sheltering from unwholesome outside influences, started babbling about 'faith'. What was up with that old scoundrel? Then I learned that Harold Simmons was sighing about 'faith' with an upper case 'F'.

On my next visit to his holding pen, Harold gurgled, "Andrew, Faith so reminds me of my granddaughter, Prudence. She needs my help."

"Who needs your help, Mr. Simmons? Prudence, I presume." Prudence being the conniving, gum-snapping, teen-age succubus who was milking Harold dry.

"No, no! Prudence is all set. It's Faith who needs me."

"Faith?"

"She's an angel."

"No doubt, but does she have a more mundane identity?"

"She's our visiting chaplain. And she's fully-trained in deep tissue massage."

Can it be, I wondered. "Where can I find this polymath?"

"You just missed her, but she'll be here tomorrow morning at eleven."

I walked into his room at 10:45. Without knocking.

"Would you care to join us in morning prayer, Mr. Millard?" said a stunning brunette who looked as though she'd been performing mouth-to-mouth on my customer.

"And who, pray tell, are you?" As I asked this rhetorical question I observed the she-devil withdrawing her hand from beneath Harold's coverlet.

"I am Faith Roberts, and I'm hurt you don't remember me from Clare Lawrence's service."

I could see why Harold was besotted. The witch had dialed down her rack and transformed herself into an almost exact replica of his granddaughter. She must have studied Harold's bedside photo of Prudence. Same bob. Same hair color. Same falsely wholesome suburban looks.

"Six years ago, you were a blond, Pokey, and, in case you don't know it, I am Harold Simmons's attorney and sole trustee."

"Really? Mr. Simmons tells me you are one of his *former* advisors. Am I correct?"

"You are not, but anything further would, as you can appreciate, be privileged information." Old man Simmons's head was swiveling back and forth between us. Yes, he was out of it, but he'd picked up the bad vibes. As for me, I was off this gravy train if I didn't join the prayer group or help out under the blanket.

In fact, I was overtaken by events.

Two months later, Faith Roberts sold that booby a million-dollar annuity issued by one of her church's affiliates. I knew this because I wrote the frigging check. Then he died. I'm not sure he collected a single payment. That deal will get her a bishopric, or diocesan salesperson of the year, or both.

When confronted by my charge of undue influence, she responded with affected gravitas and barely concealed delight.

"Undue influence? Come now, Andrew. If you like, I'll send you my videotape of an entirely competent Harold Simmons executing his new will while complaining loudly and lucidly about you and your slippery ways. Anything else, Andrew? May I call you Andrew?"

"You bet there is, Pokey. I'm reporting you. You're about to get your sneaky ass defrocked."

"Enough, Andrew. My research among a representative cross section of female Curtis and Perkins employees tells me you are a notorious if usually unsuccessful defrocker. The next time we meet I expect to be wearing purple. Until then, may God bless you and keep you."

On another subject, it looks as though Curtis is taking a tentative step forward. After 17 brown years, we're moving into a glass tower erected atop a squat granite structure. The building puts me in mind of a Great Pyrenees doing it to a dachshund.

It took imagination and perseverance to make my timid law firm step up to the plate and borrow 20,000,000 smackers. I seized the initiative and obtained fabulous terms. Little by way of principal payments until the loan matures in 2004. And that's a long way off. Then we're looking at a manageable balloon payment. The mere $2,000,000 in objets d'art I've persuaded the management committee to buy will in 15 years have appreciated enough to repay the entire outstanding balance of our loan. The art market's hot, and if worse comes to worst, we can unload it on the high-flying Asians.

Curtis must get going if it's to remain in (Eliot's view) or return to (my view) the first tier in Boston. We need a complete upgrading of our telephone and computer systems, not to mention our attorneys. Our décor is an insult to all but the mediocrities we're now hiring. We've gotten nondescript. Too beige. Too beat-up.

My deal is brilliantly conceived and implemented. One of our partners is a director of sleepy Devonshire Trust. I suggested the bank establish a law firm lending group. This is an untapped and potentially lucrative market. Until now, firms have required little capital and have extracted what was needed from their newest partners. Times have changed. Firms are expanding, and the current technology costs more than rebuilt Smith Coronas. Then there's leasehold improvements. You can't finance this from current earnings without the partners screaming about their shrunken pay checks.

If we have to be in hock, I'm delighted it's to Devonshire, a stagnant outfit whose top brass are clones of our older partners. No way Devonshire's going to mess with Curtis. It would be like friendly fire or white-on-white crime.

The transaction's a winner for both institutions. A 15-year deal is almost unheard of for a bank, but Devonshire's eager to crack the longer-term market. Interest-only for eight years and they're giving us a floating rate—prime plus a mere 25 basis points. The negotiations were a breeze, but I made the mistake of showing Eliot the term sheet.

The next day he got back to me with four single-spaced pages of niggles. Really. He suggested my loan was too aggressive, representing, as it did, at least three times our 12/31/88 net worth. "So what," said I. "If Devonshire wants to give me this much dough, I'm grabbing it."

He also pointed to what he said was a 'ridiculously relaxed' coverage ratio. Hell's teeth. I wouldn't know a slack coverage ratio from a tight-assed one. The loan officer handed me the cookie jar. Naturally I dug in. I asked Eliot whose side he was on. In the starchy tone, he uses when he's being an A.H., he said, "It's a mistake when things come too easily, and the bank is doing us no favors by not imposing some discipline." That was worse than being back in Chapel.

I'm not even sure I read all of Eliot's nit-picking before I signed the note. We had our money, and in short order we had some glorious art. I've hung a valuable de Kooning in my room and an inexpensive print of Nelson's flagship, H.M.S. *Victory*, outside Eliot's. I can see Horatio Lawrence on his quarterdeck signaling, "Curtis and Perkins expects that every man will do his diary."

Lest I forget.

Along with the blessed decline in 'professionalism' encouraged by *Bates v. Arizona*, my hustle was discovered by the yellow press. Why not? We're not newsworthy, but there are over a million of us in this fortunate land, and we relish tittle-tattle about our confreres almost as much as hyperbole about ourselves.

So I jumped at the opportunity to become an undercover stringer for *The American Advocate*. My beat: New England, ex. Connecticut. My subject: innuendo. My nom de plume: "Hearsay." My sources: the disgruntled. My identity: a closely guarded secret. Think Swiss bank accounts. Best of all, my series on troubled firms titled 'Sucking Wind' is, I am assured, the first piece read every month.

Just for the nuts of it, I wrote up one of Eliot's rare noteworthy transactions. "Have you seen the current issue of *A.A.*?" I asked him.

"I never look at that rag," he sniffed.

Boy did Mister Great Books change his tune when I sent him the article. And yes, he had it clipped, photocopied, circulated, and framed.

40

WELL, WE'VE moved again—to even fancier, more expensive space. At least we're still on State Street. Unfortunately, we've done it at what looks like the top of the real estate market. Our rent is astronomical. We've got yet more glass and chrome, plus a ton of over-priced art and furniture purchased by Millard with the proceeds of our borrowing. We're deeply in debt, and I don't like those covenants. I gave Millard a detailed memorandum setting out my concerns, but he blew me off and closed. He was playing renaissance lawyer, someone who could do it all, not a narrow, blinkered specialist like yours truly.

Worst of all was Millard's persuading the management committee to buy a condo.

"Are you nuts?" I asked him.

"Not at all, Eliot. We don't have the cot room any longer, and we need a place to put up our visiting firewomen."

My new corner office (nearly 17 feet on a side) is nothing short of palatial. It's also an obscene waste of money. I'd much prefer to have a modest room and take home the difference in rent. But if we have them, why shouldn't one of them be mine, even though I've just turned 52? I'm on the southeast corner with a glorious view over Logan and out to sea. Below me is the elevated highway that's scheduled for demolition in about 10 years. My digs are on our top floor, and visitors invariably ask how I can concentrate. Millard is two floors down, with an office on the northwest corner. I enjoy teasing him. "Andrew," I say, "it's just as prestigious to look out on the western suburbs as it is to see the harbor, the islands, and the ocean. Besides, if a LNG tanker should explode on its way up the Mystic River, I'd be the first to go. The fact is, we corporate lawyers rule."

One of the amazing features of my location is the high-altitude fauna. Jeannette could care less, but I know Clare would be intrigued. First, the spiders. How did they get here? They spin their webs in the corners of the window frames, and you can see from the insect corpses that, at least in the warm months, there's a plentiful food supply. I have taped signs to the windows asking the cleaners not to mash them with their squeegees. If my spiders and I are both present when the window washers appear, I beat on the glass, point at them and make what I hope will be understood as 'spare them' gestures.

We also have ladybugs. Charming but infrequent visitors whose backs are more yellow than orange. Some special high-altitude variety? I'll have to look them up in a field guide. Most fascinating are the peregrine falcons. They roost inside the peak of the Custom House Tower. During the nesting season, they wrap our building in their exuberant orbits. I know that somewhere Clare is soaring.

41

WHILE MY room's location may not have been perfect (I could be observed from several adjacent buildings), its interior most assuredly was. It trumpeted to the world that this was the domain of a man to be reckoned with. Among lawyers' offices, it was unique. Even those who should know better spend their careers in cluttered rabbit warrens decorated with exploding red-rope folders and third-rate prints of tediously familiar golf holes.

But now I have secured more suitable quarters with an unobstructed view of the harbor. My furniture is museum quality, 18th century American. I purchased it, and a cottage on the North Shore, from estates at prices my envious colleagues claim were below fair market value. My favorite is a Hepplewhite mahogany inlaid card table. One of my executive director friends has loaned me a glorious antique Persian Doroush and a pair of lesser Gilbert Stuarts which I allow visitors to believe are family portraits.

The impression I seek is enhanced by two borrowed Impressionists. I have avoided Fitz Hugh Lane and his seafaring ilk. Ships are a cliché in Boston. A marble bust of Nero sits on the credenza behind my desk. When I'm feeling frisky, Nero becomes my hat rack. All I lack is a private john with an ocean view where I can reflect and relax as I wait for the miracle to occur.

Books are an essential part of my setting. They help define me. The treatises proclaim my wide-ranging expertise, the bound Sotheby's catalogues blazon forth my taste, and the *Social Registers* reassure the right sort they've come to the right place. Yes, I'm into lily-gilding, but would it be too much if a copy of *Debrett's* were seen peeking from my bookcase?

The final touch is a rosewood cabinet for my expanding collection of field day trophies, which, thanks to Ruth, sparkle.

There's another thing about our new offices. Sometimes I have trouble breathing. I'm still bothered by allergies and asthma. So I never go anywhere without my inhaler, and I keep a spare in my desk. Eliot uses one occasionally, so I know where to go if mine runs out or is mislaid.

While life on State Street is improving, the same cannot be said about the home front. Sometimes you've got to clean house and muck out the stables, no matter how disagreeable the task. You owe it to yourself. Well before the business community became enamored of Jack Welch's system of ranking underlings, I developed something quite like it. I rate everyone within my sphere of influence as an A, B, or C. You pamper As. You tolerate Bs—but not forever. Up or out. As for Cs, they're gone.

Sadly for her, Alice has slipped into the third tier. Game over. Alice's undressage has long since ceased to excite. To use one of her threadbare expressions, Alice has become 'redundant and unnecessary'. What's more, I no longer get to dip into her deep pockets. That's the clincher. I rather enjoy being a kept man, but I must be kept at more than the minimum wage. Since the Edmundses will never allow Arthur or Stanley to sink to his rightful level in the social order, I have only myself to consider. My comp's increasing, and Alice is ungenerous. Q.E.D. Even worse, if possible: a while back she gave our house a name—a name that's too infra dig to divulge. Cruelty is often easier to endure than bad taste.

Most people dread it, but not I. I almost look forward to calling my glib, cheery divorce lawyer. We're growing old together, and I'm terrified he'll retire. I may need his services after I've been shunted off to assisted living. Well, like the groundhog, Herby emerged from his burrow, failed to see his shadow, worked his no-fault magic in Norfolk Probate, and a month later I was free to embark on my next adventure with no financial obligations to Alice or the lads. Bye-bye Mane Street.

I allowed Ruth to take me to dinner the night my divorce became final. She insisted. Ruth's been on a roll. Indispensable at work and play. She's taking more Harvard Extension School courses—would you believe Renaissance Art—and has dropped five pounds even though she's always been fine in that department. I'm not aroused by angular.

The following week, I directed my attention to Lucy, one of our employment law partners. She specializes in defending beleaguered businesses against their disaffected female employees. A woman is useful in that line of work. Good optics. Lucy is young, divorced, driven, and childless. She enjoys the earthier forms of congress. If we married, I'd be set in my billfold and my britches. In reality, we'd be DINKS since the Edmundses' trusts will provide for Arthur and Stanley whether or not they ever bestir themselves.

Is it now time to be Ruthless? Here's the way I see it in 1989. Ruth says she's devoted to me. Should I believe her? After a couple pops, Mother said junk like that. Yes, she tolerates my wanderings, but what if we married? She'd have leverage. But not if I hit her with an even nastier prenup than the one old man Edmunds laid on me. For a moment, I lost focus and resolve. I considered Ruth for promotion. Something I'd never done before. Can I do better? Will I ever experience her warmth and kindness with anyone else?

Why should I distrust her? She's never lied to me, as best I can tell. She hasn't been abrupt, unkind, or rude. Odd, when you think about it. She's stayed in a relationship from which others might have fled. Why? Because she has so few options? Because I confer status?

Why make trouble for myself? Ruth and I still have fun together, even though I sometimes require visual aids to prime the pump. She's lost interest in grass, won't do coke, has gotten modest, but is still affectionate. She loves pampering me in Harbor View, the firm's new condo. Sometimes she cooks there. But Ruth's getting on and I am intoxicated by the current fashion of exposing a circle of flesh between the bottom of the tops and the top of the low riders. Sometimes it's firm. Sometimes well-marbled. Like Kobe beef. The different tones and textures. The variety, ranging from silky smooth to faintly fuzzy. A fragment of a tattoo. Cast me adrift in midriffs.

So what's not to like about my arrangement with Lucy? Plenty. She's moved to the office next to mine and insists we commute together. If Lucy works late, I have to wait for her. Then we have cold take-out for dinner. She wants me to fire Ruth. My mistress is a jealous lawyer.

42

SOMETHING STARTLING happened at the end of the decade. In December 1989 Millard was elected to our management committee. It's cuckoo. He's never held a leadership position in his life. Anywhere. What's it mean for the firm? Who knows, but after I asked myself what Clare would recommend, I decided to be welcoming since we were going to be on the committee together until my term expired.

I invited him to lunch. My treat, so Millard ordered two doubles. We had a nice talk. Although I didn't bring it up, both of us knew he was the only person who had ever campaigned for the committee. I appealed to his better angels. I told him we'd known each other for almost 40 years, and like everyone, he had a good side and a less good side. If he cultivated the former, he could, I said, do wonders for C&P. He's a talented fellow after all. We covered a lot of ground, and I believe, despite our disagreements, we'll work well together. At least I thought so until he thanked me for my 'lecture', stuck me for his third double, and announced, "OK, E-Man, I'm outta here. Gotta feed the beast."

I hope it doesn't get out of hand, but Millard's first act after his election was to increase the budget of the marketing committee which he's chaired since *Bates v. Arizona*. At the same time, he added pretty Heather Gorse, our new ERISA partner, and requisitioned additional travel funds. This must be monitored and contained.

He surpassed himself at his first management committee meeting by declaring, "We're doing it all wrong. We need stronger leadership."

That got our attention.

"Enlighten us, Andrew," someone said.

"We're falling behind. It takes too damn long for our overpaid associates to become self-sustaining—at least 10 to 15 years—and most of them never do. Look at the record. We may average one rainmaker every other class. Not nearly good enough. Look at George Steinbrenner. We need to jump into the market and hire some big hitters. Make a splash in *The American Advocate*."

I shook my head.

Millard glowered at me. "*A.A.*'s rankings rule. You're written off if you're not at the top. And thou knowest this, Mr. Lawrence."

"Are you telling us to turn ourselves inside out to look good in A.A.?"

"In a word, 'yes'. Everyone else does. We may have a chance to catch up. We still have a decent name. It might be good enough to attract some players."

But those players may destroy it, I thought. Millard wasn't finished. He smacked the table and exclaimed, "I've got it."

The room went silent.

"Tax shelters. Our new El Dorado."

None of us had a clue what he meant, but my fellow committee members nodded in solemn agreement. Oh boy.

43

SOMETHING'S SPOILING my managerial triumphs. Old Faithless has never acted this way. Generally positive and upbeat. Seldom moody. Last night he got me up three times and then staged an accident, forcing me to rummage around in the dark for a dry pair of knickers. We need to talk. He isn't shy about expressing himself. He loves puns, pranks, and quips. He's generally grateful. And why not? I've been more than a good provider. Sometimes I hear him purring in my pants.

Now he's Mister Grumpy. He's outraged by my current offerings, has expressed dissatisfaction with dear old Ruth, and is noncommittal about Lucy. He tells me in no uncertain terms, "You may be slowing down, but I'm not. You may need an occasional nap, but I don't. What if I live on after your death? What if I'm buried alive? Have you considered how I might alert those on the surface? Why are you putting me on reduced rations? Once a week. Sometimes every other week. Come on."

Old Faithless is no longer happy with his nickname. It was amusing 30 years ago. Now he's threatening a boxer rebellion. The 'Old' O.F. said, was drawing unwanted attention to his sparse, graying thatch. I saw no reason to tell him he'd needed implants and a dye job for years. A fresh start was called for. Being a Yankees fan, I was tempted by 'A-Rod', but settled on 'False Staff'.

Meanwhile, my dear goddaughter has tried to cheer up Daddy by going out with Quintus's persistent friend, Sam Morris. He makes even Arthur and Stanley look like possibilities. When I got wind of her doings, I told Cecilia I was taking her in hand. I hoped she wasn't becoming too attached to that boy—Sam has been out of his low-watt college for two years.

I called her at the museum. "Ceci, my dear, Sam's a loser. Not in your league. He might once have survived in a drowsy bank or hung on for a while peddling life insurance to clubmates, but he isn't nearly right for my goddaughter." A pause to let that sink in.

"His prospects are nil, and while he may seem flush now, his puny income stream won't float a dinghy in his 40s.

"Here's a proposition, Ceci. As you know, I'm not one to underrate myself, but I can say, in all modesty, I understand men. Women are challenging mysteries. As to them, I rely on Confucius who observed, 'Treat them in a friendly manner, and they become impertinent; keep them at a distance, and they take offense.' However, I can see through guys. I'm uniquely qualified to vet your prospects and hereby volunteer to be your gatekeeper."

"Like St. Peter?"

"Yes. And furthermore, stop wasting yourself as an unpaid assistant to some nobody curator in decorative arts. If you're going to stay at the Museum of Fine Arts, hold out for European paintings at the very least.

"Ceci dear, you can write your own ticket. You've got brains, charm, and only the most miniaturized chip on your shoulder. It's all yours as long as you don't allow anyone to clip your wings."

I could tell there was more. "Ceci, you're holding something back, aren't you?"

"Yes, Andrew. Quintus, as you call him, who's been sitting on his tail for a year, took the law boards and really screwed up. Just for laughs I did too, and guess what?"

"I don't have to. Are you going to tell him and Daddy?"

"Undecided."

"Don't tell me you're thinking of law school?"

"F-no. I've listened to you."

"Shall we work on this together?"

"I'd like that."

"My door's always open, Ceci. I was somewhat mixed up at your age. And remember this—I hear you even if nobody else does."

Ceci held her tongue, but I pictured those eyes saying, "Thank you, dear Andrew."

Ah yes, young women melt when the warm-hearted sage opens up to them in ways he never has to his other handmaidens. They think to themselves: *He has revealed his innermost secrets knowing they are safe in my enfolding heart. I am among the elect. Maybe he'll take me on as his summer intern. Such a darling cabin. Such a pretty lake.*

44

"THERE'S NO fucking way I'm subsidizing those…" That's exactly what Millard blurted out at a management committee meeting. I was ashamed for him. Then he regained his composure just before saying something terribly unkind about a majority of our partners. How could he have lost control and exposed himself so completely? I hadn't wanted to trap Millard or make him look bad. My idea was a natural. Something that could only improve morale and ultimately have a positive effect on our net income.

In my view, the firm's financial results for 1990 were unlikely to match those of the previous few years. The economy appeared to be weakening. There had been problems with real estate loans across the country. An informal survey of my partners indicated there wasn't much in the pipeline. On the corporate side, our sources told me they weren't seeing new term sheets. Even more ominous: the investment bankers were uncharacteristically quiet. They only called to remind us of their existence with tasteless jokes. The next few quarters looked grim. Millard didn't see it that way.

"Look," he said, "the '80s were great, and the '90s look to be better. Gimme a smile, Eliot."

"Yes, but what about 'Black Monday' and the S&L mess? What's to prevent reoccurrences?"

"Come on, Mister Half Empty, the first was a one-time fluke caused by program trading, and the S&Ls taught us a relatively inexpensive lesson. We learned how to rein in our banking brethren and forestall future bailouts."

I was still worried, so I decided it would be helpful to the firm if those on the management committee who were in level six or higher of our 10-tier compensation ladder agreed to take a voluntary one-step reduction in their 1990 compensation. This would benefit everyone below them, and be a nice signal from the most influential and highly-compensated partners. Partnerships work best when those at the top don't grab every nickel they might legitimately claim.

I had pre-cleared my plan with one of the older members of the management committee. He'd been supportive, and if I'd anticipated Millard's objection I would have spoken to him beforehand. As it was, Millard's eruption strengthened the resolve of the more self-seeking younger members who I knew would be opposed. I'd assumed they could be shamed into acceptance if we elders presented a united front.

My proposal was roundly defeated. Millard was irked, so much so the managing partner felt obliged to say he saw no reason for Millard to take a hit. With a straight face, he told us Millard was underpaid. "There is considerable support in this room for giving Andrew Millard more money," he said. Millard's smirk returned. I'll never forget his outburst. If I were more of a wit, I might have compared his inspirational utterance to those of Patrick Henry, Nathan Hale, and John Paul Jones.

If that weren't enough, I'm getting push-back on my bills. The days of the one sentence, one-number statements sent out by Mr. Clark are long gone.

Now we write essays and, worse, furnish our computer print-outs. It's not that I have anything to hide, but this practice makes me uncomfortable. It suggests a lack of trust. I suppose that's not unreasonable when we have inexperienced associates with hourly rates higher than Mr. Clark's in his final year. Itemizing disbursements is equally fraught. Why, the clients are asking, should they be stuck with so many meals, taxis, and over-market copying charges? And, by the way, what's included under: 'Miscellaneous'?

Millard guffaws. "You're an idiot to send your customers the raw data. Of course, they're going to howl. The clay requires careful shaping, firing, and polishing. Wise up, pal. You gotta camouflage those disbursements.

"And don't forget to edit your print-outs. If Jones claims he had a half hour conference with Smith on a given date, but Smith doesn't record it, your beady-eyed customers will naturally assume Jones is padding, not that Smith forgot their chat, which, if it actually occurred, was probably about sports or nookie."

If that weren't enough, I'm going through a rough patch. Yesterday, I awoke in a funk. Was she ever really mine? What about that damn skier (Millard refers to him as 'The Mogul of the moguls'), the guy Clare was 'getting over' when we met in Arizona?

45

WHAT FUN I'm having. It delights me to observe Eliot beginning to experience self-doubt. It must be anxious-making to realize you've stalled in your fifties and there's no place to turn.

Life is about numbers. At work, it's collections. To hell with the hours if you've got the dollars and are certain of hanging onto them. The managing partner can scream for more and, if I'm in the mood, I may oblige him. It doesn't matter a damn, because I don't bill my trust customers on an hourly basis. I take my cut and get exactly the same amount whatever I dictate to Ruth. In fact, I feel compelled to record at least 2,000 hours so I won't be seen as thumbing my nose at the system and those chumps chained to the time clock. Would it be seen as provocative, I wonder, if I reported exactly 2,000 billable hours for several years in a row?

Other numbers are becoming increasingly significant: pulse, blood pressure, HDL, and LDL. Like my Curtis numbers, these are outstanding. At least all but one of them. In fact, my doctor compliments me on my tiny prostate number. I only wish he could examine me in a more dignified, less intrusive fashion. How about a semi-colonoscopy? And what's this nonsense about staying flexible and hydrated? Am I supposed to spend my remaining days stretching and peeing?

Actually, I'm suspicious of my primary care guy. We're the same age, but I'm healthier. He has it in for me. At my last physical the gloomy Celt said, "Andrew, you're in pretty good working order, but you've reached the age where something can come out of left field and take you down." He yearns to outlive me, and I wonder whether he's taking action to bring that to pass. Is he prescribing the right stuff in correct quantities? Is he using the latest tests and procedures? If so, why haven't I gotten any of those new scans?

My grumbling bore fruit. Dr. Doom ordered up a full-body MRI. All I could think as I was slid into that constricted cylinder was, why in heaven's name did Prince Charles ever want to become a tampon?

Contrary to my initial pessimism about partnership, I am finding many intangible benefits accruing to me, the fastest-rising star at Curtis. These are entirely apart from my compensation. That crossed the half-million-dollar mark in 1992. The same year that Lucy and I took the plunge. Her daddy's no Edmunds so I settled for one of those barefoot in the grass, asthma-inducing cheapies. Very cute when you're 55. Are they legally binding, I wonder?

So it was I found myself at one with the mosquitos and ticks in the bosky gathering place of a Wampanoag sept whose lobbyists were, as Lucy and I mumbled our vows, hustling legislators to replace the sacred oaks with blackjack, craps, slots, and hookers. Despite this hallowed setting, Lucy was unmoved by the epithalamium I composed and recited. What can I expect from such a union but West Nile Virus or Lyme disease?

Lucy herself marks a significant break with my past. She is the first of my wives with earned income. I didn't miss Squire Edmunds, but it was faintly depressing to marry into a family which had never heard of a prenup.

Mother missed this one too, and I was unable to decipher the spidery writing on her sympathy card. Was she being ironic? Confused? I'll never know because she expired a month or two later with a lifetime attendance average of .250. What's more, I wasn't invited to her last two, neither of which featured Seton. Didn't even get advance notice. Not a problem. I can understand her wishing to minimize the time her intendeds had for backsliding.

It's all good, though. Alice's family is underwriting our two misfits, and I am obligated to pay her nothing. Lucy has nary a dependent and is ungenerous by nature, so combining our receipts from Curtis, we're able to squeeze by on a little under a million a year.

Ruth's a mess. After attending weddings two and three—she got tiddly at the Edmunds reception—Ruth opted out of number four. Nor did she provide her traditional, pre-nuptial sendoff.

When we returned from our honeymoon—Lucy was on the phone to Wall Street the whole time—I was greeted by a middle-aged personal assistant with lank, untinted hair.

I summoned her to my office. "What's become of the heels, the perfume, the inspiring skirts, and the uplifting lingerie? Why is your dear chest at half-mast? Why have you gone Amish on me, Ruthie?"

All I got was a sidelong glance as she padded away in her brown flats.

So what. I'm on the rise and, as a result of my elevated status, I occupy people's minds. They must consider my moods. Will I be sharp and testy or warm and folksy? Will it be hauteur or my winning common touch?

In short, people must listen to him, defer to him, and accommodate him. They must solicit his opinions and applaud them as inspired. They must assess his likely reaction before advancing views of their own. And scramble backwards if he frowns. They must avoid subjects known to upset him. They must provide the setting in which he can exercise his genius. He must be soothed and made to feel secure, serene, beloved, and respected. Yes, it's so natural to slip into the third person.

I have attained a god-like, if not yet mythic, status. Though I'm not yet rich, I'm on my way to becoming so, at least by Boston law firm standards. Unlike my lower-tier partners whose unchecked libidos bring fines and humiliation, I am immune, above the law. My collections have earned me countless harassment credits. They're like membership awards for big spenders. And what's this I hear about 'grooming'? I mastered the art long before it was formally catalogued.

I am inspired. "Why," I just asked myself, "shouldn't I be in charge of this lash-up?" Yes, we have a managing partner, had him forever, it seems. Simon is a sour fellow with close-set eyes and a pinched mouth. His natural expression is a scowl that compresses his smallish features most unbecomingly.

Simon's acidity is difficult to understand. Being only one generation removed from the bog, the spuds, and the grub hoe, he's gone further than most people of his background and ability. Simon's a natural Mr. Inside. He should focus on what he does best: applying the knout and cutting costs. His highest and best use is to be a model of relentless output. Sequester him in a glass-walled space where the world can watch him work. Push food under his door. Empty his bucket daily. Litigators must be isolated.

It won't be necessary to amend the Partnership Agreement, which speaks of the management committee electing the firm's managing partner(s). Love that '(s)'. Why have we always had just one, and such a one? Simon has done everything in his power, short of deifying himself, to extend his 12-year reign. He has stacked the management committee and, under the guise of stimulating free speech, has been inventive in stifling it. Makes sense to me.

Now is the hour. "There is a tide in the affairs of men…" I can pull together the necessary majority of the management committee with or without Eliot's help. My people are eager to talk me up. I will make it happen at the meeting two weeks hence. It will be teed up in advance. I will be begged to accept. I will feign surprise. I will pause. I will reflect. Finally, moved by the 'spontaneous' groundswell of support, I will accept.

Should I have a triumph? Celebratory games? A royal progress through my realm bestowing knighthoods and pardons? No, I will content myself with a proclamation telling my subjects I am honored and looking forward to a warmly collaborative relationship with Simon. Then I will write the creep out of the script before he does it to me.

However, there is, there always is, a fly in the petroleum jelly. Her name is Lucy. My beloved who insists her office be next to mine. Lucy, whose acute hearing has caused me to purchase a white noise machine to mask private conversations that are clearly audible through our building's cut-rate construction. Lucy, who, my agents inform me, has informers everywhere. She'd like to fit False Staff with a tracking device linked to a global positioning system. All we share are certain primitive needs which once included each other. At least there's always Jeannette. And, in a pinch, Ruth. Were it not for them, it might have been (actually it has been, but only infrequently) those massages with the happy endings.

But will Jeannette, Ruth, and a changing cast of understudies be enough? This is what can happen if you get lazy. We're all tempted by the low-hanging Lucys. She was only one floor away. Now I'm caught in a choke collar. No privacy. No maneuvering room.

Ah Lucy, what's curtailed our coupling? There's the rub—or the lack thereof. You wear green skin cream to bed. And ear plugs. And a mask. You could be the ghastly byproduct of a one night stand between The Lone Ranger and a mud-caked inhabitant of New Guinea. Your hair, lashed tightly to your skull, is off limits. So are all my favorite haunts. Maybe I can touch your shins. You are tense. Stringy. Thinking about what you'll wear at next weekend's benefit for Weston's homeless.

While I'm moaning low about Lucy, there's something else. Ruth's presented me with an ultimatum. My initial reaction: that's lèse majesté. Then: what spirit, shades of my young sweetie. Finally, she wouldn't dare. Last week I found this letter on my desk.

> *My Love:*   *November 13, 1992*
>
> *Please take a moment to read this. It's Friday the thirteenth, and I'm awfully blue.*
>
> *Do I sense that what we had between us has almost died? How can it be? Don't you remember kissing my hands when I was going on about how blotchy they'd become? That was only a couple of months ago.*
>
> *No, I'm not as pretty as I was (at least you used to say I was pretty).* You're right about something else. I have become more inhibited. So would you if you had my body. I'm getting too old to play the slut.*
>
> *I still think I could make—or should I say 'could have made'— you happy. Maybe I'm the only one who can. None of your other women have. Have you ever told anyone else about Edward, 'Mother', and your bad dreams? You deserve to be happy. So do I. Everybody does. You could love me if you wanted to. You've been with me longer than anyone else. Don't our years together count for anything?*
>
> *I know you better than you think and maybe better than*

anyone else. Despite your wit and charm, you've never been happy. I could change that. I've thought so ever since you rescued me from that creep, 'Attorney Thomas'. You did something wonderful for me, and I have never stopped being grateful to you. And loving you.

You've got to know by now I'm not a gold digger. I have no dependents, and I've saved enough money to take care of myself and leave a little something to my sister's kids. In fact, I'm rather proud of being financially independent, which is more than some of your partners can say. You know I'm not a social climber. It would be too high a climb. I'd need oxygen.

I can hear you saying, "Get to the point, old girl." So here it is. I cannot continue as we are. It's too painful. I'm becoming less attractive. You're becoming more. I hope I'm wrong, but I sense you'd like me to disappear. If not, say so. NOTHING would make me happier. I'll stay with you forever, but only as your wife. Otherwise, I'm going to accept the offer I've gotten from Baker & Richards, and you'll see no more of me. What's more, I promise not to cause a fuss on my way out the door.

Your Ruthie

* *See, I've even picked up your use of parenthetical phrases, and I'm violating your rule about putting things like this in writing.*

What to do? Not being someone who yields to pressure, I did nothing. I waited. On Monday, November 16, Ruth began work at Baker & Richards. I was stunned, but told myself, "Relax. Don't panic. Don't beg. Give yourself a couple weeks. Enjoy the holidays and bring her back in January on your own terms if that's what you want. Nobody leaves you."

It was exactly what I wanted. I was confident of success, but, just like that, Ruth was gone. Really gone. She'd taken her niece to London and, like so many jet-lagged Americans, looked the wrong way as she stepped into an intersection. She was killed instantly. By a Jag, as a matter of fact. It happened the week before Christmas. No warning. Suicide?

Maybe not. She'd been carrying Christmas presents.

She wouldn't do that to her niece. Then again, the niece was a no-nonsense emergency room nurse. She'd be able to cope.

What about those nuns? They must have drummed it into Ruth's head that suicide isn't an option.

Had one of the presents been for me?

Now there's another empty space in the foreground of the canvas. Next to the void Clare and Malcolm once occupied. Malcolm's ashes are on my desk. They will accompany me to the hereafter. My Clare's gone too.

Other ugly thoughts. Could this incident reflect badly on me? Might Ruth's letter have found its way to her nephew, the Boston flatfoot? Can I get something on him? He must have a few skeletons in the trunk of his Caddy, which he can't possibly afford on his cop's salary.

I never made any promises. She made too much of my little gifts. I suppose I could have given her more of my time, but she was aware of my growing practice and new administrative duties. Admittedly, I said nothing about calling it quits. I probably should not have used that business about being 'confused' and needing 'a little space', and maybe I shouldn't have referred to my intermittent escapades as 'cries for help', although that line's worked before.

Should I have helped her financially? Negative. She was paid a competitive salary. Ruth was frugal, had few needs, and managed to put away much of what she earned. Better than me in that respect. She was well-off, or at least well enough off. Throwing money at the situation would have created a bad precedent and caused problems for my colleagues. Ruth seemed to be approaching middle age with equanimity and a seemly resignation.

Besides, Ruth had her consolations: a mixed-breed dog and her sister's kids. She had fading photos of two freckled oafs (Or is it oaves?) pinned to the corkboard at her workstation. The only snapshot I ever identified was the one of her nephew, the cop. He's a large brute.

I missed Ruth's funeral. However, I sent an attractive assortment of cut flowers and made sure to include a card which I signed,

"Sincerely, A. Millard." No point in being sappy. I've got nothing to be ashamed of. One of our city's most celebrated thugs got it right: "I can't change nuthin' so why should I beat myself up ovah it?"

I had other reasons for staying away. Remembering my mawkish reaction at Clare's service, I didn't wish an embarrassing repetition. Certain hymns upset me. I snuffled at Mother's ill-attended funeral, not because I missed her, but because I didn't.

46

I WENT to Ruth's wake and funeral. What a tragic business. I was nearly overcome with yearning. It's so unpredictable, triggered by almost anything. It comes at me in waves. I'm alternately breathless, sleepless, and restless. Sometimes there's a dull ache, sometimes a sharp one. I engage in meaningless tasks like shining my shoes. I've taken up cooking. Yesterday I baked a cake. Really. Eating it was like being trapped in a dust storm. I am unable to focus and find myself experiencing many of the symptoms I had when obsessing over the relatively inconsequential matter of partnership. People assume I'm fine by now. I'm not. Is this like combat? Something that can only be discussed with those who've been through it?

Millard was a no-show. Speaking of Millard, I just heard the darndest thing. He had some kind of accident right after Ruth's passing. Nobody's seen him for a week or so. I checked it out with Eileen, our all-knowing receptionist. She told me Millard appeared in the office at the unmillardish hour of 8:00 a.m. last Monday. He was sporting a shiner and a split lip. Eileen couldn't tell whether he'd also lost a tooth.

Eileen said she stared at Millard and he muttered about running into a door. Knowing Eileen, she probably said something fresh like, "That must have been a really pissed-off door." Millard never even took off his overcoat. He just picked up some papers and disappeared, telling Eileen he'd be working at home for a while.

Now Millard's back, but he's keeping mum.

47

I WAS fucking bushwhacked last week. Sucker punched by a low-life. After leaving the office, I was approached by a troll in a scally cap and a Pats windbreaker. What was a slug like that doing in the financial district at night? Why was he walking toward me so purposefully? Where were his manners? It must have been a case of mistaken identity or a supremely aggressive panhandler. I assumed I'd have to buy him off. He stopped in front of me as I was reaching for my wallet.

"Andrew Mehlaad?" he asked.

I liked neither his pronunciation nor his tone of voice and replied, "It's Mi-llărd. And what exactly can I do for you?"

I was taken aback when he replied, "You already done it, shit-head."

Then, without warning or provocation, the ape assaulted me. Despite a heroic defense, I found myself on the sidewalk bleeding all over one of my newest suits and manipulating a loose front tooth. And yes, I was in considerable pain. My assailant seemed in no rush to depart.

"Don't be thinking you've seen the last of me, scumbag." With that, he and his porcine mug vanished into the night.

I'd guessed right. He was an older version of the grinning lunk in the photo on Ruth's desk. The funny thing is—if he hadn't just kicked the crap out of me, I'd have told him I missed Ruthie as much as he did.

What am I supposed to do now? Prosecute a Boston cop? Sure. Where do you find protection when your protectors are rotten? I want to kill the bastard, but I'm not a violent person, and I'm not sure how you find someone else to do it.

I ached for several days. Nobody's walloped me with such gusto since Mother. I can't have been more than six, maybe seven. Father was in England holding back the Hun. I was home defending the hearth. Mother was taking a shower. Probably getting ready for a date, and I suppose I was curious. So I pulled open the curtain and took a gander. Don't remember much after that except I wound up on the john floor with ringing ears. No biggie. Everyone's entitled to privacy, but something's always baffled me; it's not as though I saw anything that a lot of guys hadn't seen already.

Another result of that run-in with the fuzz: my damned nightmares flooded back. Having to piss in the night makes this especially unpleasant since I now get to experience them more than once.

One of them goes like this.

She smiles. I do too. I'll have her phone number, presumably the 212 area code, before the seat belt sign's off. She is so deliciously unwrappable in her heels, her blonde French twisted hair and her crisp, sky-blue Pan Am uniform which complements her azure eyes. Oh for that golden age when no stews needed liposuction.

We're pushing back from the stand when, without a word from me, she's pouring a refill.

"There's more where that came from, Mr. Millard."

"Call me Andy, Clipper Maid." This will be the flight on which I'm inducted into the 30,000-foot club.

Less than 20 minutes late for takeoff. Not bad for Heathrow. Clipper Maid has taken the empty seat beside me. Like a tray table at takeoff, False Staff's in the 'full upright and locked position'. Maybe we won't have to contort ourselves in a tiny loo. I'm not so limber any more.

Our Chuck Yeager wannabe comes up on the p.a. system to announce we've reached 31,000 feet, our 'crewzin attitude'. Clipper Maid's in the aisle holding up a bottle of burgundy for my approval. Accompaniment for the discouraged roast beef and Yorkshire pudding she's nuked and set before me. The neeps look revolting and taste worse.

The explosion comes as an ugly surprise, always in the middle of a mouthful. Several unpleasant things occur simultaneously. Shock waves, darkness, decompression, a calamitous drop in temperature, and tornado-like winds accompanied by hideous tearing sounds.

Clipper Maid levitates towards me from the galley. I reach for her, but she ricochets off a seat and disappears. Though I'm still strapped in, I turn and look. There's nothing behind me but a few rows of seats and the black December sky.

As a child, I was addicted to Saturday afternoon double features. Now I have a second aviation drama to roil my sleep. It plays opposite my old standby, *P-47 Down*.

I pass out. Falling through warmer, more oxygen-rich air, I revive. As do many of my unfortunate companions, one of whom is mumbling to her crucifix. Our little capsule's in a vertical dive. I'm howling. For what? I don't know, but not for Mother. Worse, I'm covered with turnips and gravy. Does my life flash before me? Negative.

I've disgraced myself in the same way I did as a fourth former.

Somehow I realize the journey from detonation to Lockerbie is going to take a while and I'm about to experience every bloody (poor choice of words) second.

Then I hear two familiar voices across the aisle. Eliot says, "Don't worry, Sweetie," and Clare replies, "I'm not, Darling; we're together."

48

SOMETIMES EVENTS move with great rapidity, even at C&P. Big news. Millard has been elected co-managing partner. It happened at last week's management committee meeting. I was caught off guard. Millard isn't right for the job, but how to react? I couldn't object. He's regarded as my best friend. More important, I could count. Millard had the votes. And to think Simon once had the committee under his thumb. If Millard wanted the position, it was his even if Simon and I voted 'no'.

A Millard lackey gave an unconvincing speech about how stressful the managing partner's job had become and "how burdensome it is for one person, particularly someone with as lucrative a practice as Simon's". Another puppet noted "the desirability of having two people with complementary abilities. Simon's gift with numbers and his understanding of our nuts and bolts will be balanced by Millard's people skills, his connections, and his smooth, extroverted nature. We can't help but be a stronger, more vibrant firm."

I sat back and took it all in. What a crock. I wanted to applaud and call for encores. Simon, whom I've never considered a particular friend or ally, looked at me and shrugged. Since it was a done deal, I decided it would be better for the firm if the decision were unanimous. Millard excused himself and left the room. There was no discussion. A vote was taken. Unanimous. I was detailed to find him and bring him back. He hadn't gone far.

Maybe I'm the one off-base. Have I misjudged the temper of the times and lost the ability to be of use to my firm? In any case, I hope C&P flourishes because it's becoming more and more important to me. I had another big loss recently. Grammy just died. Papa had preceded her by four years. It feels so empty with both of my parents gone. I have stepped into eternity's on-deck circle.

Now it's 1993; Eliot and Ceci are both out of the nest. I haven't seen much of them since Jeannette and I got married. Maybe it's understandable. They miss their mother. And now their last grandparent's dead. They may think Jeannette's trying to take over, even though I keep telling them nobody can replace their mother. There's also the difficulty about their closeness in age. Jeannette, who is only nine years older than Eliot, may seem like a rival. There's a lot of resentment in the air. Jeannette's furious about never getting anniversary cards, while the kids grumble about her ignoring their birthdays.

Am I stating the obvious when I suggest that Jeannette is not trying to supplant my children's dear mother? In reality, Jeannette's not a bit maternal. There is no talk about our trying again after her miscarriage. She laughed when I raised the subject of adoption. Jeannette doesn't want a pet, not even a cat. I'm sure things will get worked out between Jeannette and the children, but you can't expect it to happen overnight.

I'd be more optimistic about relationships among Jeannette and my kids if I didn't sense a cooling of Jeannette's affection towards me. Jeannette and I have been together for seven years now, and my children are beginning to ask me rather pointed questions. "When did you two stop vacationing together? What's become of your old friends?" A few weeks ago, young Eliot offered to "relieve" me of my seldom-used symphony tickets.

I'm probably exaggerating, but it seems as if Jeannette and I are seeing less and less of each other. The persistent divorcée, who bothered me at Clare's service and may be starting Alzheimer's, invariably asks, "Are you really happy, Eliot? Are you really getting what you need?"

"Who does?" I'm tempted to respond.

Often Jeannette's got some evening activity that brings her home late or causes her to sleep over at a friend's place. I've got to be in bed by 10 at the latest to be worth a darn at the office.

Jeannette's done some expensive remodeling and built a suite with a private entrance in the back of our house. It has a nice view of our garden and the Charles. She grabbed what used to be the servants' quarters and knocked out enough walls, partitions, and other structural elements to make me wonder whether 118 would collapse. And why does she need a king-size bed to which I (the ostensible king) am never invited? Didn't something like this happen between Millard and Maud?

As it happens, Jeannette and I seldom share the same bedroom. Once again, I'm sleeping alone in my old place. Clare's side of our bed awaits her return.

Despite her expensive remodeling, Jeannette dislikes 118 Beacon Street. She says it's a dump and wants us (or maybe just her?) to move into one of those expensive condos at the Four Seasons. I don't give a hoot about a concierge, and I don't want to enter my home in an elevator. In the meantime, poor old 118 has taken a beating. Jeannette's punched through the walls and put in huge, ostentatious picture windows. We live in a fish bowl where the fish are eating one another. Even worse, she's tried, unsuccessfully I might add, to eradicate all traces of Clare.

There's more. When we're together, Jeannette and I have less and less to talk about. This never happened with Clare. Our infrequent conversations are combative. If I say 'up', Jeannette says 'down', and so it goes. Everyone notices. We're receiving fewer dinner invitations.

I should stop complaining, but before I do, I must confess to missing, among other things, the everyday intimacies Clare and I shared. We had pet names for each other. Names that changed over time. We touched each other a lot. This isn't happening with Jeannette. Endearments? When she's feeling affectionate, I'm 'El', the name New Yorkers had for their elevated railway. It could be worse. Maybe she'll include my middle initial and start calling me 'Eel'. I hate returning to a dark house and an empty refrigerator.

Then there's this dream. When Clare was alive I had a recurrent nightmare. I was married to someone else. I'd lost contact with Clare. I didn't know where she lived and had no phone number. I worried that as time passed she'd forget me and be snapped up by another guy. That I'd spend the rest of my life with this stranger in bed with me. At last I'd wake up, and Clare would be next to me, just where she was supposed to be. I still have that dream, but now it's all too real.

Jeannette and I need to *talk*, something I dread and avoid. So, it turns out, does she.

Over decaf (Jeannette was having a brandy) following another expensive dinner at the Ritz, I said, "Jeannette, shouldn't we think about counseling?"

"About what?"

"About us."

"Well, what about us? We're no worse than most couples." Jeannette signaled for a second Hennessy.

"We don't see each other much, and we're not getting on."

"And whose fault is that? You're always working late or away on one of your deals. How about changing your habits?"

"I can't, Jeannette. Institutional clients insist their attorneys are always available. Besides, I'm our primary bread winner."

"Yeah, but it's Wonder Bread."

"What do you mean by that?"

"You know damn well what I mean. I'm getting that managing directorship and everything that goes with it. What you're providing may have been sufficient for the incomparable Clare. Not for me. You can't even afford the Hummels I've been asking for."

"Jeannette, I'm doing just fine at Curtis and Perkins."

"OK. Not terrible, but not great either. I've heard you're not keeping up. Your collections are flattening which means, in a rising tide, you're sinking. You're not bringing home much bacon, and we're living kinda low on the hog. You'll never make really big bucks at that place."

Jeannette had almost drained her brandy. I called for the check before she could order a third. I'll try the counseling idea again, but where's she getting that information about me and the firm?

I almost forgot. Splendid news. As I'd hoped, Ceci announced her engagement to Sam Morris, a wonderful boy whom I've known since he and Eliot went to Dexter. Too bad he never made it to Harvard, but Millard didn't either and look at him. Sam's going places.

Why, I keep asking myself, won't young (actually, not so young) Eliot get moving on the matrimonial front? If he waits too long, he'll never find a girl of child-bearing age, and I won't have another Eliot Lawrence with whom to play catch. I suppose I shouldn't complain. Even though he didn't go to my law school, he's doing nicely at Baker & Richards, the firm where Ruth Donohue was working when she died. Despite Ceci's snarking about favoritism, I'm delighted to have helped him get that job.

With all the disappointments in my private life, it's lucky my practice continues to be so rewarding. It's not easy though, and sometimes I get concerned about my partners and the direction we're headed. Given the constant emphasis on collections, I'm sure that some of them would provide whatever legal opinion it took to close a deal and collect their fee. It's not just personal liability that scares me. If the firm is disgraced, my clients will have no choice but to take their business elsewhere, whatever they may think of me. That's what horrifies me about tax shelter work.

I should drop this subject. Stop flogging myself. But sometimes I feel as though I'm barely hanging on. Corporations are keeping so much business that used to go to places like C&P, and they're sending their routine work, like bank loans, to smaller firms with more reasonable rates, lower overheads, and, it must be said, lesser lawyers.

Thankfully, my stock in trade is a combination of public offerings, which require a precise knowledge of federal and state securities laws, and complex, heavily negotiated transactions with institutional investors. Ferraris, not Fords. Nothing's certain, however. Prospectuses are becoming little more than cover sheets to annual reports, and standardized forms are seeping into my private deals. As Millard says, "Despite your pitiful attempts to curry favor, your work's bound for Mumbai."

49

BOO HOO, Eliot. The times they be changing. Mergers, acquisitions, a faster pace, and the grim reaper dissolve relationships which, in Ez Clark's day, were damn near eternal. As for my competition, I underprice the investment company MBAs and out-perform the trust company dolts. I'm golden for a couple more decades and, after that, "Hasta la vista, baby!"

Yes, it's true. In May of 1993, Ceci got engaged to Samuel Perry Morris. What in God's name will they talk about? She must think Eliot needs cheering up. When I heard of this disaster, I summoned her to lunch at my eating club. The club where her deadly engagement party took place and her reception will inevitably be held.

"My darling girl, I know you're trying to please your father, whose Mama just died and whose marriage is in the crapper, but please stop short-changing yourself."

Then I treated her to some of William Blake's 'indulge yourself' aphorisms.

"Sam," I said, "will always be inadequate in certain vital respects, but all is not necessarily lost if you act with dispatch.

"With a little coaching, dear Ceci, I could help you help that dunce achieve his limited upside." She kept wringing her hands, shook her head, and changed the subject, but not, it seemed to me, with the same solemn finality as her mother.

"Promise me this, at least. Make it a long engagement. Give everyone a good look at your intended.

"I can't bear the idea of you getting trapped and submerged like your mom."

That produced a sharp look, but I continued, "At least you're out of decorative arts. Not that private banking's a big step up. It could be a ticket to b-school, but till then you've got to kiss up to money—new and old."

She grimaced. I pressed on, "You need someone of consequence to recognize and appreciate you for what you are. I'm being serious for a moment. Sam's not the one.

"One more observation before I sign off."

"Yes?"

"You can't be expected to realize it now, Ceci, but the people one's grown up with all tend to look OK, at least through college. Then the brutal weeding-out begins.

"In a decade Sam'll be passed over and bitter, clinging to a few items of inherited furniture while infecting those around him. And there's nothing you can do to help him. He's limited. Though it always comes as a shock to them, the Sammies of this world haven't gotten free rides since the Depression.

"Chaff like him just blows away." For emphasis, I blew across my open hand.

Time to lighten up.

No discussion of the '90s can omit at least a passing reference to the repeal of the dress code. But first a medical update. The wounds incurred in my battle with the cop have healed beautifully. Plus, my tooth stayed put and didn't turn gray.

The collapse of sartorial standards began with casual Fridays as an effort to loosen up the workplace. It turned out to be the camel's nose under the tent. Casual Friday was, in short order, succeeded by year-round dishabille. A pitiful effort by the corporate lawyers to look more like (and bond with) their out-of-it, high-tech geek customers. Alarmingly, this wretched look has survived the demise of the dot-coms that spawned it.

Eliot never noticed. He hasn't changed his appearance in any respect, though he's got the money to do so. He looks as he did when he got out of Harvard, and he's continued to buy his clothes off the rack at the clubby Cambridge store he patronized as an undergraduate. But being Eliot, he only shows up for its semi-annual sales.

Which reminds me. Not long ago, Eliot appeared on a Monday morning in a new suit. For once, my pal looked crisp. It wasn't quite

Wall Street; brown just isn't. His belt looked like something salvaged from a tack room, but his trousers had a sharp crease and the jacket hung nicely. He wore this ensemble for the entire week, then two more. As it was starting its fourth, it clung to his frame like a second skin, and there at the base of the fly was an unmistakable yellow semi-circle.

This must be avoided. Even in Boston, where the Brahmins and the Untouchables are sometimes indistinguishable. Sadly, Eliot's slipping. Clare would never have let him leave the house looking like a rag picker. This could not be allowed to continue. Approaching Eliot as he exited the john, I stopped, caught his eye, stared at his golden crescent and inquired, "Ever hear of dry cleaners, Beau?"

Another '90s issue is growth. Starting in the late 1980s, our consultants warned us of the dangers confronting mid-sized firms trying to maintain a general practice and be all things to all people.

Not to worry, docile shipmates, Admiral Millard has the con. Simon grumbles occasionally, but basically, he's content to cede command to me and beaver away on his briefs in a forsaken corner of our library. Despite Eliot's pitiful muttering, we are implementing my Operation Instant Earnings. I dig up laterals like truffles, sniff them, and hire them. I'm quite proud of our latest, whom I've installed as the head of our environmental practice. He may be a crock, but he's our crock, as are his three million in collections. Just you wait, Eliot. There's more to come.

As for me, I'm sitting pretty. My practice is highly portable. Better yet, I'm doing the work of a trust officer but making at least five times as much. It would be exaggerating to say I keep bankers' hours. I think of myself as a lily. I toil not neither do I spin, yet even Ez Clark in all his glory was not arrayed like me.

Meanwhile, Eliot continues to catch all the breaks. Beginning in grade school, he's been coddled by a host of mentors, counselors, and cheerleaders. When Eliot's seniors at Curtis died off, they were replaced by a horde of eager young boot-lickers, jostling for precedence and the first crack at his solid—though declining—practice. To this day, they keep him out of trouble, guffaw on cue at his pitiful jokes, and struggle to give him the impression he hasn't lost a step.

Even more annoying is the nagging suspicion there are some who think I owe a lot to Eliot. What's he been saying?

I should strike the preceding paragraph. Yes, Eliot's caught more than his share of breaks, but then he hooked, boated, and ingested the mercury-laden Jeannette.

As she confided to me recently, "I just lifted my latest beaver embargo. No nookie until Mr. Horny stopped being such a tightwad.

"It took me a month of 'you don't love me's', several sentences (to be served consecutively) to the guest room, and, I am certain, more than a handful of single-handed hand jobs before El surrendered his gold card and was suitably rewarded."

50

OH, WELL, perhaps Jeannette will allow me to get a housebroken puppy or, if not, a grown dog. I grew up with dogs, but I haven't had a pet since Sandra died and Spooky ran away. Millard's always had a terrier. There are such responsible dog-walking services these days. My pooch wouldn't be a burden to either of us, and I'd be happy to look after it when I got home. What's the most affectionate breed? I need affection. If I get one, I plan to name it 'Magnifidog'. Why should cats get all the credit?

I'm told Jack Russells are the way to go if you want a relationship and are willing to put something into it. Jeannette's response to my musings about a Jack was, "You get one of those yappy things and I'll make your life miserable." I can be somewhat dense at times, but a light went on when Jeannette said that. If I recalled correctly, it was the very expression Millard said was used by his anonymous 'hottie' who was supposedly *not* Jeannette.

To make matters worse, I've just been burned by Millard's newest lateral.

It began with a call from Ernie, the general counsel of a New York Stock Exchange company headquartered outside Boston. For years, he's been a reliable source of transactions. Not that many and not that big, but still a valued client with a promising upside. And he's never made me put on one of those stressful beauty contests.

His call was about a potentially huge environmental matter, one for which I could justifiably claim credit. A nice windfall.

As it happened, I was on vacation (an unhappy week in London with Jeannette, who must have spent at least $10,000 on herself, one of those 'make-things-better' trips that never do) when Ernie phoned. The floater sitting in for my secretary didn't try to contact me. Instead, thinking she was being resourceful, she directed the call to J, our senior environmental lawyer, someone Millard brought in because we were thin in that expanding practice area.

By the time of Ernie's call, most of us realized J was a mistake. It happens a lot with laterals. Unless some of your most trustworthy partners can personally vouch for the fellow, it's a crap shoot. Not only was J boastful, but he was likely to cost us a bundle because he was devious and dim. As the rating agencies would say, he was 'below investment grade'.

I almost forgot the outrageous amounts he charged us for what he claimed was marketing. In fact, we were underwriting his adulteries with M (the associate he brought with him). Our bookkeepers caught on to him quickly, but the clown was without shame. The next month he'd be at it again. Naturally enough, his claim of three million in collections was, like everything else about him, vastly inflated.

J showed his colors when we interviewed him in a management committee meeting. It became terribly awkward when Ted, irked with J's endless self-promotion, interrupted him with, "What were your grades?" This was after Ted asked him how he'd done at law school and J replied, "Beautifully."

That's not a question I'd have asked someone who'd earned his spurs. I'd been prepared to cut J some slack until he answered, "I don't remember." So much for him. You're as likely to forget your grades as your service number if you've been in the military. Not missing a beat, J assured us that, in short order, he'd be "occupying a leadership position at Curtis and Perkins". We hired this lunk over my strenuous objections. Ted abstained, but Millard and his lap dogs had their way.

Regarding himself as the consummate rainmaker, J made a date with Ernie for the next day. Since nobody was his equal, and so he wouldn't have to share credit with others, J went alone. Hours later, Ernie tracked me down in London. It was an Ernie I'd never heard before, "Nothing, absolutely nothing, would induce me to hire your firm, not if it were the only one in Boston."

"Ernie, what are you talking about? I'm afraid I've just woken up."

"The environmental matter I called about. What do you think I'm talking about… and how could you send me that buffoon? You make me doubt you, Eliot."

A close call. Luckily, I was able to straighten things out. We lost what would have been a high-profile matter, but I was able to preserve the relationship (barely) and the deals resumed. However, J cost us. Another Boston firm got Ernie's environmental business and competes against me for other work.

On a hunch, I had our investigative services guy do a little spadework on J, something Millard hadn't bothered doing. And guess what? He discovered a sexual harassment case and some unsavory financial information. It was hearsay but entirely consistent with what I'd observed. I got this intel to the management committee. J read the tea leaves correctly. He hornswoggled another firm into hiring him and fled with his camp follower.

At subsequent management committee meetings, I reminded Millard of the arcane concept of due diligence. It feels good to be vindicated. And win one for a change. Millard and I have our differences over firm business, but our personal relationship remains solid, I believe.

51

BECAUSE THERE'S no one but me with any flair, I've taken it upon myself to orchestrate the firm's 100th anniversary celebration. After consultation with my traveling companion, Ms. Gorse, I've jazzed up our tatty marketing brochures by adding photographs of the department heads, full page in my case. Given the Latinate nature of our profession, I'm thinking '*Primus Inter Pares*' would go nicely beneath my portrait.

Then there's Eliot. Our boy stood up at a partners' meeting and trashed my hiring program. I graciously admitted that Jack may not have panned out, but my colleagues understand that certainty about laterals is elusive. Candor is rare in this sphere, and recommendations are utterly unreliable. No firm wants to admit it lost a star, sheltered a shitbird, or worse, got sued for coming clean. So they lie. Or clam up. Who wouldn't?

Next, he delivered one of his tiresome fatwas against the marketing program I had personally devised for our centennial. "Undignified and untruthful," thundered the Old Testament Eliot. Curtis remains a polite firm, and Eliot is still accorded a degree of deference, so nobody shouted him down. I was tempted to cry out, "Get a grip, Eliot. Get laid. Take some valium. Have a drink." But why be provocative? People were snickering. No worries about him unseating me. Eliot is self-destructing on his own.

He's steamed up because I've beaten him to the punch and have actually made something of our 100th. It's more than he can stand, and he's particularly overwrought about our new stationery and one of my favorite bits of flummery. It reads as follows, "Curtis and Perkins has maintained its position as one of the country's leading law firms for over 100 years." If candor's required, we can go with, "A century of mediocrity at premium prices." Taking it all into account, I have a new lease on life. Strike that—I have full fee simple ownership.

While reasonable minds can differ about the benefits of various management techniques, there can be no argument about the delight and efficacy of inflicting yuletide terror. I am the perfect Father Christmas, and Simon is a willing Grinch. The first three weeks of December are a time of dread. We are awash in cash and anxiety. It's not unusual for December to account for 20% of our annual revenue and a considerably larger percentage of our nervous breakdowns. December is compensation time. The time we punish the malcontents and remember the greediest.

I am reminded of the poster I liberated from the recruiting office so many years ago. It features a D.I. roaring, "The beatings will continue until morale improves."

Our all-hands Holiday Party takes place early in the month. Wearing my traditional Santa tie, I flit from group to group dispensing good cheer and inviting the doffing of cloth caps. A touch of Andy in the night, not that anyone would dare call me Andy.

Even more jolly are the one-on-one compensation interviews where everyone is given the chance to grovel and plead his case. I think of them as show trials. Who will crack and turn on his fellows claiming credit for dollars in someone else's column? Who will whimper and beg me to forgive a sorry twelve months by sniveling about deaths, illnesses, and other irrelevancies? Who will hand in a written apologia? Who cares? I made the compensation decisions back in October when I took my first look at the September 30 numbers.

Most of my colleagues would avert their eyes should I initiate a dalliance with their unappetizing wives. I would do likewise in their circumstances. What's wrong with being a toady? You may get kissed by a princess.

Perhaps I'll order my favorite lickspittle to rename his money-pit sailboat the *Yes, Andrew*. Each time he bends his knee, he can think of it as another few dollars towards a new jib. How I treasure my blandishers and praise-singers. Despite their preening and posturing, when, as one might say in Russia, pushkin comes to shovekin, most of my partners are lie-down guys.

Once again, I have strayed. Let me describe our traditional Holiday lunch. Stop! I've had it with political correctness. Strike 'Holiday', and insert 'Christmas'.

Depending on your compensation message, you will either gobble up clams, shrimp, and oysters—while radiating good cheer, or, being aggrieved, you will absent yourself and hope your sulk causes anxiety among the higher-ups. I wax rhapsodic at the Christmas lunch, gliding gracefully around the room pulling people together, enveloping them in me, sharing myself with them. After the entrée, I strike an empty glass. Instant silence. I direct Simon to speak first. Five minutes of banalities. Excruciating.

Then me. I unleash my charm. I declare how much this party means to me personally, how it's my 'favorite event of the year'. I pause to allow this absurdity to sink in. My pace and timing are riveting. My smile is dazzling in the dark-paneled room. "Yes, I am honored and humbled to be the managing partner of a venerable firm composed of such able (mediocre), interesting (tedious), and high-minded (money-grubbing) men and women." Scattered applause. Several "hear, hears"! I emote about the importance of preserving our firm culture. What a hoot. We have the culture of the Donner party.

A swallow of passable burgundy. We must do better. I flow on seamlessly. Each mot is bonner than the last. First, a moment of silence in memory of the year's fallen. Then the obligatory tipping of my hat to the surviving geriatrics on whose once-sturdy shoulders this strong (rickety) edifice was built. And there they are with their implanted electronics—rheumy, tipsy, aromatic, and unkempt—gathered at the table nearest the john. Their centerpiece should be an air freshener. You can spot them by their rumpled suits, stained ties, ill-cropped hair, and large-lensed, out-of-fashion aviator glasses. Could we seat them in an adjacent room? An adjacent firm? A rendering plant? I see them gazing about, helping each other identify the newer partners and repeating what was just said for the benefit of their impaired pals. I declare my respect and affection for these decrepits. Perhaps I can cut pension costs by eliminating their free flu shots. Hold that thought.

So, while I'm chipping away at the expenses and pumping up the bottom line, what about this? Strip the geezers of their offices (I'd already gotten them doubled-up) and entomb the lot of them in a cozy, asbestos-filled interior space equipped with toddler's furniture acquired on the cheap from redundant elementary schools. Throw in a sand box, colorful digging tools, and washable, large-print pleadings. Hire a strict au pair to break up their quarrels and make sure they don't pee-pee in the sand.

God, what a bore. Next year I'm spicing things up with my presentation of the 'Time's Wingèd Chariot Padded Hours Award' to that partner with the highest, least plausible total. My first winner will be the dude who sticks customers with the time he spends watching porn on his office computer. Should I rethink my decision not to have one of those devices mar the perfection of my room?

Eliot, meanwhile, has become so 'yesterday', so marginalized, so negative. And it isn't over compensation, usually the main cause of friction. Eliot's is still just fine. While I earned significantly more, Eliot took home 700,000 smackers for 1998—though he won't do so much longer if I have my way. Pitiful, past-tense Eliot. He's Galahad. I'm 'Galahave'.

52

MILLARD'S BEING too quiet. He's up to something. So I called Buzz Townsend, a pal at another shop.

Buzz is a rarity: a tax lawyer who actually communicates and doesn't just recite from the Code.

In answer to my question about tax shelter work, Buzz replied, "Steer clear; it's a plague. That is all you need to know."

I wish Buzz were here. The two of us might be able to derail this beast. "I need some ammo, Buzz. One of our guys is dragging us into this."

"Millard?"

"Yup."

"First of all, know this: it's damn lucrative."

"I figured."

"OK. Here's the deal. A bunch of the accounting firms are peddling this junk to guys who've just made a killing and want to screw Uncle. Here's their pitch: 'Our Innovative Products Group has devised a number of foolproof strategies to reduce your tax exposure. Interested?' You can imagine the response."

"And then?"

"I'll spare you the gory details, but the keys to outfoxing the IRS are complexity and misdirection."

"Some specifics, please."

"OK, it's alchemy. The promoters create a couple reputable-sounding partnerships using untainted names like, say, 'fidelity'. The partnerships are merely facades, think sets in a low-budget Western. They exist solely to engage in sham transactions designed to generate paper losses, and before you can cry 'fraud', capital gains have vanished and, if you're double-dipping, so has ordinary income. Nifty, right?"

"But none of this works if there's no business purpose."

"Indeed. But the promoters have this covered, or so they claim."

"Is this tax planning or tax fraud?"

"Unquestionably the latter. And it all comes unglued if the IRS picks it up on audit. It's essential to bury the bodies deep in the schedules to the return."

"What's our role?"

"I was afraid you'd never ask. Law firms make it all possible. Without a so-called 'clean' legal opinion, these deals don't happen. Your firm would be the enabler, and knowing what it knows, up the creek if it hits the fan. Enough clichés for now?"

"Yes, but I'll be back to you again."

Now for a piece of wonderful 1998 news. Ceci and Sam Morris got married. Clare would approve. What's more, Ceci has finally stopped using the 'F' word. Why does it take children so much longer to grow up these days? The service (Trinity) and the reception (my favorite club) both went off smoothly, even though Jeannette was more of an onlooker than a participant, and Ceci seemed reluctant to waltz with me.

Millard overindulged, and I heard him (Was I supposed to?) characterizing Sam as 'beneath deficient'.

He told one of our guests the 'gifted' Ceci was too good for Sam, and predicted their marriage wouldn't last a year.

What can I say? Of course, Ceci's too good for anyone, but I'm convinced she and Sam will be happy together. And, in my book, Sam's quite underrated.

I can guess what made Millard so ill-tempered at Ceci's wedding. The day of the rehearsal dinner he barged into my office.

"Can you get me someone smart to handle a SEC disciplinary proceeding?" he said.

"Do I know the client?" I asked him.

"Come on, E, ever hear of confidentiality?"

I gave Millard several names, and he left. I bet anything it's Arthur again.

To mitigate the loss of Ceci, I bought a Jack Russell. Lizzie is now full grown and tips the scales at a mighty 10 pounds. People think she's still a puppy. When I first saw her, she was the size of a squirrel. I hadn't told Jeannette, and, as expected, she was fit to be tied. She remains so even after I promised to take complete responsibility. Besides, I don't want Jeannette bringing up Lizzie. She'll have her growling in no time. It was fine by me when Jeannette banned Lizzie from her end of the house. But then she suggested a crate in the cellar. No way.

My $500 got me an eager pal who likes playing ball, sneaking into Mount Auburn to visit Clare, and protecting me from other dogs. When we're not hacking around together, Lizzie enjoys following the sun as it moves from room to room in 118. She greets me effusively every evening, and when I leave for work she interposes herself between me and the door, drops one of her balls at my feet, and looks up expectantly. Of late, she's learned to find me when she needs to go out. Her favorite perch is my pillow, which, for some reason, she enjoys licking. What's more, Lizzie 'gets it'. On one of those infrequent occasions when Jeannette and I tried sleeping together, Lizzie lay down between us. She willingly absorbed our bad energy. Like those lead aprons you wear for x-rays.

At least I have good taste in dogs. At one point, I considered buying a collie and naming him 'Melan'.

My Clare dreams return. Not the happy ones. The one with the suave skier who Millard suggests was the love of her life. Is my subconscious (Or is it my unconscious?) telling me something? Would this dream keep recurring if there weren't something to it? The residue of Millard's poison lingers.

53

BACK TO business. One of my first acts on assuming the orb and scepter was to rip the photos of our dour, deceased partners off the wall of our main conference room. Who wants them staring down their endless noses at us, their unworthy successors? Next, I established a lesser caste. I drew my inspiration from the religion courses Eliot and I took in boarding school. Here's the deal. You labor seven years at the end of which, if you've survived, you get Leah, the homely older sister—a.k.a. a junior partnership. The bottom line is you remain an untenured salaryman. If you still crave lovely Rachel, you toil onward, but there are no guarantees as to the length of your servitude or Rachel's ultimate availability.

Now to my role as the good shepherd. I promised myself on taking office I would not permit my herd to outgrow its pasturage. Conservationists and environmentalists all acknowledge the necessity of periodic trimming and culling. It keeps the orchard and the flock vigorous. As the Benedictines say: *Succisa virescit*—pruned, it grows again.

Here's how it works. I maintain a 'hit list'. The appearance of a new name at the top triggers a series of events not unlike those which follow the shifting of tectonic plates. First, there's a period of depersonalization; demonization is too strong a word. But clearly, whoever he is, he's diseased. The uncontaminated must distance themselves.

Then the action items. Step one is designed to provoke a heightened sense of insecurity. The weapon of choice is the dreaded Millard visit.

I enjoy standing in the doorway and calling out a cheery, "Knock, knock." Someday, I'm going to scream, "Bend over and spread 'em!"

As the supplicant's face turns towards me, fear blots out annoyance. I love that.

He's wondering, how badly have I fucked up? Have I pissed off the managing partner by looking irked at his interruption?

He's trying to read me, but being fluent in several body languages and scores of dialects I render myself indecipherable. Like Linear A.

"Got a minute?" I inquire. You're fucking right you do, I'm tempted to add.

A tentative, sometimes quavering, "Sure."

I can see the wheels turning. What can be on his mind? Millard doesn't make social calls.

I sense the pulse spiking as the tethered goat reviews his manifold sins and wickednesses.

What has the all-knowing Millard discovered? My padded hours? A bit of unpartnerly customer-poaching? Funny business on my tax returns? The secrets in my credenza? Those Polaroids? Some totally consensual hijinks? Is our malpractice carrier on to me?

To me all hearts are open, all desires known, and from me no secrets are hid. Even the most self-assured are rattled. I love watching their eyes. Seeing them skitter about. I observe the tightening facial muscles, the fingers drumming on the blotter, the arranging and rearranging of pencils. I particularly relish their stuttering denials of offenses of which I was unaware.

I begin by beating around the bush. My trademarked boyish grin. A few pleasantries. Perhaps a question or two suggested by a photograph on his desk. This reminds him of his dependence on my good will. Without it, his children and livestock will starve. I sense the acid gnawing at his stomach lining. How should I play it? Like a seasoned pitcher, I vary velocity and location. I lull them with junk, and then bring the heat. I enjoy seeing people tremble and lean away when I crank up the decibel level and intensify eye contact. It won't be long until someone soils himself in my presence. Inducing tears has become routine.

I'm a great believer in props. Would I be overdoing it to place a loaded pistol on the condemned's desk as I leave his office?

When visiting, I encourage people to answer their phones. It's a test. How quickly can they disengage without offending either me or the caller? Meanwhile, the chump is signaling me with an agitated series of twitches, scribbled notes, and gestures, the most frequent of which is an index finger almost touching the adjacent thumb, the universal sign of a nearly-concluded call. I never flash him the 'I'll-leave-and-come-back-in-a-few-minutes' signal.

Much planning goes into my visits. Should I call ahead or just swoop in out of the sun? One of my favorite variations is to set up a visit but not tell the visitee its subject, or if I do, change it when I arrive. Sometimes, I employ the tactic of repeated postponements. Then there's the question of whether to bring Simon. When someone hears that both of us are coming, he's inclined to kneel quietly with his head on the block. Anything to avoid the stake. When it's just me—anxiety and uncertainty. A Simon solo? Contact Amnesty International.

Yes, Simon's a limited-purpose tool. He's incapable of delivering good news. After 30 seconds of praise and a half-hour of 'constructive' criticism, the listener is ready to bite down hard on his cyanide capsule.

My colleagues are such pukes. If I ever want to play hardball with Curtis, I'll go to the media. Then I'll dress in a tattered three-piece suit and huddle on the sidewalk outside 50 State Street. Duncan, Malcolm's successor, and his empty bowl will be there with me. My highly visible sign will read 'Wrongfully Discharged Curtis and Perkins Partner. No pension. Clean. Sober. Will photocopy, collate, and staple for food'.

As the facilitator at one of our retreats said, "Lead, follow, or get out of the way." Eliot has done none of these things. He's tried to thwart me.

54

I AM not a fan of Millard's management style, and our differences came to a head over a partnership election. Don Worthington, one of our marginal contract partners, was again being considered for elevation. Millard was scathing. "This guy's no rainmaker, barely a mist maker."

Normally, a contract partner makes it, or not, in two years. After his second year, Simon and Millard persuaded the management committee to defer Worthington for another year to see if he could hit certain targets—eighteen hundred billable hours and a million in collections. Fat chance, thought Millard and his cronies, but damned if Worthington didn't do it. Millard's compliant CFO was unable to invalidate a single number.

Simon and Millard were undaunted. At the next management committee meeting they said Worthington's numbers weren't 'sustainable', so we should put him on hold for at least another year. Millard turned to his stooges. Their bobble heads nodded in unison. Then I stuck my oar in. "Didn't we make a deal? Didn't we give him our word?"

The nodding ceased. Millard's chorus line looked to him for a cue. He conceded the point with apparent good grace. But that was it for me. The following year (2000) the Dow hit its high of 11,722, and I rotated off the management committee. In 2001 when I was once again eligible for election, it didn't happen.

Another anxious call to Buzz. "Tell me again, what's our role in tax shelter deals?"

"Law firms are the last line of defense. They provide the opinion which, if the evader's picked up on audit, will save his ass from penalties or worse. It comes down to four magic words. The chiseler's pretty much off the hook if the opinion concludes, as it always does—after pages of bogus analysis—that it's 'more likely than not' the scheme complies with the Code."

"Aren't there risks for the opinion writers?"

"Damn right, but so far it's paid off handsomely. Our canny brethren figure they've covered their asses by relying on the affidavits they've drafted and their clients have signed, everyone knowing them to be false. Really pretty."

"What would you do if your firm hired one of these creeps?"

"I'd be on the horn to my pal, Eliot Lawrence, begging for sanctuary. What we've got here is the flip side of generic accounting fraud where the game is to overstate the good: assets and revenue—while downplaying negatives: liabilities and expenses. Here you manufacture losses. That's why the high priests of this racket tend to be CPAs with law degrees.

"You never have to wonder whether these guys'll put out. The only question is price. Think of an old-time cat house with the solicitors lolling about in their gartered lingerie.

"Your pal Millard would appreciate that image."

55

THE YEAR 2000 brought me yet more personal triumphs. I had the following added to our letterhead: 'Our Third Century of Service to Boston and Beyond'. My hourly rate reached 500 bucks. A fine number, and I expect to hit 1,000 before I call it quits. New York, I would estimate, is no more than eight or so years from that impressive milestone, and Boston always creeps along behind after a discreet interval. We raise our rates every year. It's like printing money. All the big firms do it. If you, the customer, want the best, or those who've persuaded you they're the best, you grimace and fork it over.

I mustn't forget Cecilia. She and Sam remain in their respective ruts. "I'd be happy to introduce you to Herby," I told her. "He's my friendly, efficient, and reasonably-priced family lawyer. Better make your move before you turn 40, Ceci dear."

She didn't say yes, but she didn't say no. I ran out of time with her mama, but that won't happen again.

Now to other matters.

The millennium was great. I made off with $1,250,000 for 2000. Much wampum for the chief. Even better, disobliging Eliot slid to $650,000. When he drops below half a million, he'll be eligible for benefits under our 'No Lawyer Left Behind' program. I look forward to buying $6,000 shower curtains like Dennis Kozlowski, and charging them to client disbursements. Also, I still want to be an insider. To have Enron opportunities like my namesake, Andrew Fastow. I'll get in and out fast, taking with me buckets of tax-free income from innovative, off-shore, off-balance sheet transactions. Who says, "No man is a Cayman Island?"

As we enter the new century, I've reminded Eliot of his sad-sack predictions for the '90s. Asia's looking sick, but who gives a damn. Serves them right for being so grabby in the '80s. We've had a decade of growth, zippo inflation, and a Dow which, when graphed, looks like Old Faithless in his salad days. Some good legislation as well. Down came those antiquated Glass-Steagall firewalls. Banks, brokers, and insurers can, at last, crawl around in each other's jeans. Greenspan's tamed the business cycle; we've achieved a 'new paradigm'.

Now I'm asking myself what I can do for my firm. I am dutybound to burnish its most valuable asset. Myself. I must get more exposure. I need a larger stage, but must proceed judiciously. In some quarters there's a lingering feeling it's unseemly for lawyers to seek the limelight. Ha! We ache for center stage. Hence those 'Best Lawyers' lists. We are too well understood. I need to befriend the media, and, I've begun by feeding choice morsels to Philip Barnes, a business columnist. He's hungry and, therefore, easy pickings.

I completed Phil's subornation by providing him with a free estate plan and getting him into an over-subscribed hedge fund even though he couldn't come close to making the minimum investment. His returns have been fabulous. "How," he asked, "can I repay you? A nice puff piece about Curtis?" Nah, you see this junk all the time now. Every outfit yelling, please notice us. We do worthwhile things. We're not just money grubbers like our competitors.

No, if there's a story at Curtis, it's me. But where's the hook? Then came 9/11. My heaven-sent angle. Once again it was time for me to leave my fields and take up arms against Rome's enemies as I had tried to do 32 years earlier. I offered my sword to my country. Homeland Security. CIA. USMC. I wrote letters. I made phone calls. All the while knowing I was too long in the tooth. Guess what? The word got out. I didn't have to call Phil. He contacted me and brought a photographer with him to my office.

Before they came, I did a little redecorating. I secreted my priceless oils. I borrowed a large Old Glory and stood it behind my desk, slightly off-center so it would be visible over my shoulder. This theme was enhanced by a reproduction of the Suribachi flag raising and the withdrawal from 'The Reservoir'. I supplemented my militaria with most of the firm's 'good deeds' plaques, certificates, and testimonials. There weren't many, but what we had I snatched off other walls and hung in my office. Being a good family man, I found a 10" x 12" photo of Arthur and Stanley for my desk. It was taken years ago, before they'd been found wanting. I am big news, and would be even more compelling had Lucy been on one of the 9/11 aircraft.

My portrait in the *Boston Bar Journal* would do credit to Holbein. There I am, magisterial in a sumptuous three-piece suit complete with a gold watch chain dangling from which is the Phi Beta Kappa key I came across in a dead customer's stud box. All I lacked was a touch of ermine. Eliot had the nerve to say I was beginning to remind him of William Howard Taft. Most unfair. I can still, without bending too far, catch a glimpse of False Staff's russet tip.

Finally, I am hot. Unsurprisingly, lawyers seldom are. I am swamped with requests to appear, to speak, to advise, to moderate, and to be fêted. Now I'm beginning to mutate. I, who still admire Nixon, his Republican successors being pale imitations, am now an Independent. I can 'pass' in Cambridge and revile 'W' and 'Rummy' with the best of them.

Since my newspaper profile, I am a welcome contributor to its op-ed page. I inveigh against corruption in all its guises: in sports, politics, business, and the church. No organization or individual is safe from my balanced scrutiny. In my questioning of traditional gender roles and hierarchies of power, I stand four square for fair play. Turn the glass ceiling into a retractable roof and dissolve the old boys' network. Don't overturn that abortion case.

If only I could plausibly claim to have battled bigotry and injustice in a distant jurisdiction where the truth would stay buried.

Through it all, I observe Eliot observing me. He looks awe-struck.

And yes, my headhunter's gaffed a keeper. Henry (he prefers Henri) Giroux is a big hitter from a well-known, if not well-regarded, New York firm. We're not talking Cravath here. Henry's getting anxious. His way to the top is blocked.

He's assured me that if he moved to a reputable Boston shop, he could more than double his collections by dropping his opinion price from 50 to 40K. That would be a cool $4,000,000 per annum if he only did what he's already doing. This is a no-brainer.

Henry's taken by our untarnished (his word) reputation. Virginity or its simulacrum is essential in his game. He must work his magic in unspoiled landscapes. Not that I'd want him packing my parachute, but Henry's plausible in person and on paper. He winks warmly, does an effusive two-handed handshake, and has cultivated just enough gray hairs. Even the moustache works. He dresses stylishly: Milan with a touch of Savile Row. I'm getting myself a pair (or two) of those monk strap shoes.

Henry's CV is perfect. He practices before all varieties of courts and agencies. He represents natural persons and artificial entities. He's joined everything, plus he teaches, publishes, edits, advises, and smiles. Best of all: he has no convictions.

56

WHY DO I stay at C&P? Millard's running amok. He's becoming more and more himself. My influence and compensation are declining. I'm not sure I'm still wanted, and I hate being defined by my collections. My hourly rate is obscene. When I started, five dollars would get a client fifteen minutes of my time. Now it's about 30 seconds. I dislike moaning low. Things will look better soon.

Or will they? I've never been less excited by my work. It's one deal after another. All of them contentious and stressful. I'm endlessly rearguing the same issues with increasingly rude and youthful adversaries. Lately, I've been playing mind games, telling myself that for each additional year I spend at C&P, I'll be granted another rewarding, Alzheimer-free year of life. But what would I do with this gift? Jeannette has no wish to spend time with me, and I will not allow myself to become a burden to Eliot and Ceci.

At times like this, I find myself recalling Millard's provocative banter. He enjoyed asking me whether Clare had 'unloaded' me yet. I'd shake my head, and he'd follow up with something like, "Why on earth not?" I was never able to give him any cogent reasons. Now and again, he'd ask Clare this question in my presence.

"Stop it, Andrew," she'd playfully reply.

But was there more than playfulness in her tone? And what had my darling meant when she said on her death bed that Millard had 'pestered' her for years? Was it pestering or attention she'd enjoyed and perhaps invited? And what about that Jean-Claude Killy lookalike? Even though I got pretty good at selecting the correct wax, I'm not sure our tame cross-country outings ever quite measured up.

I've got to admit it: my children have paid their dues, daddy-wise.

Ceci never allows me to forget what she refers to as the 'teeth-gnashing enthusiasms' I inflicted on her when she was young.

"Don't you remember, Daddy—those years of making maple syrup? The summer you had all four of us on adjacent hilltops waving semaphore flags?" I could never understand Ceci's resistance. It would be a useful skill to possess in the event of an emergency. She reminds me of the times I'd get home late and hide behind my newspaper. I remind her of the times she hid the sports section. Then there was our recorder quartet which, at the children's request, Clare finally suggested we disband. My only good news is that young Eliot finally married Wendy, the nice girl who'd pursued him since they were classmates in day school. Maybe I'll write about her later.

Jeannette's worse. She doesn't even fake it. A few weeks ago, Hank, my jogging buddy, and I had just completed a brisk bad weather trot along the Charles. We were hanging out in 118's kitchen when Jeannette appeared. I started to tell her about what we'd seen on our exhilarating nine-minute-per-mile run. I'm fascinated by the return of fish-eating birds as the Charles becomes cleaner. Jeannette stared at the soggy clothing we'd dropped on the floor, gave Hank a thin smile, and said she'd be gone for the rest of the day.

So how will I entertain myself? There are scores of books I should read, but never will. Austen. Trollope. And if I did, so what? This isn't the way a modestly successful career is supposed to end. Full stop. I've become a whiner. I'm only partially joking when I say I'm an advocate of the unexamined life. Look what happens if you take a peek.

I've just heard of something called identity theft. Anybody who wants mine can help himself.

It's disappointing and shame-making to be off the management committee after so many years. It wouldn't matter if Clare were still here. She'd probably say that without me the committee's a joke. And I might believe her. As it is, I've got too much time on my hands. I had to sit out 2000, but not getting elected in 2001 hurt. I should relax and give others a chance. I'll be back on in a few years. But no campaigning. The fact is, I can't abide change and loss. I get upset when the recorded message says the moving walkway is coming to an end.

Should I retire? Depart on my own terms before my ensign's shot away? What would I do? Even if Clare were still alive I'd have to show a little consideration and not become a total nuisance. Just because my day job ended didn't mean I could expect her to entertain me 24/7. As the saying goes, 'For better or for worse, but not for lunch.'

Poor Princess Margaret just died. That got me wondering whether Clare spent her life trying to forget her own Group Captain Townsend.

If I hung it up now, I'd organize my files, clean my closet, reshelve my books, and—then what? Genealogy? Drink and anti-depressants? It's terrifying. Just last night I dreamed of solving a legal problem and woke up happy. How bad is that?

Can it get worse? Yes. Ceci and Sam Morris have separated. Married in 1998. Divorced in 2002? I don't like that one bit, and I've told Ceci so in no uncertain terms. Millard is supportive, she says. Evidently, he has introduced her to his slimy divorce lawyer; he's called Herby, and he wears a pinky ring.

I dreaded it, but there was only one thing to do. A gentle father-daughter talk over a quiet lunch at my quiet club. Where we could sort matters out in relative privacy. Ceci resisted. I persisted.

There were rather too many people in the dining room. Odd for a Tuesday. Worse, I knew most of them. We should have met in my office behind closed doors, but I wanted a drama there even less. We got off to a bad start with Ceci complaining about 'being dragged to this hospice'.

After we'd gotten our drinks and ordered, I bit the bullet. "Have you and Sam considered couples' therapy?" I could see words forming on her lips, but I raised a finger and continued, "Sam's…"

"Daddy, you can be such a FUCKING ASSSSHOLE!"

Every table went mute. Watery eyes in aged heads on arthritic necks rotated in our direction, then dropped quickly back to their plates.

"All you fucking care about are your collections, your schools, your clubs, your dumb-ass teams, and the dauphin. Your goddamn fantasy world. Your dreams of glory."

The waiters bowed their heads and scuttled for the kitchen.

"Mom's been gone for nearly 20 years. She's not coming back. Ever. But I'm here, for Chrissake, and you're always mistaking me for her. I'm not your docile, self-effacing, 1950s wife."

"Don't you dare talk about your mother that way."

"My sainted mother… The woman you scarcely noticed until you canonized her. What about inconsequential me?"

Ceci, whose color was terrible, gulped down the rest of her martini and signaled impatiently for another. But the only waiter in the room had turned to stone.

"Wake up, Daddy. Jeannette's servicing most of Beacon Hill. She's more reliable than Edison. And, while we're at it, stop calling me Ceci. In case you haven't noticed, I'm not in diapers."

"But Ceci, your godfather calls you that."

"Yeah, but he's not my father."

The dining room was emptying fast.

"Oh, fuck it," said Cecilia as, in violation of club rules, she lit a cigarette.

Then she started crying.

What on earth have I done? How many daughters call their father that? And what a terrible thing to say about her stepmother. Did she have a few drinks before joining me? Does she have a booze problem? It wasn't for nothing her maternal grandfather was known as 'Old Grandad'.

Is Ceci paying me back for the game we played on those seemingly endless summer car rides to and from Prouts Neck when she was very little and very gabby? I let her in on a secret: human beings have a lifetime quota of a million words, so it's important not to use them up too soon. Living in silence for your last few decades isn't any fun.

What should I do next, aside from deleting most of what my daughter just said? Easy answer. Nothing. It will blow over. Treat her outbursts like summer thunderstorms. I guess I was premature about Ceci's dropping the 'F' word.

At least I still have Lizzie. I'll never forget the night I got back late and found her outside on the steps. Jeannette's handiwork, though I can't prove it. Dear Lizzie. Any other Jack Russell would have vanished forever in pursuit of a squirrel.

57

BRAVO. BOUND to happen. Ceci needed bucking up so I took her to lunch at Trattoria Angiolino. She accepted my present, an anthology of Charles Addams cartoons, but it wasn't enough to drive away the clouds. The sun burst through when I said, "Ceci, you've got to get out of Dodge."

"What are you talking about? Daddy'd have a fit."

"Would you be interested in moving to godless Gotham and working as a paralegal in one of Wall Street's fanciest law firms or, if you'd prefer, with Monsieur de Montebello at the Metropolitan?"

"You can make that happen?"

"Indeed, I can."

"But where would I lay me down to sleep?"

"Got it covered. I have a customer whose widowed Mama would love some company in her echoing Fifth Avenue duplex. Close to the Frick. And there's no diaper-changing involved. What say you?"

"How soon?"

"Whenever you like."

"Thank you, Andrew. If I ever get hitched again, you're giving me away."

"Nothing would please me more, dear Ceci, but I couldn't. Think what it would do to Papa."

And now a painful aside. I am flourishing, but the same cannot be said about the boys. Yes, I have avoided the subject in the vain hope they'd get their shit together and not smear it all over New England. When they were little I predicted they'd attain Ceci's eight-year-old level by their early teens. Not so. I'd been blinded by paternal love. My lads were born on third base and immediately picked off.

Eliot loved twisting the blade with his oh so concerned questions about my boys' well-being and educational progress. Now I find his considerate silence even worse.

Yes, there's a lot to overlook, but it's hardly my doing. I've been an excellent father. My boys have wanted for nothing. The most prestigious schools, at least initially. The best tutoring money could buy. I wish things were turning out better for them, but they've been given every opportunity. Arthur tends to blame others, claiming to be the victim of a vast multi-winged conspiracy, to which I respond, without attribution, "The fault, dear Arthur, is not in our stars, but in ourselves, that we are underlings."

Can I help it if they've been dazzled and stunted by their illustrious father?

Shortly after Arthur's birth, we hired the formidable Perdita. She stayed with us until Stan went away to school at age 13 (just as Eliot and I had). Perdita took over, feeding the boys, exercising them when they were young, and transporting them to and from Sunday School and Norfolk Country Day when they were older. Perdita read to them, and I can't understand why they've failed to develop a liking for books. At the time I assumed they were merely slow, not stupid. Since then I've learned stupidity doesn't exist. It's always something else. And when that something else is finally named and classified as a disability, it is embraced by those theretofore regarded as *dummkopfs*.

Do my beloved boys have multiple disabilities or an all-encompassing one? They are hopeless in reading comprehension, oral expression, written expression, writing mechanics, spelling, and all forms of math.

I recall hoping that by early adolescence they might, like the great apes, be able to use simple tools.

Arthur and Stanley both received expensive instruction in golf, tennis, sailing, and, it goes without saying, riding. I taught them the fundamentals of backgammon. Their behavior, starting as adolescents, could not have come as a greater surprise. Though I'm not made of money, my broker never fails to transfer at least $100 to each of them on their birthdays. Do they remember mine? Or Father's Day?

After three boarding schools of diminishing social and academic standing, one detox unit, and two years at a junior college with a 100% acceptance rate for those paying full freight, I thought Arthur might have found himself. Though he'd spit the bit at several offices where I found him work, he seemed to have caught on as a trainee in the Dover branch of a national brokerage house. But Arthur has the habit of wearing his bloodlines on both sleeves. He chose to live near his office in a town none of his young colleagues could afford. He considered his fellow clerks to be beneath him. They noticed. This was only a way station for Arthur. Soon he would be enthroned in a downtown corner office like mine while they withered in the burbs. He wouldn't be in his lowly position much longer. In that, my boy was prescient.

Since being canned, Arthur has resumed his life in the squirearchy, clinging to his wastrel chums, dropping names, smoking cigars, dulling—if that's possible—his senses, and wondering whether he should take up polo or go into private equity. Arthur's schemes all require money, so in 1995 he married Bethany, a direct descendant of one of Bermuda's original Forty Thieves. Alas, Bethany's net worth was not as advertised. Does that sound familiar? As I am writing this several years later, Arthur and Bethany are experiencing the pre-breakup discontent I've become so expert at recognizing. Too bad. I rather like Bethany. She's kept me supplied with Talbot Brothers CDs.

I can remember when I thought Arthur might succeed at something. He came to me one night in his fourth-grade year and said, "Dad, I got into a little jam at school today." I frowned. Arthur continued, "But I paid one of the scholarship kids five bucks to take the rap."

Finally, a chance for some hands-on training.

"Smart move, Son, but where did you get the dough?"

"Mom makes sure I carry at least 50 bucks in small bills. For emergencies, she says."

What really browned me off was Alice's being more generous to the boys than to me.

Stan made Arthur look like a Phi Beta Kappa. Starting one rung further down the scholastic ladder, he lasted but two years at a recognized boarding school before being taken on by an experimental, minimum security establishment for troubled boys from good families. That's a growth industry. A school to which my desperate father-in-law made a high five-figure contribution. It is located off the beaten path in Maine. New Beginnings takes the position, publicly at least, that no boy is beyond hope. Stan caused the faculty to rethink this core assumption.

The school was founded by a retired teacher who for many years enjoyed success with reclamation projects. He created a habitat where recidivists and hard cases received the personal attention that would have taxed, if not paralyzed, the faculty of a conventional institution. The school's staff consisted of its founder and three husky, optimistic male teachers charged with controlling six felonious adolescents. Everyone cooked, cleaned, gardened, painted, and chopped firewood. Not much reading. No math. The athletic program was touch football, pond hockey, and tennis on a dirt court. Stan learned survival skills. Along with growing vegetables and weed, he cultivated his disgust with his parents, his brother, and what he characterized as the materialistic Western culture into which he'd been 'thrust'.

At least ponytailed Stan isn't costing me much. After 'graduating'—Stan made the diplomas as part of his calligraphy course—and flirting with several limp Eastern religions, he persuaded his mother's trustee to distribute sufficient funds to purchase a 100-acre tract in the Maine woods on which he established a commune stocked with gullible, well-to-do followers who acknowledged him as their temporal and spiritual lord and signed over their worldly goods. This regressive branch of the de Peyster line will, I'm afraid, be carried on by three (present count) illegitimate children, each with a different mommy, who are shod in beaded moccasins fashioned from the hides of jacked deer, which Stan, in a rare entrepreneurial spasm, is trying to sell to L.L. Bean.

Can I persuade my two stalwarts and their progeny to drop 'Millard' and adopt 'Edmunds' as their surname?

One other thing. This epic is well beyond their grasp, but to me it's a joy forever. It is to be shared with the world. When I find a moment, I'll anoint the fortunate agent. It must be released at once, but I want nobody missing my subsequent coups and conquests. The solution is obvious. A second volume, a few years hence. A third near the end, wrapping everything up. My benediction. Yes, a trilogy.

So much for my seed and an aside about my friend's. Quintus's dowdy wife doesn't come close to matching his dear mother. The Lawrence downturn continues.

Meanwhile, my star keeps ascending. Having begun my legal career in reduced circumstances, I am now a gentleman of independent means, soon to be further enriched by my hefty cut of our tax-shelter practice.

For those of us with our wits about us, age brings boundless opportunities. Only our contemporaries really know us, and if most of them are dead or gaga, we're free to dissemble, to recreate ourselves, and to garner the respect that's unfairly eluded us. Even bankruptcy lawyers have been known to resurrect themselves.

Being venerated comes easily. An avuncular look and a self-effacing manner are enough to offset decades of sketchy conduct. Dimly remembered episodes of tax fraud, malpractice, customer-kidnapping, betrayal, and sexual harassment, as it's now called, take on a warm rosy patina, evoking chuckles, not outrage. Selfishness and greed are givens and, therefore, disregarded.

Attention to detail is essential, however. The challenge is to be taken for a slightly befuddled professor, not a vagrant. A few food stains on the signature tattersall vest will always be tolerated, but it's imperative to maintain minimum standards of personal hygiene and appearance. Instruct your barber to institute a rigorous defoliation program, check your fly regularly but not so often you're arrested, remember to chew with your mouth closed, use your napkin constantly, floss at least twice daily, and never overestimate the capacity of your bladder or lower intestine.

Onward!

Next year, 2004, should be a world-beater. Giroux will be on board by the end of the first quarter. He tells me his sources are delighted with his proposed move and promise an even more robust deal flow.

Since he's getting a contract partnership, a vote of the partners is unnecessary. Sorry about that, Eliot. One other thing: Giroux bragged about participating in his own scams. He invited me to join the fun. Dumb move. Now I've got him by the short and curlies. Any lip from M. Giroux and I go to the IRS. And collect a handsome bounty.

Back to *mon ami*. Whenever I'm bored, I give him a tweak. Remind him I'm still around and still on top. Last week I grabbed him after a partners' meeting. I forgot to mention it, but we're now paying attendees 100 bucks a pop, and I'm guessing most of us treat it as a tax-free trifle. If you stay till the end, the paymaster will hand you a crisp Ben Franklin as you leave. Much like the Marine Corps, where, according to Eliot, the snuffies marched up to a blanket-covered table, snapped to attention, and received a month's pay in cash.

"Just a thought, Eliot, but if Jeannette's giving you grief, you might think about getting her a nightgown at the shop on Newbury Street where you bought Clare's."

He'll gnaw on that for years.

58

IT'S INEXPLICABLE. Desirable women, certainly those over 30 years my junior, never chat me up. Most stare me down. If I catch their eye at a party, something I generally avoid, they will look through me, dive into the hors d'oeuvres, or take evasive action like an aircraft caught in a missile lock. I'm waiting for one of them to scatter chaff. If the "I'm not here, I'm invisible" approach fails, they'll begin an animated conversation with anyone at hand, however unpromising. They probably know I'm a corporate lawyer and may think I'll lecture them on, say, secured transactions.

Whenever a beautiful woman is more than civil, I soon discover it has little to do with me. She's been abandoned. Her baby is sick. She's lost her father. Something like that.

It all changed yesterday at the June 11, 2004 firm cocktail party, one of those ineffective morale builders, complete with exhortations from our managing partners. I sometimes attend so as to catch up with my peers and favorite retirees. As usual, my friends and I—being shunned by today's movers and shakers—formed a protective cluster of aged herbivores. We were a five-minute struggle from the bar. Had we been gently herded to the sidelines so we wouldn't discourage the newer hires? As the French put it, "*Qui sait?*" I was having a quiet, friendly time with my contemporaries. That was the most I could reasonably expect from such an event. While women my age like to talk about their grandchildren, we gab about our bodies and their discontents. I was particularly glad to see Tony, who had just gotten a pacemaker.

Imagine my surprise when Dawn Peterson, wineglass in hand, walked over to me. I was more than surprised. I was thrilled and excited. And curious. As the young would say, 'stoked'. Surely, she'd just paused for a moment on her way to someone or somewhere else. Dawn, one of our most promising trusts and estates associates, is a striking dark-haired woman whose features are transformed from severe to radiant by a smile. I wish I could do her justice, but, as usual, words fail me. What's important is that I appeared to be her destination. Maybe she hadn't just found herself in my vicinity and felt obliged to favor me with a few moments of perfunctory office chatter. For some reason, probably pity, she'd navigated the crush to be with me. Did she think I still mattered here?

What made this nicer was she worked in Millard's department. It would have made sense to get into his good graces. That wouldn't be difficult. Millard nearly salivates whenever someone mentions her name. I've heard so many wonderful things about Dawn. Kind. Smart. Funny. Industrious. A great future. Attached? Not sure. Someone told me she'd worked for VISTA in Appalachia. That reminded me of Clare. I'd heard Dawn came here because Millard, who interviewed her at law school, said we did a lot of pro bono work. Maybe she wanted to ask me about that. Should I tell her the disillusioning truth?

What could I possibly mean to this spectacular young woman? I intend to be positive. Dawn was close—'in my space' as Cecilia would say. I gave her a little breathing room so she could move on if she wished livelier company. Praise be, she stayed put. In fact, she advanced half a pace. Her generally serious face was alight. It must have been the wine. Who cares? I know I was grinning at her like the village idiot. Oh for a more mature expression. Complex. Magnetic. More Millard-like. Not a sappy Alfred E. Neuman grin. Soon I was struggling for words. It didn't seem to matter. Dawn took the lead and kept the conversational ball in play. That was thoughtful.

At one point she asked me to hold her glass while she did something with her hair. When I gave it back to her, she said, "Thank you, Eliot." I was thrilled to be helpful.

I delighted in her proximity. My only thought: *Don't let this end*. I wanted to move closer but dared not. We were in a gentle evening breeze. She had Clare's clean, non-smell, smell. Strands of Dawn's hair drifted across my face. I didn't brush them away. We were nearly touching. Time stopped. Then I noticed Millard observing us. He gave me one of his sardonic looks. I knew what he was thinking, but he was wrong. He was judging others by himself. Millard, the troublemaker, with the uncanny knack of being able to poison anything, had sidled over to us, but was momentarily silent.

Thinking of Millard reminds me of the tax shelter hyenas who were just profiled in *The American Advocate.* That's generally a harbinger of doom. In the meantime, Buzz keeps the emails coming. The last one read, 'Jenkens and Gilchrist, one of the biggest players in this sordid game, got nailed last year by the IRS. The rats are scampering down the hawsers. I wish there were a way to short law firms. I'd do J&G in a heartbeat.' Millard must be stopped before he ruins everything.

Perhaps Millard's expression was caused by Dawn's lovely dress. It reminded me of something worn by a Jane Austen heroine in a Merchant-Ivory movie. Innocent and simple, but when seen on the right person, wildly seductive. Low cut, in that alluring fashion. Is it called 'empire'? I wish I could remember its color. Some shade of blue. Yes, I'm a swine. It wasn't the dress. It was what was beneath it. More than a suggestion of quite perfect… stop. How to stare without seeming to? Staring's never cool. Particularly by a geezer. Not that I ever stare.

I tried to be subtle, to make eye contact, then to look elsewhere before allowing myself yet another quick glance. I yearned to see all of her. Was she wearing one of those garments that shoves everything upwards? What could I say that wouldn't bore or give offense? That wouldn't have people calling me 'Humbert' Lawrence?

Quel lunk. I'm unsure about the color of Dawn's dress,* and I've no idea what it was made of. I've never been good with materials and fabrics. In fact, I'm proud of myself for using 'fabric' rather than 'cloth'.

This ignorance extends to plants, birds, and the rest of the natural world. I'm clear about seagulls, pigeons, robins, blue jays, and cardinals. Actually, I've learned to identify a cardinal's song. I almost

---

* Since it was driving me nuts, I looked it up. Cobalt.

omitted sparrows. I can identify them too. That's pretty much it for our fine-feathered friends. I do better on animals. As for Dawn's dress, I know it was not felt, flannel, wool, leather, spandex, or Gore-Tex, but that leaves a lot of possibilities. Was it natural or synthetic? All I know is my thoughts were sinful. Millard would like that last bit about sin and synthetic.

I know it sounds like "I could have danced all night", but I could have stood there all night. Though sunrise was hours away, Dawn had to be off. Why? She never said. Instead she smiled, apologized, and left me. When would we talk again? When would I see her in that dress? Feel her hair?

A horrid thought. Am I seen as a lech? I choose to believe I'm invisible, but having been here so long I suppose I've picked up some kind of reputation. Everyone does. Oh, dear.

59

I'VE SELDOM observed a desirable woman behave in such an aberrant fashion. Was she bewitched? Like a character in *A Midsummer's Night's Dream*? It's not as though Eliot's literally an ass. He's my friend, after all. Even if he's engaged in a *folie à un*. Had Dawn been a fox of the four-legged variety, I would have said she had rabies. And why, may I ask, isn't she kissing up to me, the big hitter, the only hitter, in her department? What gives? Must have been a sympathy thing.

Larry Thorndike's the only person more ludicrous than Eliot. Until recently, Larry always did what was expected of him. The right college, the right clubs, and a dutiful, androgynous debutante with whom he sired more of the same. I'm pleased to say people like me have always annoyed Larry. To Larry, the Millards of the world are wrong-headed. He knows they're laughing at him and finds that outrageous.

For nearly 60 years, Larry's life has been one of quiet desperation. Now it's noisy and frantic, but equally desperate. Larry shows what happens when you peak too soon. In our boarding school, where a premium was placed on piety, docility, and a large body, Larry was the beau ideal of the slow-witted masters who were profoundly suspicious of adolescents like me who outsmarted them.

Larry's a really dumb Eliot. Our school showered him with awards—even if all of them were for athletics or 'school spirit'. Larry was led to believe his prizes heralded a glowing future. It was all an innocent falsehood perpetrated by the unworldly on the uncooked.

Understandably, it's corrosive to see others, particularly the trouble-makers, the slackers, and those you'd written off 50 years ago, in possession of life's spoils. It's worse to see these rotters come back to reunions and charm the doddering masters who had, quite properly, scourged them as schoolboys. Somehow, somewhere, something had gone awry. Larry's no longer the coin of the realm, and he knows it. So, he retreats to his club, where he's revered as a raconteur by those of comparable intelligence.

Well, Larry has awakened. Deprived of a mid-life crisis by timidity and the constraints of his background, the aged satyr is kicking up his hooves with a lackluster late-life crisis. No going quietly for our gratingly-hearty Larry. Observe him at parties with someone young. Much thudding, heavy breathing, and braying.

Watch yourself, Eliot.

60

MILLARD, WHO'S still furious that Larry Thorndike got into Harvard, is getting a kick out of comparing me to him. I've known Larry since we were children. Despite a few surface similarities, it's totally unfair. Larry's really insular, even by my standards. He boasts of his eye-opening year in the unfamiliar and, therefore, terrifying wilds of Manhattan's Upper East Side where he met exotics such as Methodists and washed out of law school.

Enough of that. Let's go, Eliot. Show some initiative. You can arrange to see her. You're an important partner. At least you were once. The age difference wouldn't faze Millard. Would I want to see Dawn again if there was no hope of touching her? I think so, but let the record show I do want to touch her, touch her all over as it happens. Oh God, did I really write that? Delete.

OK. So we get together again. What then? What can I dream up to entertain or amuse her? Stay away from military history. That's been a flop.

Be suave. Stop being so leaden. Such a 'wet'. Millard would have seized the moment and seized Dawn as well. What would he have said when he felt her hair on his cheek? Maybe something like, "Let's get out of here. Now. Take a drive. In my Porsche. Dinner's on me. How about it?" But that doesn't sound like me. Besides, Volvos aren't cool.

Maybe I don't need some transparent pretext to see her again. We have lots to talk about. When Dawn spoke to me I tried to focus on her words. I remember much of what she told me about herself, her work, her family, and her education. Enough to start another conversation.

It is difficult to avoid inappropriate fantasies. I see her without clothes. I see myself assisting in their removal. I see her smiling as I do so. Maybe even helping when I fumble with the more challenging fastenings. More smut. Stop it!

Recently, I was dragged by Jeannette to a black-tie charity event at the Museum of Fine Arts. I dread these occasions. They cost a mint, and are all about Jeannette's getting more 'exposure' (in addition to that afforded by the dresses she selects for her public displays) and me being importuned to invade capital and buy the board seat she claims Millard could get her. I'm not sure this is prudent. Having Jeannette better known is unlikely to benefit her, my children, C&P, or me.

Oh, there's something else. She never fails to be photographed in the hip pocket of the most important man in the room who, alas, is never Eliot Lawrence and, thankfully, is seldom Andrew Millard. The big shots haven't got a prayer. Jeannette's like a jungle cat crouching on a limb over a water-hole. Soon 118 Beacon will be forced to accommodate yet another over-sized, silver-framed image of "the vivacious, stunning, ubiquitous Jeannette Lawrence", wine glass in hand, looking, I hate to say it, a trifle cheesy.

Tired of pretending, I wandered off into another gallery, where I saw an Indian painting portraying the 'king of carnal love' entwined with his lover. They are sprawled on a lotus. But what are the chances of experiencing something like that twice in a lifetime?

I daydream. What if Dawn saw me in the altogether? What if she saw me in the Michelangelo underwear Millard gave me? Very problematic. I'm passable in a suit and tie, but now my fabric hangs more pleasingly than my flesh. Just recently, I noticed my third belt hole has migrated to where the fourth used to be. It may be best to avoid mirrors and think less about myself. Millard is still cocky about his body that, objectively speaking, is worse looking than mine. I'm sure this attitude underlies much of his success.

Not that Jeannette noticed, but I was in a state when I got home from the C&P party. I knew I'd be unable to sleep, so I took a pill. I do this sometimes to help me nod off on trans-Atlantic flights. I just want it understood, however, that I am in no way, shape, or form a druggie. Anyway, I dreamed about Dawn, but when I woke up, I couldn't say whether or not we'd made love. I had a wonderful sense of well-being, but no specific memory of what we did or didn't do. Twenty years ago, I'd have awakened in a puddle.

I first noticed this development a couple years ago. In the old days, most of my dreams would have received an 'X' under the motion picture industry's previous rating system. Now, all but my upsetting dreams about Clare would only get a 'PG'. They are gentler and less graphic. Do I like this compromise? My triumphs are less satisfying, but my nightmares are less terrifying. Merely frustrating or annoying, and sometimes, though I hate to admit it, boring.

As a child I developed the ability to wake myself just before being spitted on the bayonet of a screaming Jap, as we called them. Since my father was in the Pacific and I was the man of the house, it would have been unseemly to jump into bed with Mom. So I toughed it out, ignoring the monsters hiding under my bed. Those terrors are faint memories, but others have replaced them.

A few days later, actually it was Tuesday, June 15, I stopped by Dawn's office. Dropping in wasn't as easy or casual as I've made it sound. More like a plunge off a dock in Maine. You know you'll be pleased with yourself once you've done it. I felt wild and reckless, although Millard would probably have said 'mild and feckless'.

I recycled some of the subjects I'd remembered from our happy moments together. Mostly office gossip. A little about her interest in cats. I mentioned Spooky. It's a shame there are so many areas of current interest in which I'm virtually illiterate—like technology and the vast bulk of popular culture. Never mind.

Somehow, we started talking about lunch. Did I manage that on my own? It seems inconceivable. However, it was lunch as a concept, not a lunch we were actually going to have together. There was still hope. Keep the ball in play. No unforced errors. Neither of us, it turns out, can abide the claustrophobic atmosphere of our firm's cafeteria, a windowless, low-ceilinged interior space.

Dawn dislikes the food as well. Too heavy. It has always seemed adequate to me, but I was looking for common ground so I denounced it at length even throwing in a few gratuitously uncomplimentary remarks about the service. At that point, I would have stooped to anything. I was nursing a tiny flame, and thinking of

Jack London's nameless protagonist who froze to death in the Yukon when snow extinguished his campfire.

I slunk forward like a border collie, my belly close to the ground. Then inspiration. A forceful, vigorous verb occurred to me, "What say we grab lunch sometime?" Not missing a beat, I advanced at least three feet and started on about the pleasures of al fresco (I think she was impressed by my use of that expression) dining during the nice summer months. She conceded that eating outdoors was nice. In fact, she knew of a nice place. Am I using 'nice' too often? It was now or never.

Springing from the underbrush, I barked, "Let's do it," and had the moxie to follow up with, "sometime soon." *Nicely done*, I thought to myself. Millard, the master stalker, would have approved.

To my amazed delight, she replied, "It's a date." That was a cinch, Eliot, you devil, you. My first tentative step toward roguedom and, perhaps, happiness. Then I realized that technically it wasn't a date. No date had been set. At most we had an unenforceable oral understanding, an agreement in principle, but far be it for me to niggle, or quibble, or suggest we reduce it to writing.

It would have been unwise to allow Dawn to think her acceptance had come as a surprise. As an experienced negotiator, I knew we'd been at the table long enough. I beat feet. If I'd been Millard I might have winked at her. Do I know how to wink properly? Would it look like a tic? I smiled instead. At least I hope I did.

Returning to my office, I couldn't help cataloguing the witticisms that hadn't occurred to me at the time. Why can't I think of anything besides Dawn? What about the Sox? It's early, but they're looking strong. They're within striking distance of the Yankees. Surely, the wild card's in the bag. If our shaky pitching doesn't collapse. Who cares? If the devil appeared before me I'd have consigned the Sox to the cellar for eternity in exchange for more time with Dawn. I'm proud of my composure. I gave it a few days. Let her sweat a little. I made her wait until Friday, June 18.

Friday morning (I held off until 10:30 a.m.) found me standing in her doorway as though by coincidence. I uttered the coolest "Hey" and asked her whether she was 'booked up' for that very day. If she turned me down, she'd feel remorse and give me the opportunity to be cheerful, understanding, non-threatening, and gallant. I waited. I was relaxed. The ball was in her court.

She was, in fact, 'booked up'. However, with but the slightest pause she added, "What about next week?" Not next month, not next year but next week—and it was already Friday of this week. Ecstasy! Well, that's somewhat premature, but certainly boundless joy. Don't blow it now. I almost blurted out, "How's Monday?" Instead, I studied my almost empty engagement book and asked whether Wednesday 'worked for her'. I was pleased with my use of the current vernacular.

Wednesday did work for her. I searched her face for signs of reservations. Ha. Ha. I saw none. My final touch was to leave the time of our lunch entirely in her hands. I told her I had 'a fair amount' of free time on Wednesday and she should 'stick her nose' into my office whenever she was ready. Was I a smoothie, or what? Time to pull up stakes. Don't be a noodge or a pest.

So, there it stood. The rest of Friday, the weekend, then Monday and Tuesday. An eternity. Did she agree to eat with me on a dare? On a bet? Did she tell anyone about us? Us?

There's a small dark cloud. Jeannette. She's got some temper and, despite her business success (she's selling some new financial products I don't fully understand), she hasn't mellowed one bit. Am I over-dramatizing? If I wish to play the old fool, I'll do so. Nothing has happened, and it's a good bet nothing will. Ever. When I consider this matter in the clear light of my office, the likelihood of impropriety is absurd. I am more concerned with what Clare may be thinking.

It's becoming clear to me, and I'm sure it's been obvious to Jeannette for ages that the time for a peaceful solution or a negotiated settlement has passed. All that remains is to provoke and then document the incident(s) entitling one or both of us to end it. The result's inevitable. The fight's gone out of me. I can't go on this way. That's why this interlude with Dawn has made me feel so alive. The way I used to feel with Clare. So what if I'm still off the management committee.

OK. I gave it yet another try with Jeannette. We celebrated her promotion at the Four Seasons. Even more expensive than the Ritz, which Jeannette considers 'old and dumpy'. Is there a Three Seasons anywhere?

I ordered a nice champagne, not the most expensive, but more than adequate.

I toasted Jeannette, "Congratulations, dear, a managing directorship is a marvelous achievement. You worked hard for it, and you deserve it. Now you won't have to go on all those trips."

"You outta your mind? It's gonna get worse."

"Why?"

"Christ, Eliot. Same deal as yours. Making MD's just the start. I can't put my feet up. We eat what we kill."

"And you're a hungry girl, aren't you?"

"Damn right."

"I'd hoped we'd finally see more of Ceci and young Eliot."

"Why should I?" A frown. "Neither of them's ever reached out to me, the wicked stepmother."

Should I keep trying? Why bother? It's no fun living with someone who scares you. Besides, I care less and less about what she may or may not have done.

Just the other day Millard suggested I get Jeannette the latest P.D. James novel. Then he corrected himself, "Sorry, Eliot. She was one of Clare's favorites. Too much for Jeannette. No pictures."

From where I sit, it looks as though Millard's marriage may be as far gone as mine. Maybe I can cadge some meals from young Eliot and Wendy, who is at last looking quite preggers. With luck, I'll have someone to play catch with in a few years. As for Millard, he's come up with an inventive escape route. It's all about his children. Lucy's no good with Arthur and Stanley. She doesn't care for them. She barely tolerates them. Here's another instance where a childless woman makes a lousy stepmother. I had trouble keeping a straight face when Millard laid this on me.

I can't seem to win for losing with Ceci. Instead of cooling off, she's getting more unreasonable. Am I to blame for everything? Am I too controlling, too detached, or both? The last time she was home from her New York paralegal job, she said, "Since I got my fucking magna from Yale, you've either ignored me or intimated I'd look swell in a burka." I can't stand her swearing. Sometimes my own daughter frightens me. I'm becoming a mouse.

The low-pressure area is lingering, and as I write these words during the weekend before my lunch with Dawn, I'm finding 118 Beacon to be much as Clare originally anticipated—dark and lonely. It is also quite changed in appearance and atmosphere. It's not all bad, however. When I go, Eliot and Ceci will have themselves a mid-seven-figure asset, and the soapstone sink, having hidden in the alders at Prouts Neck for three decades, is theirs for the asking.

And, if this weren't enough, there's a rumor drifting up from the secretaries that Millard's writing off his bills to certain preferred female clients. My informant told me this typically occurs on the Tuesdays following three-day weekends. It might have been better if I'd let this matter ride, but I seem unable to pick my battles.

"Why should we, your partners, finance your goat-like conduct?" I asked him. "You personally owe me about 3% of those write-offs."

"No way. You've been nowhere near 3% for ages."

"How long's this been going on, Andrew?"

"Come on, Tiger. Get a life. Don't you do occasional favors? Aren't we all trying to ingratiate ourselves with important customers, whether they wear boxers or thongs? Am I right?"

"No, you are not. I do it once in a very great while for the good of our firm to retain important, institutional clients."

All he said as he gave me a dismissive wave was, "Puh-leez."

61

SOMETIMES ELIOT'S not completely oblivious. He has correctly perceived it's 'so over' between him and Jeannette. Just like my union. I suppose I could have twigged to this sooner. Lucy telling me, "I like you best when you're sick," might have been a tip-off.

And now Jeannette's getting balky. Her generation doesn't appreciate what they've been given. After all my mentoring, you'd think I'd be entitled to a perpetual tenancy between her legs. However, it's clear my Beacon Hill townhouse, from which Lucy moved last year, is no longer Jeannette's favorite playground. What's she saving it for? It's not like she's a marathoner with only a few world-class races in her. Nor is that area of a woman's body susceptible to stress fractures or overuse injuries.

Jeannette's brutally frank. She said, "I've cut Eliot back to semi-annual quickies. I pay off every six months, just like his damn bonds. Not bad, considering he may have given me a grand total of three less-than-earth-moving orgasms."

If I smirk, she narrows her eyes, fixes me with her reptilian stare, and begins critiquing my ardor and technique. Then she gets off on what she terms my "need for pharmaceutical assistance". I made the mistake of telling Jeannette about renaming Old Faithless. She said, "You should have consulted Disney, not the Bard, and named him Droopy."

Jeannette's been suspiciously quiet in the sack of late. No thrashing. No crying out. No rosy after-glow. Our romps are infrequent and impersonal. They remind me of my transcendent coming-of-age experience. Jeannette's out of bed, into the john and through the door before I've got my slippers on. Yes, I'm wearing slippers now. When I remember what she liked doing and the unladylike acts she demanded from me (we were like tongue-and-groove planking), I sigh and almost blush.

Jeannette made me squirm when she described 'El's' fumbling efforts to liven up proceedings between the sheets. Eliot, it seems, had read about a new position promising seismic results. Jeannette's tough. This is how she put it: "Remember those old diagrams that taught you to dance by moving your feet from one numbered box to the next? Well here comes Arthur Murray Lawrence. In a tone more suited to the boardroom than the bedroom, he says, 'I place my full weight on you, and you wrap your legs around me, resting your ankles on my calves. OK, so far? Then I insert…'"

Soon after one of our own less-memorable outings (it was during that sticky phase when your will to resist's been eroded), Jeannette, in a rare pensive moment, said to me, "You know something, Lover Boy, I need a new start. Life's passing me by." She was in one of those raggy moods selfish women can slip into. Inexplicable. The sun was streaming through the windows of her Eliot-proof private suite at 118 Beacon, the rhododendrons were in bloom, and we'd taken care of business. Life was good.

"You'd be alluring in black as the well-off widow Lawrence, but you might be disappointed if you and Eliot end up in divorce court," I said. "Even with my pal Herby at your side." Nothing like ejecting a load to make me feel expansive.

"And why would that be?" Jeannette asked.

"Justice may be blind, but that doesn't mean all probate judges are."

Jeannette retorted, "I've got plans, Sweet Meat. But I need coaching and you're the man." She paused, gave me one of her looks, and said, "Help me get a license to carry."

Sweet Jesus. Where the hell was Jeannette going with this? I've never seen the still-appetizing Jeannette more excited. So excited, in fact, she lowered her head towards drowsy False Staff, and I recall hoping, at last, after all these years…

Wrong. She just blew a raspberry on my tummy.

Then she got scary. At times like this Jeannette has the merciless eyes of a raptor.

"Would you help plan my next move, *Liebchen*?"

Like an idiot, I responded with good cheer, "I'll consider it if you do something first." I'm a 'take-no-prisoners' bargainer, and I didn't even offer the customary assurances about a no-fire zone, as I proffered my 'amuse-bouche'.

And damned if she didn't set to work like an alchemist trying to transmute rope into rebar. Thank you, Mr. Pfizer.

Jeannette shook me awake from my brief nap. "OK, Hot Stuff, how about this?"

I was about to make with another wise-ass response, but suddenly it was icy in Jeannette's no-longer-cozy hideaway. False Staff wasn't amused either. He was diving for cover like one of those 19th century cannons on retractable carriages.

Whatever it was, I didn't want to hear it. Not after what I'd espied in the drawer of her bedside table. All I'm saying is, it wasn't a Gideon bible. I cleared my throat a few times and took a couple hits from my ever-present inhaler.

Coolness was required. "Listen, *Schatzi*, give me a rain check. I've got a client conference in 15 minutes. Gotta run." This distracted her. I was out of there and haven't been back.

Reflecting on this later, I realized I'd overreacted. I shouldn't have gotten so flustered. No biggie. Jeannette's just kinda twisted. There's no reason to tip off Eliot, not that I could have without blowing, so to speak, my cover.

In the interest of closure, there should perhaps be another word or two about Lucy, whose departure from my life went almost unnoticed. She's still at Curtis, and it will be challenging to fire someone with $2,000,000 in collections. It's incongruous being the one cast aside. I've never experienced this before and, while it's not exactly painful, it is perplexing. Maybe she and Maud would hit it off.

62

I'M GETTING ahead of myself by feeling badly about leading a double life. At most, I'm leading barely one and one-quarter lives. If that. I wouldn't be much good at a double life anyway. First of all, I've had no practice. Second, I'm getting forgetful and would be likely to botch my alibi. Millard could help. At what price, though? He'd have a field day making fun of me. What if I told him I was inquiring on behalf of an unnamed friend? Would he see through me?

No. Avoid Millard. He's notoriously indiscreet. This is part of his charm unless, of course, he's dining out on you. My story would be all over town in no time.

"But soft" (as they said in Elizabethan dramas), Millard has told me of the ploys he used in his prime, when he had women stashed over much of eastern Massachusetts. Whenever I think of Millard, the high flyer, in those endless '60s summer nights, I am reminded of the Battle of Britain movies we saw as boys. The scene: Summer of 1940, an operations room, Royal Air Force Fighter Command, harried NCOs in heavy, poorly-cut blue uniforms moving facsimiles of Jerry aircraft across a giant table map of England. Horrific casualties. Mugs of tea. Stiff upper lips. Laconic after-action reports: "Awfully hard luck on the 21st."

Tracking Millard was as challenging as keeping tabs on the Luftwaffe. Last seen in Boston heading west, then a report he was spotted in Duxbury, when actually he was picnicking on Singing Beach with some well-chilled but lousy champagne. Millard has always been a skinflint; he uses a label maker to increase the apparent price of every bottle he buys.

Now I find myself trying to recall Millard's gambits. He never discloses his current antics, always pretending to have reformed.

He's lost the urge. He's become a truth-teller. His friends are in stitches.

I once asked him whether he was ashamed of being a liar and a sneak. He gave me a patronizing look and replied, "That's how it's done, *Mon Brave*."

What should I wear to lunch on Wednesday? What does it matter? I peaked in the Casanova department before I turned nine. I remember no feelings of awkwardness or self-consciousness in those days. Talking to girls didn't frighten me. I don't know why this was so, nor can I explain why it changed. I had no idea what I looked like. It wasn't a concern, and girls seemed OK with me as well.

I spent a lot of time with Heidi, my third-grade girlfriend, and remember how comfortable we were together. This was before the onset of acne, anxiety, and adolescence when I lost the ability to do anything but stand and stare. Now I've regressed to that condition.

Did Heidi and I ever touch? I doubt it. We never kissed. I never dared to try. We certainly didn't play doctor or spin-the-bottle. Would she have gone for that? Most unlikely. I know what I want. Another Clare.

Why wasn't I warned that infatuation isn't restricted to children? What a nasty surprise. Like waking up with pinkeye in your 60s. Think about the Sox. Or your children, for pete's sake. Anything but that gossamer dress and the lovely body inside it. Will she wear it for me again? No, you idiot. She wasn't wearing it for you then. If I see her in it now, I'll be better defended. Oh, to live sedately, without this constant tumult.

I've heard it can get worse. Cupid has no respect for the lame and the halt. Stories have come to me about desperate groping and fumbling in nursing homes. Jealousy and anger, and even STDs, in the assisted living wing. Lust while on life support. Failing hearts that have been broken and rebroken are broken yet again.

How will it go at lunch? Should I order a drink? It's a weekday. Would she like a drink? Would she be suspicious or offended? What, if I used the light-hearted word 'libation'? Suggest a spritzer. Relatively harmless unless she had several. Now you're talking. That's a possibility. No, it's not. I don't want her thinking the wrong thing. Or do I? Stop it. I'm beginning to sound like Millard, and that won't get me anywhere with Dawn.

Back to my worries. It will be terrible if Giroux's indicted after he gets here. Can we get the IRS after him before he arrives? Buzz says he'll look into it.

I can't understand why nobody opposed Giroux's hiring. Probably because Millard controls our compensation decisions. I know why I didn't howl. I didn't want his guard up. In fact, I told him later that Giroux could really help our bottom line. Aren't I the born conspirator?

After the meeting, I spoke to X, one of my tax partners. Someone who understands this nasty business. I'm not mentioning his name. This document isn't going anywhere, but I'm not bad-mouthing a member of my firm.

"Why didn't you object to Giroux?" I asked him. "You know what he's doing."

"In the first place, my name's not Eliot Estabrook Lawrence the tenth, or whatever you are."

I was stunned by his rudeness.

"In the second place, I am, unlike yourself, a humble service partner, a cowed member of a clientless caste, a mendicant who depends on the kindness of others, and whose primary source of business is Chairman Maollard."

I'd never heard that one.

"Yes, I am only a plebian with tuition bills and a modest sailboat whose hull I must scrape myself. Here I am, a cringing wretch, clinging to the third rung of a ten-rung compensation ladder where rungs one and two are reserved for the newly-admitted and the nearly-departed. Any further questions, my liege?"

He hung up before I could answer.

63

I'VE TRIED not to dwell on it, but this winter (Monday, January 16, 2004 to be precise) James (never Jim) Fulham, who we'd rustled from a lesser (as in less profitable) firm, took his private equity group over to Baker & Richards. The same damn outfit Ruth went to. As did Quintus. He made partner a few years ago, and, given the financial disparity between the firms, he may be out-earning me.

Seven partners, 10 associates, assorted other ranks, and over $18,000,000 in 2003 collections bugged out with no warning. Those slime balls defected within a week of receiving their bloated bonus checks. I'm not sure I'd care if it weren't for that damn loan from Devonshire Trust, now AmeriCorp. The departure of Fulham and his fellow-ferrets shouldn't be fatal, but it's a red flag to our lender and our customers, not to mention our other lawyers with itchy feet.

The media are all over it. There's nothing more entertaining than covering lawyers mud wrestling. It makes everyone else feel good about themselves. I've seen the same effing picture of Fulham in four publications. He's getting more exposure than me. There he is, the smarmy Judas, wearing a self-satisfied smirk, surrounded by his sixteen fellow travelers. I disliked Fulham from the moment I saw him. Peevish. Petty. Always looking out for number one. There's another photo that's even worse. It's a portrait of that phony in his tinted, sculpted hair with his chin supported between thumb and index finger. He's doing his damnedest to look distinguished while favoring us with his sickening 'hire me' expression.

Now he's telling the world how much he loved—no, loves—Curtis and how much he hopes the firm will survive. A nice touch. "They forced my hand," says Fulham. "I had no choice. I had to look out for my team. It wasn't about me." My ass.

We hadn't implemented the business practices necessary to survive in today's competitive atmosphere. Funny to hear that crap from someone else. Yes, he went on, Curtis and Perkins, a fine 'old' firm, was making 'some' progress under Andrew Millard, its 'able' (condescending pecker head) managing partner but it was a case of 'too little, too late'. This was, in Fulham's words, a 'more in sorrow than in anger' decision. Curtis and Perkins's 'nice guy ethos' was inhibiting the required reforms. He even had the stones to talk about his 'heavy heart'. I almost admired him since I'm always invoking the same organ.

Since there was nothing more he and his 'team' could do within a reasonable timeframe (the miserable dick hadn't done squat except say he was gone), Fulham's jackals owed it to their customers to find a stronger 'guess what' from which to screw them. You got it: 'platform'. Cliché du jour.

The Fulham Group would have the necessary resources and support at Baker & Richards, a larger, more 'vibrant' firm with NIP that just happened to be about $300,000 more than ours. To the layperson: NIP stands for net income per partner, and don't ask me what happened to the second 'P'. NIP rules, and all one needs to know is this—NIP is the partnership equivalent of earnings per share, with the partners being the shares. A trick to remember: reduce the number of shares, *i.e.* unload unproductive partners, and presto—a flat bottom line generates higher NIP.

"Not that this is about money," said Fulham.

However, when one of the business reporters pressed him, he admitted, "Yes, my team's financial contributions were inadequately recognized at Curtis and Perkins." Some lawyers revolt me.

In fact, the press was more interested in the damage done to Curtis than they were in the creeps who'd just hit the jackpot. With an uncanny instinct for the jugular, my erstwhile friend Barnes phoned the clown who'd make us look the worst. Eliot, who could be counted on to spout the passé pieties. He came through, rambling on about disloyalty, selfishness, greed and the failure by Fulham to respect the fact that other lawyers had pulled Curtis through slow times in the past. Eliot was adept at pouring kerosene on the flames. He succeeded in making Fulham look like a swine, himself look like an ass, and me look as though I'd lost control.

Then the AmeriCorp goons came calling. Not our madras-wearing schoolmates who'd shoved money at us. They were long gone. Handed paper parachutes and pushed. These were the Bronx hard asses. The usurers. The workout thugs from the back offices with linoleum floors. The closet squad you never see at closing dinners or golf tournaments. The wide-belt, narrow necktie, square-toe shoes gang. To them, maintaining a relationship with a venerable Boston law firm meant zip. Their knee cappers didn't mince words.

No more matey talk about rolling over our loan even though we were current. The Fulham defection was a default under the covenant requiring a minimum number of equity partners. Our loan was put on a demand basis, our interest rate was increased to prime plus 500 basis points, and the bank took a security interest in everything not hocked to others. That once faraway balloon payment is about to explode in my face.

Now an aggressive repayment schedule has us driving domestic cars and shrink-wrapping our boats, including the *Yes, Andrew*. To complete our humiliation, the equity partners must sign joint and several guarantees of the entire $15,000,000, thus overriding the forgiving provisions I'd originally negotiated. And, finally, that art I'd bought in '89 hasn't done squat. The Japs, who I'd counted on to take it off my hands if things went sideways, are busted. Where is Ruth or a trustworthy wife when I need to hide assets?

Still on the firm: there's another weak spot. Hiring. When I arrived at Curtis, we had a subspecialty—declining families. We were experts at selecting the last withered shoot from the expiring plant. We took those simpletons because of their grandfathers' accomplishments and the hope their daddies would send us business. It never happened. The poor saplings were unable to stand without stakes and guy wires. Sooner rather than later, they were off to the failed associates' pulp mill. Eliot and I were the exceptions who proved the rule. Since then, we've traded down socially without any appreciable uptick in talent.

Last year was typical. We interviewed nearly 300 subprime prospects from 17 (!) law schools. We made over 70 offers and received 11 acceptances (eight of whom were women). Grim. I remember when our yield from the top schools was over 75%. We need people on our hiring committee who can sell mutton dressed up as lamb.

And, while I'm at it, where am I supposed to put my newest field day trophies? They're now pewter, a dismal gray alloy of tin and lead. Quite appropriate, actually, since most of us are dross, not sterling. Another uplifting change: the partners' retirement parties, once held at the most discriminating clubs, have become forlorn cake and boxed-wine wakes in our main conference room. The attendees: a mob of sullen rankers held there at bayonet point. Worse than those May Day rallies. As a surveyor with a malfunctioning instrument might say, "*Sic transit…*"

Even worse, I'm back on the coffin nails. Not too bright if you've got asthma. I'd damn near broken the habit, getting down to no more than the few a day I cadged from our more obliging secretaries.

What's Eliot up to during all of this? He's smelling the fucking roses. That's what. Time to introduce the canker.

64

I NEED a plan. What about this? Enlist Millard as my coach, as my voice. Have him be my Cyrano. On the plus side, Millard has Cyrano's way with words, and he's had notable success with the ladies. Yes, he's got panache, but he lacks Cyrano's nobility. If it amused him, he'd think nothing of grabbing Dawn for himself. I saw the way he was leering at her.

Millard once said, "Ten seconds of my full candle power and the woman's mine. She'll try turning away, but she'll always look back and there I'll be, high beams blazing."

I'd make a perfect tongue-tied Christian de Neuvillette, the earnest dim bulb for whom Cyrano acted as proxy, but there the similarity ends. Christian was young and handsome, and it's unlikely Millard would risk much for love or honor. Drop the Cyrano idea. Millard's unreliable, and the story turns out badly for everyone. In the end Dawn/Roxanne realizes she's always loved Millard/Cyrano. That would be bad enough, but by then both Cyrano and Christian are dead.

When someone daydreams the way I've been doing lately, I assume he reaches the critical moment when the object of his desire sees him in the buff. Most men probably figure this will arouse their ladies. Millard would. I have no such illusions. While I might pass muster in a dim light among octogenarians with glaucoma, the same cannot be true with an ardent clear-eyed woman in her prime.

Hair is a problem. The gray I once craved is betraying me. Even worse, hair's vanishing from where it belongs and sprouting like kudzu in places best left bare. I need both fertilizers and defoliants. I am cast down when I compare my shiny dome with Millard's luxuriant crown which has somehow retained its original color,

But even Millard, who's been chewing his fingernails since AmeriCorp jumped us, complains. He talks openly about his 'Bermuda triangle' where hair loss is occurring 'in an absurdly symmetrical pattern'. "My once-flourishing first-growth forest looks like a drought-stricken wheat field. What's to be done about this parched landscape?" asks my friend. "Implants would accentuate the unnatural agricultural look. Should I consider a brush fire to stimulate new growth?"

Then there's gravity. Parts of me normally covered and, therefore, invisible, are experiencing their own depressing transformations. I refer specifically to my hindquarters, which hang listlessly like the drooping sails of a becalmed square-rigger. At least my stomach is reasonably flat. Millard's looks like a well-set spinnaker.

In addition, I've noticed my body's constituent parts are no longer cooperating with each other. Once they worked in harmony. Not anymore. Limbs and organs that break down are abandoned by the side of the trail. As my drill instructor described the Army's Second Division in Korea, "They left behind everyone they could fucking find." My heart doesn't give a hoot about my lungs, and my chest disregards my lower back. My innards refuse to curb my cholesterol. I've held this alliance together for years. Now it's like post-Tito Yugoslavia. What's more, I'm making puddles under the urinals and rolling rather than carrying my suitcases. Enough self-flagellation. Despite everything, I feel revitalized. The firm and its problems seem remote.

65

JEANNETTE INFORMS me my pal is alarmed by his physical deterioration. Well, he should be. Even I have experienced some subsidence. In fact, people have ceased underestimating my age. But I have glorious memories. And, as it happens, a not-so-glorious one. I was in my bedroom with the door closed. Reading comics. Probably *Blackhawk*. It was late, and it would have been logical to assume I was asleep. But I wasn't. So, I overheard Mother refer to me as 'FATSO' (fat repelled and terrified her). No biggie. That sobriquet kept me trim for decades. Now I am on the 'husky' side. 'Plump' and 'stout' are too eunuch-like.

Of late, however, I've been prey to melancholy. It's tragic I was never captured on canvas in my prime. Alternatively, I see a larger-than-life statue in glowing red marble. I am regal in my armor. I can hear cries of delight and sharp intakes of breath, when centuries later I am unearthed from a shady cypress grove. "O Attic shape!"

I'm gently sponged by lusty, adoring peasant girls, smuggled to the Getty, and, finally, after heated negotiations, repatriated. What classic harmony! What dynamic tension between my beauty and my majesty! My votaries whisper, "More lovely than Apollo, more dreadful than Ares."

No. Strike that. I am sculpted in white marble. In the buff. Smooth and hairless. As though I'd just gotten a full-body Brazilian. Regard my articulated veins and musculature. I am Michelangelo's magnificent marble David, not Donatello's poofy bronze travesty. Observe my engine of desire. Saved from the puritanical Christians who depeckered the heroes of antiquity, lopping off the one organ that, even if it belonged to a saint, offered no hope of either salvation or temporal power. Despite this doctrinal absurdity, mine would, I am certain, have found its way into a reliquary. Generations would have gazed upon me and my memorable member; men with awe and envy; women modestly or boldly depending on their inclinations; none with indifference.

Alas, tempus has done what tempus does. Should I end it now, not by falling on my sword—ouch—but with an overdose of an ED remedy? False Staff would enter the hereafter standing tall. However, that would discommode the undertaker. He'd have to top False Staff with a chain saw in order to close the casket. Alternatively, he could install a Plexiglas observation cupola in the lid, kind of like a Jules Verne submersible.

Now's the time to strike. While Eliot is, as usual, blissfully unsuspecting. Being the petitioner, I agreed to meet him in his cluttered, trophy-less room.

A stack of months-old documents teetered on the edge of his single guest chair. Eliot looked up, grinned Eliotishly, and noticed there was no place for me to sit. After a moment's rummaging, he produced a virginal red-rope, one that didn't have the stretch marks of those distended by too many closings. After stuffing it, he added it to one of his piles, which, at present rates of growth, will eventually cut off his view of the harbor.

"What's shakin'?" asked the newly-hip Eliot Lawrence.

"Since you were good enough to support Henri Giroux, there's someone else I'd like to run by you."

"Run him or walk him, my friend," said the implausibly cocksure Eliot.

"It's about our investment philosophy."

"Yes, I know. *Harvard College v. Amory*. Eighteen something. The prudent man rule."

"Nice work, E. That said, there's someone you've got to meet."

"Who?"

"Someone who'll give us a shot in the arm, a kick in the ass, you name it. Like our other laterals. Juice up our performance and stop the bleeding."

"The bleeding?"

"Roger your last. A bunch of my customers are kvetching about their returns, and a handful have had the temerity to walk. As for smart new money… not happening if I've got to level with them about how we're doing."

"Who's our newest savior?"

"A kid named Roddy Slice. Almost 40. He's about to make managing director at a big-time Wall Street operation. We've got to grab him first. We need someone sharp and with-it, and we need him, and I mean him, fast. Not a dame. Not another plodder from a bank's trust department."

"What'll he cost us?"

"Low seven-figure signing bonus, tier 10 dollars, annual performance bonuses, complete investment discretion and, if I could figure out how to take this joint public, options."

"Nothing else?"

"Please, Eliot, don't fuck with me. Not now. I'm serious. We're hemorrhaging worse than the Hapsburgs."

"But why me? It's your racket."

"Yeah, yeah, but for reasons that continue to escape me, people around here will ask me what you think. So, for Chrissake, at least talk to him. For your pal Andrew's sake… for old time's sake…for whatever."

"OK, but only if you can assure me he's not another Jack Lucas."

"Thanks. Consider yourself assured." God, how I hate crawling. I thought I was past that.

66

WITH NO chemical assistance, I feel rejuvenated. Restrain yourself, Mr. Lawrence. It would be unseemly to be observed skipping down the corridors. I haven't felt this way since I pursued dearest Clare in the Arizona desert. No more killing time by cooking. Cooking's on the back burner. Ha. Ha. Cool it, Long Ball. Even the remote Jeannette has noticed your buoyant mood. She's probably worried you'll "jump her bones", to use one of Millard's crude expressions. She needn't be concerned.

The day of our lunch arrived at last. Using a new blade, I shaved with particular care while asking myself, "What are you on?" Am I as vain as Millard? I've let Dawn pick the time of our lunch. When I was courting Clare I made those calls, but that was then. This way, Dawn will be more engaged and empowered.

I thought I recalled her saying she knew of a place by the harbor, but, just in case, I've taken the precaution of reconning a part of town I haven't visited since the beginning of the Big Dig. Far better to be decisive than to lose face by floundering, particularly in a seafood restaurant. Ha. Ha. The place I've tentatively selected is perfect. Left to my own devices, I usually eat at my club or a sub shop, but Dawn will expect a clean, airy establishment where we can 'dine' either in or out depending on the weather. She'll require an up-to-date menu with an array of low-carb selections. Her lovely figure cannot be an accident. That's given me an idea for another topic of conversation. Healthy eating. This will flow naturally into a discussion of the benefits of exercise and, were I Millard, the relationship between fitness and sexual performance. Here I go again. Dream on.

It was getting on towards one o'clock when Dawn called to say she was 'good to go' but didn't have much time. Oh boy. What did that mean? Was she begging off? No, but this might put us under pressure. What do I know about speed dating?

We left together in the same elevator, and that, I thought, was bold. I was relaxed, and so was Dawn, but probably for different reasons. For me, it was *'honi soit qui mal y pense'*, a defiant proclamation of bona fides. For her, it was no biggie, probably nothing more than honoring an improvident commitment. Dawn looked different today. No longer the moonlit enchantress, but wonderful to be with, nevertheless. Lovely black hair; strong, interesting features; and a powerful red lipstick that matched her vivid silk (I think) blouse. A delicate blouse, the contours of which I studied for reminders of what I'd seen exactly nine nights before. A heart-stopping smile that lost nothing in daylight. White, pleated skirt. Pretty sandals. Wow.

Sometimes I look silly, and this was one of those times. There I was walking down State Street with a beautiful young woman nobody could possibly mistake for a relative. I'm not being modest. Just realistic. How can I forget an incident at my last boarding school reunion, where Millard skipped my 'Giving Back' discussion group and tried to organize one of his own called, 'Our Peckers, Our Prostates?' This was after he rolled out his "Which-first-wife-looks-most-like-a-third-wife" contest.

Millard and I were going to visit the new hockey rink. We'd taken a wrong turn, stopped, and bumped into each other as we set off in different directions. I sensed we were being observed, and when I looked up, I saw three girls giggling at us.

Our school had gone coed years earlier. That was fine, but those young ladies hurt my feelings. Yes, I was wearing a dopey bucket hat, and, yes, I had a bandage on my face covering a recent shaving accident, but were we, was I, *that* pathetic?

Millard ignored them. "They can't be laughing at me," he'd have said. He was wrong, I'm afraid, but summoning his instinctive self-assurance, I squared my shoulders, picked up my head, and looking to neither side, strode like a boulevardier toward the harbor with Dawn.

I had memorized a list of interesting talking points. Being somewhat on edge, I considered putting them on an index card in an easy-to-remember sequence. What a turkey. I even thought about scribbling a few reminders on a wrist band, the way quarterbacks do with their plays.

Evidently, Dawn forgot she told me about having a favorite waterfront restaurant. A bad omen. She was happy to eat anywhere. Implicit was the unstated, as long as it's not too far away and the service is fast. So be it. Maybe Dawn didn't put much thought into our tryst. Did she wish to stay at her desk resolving whatever problems were impinging on our time together?

We went to the restaurant I'd already scouted and sat outdoors under a clean striped umbrella. Dirty umbrellas ruin my mood and raise concerns about the cleanliness of the kitchen. This one was immaculate. It was a heavenly June day with low humidity. A soft sea breeze. Temperature in the mid-seventies. A couple billowy clouds. Cumulus? Who cares? Even the pigeons, gulls, and sparrows contributed to the atmosphere in a positive fashion.

67

ALL I could say when Eliot described his lunch with Dawn was, "Jejune is bustin' out all over."

But rest assured, Millard. His revels now are ending. Eliot's a sitting duck and I am an unsportsmanlike duck hunter. Just a few suggestions, trifles really, and his over-active imagination will do the rest.

And let the record show, Eliot's not the only cool kid enjoying our fine spring weather. Wouldn't it have been something if we'd bumped into each other on the waterfront, you with your friend and me with mine? She was up from New York and, still being pissed off at Papa, was staying with Wendy, Quintus, and Sextus. Cruel of me, but I couldn't help thinking of Justice Holmes's observation, "Three generations of imbeciles are enough."

Since it was almost summer, I ordered a round of gin and tonics.

"So, Ceci, how's it going?"

"Let me at least get settled before the grilling starts. Sometimes I think you're spying for my father."

The drinks arrived. We touched glasses.

"Not so, but allow me to summarize: you've done the museum thing, dabbled in private banking, killed time in your school's development office, and now you're getting a taste of the law. Nice turnaround, and here's to you."

"Thank you, temporal and spiritual adviser."

"Are you enjoying yourself?"

"I wouldn't say that, but I'm sure I could do it, and do it successfully."

"I agree. Now, your—social—life. What's happening on that front?"

"Damn little. I've been out with every eligible guy in Boston."

"New York?"

"I'm sick to death of sweaty stalkers dropping their yoga mats just upwind from my quiet space and then going 'Om' at me for the rest of the class."

Back to my risotto. It's impossible to sit with Ceci without being reminded of the fruit of my loins. Arthur and Stanley are fretting they won't survive the life estate my next and presumably youthful spouse will almost certainly extract from me. They natter on about the nuisance of arranging for my care and tidying up after my death. As though they'll have any say in these matters.

Wake up, coach. "How do you see your future, my dear?"

"As you well know, counselor, I see myself at a prestigious organization. I'm highly compensated and respected. I am someone to be cherished and indulged."

"So do I."

My sons' hearts would sing if I moved to a rent-controlled basement apartment and purchased my casket. They would be euphoric if I disposed of my property to them now, dropped my club memberships, stopped traveling, ceased all exercise, increased my intake of booze, carcinogens, and artery-clogging fats, eliminated all health care expenses, other than infrequent bulk purchases of generic drugs, and then set out for the East with my begging bowl.

They browbeat me about my lifestyle, implying, not incorrectly, that it's depleting their inheritance. They whine about receiving 'our shares now', failing to realize the income from 'their shares' assures my comfort. Do all grown children insist their vigorous daddies execute DNRs? If mine were brighter, they'd devise a DNDA (Do Not Do Anything).

I snapped back into the now when Ceci set down her drink and stared at me.

"I haven't discussed this with the men in my family, but I'm thinking of law school even though I'm damn near 40. Am I nuts?"

"The law schools love women with brains and real life experience. And, no matter what they say in places like Cambridge, beauty is not a disqualifier. Remember Reese Witherspoon in *Legally Blonde*. You'll knock 'em dead."

"I won't look foolish?"

"Absolutely not, Dearie. Check out what I'm saying with any of the lawyers you work for."

"You're sure?"

"Would you like a hand with the process?"

"Whose hand?"

"Mine."

A thoughtful pause. "Of course."

Is this what's come to be known as 'grooming'?

Meanwhile, what gives with Giroux? Where the fuck's he at? He was due here by the end of May—at the latest. He's delayed his arrival twice already. What's that crap about 'cleaning up a few odds and ends'? Is Eliot of the furrowed brows micturating in my punch bowl? It was so unlike him talking-up Giroux after that partners' meeting. He's never in favor of anything, and he's a sorry liar. Doesn't matter, though. There's no way he can screw this up—or down.

68

WHAT A nice surprise. No sooner had we sat down than Dawn handed me a page from the *Globe*. It contained an interesting piece I'd missed about Harvard's baseball coach. Then I noticed the adjacent article, which spoke of a research project on elderly men with enlarged prostates. Its headline read, 'Waking at Night to Urinate?' Which was meant for me? It was, without doubt, the baseball story, and she was being sweetly considerate.

Dawn is easy to talk to. I was spared fumbling when she said she and a friend of undisclosed gender were going to Paris in August. Was it a man? I hope not, but I shall remain positive. It's a little early in our relationship for jealousy. It was to be her first time in Paris. Since the city's nearly empty then, the resourceful Dawn went online and found an attractive rate at a five-star hotel, a hotel at which I have stayed. At full freight I might add. Was it boastful of me to tell her so? Was she impressed?

Having been to Paris, I was in a position to be both wise and helpful. I offered to loan her my guidebooks. She accepted with pleasure. Should I bring them tomorrow? How would that be interpreted? Hopelessly overanxious? Would it even register? Am I over-thinking everything? In this regard, I'm distressed when I realize women can see through so many of us. But that's other men. I'm no open book.

As we talked, I paid close attention to what Dawn said about her friend. Uh oh. It was a he. You don't travel abroad with a casual acquaintance. Or do you? Sometimes I wonder if I'm a little old fashioned. It would have been fun if I'd had a lady pal in Florence. Evidently, Dawn decided when and where they were going. Did she wear the pants? Perhaps the bloom is off their rose. I'm becoming too Millard.

Our conversation flowed along so effortlessly we neglected our menus. And I'd forgotten to see whether we were being observed. Not that I was concerned. As it happened, I saw no one I recognized. Our waiter arrived. He called himself our server and insisted on telling us his Christian name. In fact, he was concentrating on Dawn. He crouched beside her. I was momentarily flustered, and before I could suggest a more adventurous drink, Dawn ordered iced tea.

If I'd had my wits about me I would have taken charge, ordered wine (maybe even red wine) or a silly mixed drink, perhaps one with an umbrella in it, and invited her to join me. But no. The moment passed, and I settled for my usual—Diet Coke. With our waiter being unctuously attentive, Dawn ordered an anemic chef's salad (dressing on the side), and I opted for my favorite: a cheeseburger with bacon, chili, onion rings, and fries. So much for healthy eating. I should have resisted the rings, but how was I to know?

69

HAVE I been mean to Eliot of late? Mustn't alienate him. I need him to help me land Roddy. Maybe I'll cut him in on Giroux's latest, the Irish caper, where the participants grab the 'losses' and our well-compensated Hibernian straws, who aren't subject to U.S. tax, get stuck with the 'gains'.

What a hoot! Deductible Aer Lingus trips to Dublin with pints of frothy Guinness served up by ripe, red-headed Ruths, or rent boys, or tweeners for those with off-beat tastes. It's like organizing a banquet where you're obliged to offer beef, fish, and poultry.

70

I'VE BEEN so caught up with Dawn I nearly forgot about my meal with Millard and Rodney ('Roddy') Slice.

I liked that Slice wore a tie, but I'm put off by bow ties. People who wear them are self-absorbed. They regard themselves as dapper. As far as I'm concerned, a bow tie is out of place, except with a dinner jacket. And I didn't care for him fiddling with an electronic gizmo. It never left his hand, even when he was eating. Also, I'm positive he was wearing clear nail polish.

He did have impressive credentials, though. An honors graduate in economics from Columbia, a joint JD/MBA from my place followed by 15 years of increasingly prestigious jobs on Wall Street. In addition, he was a member of the Mass bar and a CFA.

"Why," I asked him, "would you leave the Big Apple just before grabbing the brass ring? And why a Boston law firm?"

"I've always wanted to run my own show, Mr. Lawrence, and, having loved my time in Cambridge, I've never stopped thinking about coming back to this neck of the woods."

"But why us, Mr. Slice?"

"Mr. Millard tells me you've got two billion under management. I'm confident I can at least double it in four or five years. And there's something else."

"Yes?"

"It'll be huge to sell Henri Giroux to our trust clients."

God save us.

Next, referring to himself as a 'quant', whatever that is, Mr. Slice assured us that under his nimble guidance we would improve returns for our trust clients without exposing them to 'material' additional risk.

He touched and retouched the usual bases: liquidity, diversification, and 'alternative' investments. He mentioned some 'complex but exciting' new products.

"What are they rated?" I asked.

"Triple-A," he shot back.

"Fine. It's enough for me if they've been blessed by Moody's and S&P."

Then Mr. Slice wrong-footed me. "I've brought along my transcripts. Would you care to look at them?"

Before I could answer, he took off on his infallible risk model and dismissed past financial calamities as curiosities from the pre-Roddy Slice dark ages. Finally, he set the hook by announcing that, with only *a slight bump* in charges to our clients, he'd be in a position to manage our personal assets for nothing.

I sensed Mr. Slice had prevailed.

Then Millard chimed in. "Want to know something else about this bright young fellow? He's got a friend who's got a friend who's best buddies with Mr. L. Yes, that one. The president of your favorite ball club."

We hired Roddy the next week. It didn't feel right to me. If I'd had a vote, it would have been thumbs down. And yes, we spiffed up our formerly low-key trust operation. Now it's called State Street Wealth Management. For what that's worth.

Back to a more agreeable subject. Dawn's coming trip to France was a conversational subtext of our lunch, something to which we could return when the words came less easily. Should I have brought up her friend? I could have gone either way on that delicate topic, but I elected to skip it. Since I'm probably older than her parents, I didn't ask about them, either.

The other big topic was Lizzie. "Would you like to hear about my pooch?" I asked her.

"Of course, Eliot. I love terriers."

Lovely! My first name just popped out. I studied her carefully. No signs of boredom. Or irony. No quick peeks at her watch. "That's wonderful. Jeannette can't stand Lizzie." That was all I had to say about my wife.

I gave Dawn the unabridged edition of my life with Lizzie. Our walks. Our games. Our conversations.

Then judging the moment to be propitious, I took a bold Millardian step and allowed as how Lizzie slept on *my* bed. I wonder if Dawn understood that meant Jeannette slept elsewhere.

Dawn seemed interested, so I pressed on. "If you'd like to meet Lizzie, I'll smuggle her into 50 State. She'd fit in a shopping bag."

Did I talk about myself too much? Did I talk too much, period? Jeannette makes no bones about my tendency to run off at the mouth and says it's getting worse. She signals me at parties by shaking her head and drawing a hand across her throat while simultaneously rolling her eyes. Others have observed this. Clare chided me more gently. Always in private. Sometimes she coached me before we went out. Was I less windy then? Won't Dawn sour on my repetitious stories? Just the way Jeannette has. Maybe my grandchildren will like them—once.

I forgot to mention that Dawn and I were sitting side by side facing the harbor. I told her I'd done this so we'd both have a good view. In fact, I'd anchored myself to leeward of her so I'd be within range of any blowing hair.

The last thing I wanted was to make Dawn anxious, so I kept a close eye on my watch.

Both of us turned out to be fast eaters. She picked at her salad, consuming the rabbit food and leaving the few good parts which I resisted spearing. I even passed on the spuds. Girls like Dawn may not fancy men who devour a whole plate of ketchup-drenched fries. I could have lingered over a coffee, but I knew we'd be off to a bad start if she began worrying about being late.

Were we noticed walking back to our office? Boston's a village, particularly the financial district if you've worked there as long as I have. It's literally impossible to go more than a few hundred yards without encountering someone you know—or, as I now find—someone familiar whose name eludes you. This goes double on a sunny spring lunch hour. Did Dawn regret we hadn't separated at the restaurant?

Then and there I made a snap decision. I wasn't returning to the office. We parted on the street. She said, and I won't forget it, "We'll have to do this again." Naturally I was thrilled, but then it occurred to me—what else could she say without being unkind? On the one hand, she could have said nothing and just thanked me. Better yet, she could have added 'soon'. Her goodbye was polite but unreadable.

We stopped. Dawn extended her right hand. No, that wouldn't do. I don't know what came over me. The Diet Coke? On an impulse, I bent and kissed her. I aimed for her cheek. She must have turned towards me (Had she meant to?) because I brushed her lips. Sweet. Delicate. Heady. And I didn't gouge her face with my glasses or bang into her teeth. It felt as though we'd been doing this forever.

Then I remembered the onion rings.

I was too wound up to analyze what I choose to think of as our date. So, I decided to take the rest of the day off. Just like that. It may not sound like me, but I've always wanted to have lunch, down a couple brewskis, and flick-out. On a weekday. While everyone else is in the office. After saying goodbye to Dawn I felt an overpowering urge to take a few hacks. And why not? You're only middle-aged once.

I used my cell phone to tell my secretary she wouldn't see me until tomorrow. I didn't even bother concocting a cover story. Did I detect a note of surprise in her voice? I think so. By the bye, I am pleased with my newest toy although I never clip it to my belt like the dweebs who strut around as though they're 'packing heat'. Yes, it took me some time to get one. It's seldom on. I don't know its number, and I only use it for occasional outgoing calls. Not that I have many people to call.

Dawn must have a cell phone. Aren't these numbers totally private? When can I ask for hers, or are you expected to wait until it's offered? I don't wish to be seen as either brash or uninterested.

All the gear was in the trunk of my turbocharged Volvo. So I saddled up, blasted over the Mystic River Bridge, and zoomed north on Route 1, hardly noticing the massage parlors. Sometimes I can hear my aluminum bat rolling around in back. Part magic wand, part Excalibur, it weighs a mere 25 ounces, and is a stunning blue and silver with its brand name in gold letters on the barrel. I'm crazy about it, but am I betraying my Louisville Sluggers? After Clare died

I stopped hitting. I bought my Easton a few years ago on a whim. It's almost unused. Because it's metal, I'm naming it 'Ding Bat'.

Helmets are required now. I selected a red one. Crimson, actually. I hadn't batted for ages, so I thought it best to start slowly. I began on an intermediate speed machine and dominated it. Next, I strode over to 'Very Fast'. I was told it was throwing at least 92 mph.

Women are unfathomable, but I've figured out pitching machines. The ball is always in the same location unless the rotating brushes are wet, in which case, go to the movies. I watch the ball coming down the chute, and start my swing before it leaves the machine. What a blast. Keep your head in there, don't stride, and watch your timing. Doing this enables me to pull it down the line. Awesome. For variety, I'll crowd the plate and go to the opposite field with a slick inside-out Jeterish (it's hard to hate him) swing. Having once again changed the outcome of the 1946 World Series, I switched sides and, batting left handed, did the same to that 1986 fiasco against the Mets. Not to mention 1967 and 1975. Take that, 1918. Bliss. I wonder if Dawn would come here. I could teach her on a slow machine.

By then I was dripping and must have looked odd in a t-shirt, suit trousers, and sneakers. Luckily, school was still in session, so there weren't any teenagers to make fun of the codger in the high-speed cage. I wish I'd been wearing my light, low-cut spikes. So much more macho than the footwear used in other sports. My last pair are in a trunk at home. I want them in my coffin when the time comes, along with the glove I used in boarding school, my first jack knife, a sweater my paternal grandmother gave me, some special honeymoon photographs, my Easton, Clare's frequently-mislaid purse, plus the compass and flashlight I will use to find her.

I was still sweaty when I turned in my helmet, so I stopped for a beer at a roadhouse. The Sox were playing a day game and kicking ass big time. Jeannette wasn't home to interrogate or ignore me. She was off on one of her due diligence trips. Millard was away too. I decided to eat in. What a lovely day. Plus, I thought up a good one for Millard. The name of an Asian baseball star. "Thai Cobb." And how about this? The name for a happy beer: "Brew Ha Ha." I bet Dawn would like that.

I poured myself a healthy scotch, microwaved some scary-looking take-out, and turned on the tube. I wonder if this journal has served its purpose. It's kept me occupied for over two decades. Maybe I'll keep on with it until I've figured out my relationship with Dawn, if I dare call it that. Then the time capsule?

So, as my colleagues are fond of saying, "What was the net-net?" All things considered, I thought it went pretty well, but Millard would have been more masterful. He'd be much further along by now. He'd have been all over her. Millard signals his interest. Why can't I? Instead, I sat there grinding on my burger and studying her face, a face I love to stare at but am unable to read.

On further reflection, it might be more effective if I put my thoughts in writing. I'm known around C&P as a polished draftsman. Every year I produce scores of well-written Note Purchase Agreements, so why should I have difficulty in expressing myself to Dawn? Letter, not email. Little thought goes into emails and, what's worse, they have a tendency to wander off the reservation.

It hasn't been easy. I began several letters, but I am still struggling to produce an appropriate salutation, not to mention a punchy first paragraph. My efforts have consumed almost half a yellow pad and several hours which would otherwise be billable. Not all of it's been wasted. I've made several decisions. Clearly 'My Dearest Dawn' is still unwarranted. So is 'Dearest Dawn'. Both greetings could ('would' is more likely) be regarded as out of order. I don't want her thinking me misguided or ill-mannered. Or pitiful. 'Dear Dawn' couldn't be faulted, but is it too alliterative? Should I just adopt the casual email approach of 'Hi'? It's friendly and youthful, but may not convey the intensity of my feelings. Perhaps that's just as well.

'After at least two dozen versions, here's the current working draft of my opening sentence:

> *Dear Dawn:*
> *In thinking about our conversation at the firm party and our nice lunch together, it occurs to me that you and I may share many of the same interests, and it would give me no end of pleasure to continue to explore with you the extent to which this might be true.*

I'm not entirely satisfied, but I've made a good start, and must remember every man of letters (Ha Ha) is blocked from time to time. Now I'm going to stop. I'll let it steep for a bit.

It's been several days since I wrote that introductory sentence, and I haven't seen Dawn again other than to sign her up to revise my estate plan. This will help us stay in touch. We've discussed my instruments, but haven't had a chance to *talk*. Can she guess the reason for my changes, particularly those concerning Jeannette? I can't seem to get any farther with my letter. I'm not sure what I want or can reasonably expect. One thing is clear. I must be more positive. And why not? The stock market continues to climb, and we appear to have won in Iraq.

Will anything 'happen' between us? I know how Millard would answer that one. What should I make of our lovely moments together? What now? Read *Pride and Prejudice* with her?

Who am I kidding? Besides myself, of course.

Just the other day, Millard said, "What a shame Clare never realized her dreams."

"What do you mean? We were blissfully happy together. You know that."

"Don't let it concern you," he said in his most offhand manner.

Clare and I shared everything. At least that's what I thought. Could she have been false? What an unworthy thought. But what did she write on the card she sent Millard? Did she ever see that skier again? Did she miss him all her life? Were there others? How did Millard learn so much about her?

71

AT LAST. August 6, 2004.

After all these years wondering whether I'd get the Jack Falstaff treatment. That she'd turn to me and say, "I know thee not, old man." Instead, it's lunch at the Ritz with Favorite Young Friend ('FYF'). I booked a bedroom overlooking the Public Garden. Just in case. I was jumpy and had fortified myself with a pre-game pop before FYF's arrival. In fact, I was soaked. It was literally running down my side. Worse, it showed. I was wearing a blue shirt.

Then I went and violated one of my (cribbed from Anthony Bourdain) sacrosanct culinary commandments: Never Ever Order the Fish Special. Today's was tarted-up branzino, unlucky successor to the disappearing Chilean sea bass.

I think we suspected this could turn into more than lunch, but we pretended otherwise. Was it a go or a no-go? Would I have to eat the cost of the room? It's easier to break the ice if you're smashed. But I wasn't. Neither was FYF.

Following the obligatory salads, our waiter brought us our third wines (actually it was FYF's second, unless she too had jumped the gun). We'd already wolfed down a couple bowls of mixed nuts. FYF preferred the cashews. So do I, but I let her have them. Anything to improve the odds.

How to raise the subject that was filling me with dread and excitement? The answer was right in front of me: a nearly empty dinner plate in the center of which was a small fillet. It had been wrapped around what had been advertised as a 'jumbo' shrimp.

All you could see of happy Mr. Shrimp was his hindquarters. The rest of him had disappeared into the branzino. Totally indecent. Filletlingus at its most depraved.

FYF and I marveled at this uninhibited pair. We looked at each other. Seconds later, we cracked up. Both of us were somewhat flushed. Had we crossed the rubicund? Time for the Ogden Nash Test.

"I propose a toast to America's greatest comic poet, a man who could express so brilliantly what, I trust, both of us are feeling: 'Home is heaven and orgies are vile. But you need an orgy once in a while.' To Mr. Nash."

"To Mr. Nash."

"Upstairs?"

FYF nodded.

We left the shrimp and the branzino to their fun and set off for ours.

Poor FYF. She'd lost her mother and a doltish husband. Dad was a lump, but I understood her. We shared a joint and sipped champagne (French for a change). I presented her with a Hermès scarf (likewise French) and sprang for more champagne (also French). By 3:00 p.m. I had my arm around her waist as we looked down on the Garden. By 3:10 p.m. I'd ingeniously transformed her scarf into a piece of intimate apparel. By 3:15 p.m. I'd removed it.

I mean, why wouldn't we at some point? Look what came of saving herself for her underdone spouse—cook-offs, misfires, and air bursts.

And wasn't I irresistible when I begged her to "lead me now into temptation."

I raised an inquiring eyebrow. "At least three mattresses," crooned the rosy FYF. "You were considerate, patient, and pleasingly vigorous—although seeing you in the raw with your one-pack abs made me think of the old line, 'It gotta be jelly 'cause jam don't shake.'"

Such unplumbed depths. I chuckled like the good sport I am. The TV was showing reruns of the Tour de France, and FYF dubbed me 'Lance'. After that, I even managed an encore.

So what's the takeaway from this happy tryst? Just this. She's mine. John Wilmot put it best,

> *But still continue as thou art,*
> *Ancient Person of my Heart.*

And to think the firm has exempted me from attending those sexual harassment sessions.

I'll let FYF's shrink figure out how her father fits into all this. He'd be beyond upset. Was she trying to *get* Dad in some sick southern gothic fashion? But this is New England, and she comes from fine Puritan stock.

Now I shall spirit her away to the Gulf. To my favorite hotel. I'm a regular. My Eggs Benedict await me every morning. The maître d' is, at least in my presence, an ardent Yankees fan. The staff is unfailingly deferential, particularly after I scourged the waitress who addressed my most recent companion with the name of her immediate predecessor.

Unlike the restless Atlantic, the Gulf of Mexico is still and empty at six on a summer morning. It's even cool, if you're out before the sun clears the palms and the hideous piles that rise above them. Little's stirring aside from a few skittish sandpipers. Perhaps a lone gleaner scouring the beach with scythe-like swings of his metal detector or a gaunt power-walker lacerating the sand with her ski poles. At this time of year, you may observe a squadron of well-drilled stingrays driving panicked bait fish to their deaths against the shore.

I went alone the last time. Never again. Early one morning, I came upon a mother and her young son gathering shells at the high-tide line. She held the bag into which he placed his offerings. Then he'd be off down the beach, but never beyond the arc of her concern.

Thankfully, I am not burdened by such memories.

As for Eliot, would he welcome me as his son-in-law?

Lately, I'm feeling an uncharacteristic warmth towards the old boy. Why? Well, for one thing he's such a gracious loser, and I am, if nothing else, a magnanimous winner. As a token of our enduring friendship, I just gave him a weekly AM and PM pill organizer. A subtle foretaste of what's in store.

The poor guy. Since leaving college he's laid a grand total of two women, married both, and lost both. Yes, I have won and won big, even if this is not yet universally acknowledged. In addition, I've made scads more money. He has never learned that in the real world, it's hard to conquer if you refuse to stoop.

But now he's slowly drifting away from me and the firm. This is disturbing. We're adversaries, even if he doesn't know it. He's supposed to keep trying and keep failing. How dare he quit on me. Outwardly, he is neither jealous of my earnings nor concerned about his own. With a nod to the great lexicographer, let me say that when a man is tired of his comp, he is tired of life.

I don't need him, but it would be useful if he helped me with AmeriCorp. It's mid-October, and the bank could offer us decent terms or call the loan tomorrow. We've limped along on a demand basis for over a year with our numbers heading south. Our quarterly floggings by the workout heavies are brutal. As I was being tongue-lashed at the last meeting, I found myself drifting back to the days when Ruth was my now and Clare my later.

I sometimes ache for Ruth, even the high-mileage 1992 model. She was the sweetest of them all. I may have undervalued sweet. She addressed me as 'My Love' in that long-ago letter. Was that what we were to each other? You weren't just sweet. You were spicy too. Like the time you said, "I've got a new name for Mr. Lawrence's horse-faced personal assistant."

I looked, expectant.

"Secretariat," you giggled.

I can still see and smell you quick marching into my office, halting in front of my desk, hiking up your skirt, thumbing down those lace nothings, executing a smart about-face, bending at the waist, and saying, quite solemnly, "Name the banker."

"Bear Stearns," I'd answer.

"Will the handsome solicitor come forward and receive his prize," you'd reply.

Thank you for helping me endure those decedents and testators, Ruthie.

And, to the end, you had great pins. Unlike boxers, whose legs go first.

Stop this mawkishness, Millard. You're a roué who never rued a day. *Je ne regrette rien.*

There's something else, however. Edward, who never got his rocks off, was born 63 years ago today. As a matter of fact, I had a run in with Ed less than a year ago when we buried Cousin Bruce of the recycled English papers. Don't ask me why I went, but I owed Bruce and thought I should check out the old gang. My grandmother shelled out for perpetual care, and I damn well wanted to make sure we were getting it.

There was Mother. Her three hubbies were elsewhere. Was she still hitting the bottle and revving-up the REMFs? And there too was Edward Van Rensselaer Millard, October 18, 1941–August 16, 1944.

Maybe it's time to stake out my site and consider my obit. There's scads of good material and an array of flattering photos. But what happens if some big shots check out when I do? Will I get stuffed into the death notices? Unthinkable.

And what happens if some essential, but till now ignored, pump, pipe, or valve shuts down, plugs up, or malfunctions? I can hear my healthy bits, including, of course, the indomitable False Staff, screaming, "Hey, asshole, get back to work. We're just fine. Stop dicking off for fuck's sake or you'll sink us all." Scary.

After planting Bruce, I went to the business office. Given my fair complexion, I put in for a shady spot. Then I learned our plot was full, and the abutting acreage was spoken for. Now what? I have no desire to hang with my old man. He's in an espresso can on a shelf near Hartford. Besides, we always fought. Where does that leave me when the music stops? Where will I go, and who will lie next to me?

And then what? Will Mother be her usual welcoming self? One of her last endearments was to address me, her successful first born, as 'Dead Ass'. Well I guess the joke's on her. Is she still pissed off at me for being alive? How about Ed? Playing the blame game, I bet. How old will he be? Will he and Mother make common cause against me? It won't matter if Edward's still under three. I'll be able to handle him. However, I can't count on the old man weighing in on my side. He never forgave me for Brown, and by the time I'd made it, he'd lost it. He probably thinks Ed would have gone to Harvard. Is that why he disinherited me and left what little he had to his undergraduate club, the one Eliot joined?

Stop with the belly aching, big guy. You're sounding like your pal. How could I have guessed in 1963 that everything would turn out so well? *A.A.*'s going to run my feature on Giroux as soon as he shows up.

Change of subject.

Francesca has reappeared. Last week we found ourselves cheek-to-cheek, so to speak, in the same elevator. She's moved back to Boston and is running the State Street office of a New York venture capital firm. She looks stunning. But older and perhaps slightly less picky. I moved closer.

While staring at my trousers, Francesca asked, "Have you missed me, Honey?"

That wicked girl noticed me noticing her chest, her anklet, and her sandals.

"Adorable Francesca, you make me forget all others, real and imagined." She tossed her hair, and I tossed mine. "Darling Creature, I even forgive you for telling me—and others—I am needy, narcissistic, and immature."

What she said was, "Such fun to see you again. Let's give it a whirl before you're beyond chemical assistance? I'll go easy, and if you experience an erection lasting more than four hours, we'll post it on Curtis's website."

Which brings me back to me.

I've got to remember that each year my annual physical has shown a gradual worsening of my cardiac risk ratio. My only bad number. No matter. We, Francesca and I, have unfinished business. Doctors be damned. To my old-fart golfer friends, I say, "A bush in the hand is worth a bird on the 18th."

So I'm taking Francesca to Fenway, and I hope she hasn't put her breasts away for the winter. However, there's something to be attended to before we gorge on brews, bratwursts, and each other.

Dawn Peterson was in chambers. As always, she was composed. Her hair was pulled back in a way that accentuated her alabaster profile. A lapis pendant hung from her neck. Almost straight down. Little makeup. Kind of 18th century. Not really my sort. She's bound to turn into one of those lace-capped, frizzy-haired hags painted by Copley and Stuart.

"Miss Peterson, we need to talk. Now."

"Talk about what, Mr. Millard?"

"Not what. Whom. Our mutual friend, Eliot Estabrook Lawrence. Who else?"

"Oh."

I believe the poised estate planner was beginning to blush. How quaint and old fashioned. "Look, I don't wish to be insensitive, but of course you like Eliot. Everyone likes Eliot. Wouldn't you agree?"

"I'm a little confused, Mr. Millard."

"Please, Dawn. Don't go all 'litigator' on me, and don't, for goodness sake, think I've been conscripted into the sex police. OK?"

"Mr. Millard, this conversation's really…"

"Stop interrupting me and stop with the injured innocence routine, although you do carry it off quite nicely. You know, I know, everyone in the office whose nookie radar, yes nookie radar, is functioning knows Eliot's smitten with you."

"I…"

"That's quite enough. It's fine. You're an elixir. He hasn't looked this chipper since the first Mrs. Lawrence. So keep on doing whatever you're doing. And you have no obligation to fill me in on the juicy details. But if you like…"

"Mr. Millard!"

"Just kidding. Don't take offense, and don't think about reporting me. My collections trump your feelings. Lastly, remember you work in my department. All I ask is this. When Eliot ceases to amuse, let him down gently. The recycling bin, not the shredder or incinerator. If you can manage it, trundle someone age-appropriate into his path, and make him think he's releasing you. He loves doing the right thing."

"Enough, please. I must ask you to…"

"Yes, it's a tall order, but you've got what it takes. A final word. This conversation never happened. Understood?"

I received a flustered nod.

She'd be such a push-over. So maybe I'll push. Eliot would have a fit when, as usual, Millard gets there firstest with the mostest.

72

I KNEW what to expect when Millard exploded into my office without knocking and screamed, "How're they hanging, Hoss? You wanna hear about my latest?"

At times like this, I have few choices. Hang up and smile, or be unacceptably rude. I hung up, but I didn't smile. What would it be: sex, money, or acclaim?

"Hey, Big Guy, remember Francesca?"

How could I not? For several hours in New York, I'd thought she'd ruined me. "Of course," I replied.

"Well, I'm taking her to Fenway to see some ass-kicking by the Bronx Bombers. Yo, baby!"

I gave him a curt nod which I trust conveyed my need to return to the lease I'd been studying. No such luck.

"And, while we're talking poontang, you might be interested to hear I've just had a date with my favorite young friend."

Millard was studying me carefully. I didn't want to give him any satisfaction, but I couldn't stop myself, "Anyone I know?" I said casually.

Running his fingers through his hair, he shook his head and began laughing, then coughing. He started turning red, pulled out his inhaler, and took several puffs. Being asthmatic myself, I knew what was happening. It kind of sneaks up on you. First the throat clearing. Next the scratchiness. Then the coughing and finally the terrifying constriction of the airways.

After settling down, Millard made for the door. As he was leaving, I noticed he'd left his inhaler on my desk. I should have called after him, but I didn't.

It may have been because I was still replaying my last two voicemails. The first was from Buzz.

"Stay alert, buddy. Tax shelters are collapsing, and law firms are folding. Justice, the IRS, and the SEC are circling. Even the Big Five have taken cover. When these babies go down, everyone starts pointing fingers, including the clients who howl they're innocents, lured into these schemes by unscrupulous professionals with assurances, written and oral, that everything was copacetic. Fend off Giroux, or look to thy malpractice policy."

I'm disregarding the second message entirely. It was from some clown affecting a James Cagney accent: "A word to the wise, Mr. Lawrence. Stop bashing Giroux. You don't want to be hurting a lot of important people, including some of your firm's best clients. That wouldn't be smart, would it?"

Hot damn. Though I've never been romanced by a headhunter, I've finally been threatened. That's something.

73

WHAT HO, Millard? The entrails foretell a fifth and final wife. I see her clearly: Brandi, a tat-splattered teenager I'm destined to meet at the take-out window of a drive-thru. She admires my Porsche and the net worth it implies. What seals the deal is my evident proximity to the hereafter.

Which leads me to my latest offering. The Dunkirk Fund. Too many of my improvident contemporaries are entering their final decade with lucre insufficient to shed their Brandies and still enjoy the comforts to which they've become accustomed.

Why must it be 'either/or?' It needn't. The Dunkirk Fund (liquid assets prudently invested in jurisdictions that respect client anonymity) enables one to evacuate and maintain standards elsewhere. Bravo, Millard. I continue to delight in my creativity. Like aged Ulysses, "Though much is taken, much abides."

I am so not missing Jeannette. Finding a magazine, not the kind you read, in her bedside table really tore it. Even though it wasn't loaded.

Another matter. About this, my chef d'ouevre. I see reviews larded with phrases beginning with 'fully', followed by a hyphen, followed in turn by 'developed', 'imagined', and 'realized'. Verbs like 'conjure' and 'depict' (the equivalent of 'show' in the Manichean universe of 'show' v. 'tell'). My absolute favorite: 'limn'. You've arrived when you're said to have 'limned'. And descriptives like 'lapidary' and 'translucent'.

74

SAY IT isn't so. Such a tired cliché. Elderly husband returns unexpectedly from a busted closing and catches his young wife… It's bad Boccaccio.

"Yo, Andrew. It's on the kitchen table. Pour one for me, and get your ancient ass in here. Check out my new playsuit.

"Sheesh. Yes, I remember you. You're my hubby, Eliot Effing Lawrence. Right?

"What's it look like I'm watching? *The Sound of Music?* A girl's gotta get herself in the mood.

"You dipshit. Look what you've done. I can't return it to Blockbuster like that.

"Get dressed? Pffft. Why don't you get undressed? Maybe something'll happen for a change.

"Yeah. You disgust me, too.

"Get out, yourself.

"I *meeeen* it, Jeannette.

"Get your hands off me.

"You're hurting me. Tony'll fix your ass.

"None of your damn business. Ouch, goddamnnit.

"Get outta my room. And close the fuckin' door.

"No way. I'm not going anywhere.

"Not now. Not anytime soon. Maybe not until you're dead.

"Think you can scare me?

"Whadda you mean, half an hour? I can't be packed that fast. You think I am? Fuckin' Houdini?

"A room at the Sheraton? Why not the Four Seasons, you cheap bastard?

"OK. OK, I'm ready. You mess with my Hummels an' Tony'll mess with you.

"That's right, asshole.

"No, I don't give a fat shit if I ever see this dump again.

"Now it'll be just you and that yappy bitch. The four-legged one.

"You better get me a condo.

"No, at the Ritz.

"You got that right. I never did. And you never gave a fat shit about anyone but her."

How sad but predictably tawdry. At last she's gone. Should I clean up Jeannette's language or delete the scene entirely? That would be the decent thing to do. Nope. Tell it like it is, or there's no point to this.

Only one remaining task. Find her a condo in the 'burbs. Sufficiently distant for me to be outside her blast radius.

75

WHAT THE fuck! Sitting on my desk when I got to work was a heavy, dazzlingly white envelope. In a punctilious, fussy, almost unfamiliar hand, it read, 'Andrew de Peyster Millard, Esquire', beneath which appeared, 'Personal & Confidential'. Crane's stationery? Of course. Black ink? What else? On the back of the envelope: '118 Beacon Street, Boston'. No self-respecting Lawrence would include the state or, perish the thought, the zip code.

So, what's the lad up to now? No, you gotta be shitting me. It read:

Dear Mr. Millard:

The other night, after consuming more than her recommended daily allowance of distilled spirits, my spouse, Jeannette Tisdale Lawrence, let slip certain matters concerning her personal life which, while not entirely surprising, were far better left unsaid and, while so doing, made a number of vulgar, invidious, ad-hominem comparisons between the two of us upon which I am disinclined to elaborate. Suffice it to say, these revelations and divers related suspicions compel me, as a gentleman, to demand satisfaction and call you out. I assume you take my meaning. Allow me to suggest the following arrangements.

<u>*Date & Time*</u>*: Friday, October 15, 2004. The traditional hour: sunrise which occurs at 6:57a.m. However, for the sake of simplicity, I suggest 7:00 a.m.*

<u>*The Place:*</u> *the 50-yard line, Harvard Stadium, Allston, Massachusetts. You can obtain access through the gate at the open end of the Stadium adjacent to the Gordon track facility.*

Weapons: Fists, bare or gloved, at your election. I shall bring with me two matched pairs of Everlasts which you are, of course, free to inspect beforehand.

Rules of Engagement: Standard boxing protocol (as promulgated by the Marquess of Queensberry) will be in effect, but the match will continue without interruption until one of us obtains satisfaction.

Seconds: Suit yourself. However, I, the offended party, shall be unaccompanied.

I trust the foregoing arrangements are satisfactory in all respects. I am stunned, disappointed, and outraged. Be there at the appointed hour or I shall seek redress at another time and place. The gauntlet has been thrown down.

Eliot Estabrook Lawrence

Fuck! Fuck! FUCK! What is that jackass thinking? What mythic hero is he playing now? Hector? Hamilton? No, both of those clowns bit the gas pipe. Maybe he's Robert the fucking Bruce at Bannockburn offing that English knight in single combat. What was the guy's name? Who gives a shit? My *nom de guerre* is Andrew, *Coeur de Lapin*. Or is this some dicked-up Monty Python skit? No, not his style.

What a frigging dork. He knows I'm a little overweight and a bit out of shape. And, who's he kidding? He doesn't give a rat's ass about la belle Jeannette. As for those "divers-related suspicions", I was just messing with him.

76

I SLEPT well last night. The first time in ages. It was her doing, of course. After a long absence, the Clare I love paid me a visit. She was wearing one of the last nightgowns I'd given her. We lay together as we always did, heart to heart.

"Don't doubt me, Dearie," she said. "Remember what we had and always will."

"Always?"

"Always. Now I must go."

"Forever?"

"Of course not, Sweetheart."

77

SCREW HIM. I'm choosing guns. That'll cool his jets. Oh Christ, no it won't. He'd accept, and I'd be fucked. Aging Galahad actually owns a matched pair of dueling pistols handed down to him by some illustrious great, great. Worse, he's probably fired the frigging things. Holy crap, didn't he shoot Expert with the .45 in the Crotch? Leave us reconsider. Swords? No way. I remember us going at it with broomsticks when I was 14 and relatively agile. Unfortunately, he was a young d'Artagnan. How about some ideas, somebody?

78

OK, I'M still enraged, but now I'm feeling like a dope. And, if I'm going to be even faintly honest with myself, I've got to admit this isn't about Jeannette. He can have her back; I'll chip in the dowry and some figurines. It's those other things.

So, here I am, standing in the middle of the field. It's drizzling, and it's almost 7:15 a.m. His email said, 'Roger your last, I'll be there at the appointed hour,' and he signed off with, 'Your once and future friend, Andrew.' If we don't do this soon, the jocks who work out by running 'stadiums' will be laughing their asses off at us. Damn! Damn! DAMN!

At last. A car. Familiar throaty rumble. That's got to be Millard's Porsche. Yes. My God, I don't believe it. His right leg's in a cast, and he's on crutches. Someone's helping him. No... but it is. Our former colleague, the lady possessing what Millard described as a "generous community chest", the irrepressible Francesca.

Now what? Duels are only fought between men of honor. In situations involving low-lives and cowards, the aggrieved party dispatches a servant to horsewhip the knave. Since I possess neither whips nor servants, I suppose this means Millard walks, as he has so many times before.

79

FRANCESCA, IN a starched, appropriately subdued (if you disregard the fishnet stockings) nurse's uniform complete with peaked cap and white cape, is attentive as, supporting me gently, she squishes across the grass towards my perplexed adversary. I sway forward, pushing bravely through the pain, my face a contorted mask, the wounded rifleman home from the hell of Iwo to sell war bonds. I'm wearing a chewed-up Marine Corps field jacket. Sewn onto the top of its left sleeve is the iconic diamond-shaped patch enclosing a blue field containing the stars of the Southern Cross and a red figure '1', embroidered onto which is a single word 'Guadalcanal'.

Semper Fi!

80

WHENEVER I see that jacket, I recall those who honored it by giving their lives for their comrades. Then a vision. Millard and a fellow Marine in a listening post. A starless night. The stench of rice paddies. Suddenly: screams, bugle calls, and rounds snapping overhead. A chicom grenade lands between them. Without hesitation, Millard throws his buddy on it.

I don't hesitate either. I saw fear and astonishment in Millard's eyes just before I knocked him ass over tea kettle and broke his nose. Now I'm experiencing a strange mixture of shame and elation. How could I have doubted her?

81

ELIOT LAWRENCE is not what he claims to be. He's a sneaky, vicious shit, and I'm going to make sure everyone knows it. I am so done with him. This is my thanks for a lifetime of friendship: I agreed to room with him in boarding school, I got him his partnership, I kept him afloat at work despite his flaccid collections, I administered psychic CPR to his unsatisfied first wife, I selflessly took charge of his difficult daughter, and I've single-handedly revived our sagging firm (speaking of which, where the fuck's Giroux?). I even set him up with Mona Tucker. It's a pity he couldn't close the deal.

In the summer of '85, just before his half-assed Harvard trip to Florence, Alice and I talked him into joining us at the Colonial Yacht Club for its Labor Day shindig. It's always been a seemly, Eliotish event. Lanterns everywhere. Jolly speeches. Endless toasts. The awarding of croquet, tennis, and sailing trophies plus subdued foxtrotting livened up with some favorite throw-backs: Charlestons and bunny hops.

Without telling him, I also invited Mona, the well-off, then-unattached fox who'd violated Eliot's space if not his person at Clare's funeral. Mona's still got that sweet spread on the Vineyard.

It was a hoot watching Mona's mating dance. There was Eliot, the Marine, retreating in disorder as he tried, with little success, to maintain a sliver of moonlight between Mona's questing groin and his own.

With no warning, the music ended. Before he was able to drag the over-heated Mona back to our table, a strapless siren stepped to the mike, aroused it, and, with a revitalized band behind her, belted out one of Frankie's all-time favorites.

> *Fly me to the moon*
> *And let me play among the stars*

Eliot wilted.

> *Let me see what spring is like*
> *On Jupiter and Mars*

Eliot's hands had fallen to his sides. He was somewhere else, and Mona was displeased.

> *Fill my heart with song*
> *And let me sing for ever more*

Eliot was reaching for something. An effing hanky.

> *You are all I long for*
> *All I worship and adore*

Christ, what a balls-up. I cut in.

Then I produced Jeannette. It looks as though she's hit her sell-by date, but she's kept him clean and healthy for 18 years. Now, he may have a shot at Dawn Peterson. All thanks to me.

Well done, Millard. Well done, indeed.

82

THE GAME began on October 18 and ended the next day when, in the bottom of the 14th, Ortiz singled home Damon for a 5-4 win sending the series back to New York with the Yankees clinging to an evaporating 3-2 lead.

To give Millard his due, he went down swinging. His bat wasn't on his shoulder, and False Staff wasn't riding the pine. He'd called in some chips and scrounged a pair of seats behind the Red Sox dugout for game five of the ALCS. He wanted to snow Francesca, who was as avid for the Sox as, I believe, she was for c**ks (now I'm sounding like him).

I can see Francesca. Taunting Jeter, spilling beer, and becoming generally overwrought. She may have been tempted to bare her breasts (she certainly loved implying them), but that's Foxborough behavior. Millard, the Yankees-lover, must have been pooped, despondent, and prepared to call it a night, but I can't imagine him admitting that to Francesca. Millard had to have been torn. Could he? At that hour? We know how he decided. Maybe a little blue pill clinched it. Millard had wanted Francesca for years, and, as we lawyers say, this was his 'last clear chance'.

Nobody but Francesca knows what happened, and, unlikely as that may seem, she's gone quiet. Like the sometimes deadly Japanese fugu fish, Francesca was the feast you remembered forever or your last supper. Here's all I know about Millard's final at-bat.

He wound up at Mass General just before sunrise on October 19, beautifully turned out in one of his bespoke suits and well-matched accessories, including a stylish pocket square and a bandaged nose. Odd shoes with little straps over the insteps. Francesca had done nicely. His shirt was tucked in, his belt buckle was centered, and the fly on his monogrammed silk boxers faced front. His cast had been cast off. He was wearing pinstripes. The way any Yankees fan would want to go.

Speaking of baseball, since the decision to hire Roddy Slice was blessed by my partners, I felt no qualms about accepting his kind offer of Sox tickets. It would, I suppose, be unfortunate for our clients to miss out on what's happening in the financial markets. Not to mention the fact that most of my partners are excited about Roddy managing their own money. I'm still dubious.

Since Millard's end was so sudden, nobody had an obituary ready. He wound up in death notices. Too bad. Maybe I'll write something later.

I have this primitive response to death. I must see the body and bid my own farewell. My sect doesn't do wakes, so it has to be a private visit. Just me and the decedent. I need to know people are doing right by the not-yet-fully-departed.

So, off I went. At least there's always parking. It was a generous, well-maintained white Victorian, a place you'd be happy to visit if it were still a private home.

Millard was in the basement. On his back atop a high table. There was a lot of makeup on his face (particularly around his nose), and his arms were outside the sheet drawn up to his chin. He was clean-shaven, but would have been outraged by what they'd done to his hair. And what were those bruises on his arms? Signs of age, or Arthur and Stanley getting theirs back?

I pulled down the sheet. His leg was fine. False Staff looked out-of-sorts.

Millard would have hated his surroundings. The absence of ornament. The stark lighting. The inhospitable brick vault. The dreadful smell. The bathroom, a mirror image of those at 23 State Street.

I played no role in Millard's send-off. I was upset but unsurprised. I've never gotten on with Lucy and am baffled and put off by Arthur and Stanley. So there I was, just another member of the congregation. Jeannette had the sense to stay away. Even if she'd come, there was a long-standing C&P tradition of the attorneys sitting together at the front of the church.

As is my wont, I was unfashionably early. I grabbed a seat on the aisle of an empty pew. And waited.

Am I too accommodating? Too detached and dispassionate? Should I have pasted Millard sooner? God knows I thought about it. But surely, after all our years together, I owed him the benefit of reasonable, perhaps even unreasonable, doubt.

Would an earlier confrontation have brought resolution? Unlikely. Only in books. Would it have brought change? Out of the question. Healing? Ha.

Would I have preferred someone else as my oldest friend? Someone more constant? More like my childhood companions—Hector, Galahad, Roland, and Robin Hood? Sure, but they might have gotten tiresome and preachy in real life. It's better they're sealed away in their bookcases where friendship, loyalty, and honor are unwavering and undying. In this world, you can only play the hand you're dealt.

My goodness, I believe that's Gloria. She looked towards me and turned away. Does she remember me, I wonder? She obviously remembers Millard.

It's funny though. Those mythic companions remain compelling. This despite more than 40 years of law.

When's the service going to begin? It's already eight minutes late. Who's that? Nice looking. One of Millard's protégés, I bet. Given her youth, a recent one. What's she thinking? *I was special.* Silly girl.

At last. Company. Someone stopped beside my pew. How wonderful. Dawn. My Maid Marian?

I slid in.

The space between us shrank as our pew filled. By the start of the service we were nearly touching. Dawn smelled lovely, just as she had the night of the C&P party.

It's embarrassing, but there I sat thinking, is there some way to prolong the service? Could I raise my hand and ask the priest to throw in communion? That would mean Dawn and I could get up, bump into each other perhaps and shuffle up to the altar together. Then I giggled. I had just recalled Millard's remark about women at funerals making him tombescent. Dawn nudged me in the ribs and went wide-eyed. She was, dare I say it, looking naughty. I gave her what I hope was a 'tell you later' expression.

I should be ashamed. Millard might still be alive if I hadn't let him walk away without his inhaler. Had its absence caused his death? Is that what I intended?

His funeral was a circus. Great people-watching. Lucy, his estranged widow, occupied the first pew. She seemed to be controlling her grief. Millard, who'd been in no rush to get divorced, told me, "I've learned it's easier to fend off the supplicants if you're already hitched."

Alice showed up as well, even though she'd unsuccessfully sued Millard to reopen their separation agreement upon learning of his marriage to a successful attorney with no dependents. Perhaps the Edmundses are running out of dough. Arthur and Stanley accompanied their mother, the former looking as though he'd just stepped out of the Stewards' Enclosure at Henley, the latter a dead ringer for the Unabomber.

Maud was there with her partner. She was daunting with her belligerent gray hair cut in the shape of a WW II German helmet. No Edith. She, I learned, has been institutionalized for over three decades but made her views known in an incoherent letter that eventually found its way to me.

Ceci was sitting up front. She must have considered herself family. Young Eliot called a couple days later and told me he'd been at a closing.

Despite a good turnout, my polished, articulate colleague would have been outraged. None of his contemporaries volunteered to speak, and his immediate family declined as well. I'd offered to do so but was turned down. Had the family believed I would do unto Millard as he would have done unto me? Instead, we had to endure Simon, once again our sole managing partner. His eulogy, awkward, blessedly brief, and seasoned with bad grammar, was like a pair of cheap pants with an elastic waistband, a one-size-fits-all *'ave atque vale'*.

In non-specific terms, Simon spoke of the firm's gratitude for Millard's "invaluable contributions", and asserted he would be "sorely missed". *What would be sore,* I wondered. There followed some generalized allusions to his 'dedication, his tireless efforts on behalf of his clients, and his sound judgment'. People were staring at each other in disbelief. I felt Dawn looking at me, but didn't trust myself enough to turn in her direction. Then, believe it or not, there were a few sentences about 'filling the big hole he had left'. Would it require a back hoe? Millard would have gagged when referred to as 'a giant' of the Massachusetts bar. On the other hand, he wouldn't have wanted his 'customers' thinking he wasn't worth every nickel they'd shelled out.

I was half expecting Simon to laud Millard's integrity.

At least Simon had the wit to excise his usual introduction where he'd tell us, "I am delighted/excited/thrilled to report…" Simon also omitted the portion of his script reserved for those who were being fired rather than interred. Nor did he urge Millard to keep in touch or wish him well in his future endeavors. If the numbers had been better, Simon would probably have delivered a summary of the firm's financial performance for the most recently completed month and the fiscal year to date, accompanied by his customary exhortation to increase billables. Simon signed off with an allusion to the strong bonds that existed between 'he and I'.

I took it upon myself to escort Dawn from the church. As I will do at our wedding. Then we're off to Bermuda. Stop! Delete.

It would have been churlish not to take her arm, so I did. The family members seemed to be having trouble arranging themselves, so Dawn and I stood together just inside the doorway. How wonderful. Dawn hadn't asked about the cause of my snickering, and I couldn't bring myself to explain it. Not then. Not there. Maybe not ever.

Don't think I was entirely passive, however. Strike while the iron is hot and the body is cold, I told myself. After steering Dawn away from the others, I blundered horribly. Trying to be someone I'm not, I put a hand on her shoulder, winked (yes, I winked), and said, "How's about we flick out… sometime soon?"

I choose to believe Dawn's silence and odd expression indicated her unfamiliarity with my outdated colloquialism (and perhaps my hopeless rhyme) rather than an unwillingness to take the next step in our relationship.

One thing was obvious. It was time for a time out. After a few minutes of labored (yes, it was labored) small talk, Dawn smiled, said she had to be off, and took her leave.

I had no time to process what had just happened, because there was Francesca.

She looked great, even if Jeannette might have said her neck had started to go. Francesca wasn't wearing those sandals so I can say nothing about toe rings. And what better place for her to find someone more durable than my defunct friend? It can't have been fun, untangling yourself from a cooling corpse.

I braced myself, expecting an angry condemnation of my thuggish behavior. I recall my initial concern about Francesca's broadcasting the news of my triumph. It's shameful, but now I'm worried she'll keep it to herself.

However, Francesca never fails to surprise. She grinned and said, "Call me any time, Rocky." She must have seen me blush, because she added, "You've probably heard it before, but, at the end, your erstwhile pal was coming and going at the same time. He departed with an expression which I hope the mortician rejiggered into something more dignified." Then, in front of everyone, she kissed me loudly and wetly. I am pleased to report this did not go unobserved.

That was it. Francesca turned and was gone. The back view was equally pleasing. A taut stern and a pair of Betty Grable-like legs. Millard enjoyed himself with Francesca and why, for that matter, shouldn't I? No. It would upset Dawn. And Clare.

While I was staring, someone stepped in front of me. It took me a moment. Stevens. We shook hands. His suit looked expensive, but how would I know?

As his executor, it was my duty to survey the contents of Millard's office. I admit being inappropriately interested in what I might discover. There's a bit of the voyeur in all of us I suppose. Millard had been adept at covering his tracks, but wouldn't he have enjoyed leaving behind hints of his misspent life? If for no other reason than to show me what I'd missed. That's probably why I'm his executor.

Standing in Copley Square after Millard's service, I thought, *Why not now*? I had nothing better to do, and wasn't eager to head home, so off I went to 50 State Street. Duty called. So did curiosity. I was excited about getting on with it in private. In addition, starting on Saturday wouldn't cut into the next week's billables.

I knew where to look first. Under his blotter. The default hideout for lawyers of a certain age. Millard and I are the only ones here who still use (used, in Millard's case) that vestige of the 19th century. His paper was blue (to match his eyes?). Mine is, and always has been, crimson. I haven't peeked under my blotter since, when? Our last office move? Back in '89?

Millard's blotter is in better shape than mine. He had the firm buy him a new one every year. Another extravagance. Mine's original issue, and, I am informed, looks it. The hole I stabbed in it after a heated conference call reminds me to keep my cool.

I peeked underneath. Among the addresses, phone numbers, and initials was a recent email. It read:

> Andrew:
> Wonderful news. I just heard from a pal at IRS that somebody's been telling tales on me, but they're being disregarded. My virginity's intact, and the store's open. With my Curtis and Perkins opinions supporting them, our deals will fly off the shelf. My sources are thrilled.
>
> And yes, your revised compensation proposal is acceptable. Three million guaranteed in year one with 500K increases in each of years two through five. You're correct. The best New York shops would never make a deal like this, but that's the cost of luring rainmakers to modest establishments like yours. For the record, some second (and below) tier New York firms have started baiting their hooks with guarantees.
>
> And now a heads-up. I haven't tipped him off, but when Roddy Slice hears of my arrangements, he'll want something similar. I can't speak for your home-grown talent, but they may become restive if not brought to heel. No doubt Eliot Lawrence will yowl ineffectually.

See you within the month. As we agreed: a top floor corner office with a harbor view. How about Lawrence's?
Cheers, Henri

Guaranteed comp? Unheard of. Unacceptable! My office? NFW!

I needed a break. So, I got a diet soda and a small bag of chips and took them to our main conference room, the one where the management committee (which now has an opening) meets. The office seemed like a morgue, and that's a bad sign on an autumn Saturday. On my way to the recycling bin, I had a surprising mood change. A cloud lifted. Maybe I can fix this place.

I returned to Millard's office and tackled his desk. Aside from the usual sludge, which I'd sift through in due course, the two objects of interest were a bulging red rope folder and one of those ledger-like books once used by anxious law students for briefing cases and taking class notes. I'd filled books like this during my first year before switching to inexpensive spiral notebooks as my confidence rose and I sensed I might survive.

But what was one of these anachronisms doing in Millard's messy desk? He'd read few of the cases and usually napped in an unassigned seat in the rare classes he deigned to attend. As for me, I felt like Alice before her trip to Wonderland, examining the little phial with 'Drink Me' on its label. There was no doubt in my mind—if this serious-looking volume could have spoken, it would have said, "Read me, Eliot."

Inside the front cover was a single sheet of paper. It read:

Yo, Eliot: Since you're reading this, I guess it means I won't be speaking at your funeral, and that's a bloody shame. I'd have given you a better send-off than you deserve and bagged some fresh pussy and new customers in the process. As I have predeceased you, let me say that I hope someone discovers the instructions for my funeral in time to implement them. [Nobody had.] *Approaching my 70s with False Staff faltering, my girth expanding, and my desires, alas, moderating, I have given thought to the hereafter. Perhaps I'll become a death-bed convert to one of Islam's less strident sects, and rate a seraglio of vigorous, appreciative former virgins. Hold the maidens. Quite overrated, I'd say. So long, for now. Your pal, A. de P. M.*

I'll be darned. It seems I was now in possession of the journal Millard had begun about the time we came to work in 1963. He started 22 years before me and kept at it intermittently until his death. Does everyone do this?

Millard's chronicle would require meticulous study at a later date. Maybe at the Thanksgiving break. Would it support his recent campaign to persuade others he'd led a worthwhile life? So many ne'er-do-wells pull that as they near the end.

Next, the bloated red rope. I slipped off its elastic strap and shook the contents onto Millard's desk. Nothing but a single envelope and scores of photographs. Many of the color ones badly faded. Odd. Considering the subject matter, they should have remained out of sight. How could I have forgotten Millard's delight in his Polaroid camera and the opportunities it presented to end-run the snoopy pharmacists?

Most of the pictures were standard snapshot-size. One of the exceptions was a formal black and white portrait of the partnership dated January 1971, the month Millard and I were admitted. It was taken at one of our regular, but now discontinued, lunches when we could all be accommodated at an oval table which filled the largest private dining room of my eating club.

There we were, seated in our customary, hierarchical fashion. At the head of the table was our senior partner, William ('Ill Will') Walters, Mr. Clark's successor and an unrepentant lamb chop hog. Mr. Walters being furthest from the camera and closest to the hereafter was a lesson in perspective. He was the point at which imaginary parallel lines seemed to converge in the background.

It was as though our seating plan had been devised by an actuary. As one's eye moves down the table from Mr. Walters, compensation is shrinking and life expectancy is increasing. The faces at the foot of the table (Millard's and mine) are larger, more animated, and in better focus. In the pictures now being taken at our dismal biennial retreats, we are arranged in rows, in no discernible order. Thank goodness. Using the old format, I'd be in Ill Will's spot and poised to take my leave.

It was at this luncheon that Millard asked Mr. Walters, who'd finally made it to the top of the letterhead, whether it wasn't time to list partners alphabetically.

Back to the porn. That's young Jane Stevens. In the buff. And there are Jane and Millard together, in the altogether. Yes, Millard had a decent-looking body back then. Even if he'd never been 'buff', there was a time when he wasn't tubby. Then a blurry shot of a motel with the ambiguous caption—'Soldiers' Field Road, the scene of the crime'. There were photos of the young Ruth Donohue in a variety of costumes, poses, and settings. I won't forget (and I'm tempted to hang onto) an enticing shot of Gloria, whose surname I've forgotten, holding a tiny hoe and wearing only her green gardening gloves.

Hardly a surprise. There's False Staff. No, it was Old Faithless back then. How did he manage some of those shots? There can't have been a third (or fourth?) person on the scene. Not even Millard would have stooped to that. Would he? Dumb question. And by the way, I was getting somewhat steamed up by this smut. Should I destroy it? No. Executors have their duties.

Painful? Of course. Surprising? Not really. There's my wife. But not the one I love. You really haven't been robbed if you care nothing for what's been stolen. I shouldn't have much trouble in Suffolk Probate. Even Herby'd fold if he held Jeannette's cards.

Like the notebook, the photos needed more attention. Before I took them home, I made a fast but thorough survey. Many breasts. Many... Many suggestive smiles. None of the women, thank God, was Clare or Ceci. How could I have doubted?

Clare would have been amused by my concerns and dispelled them immediately. She always did.

Held together by a rusted paper clip was a set of 8 x 10 glossies taken in New York nightspots during WWII. There she was, holding court at tables covered with ashtrays, empties, and other debris. Millard's mom, the oft-mentioned Roberta.

I could see why men, some men anyway, were attracted to her. She dominated the photos. Laughing mouth. Sparkling, if sometimes unfocused, eyes. Smudged lipstick. A changing cast of anonymous, slicked-back lotharios orbiting her like lifeless moons.

At the bottom of the pile I came across a really old one with a white border and scalloped edges. The boys were in navy blue bathing trunks with a white stripe down each leg. Millard, chest puffed out, was mugging at the camera while the not quite three-year-old Edward stared raptly at his big brother.

I took a short break.

Sitting back down at Millard's desk, I opened the envelope. It contained a small tape, the kind I used to leave at secretarial services before going home. The next morning I'd find it and letter-perfect copy centered on my blotter.

I unearthed Millard's dictating machine, dropped in the tape, pressed 'play' and there he was.

"Eliot, my boy. A final, final message. I've written it, revised it, crumpled it, smoothed it out, shredded it, and begun again more times than I can recall. Then I decided to dictate the damn thing. More personal, don't you think, and one can learn so much from tone and inflection.

"First off, don't you feel like a turd for sucker-punching your oldest friend? I'll answer that. Of course you do.

"Now, don't take what follows as a pathetic effort to redeem myself in your or anyone else's eyes.

"However, it comes down to this. For some unfathomable reason, she seemed to prefer you to all others. Who knows, she might not have given me the time of day if I hadn't been a long-term pal and what both of you considered a major rehabilitation project, sort of like Europe under the Marshall Plan.

"Every so often I thought I had a shot, but I may have been misreading a warm and spontaneous nature. That said, I derived keen delight from observing you writhe, secure in the knowledge that your growing doubts, your diminishing self-esteem (After all, how could any woman with options 'settle' for you when I was available?), and resultant distrust would eventually provide my opening. Didn't quite happen, damn it. It would have if she'd lived.

"Regrettably, she didn't. But you provided a diversion. Since Clare was no longer there to reassure you, I have derived a certain cold comfort from nourishing your understandable suspicions about what may have occurred between us.

"I can hear you torturing yourself. 'How can Millard know so much about my sweetie?' Simple, really. I listened. Listened to her."

There was a long pause. I thought Millard was done, but no.

"So, you can relax, Stud. You were her one and only."

An even longer pause.

"If you can believe me, that is."

83

CHANGE OF channels. It's me, Ceci, the difficult daughter.

Right after my father's accident, Dawn Peterson, his prissy protégée (I know her sort; she's probably giving head to half the mailroom) handed me the memoir he's been fussing with for years.

Included with my father's effusions was something comparable by my godfather. For my own protection, I better read both of them. Every damn page.

Andrew's scribbling was a kick until that imaginative scene at The Ritz. Talk about an unreliable narrator. Yup, he's done it again, brewed up an intergalactic shit storm. He'd be so pleased with himself. Even my unconscious father's bound to unmask FYF. I suppose he was being thoughtful in not providing an index: Lawrence, Cecilia, sex with, page __.

Yes, we had lunch together. Why not? We did that now and again.

Yes, I had a couple glasses of wine, but Andrew was snozzled when I arrived. I notice he neglected mentioning the mess he made with the horseradish and cocktail sauce as he hoovered down a double load of oysters.

Yes, he gave me a Hermès scarf. Hermès, the cunning trickster. I gave it away. Can't be too careful.

Yes, the shrimp and the branzino were being gross, and yes, I laughed, loudly I suppose, when he tickled them with his fork.

However, I do not recall the Ogden Nash couplet, AND, NO, NO, a thousand times NO, I did NOT go upstairs, downstairs, or anywhere else with him. In fact, 'up' was almost certainly beyond False Staff at that point.

Sympathy sex with a deft old dude who'd been nice to me for years? Maybe. We all have our needs. With Andrew? No way.

OK, I admit it, we were some kind of weird item (and spare me all that reaction-formation Freudian crap). Still, no way. And I spared him from realizing I wasn't what he really wanted.

While I'm at it, what gives with that dumb-ass bit from the syphilitic Earl of Rochester? Gimme a break.

Then he craps out a few months later and leaves me damn near everything he had. Is my father miffed by my sudden independence? I hope so. Moreover, he's no doubt wondering what was the *quid pro quo* for my shower of gold, and, as every lawyer knows, it's difficult to prove a negative.

After finishing Andrew's nonsense, I had a number of thoughts, one of which was to have a little fun with my sluttish stepmother and another was to toss my godfather's apologia off the Mystic River Bridge in a weighted sack. Instead, I visited my father in his room overlooking the Charles.

He'd taken uptight Dawn Peterson (Why not me?) to what he calls, with a straight face, 'The Game'. Still over-excited by Harvard's margin of victory, he fell leaving the Stadium and damn near broke his neck. Now he's recovering at Mass General. I dreaded my first visit.

What was he thinking? Andrew'd dropped some fragrant clues, and my scent hound father would be on them like… well, like a lot of things are on other things.

Each of these men had a role to play in this, the final scene of their long-running tragical/comical/historical—what? The plot is familiar. Andrew cocks a snook at my father, who bays and tugs on his leash. The hunt's on.

Predictable and entertaining, but not if you're the treed raccoon and my father's below you woofing and slobbering.

I must assume my father's studied, if not memorized, Andrew's myth. How will he deal with me, the troublesome one? Eliot Lawrence is a creature of relentless forward motion, incapable of being deflected or distracted. Regardless of cost. Andrew favored the oblique approach. Minimize casualties, at least to himself.

I was unprepared for our conversation. It wasn't that he'd aged. And 'mellowed' didn't fit either. Oddly (suspiciously?), he seemed to have no agenda.

"I was so hoping you'd come today, Cecilia."

"Of course, I came. It's the first day they'd let me."

"Joyce, this is my daughter, Cecilia. Could you get her a ginger ale and some more of these cookies?"

I'd have preferred a martini. The nurse smiled and departed. Was it now?

Evidently not.

"That was quite a game, wasn't it, Cecelia?"

"Come on. I don't give a… hoot about 'The Game'. You know that. And please for… Chrissake, call me Ceci if you'd like."

"I would, Ceci."

That's the way it began, continued, and concluded. We burbled aimlessly, drank ginger ale, ate graham crackers, and stared at a riverside scene we couldn't bring ourselves to discuss.

He asked me about my plans, and I asked him about the firm. That was like flipping a switch. Immediately and alarmingly, my father began to radiate the enthusiasm I'd come to dread as a child because it presaged another excruciatingly wholesome family project. One which he'd claim I'd remember fondly and wish to inflict (my word) on my own issue (his word). One which would cause me, but never kiss-ass Quintus, to flee or feign illness.

"I feel really energized, Ceci. Like I'm starting over. It will be challenging to straighten out the firm, but that's what we live for. Challenges. Right?"

I let that pass, but he favored me with his 'don't interrupt me' expression, so I stifled my groan and nodded mutely like an obedient girl child.

"I think I can make a difference. There's a vacancy on our management committee and, much as I disapprove of doing so, I've decided to campaign for it."

Desperate times call for desperate measures, I suppose.

Then, in what I took as a hint of a coming purge, he said, "I'm considering a change in my personal life." He paused. In an outpouring of emotion, Eliot Lawrence continued, "That young woman's a comfort to me." There was no need to identify the 'young woman'.

I sensed my father was getting tired and said so.

"You're right, Ceci... will you come see me tomorrow?"

"Of course, I will, Eliot."

He looked at me the way he does when I call him Eliot. Then he shook his head, hauled himself into a sitting position, kissed me on my forehead, and, going completely overboard, patted a shoulder. Was my father being devious? Setting me up for tomorrow? Nope. Not his way.

I was correct. He never mentioned Andrew's journal. You lucky dogs at Curtis and Perkins. Oliver Cromwell's spurring to your rescue.

Both of us drew back from charged topics. There was no point asking him why I was the bottom of the barrel, a duty dance. Nor did I reproach him for hoarding the memories of Mom and using his grief as an excuse for ignoring all else.

Two questions. How do I break it to my semi-conscious father that, based on my observations, he and the ambitious Ms. Peterson, the current Clare replacement, may view their 'relationship' somewhat differently? Second question: when can I stop faking it? Must I really act interested in the Yale-Harvard football game? C'mon. And what about all the other stuff that was drummed into me as a kid?

And now, to Andrew. Like all lawyers, he demanded the last word.

He was so eager to upstage Eliot Lawrence, despoil (Andrew's word) his women, and pollute his mind. While he couldn't take charge of his leave-taking, he planned every detail, but kept it to himself. However, the incomparable Ms. Peterson found the script for his 'apotheosis' (again, Andrew's word) and forwarded it to me. Why me? Was she being catty? Who knows, but here it is. The song the swan never sang. There is no good reason to share it with my father.

84

SINCE THERE is a relatively high likelihood the unthinkable may happen, that at some distant date the world must do without Andrew de Peyster Millard, it behooves me to make necessary preparations before that tragedy occurs. However, prior thereto, I am going to demand heroic, make that Medal of Honor heroic, measures for myself. Screw that palliative, slip away gently surrounded by your family crap. Bring on the respirators, the ventilators, and the 'ators' still on the drawing boards. I want every single minute, and I want them pain-free. Don't even consider yanking my feeding tube. And don't fill it with gruel. Make mine pureed lobster served by odalisques. Hold the effing kale and broccoli.

Also, I require a private, river-view suite at Mass General (on the floor where the Saudi royal family stays) filled with banks of the latest medical devices, manned 24/7 by the most committed honors graduates of our best medical schools.

I am developing an elaborate protocol to be observed before anyone thinks about turning off my bubble machine. I've made it as complex and foolproof as the procedures to be followed before launching our ICBMs. None of this, "We'll miss you terribly, Daddy, but nod if you'd like to go." What if some sexual fantasy caused me to twitch at just that moment? Arthur and Stanley would be wrestling for the rheostat, probably joined by Edith, Maud, Alice, Jeannette, Lucy, Ruth's shade, others who must remain nameless, and perhaps women yet unborn.

I insist on generous subsidies to my caregivers, but only so long as they keep me breathing. Even in a vegetative state.

And what shall be done with the corporeal me (if I were around to arrange myself, I would insist on an open-casket ceremony)?

I'm to be laid to rest in colorful, hypoallergenic, high thread count cerements in a burial chamber of rot-resistant larch logs. Like the Scythians prepared for their chiefs. In another age, I would have insisted on a spacious private chapel off the choir of a cathedral. A porphyry sarcophagus, I should think, with my raised likeness on its lid and mythological creatures cavorting on its sides. The inscription would be that of naval hero, Stephen Decatur: "In him, every virtue of human character was carried to its highest perfection! Columbia mourn!"

Maybe I'll lighten up and go with Ogden Nash:

> *He who is ridden by a conscience*
> *Worries about a lot of nonscience;*
> *He without benefit of scruples*
> *His fun and income soon quadruples.*

Don't even think about cremation. I'll not be soaked in accelerant, cradled in kindling, and consigned to the flames. Nor do I wish to be scattered in some weed-choked nature preserve. Blasphemy.

No, I must be intact for the Last Judgment, not like the Red Sox left fielder that some have the nerve to compare to Joe D. Is it possible to work in a cavalcade of black horses, decked out in nodding ostrich plumes followed by a riderless stallion with a pair of reversed boots in the stirrups? Or a funeral train like Lincoln's, where I can be observed and mourned?

After payment of all proper funeral and administrative expenses plus unavoidable death taxes, I direct my remaining assets be liquidated and the proceeds used to acquire gems and precious metals for the adornment of my body and the fabrication of tangibles for my afterlife, including, without limitation, a bow of burning gold and countless arrows of desire. On the assumption that 'the rich get richer' holds true in the hereafter, my three-ring binder cataloguing Curtis's wealthiest female customers is to be placed with my remains.

All pets (and the remains of former pets) I may own are to join me in my crypt, and for purposes hereof, the term 'pets' shall include any woman to whom I am, at the time, married, affianced, or otherwise attached. My only fear is I will spend eternity listening to my former wives, kissing up to customers, and competing unsuccessfully with Eliot. But maybe there's a benevolent Supreme Being who will give me Clare and FYF. And now to my final curtain call. My obsequies.

In a way, I wish I knew the date of my death. Remember that 'readiness is all' tripe? My motives are less heroic. A year before the end of the world as I know it, I would resume all the delicious but unhealthy vices I abandoned in order to prolong myself. Why expire trim and in good health? Why not bow out looking like King Farouk, merry and debauched, surrounded by the ripest belly dancers my customers' money can buy?

I see myself lolling on a sunny isle with a proud, tanned paunch overhanging my Speedo.

Damn Prometheus and his gifts:

> *Prometheus* – *I caused mortals to cease foreseeing doom.*
> *Chorus* – *What cure did you provide them with against that sickness?*
> *Prometheus* – *I placed in them blind hopes.*

Poor Eliot is a happy recipient of this gift. He will be taken by surprise. Not me.

My send-off will be staged at Trinity, the scene of my best work. The throng will assume they are in for yet another mundane rendition of Rite One from *The Burial of the Dead*. And so it will appear until the Celebrant intones, "And I will dwell in the house of the Lord for ever."

At that moment, a line of stooped, shrouded, spectral figures will rise wraithlike from behind the altar and shuffle towards the 'people', who are beginning to wonder what Millard is up to now. Breaking their silence, these dread figures begin a high, antiphonal keening. Then comes further wailing and tearing of hair followed by:

> *I sing suffering, shrieking,*
> *Shrill and sad am weeping,*

> *My life is dirges*
> *And rich in lamentations,*
> *Mine honor weeping.*

That might just do it. Having established this is not one of those dreadful 'celebrate a life' services, the chorus advances westward to the crossing where they execute crisp, alternating 90-degree left and right-hand turns until they form an evenly-spaced line directly in front of the pews. After a few moments more on death and despair, the chorus begins rending its garments.

Before the rending is complete, Trinity's massive organ segues from Bach to Sousa's *Semper Fidelis*. The chorus throws off its weeds and snaps to attention, revealing itself as a lush, multi-racial sampler of full-bodied non-virgins in sequins, glitter, pasties, fringed G-strings, anklets, bells, toe rings, and bejeweled high-heeled sandals. Strutting down the three parallel aisles like Lipizzaners, they scatter thousand-dollar gift certificates to Boston's most highly-rated escort services. Sorry, Arthur. Sorry, Stanley. Exiting the church into the setting sun, my girls proceed briskly across Copley Square, past the marathon finish line to the T station, and by a lucky fluke, find a functioning escalator to whisk them back to Parnassus in time for Happy Hour. Where I shall join them.